Tales of Asculum

Blood of
Ancient
Kings

By
V. J. O. Gardner

The **DIY** Book Festival

2013 Young Adult Catgory

Tales of Asculum
Blood of Ancient Kings
By V.J.O. Gardner

Copyright © 2010 by V.J.O. Gardner
All Rights Reserved
Please visit www.vjogardner.com

Cover Art by Katerina Davailova

First Edition – Nov 2010
Second Edition – Dec 2011 (cover change)
Third Edition – Apr 2013 (major rewrite)
Fourth Edition – Feb 2014 (cover update)

Version 4.1

Prologue

In every culture there is a history that needs to be remembered. Without remembering the past, the same mistakes are repeated. On this earth-like planet the story of the bloodline of the ancient kings of Brinley is an important one. For generations royal marriages were arranged and politically motivated. The marriage of King Hessgar and Queen Perla was to insure that the neighboring kingdom of Okiah would not invade the village of Nordam where the gemstone mines were. Their only son, Burkhart, became king when King Hessgar suddenly died. King Burkhart immediately broke his engagement to the woman his father chose for him and married the sister of one of the servants. King Burkhart increased taxes so he could lavish her with expensive clothing and jewelry. He outlawed any opposition and anyone openly speaking against him was executed. He ruled through fear. Every man was taken from his home at seventeen to spend three years in the military. If they refused they were executed.

In the fifth year of his reign, King Burkhart began hearing rumors that one of the colonels suddenly vanished. This Colonel Langward had even stood guard in the palace frequently during his military service. The official report was that he had died while on the eastern border patrol, but no body was found. Perhaps he had been killed by the dragons rumored to live to the east, but King Burkhart began hearing rumors that Langward still lived and was planning to take the throne from him. He tried having Langward found, but his brother and parents thought him dead. His wife had vanished and some mentioned her saying she didn't want to raise his child she was carrying alone. As much as he hated and even feared this Langward, that news struck his heart because his own beloved Queen Aurita was due to give birth soon. She had been so very sick while carrying his child and spent much of her time in bed.

The clash of swords and battle cries fade as one life ends and another begins. As one draws their last breath, another draws their first. A single moment in time that begins a series of events eventually affecting an entire kingdom, like ripples spreading in a pool of blood.

Chapter 1 – Life and Death

Langward stood in the open doorway as blood dripped from his sword. He heard his men coming down the hall to join him and held his left hand up.

"We come to protect you as you face him," one said.

"We want to watch as you kill him," another added.

"You cannot kill that which is already dead," he replied.

The man Langward had come to kill to gain Brinley's throne knelt on the bed with the lifeless body of his wife in his arms. The bedding was soaked with blood. King Burkhart had taken no notice of him and his men, nor had the group of women huddled around the table. There was a sudden cry from near the table and King Burkhart finally looked up and met Langward's gaze. As an infant's crying filled the room he laid his wife's body gently on the bed, kissing her lips tenderly before removing her armband. The man who had been a tyrant of a king now knelt before him holding the royal armbands and signet ring up to him. Langward wiped the blood off his sword before sheathing it.

"Aren't you going to execute him?" one of his men asked. "He needs to be punished."

"He has been judged and sentenced by a higher power," Langward replied as he took the ring and armbands from Burkhart. "It is not my place to change that sentence. Take him and clean him up. Find him some clothes and a cape."

"Yes, Sir," the men answered and took Burkhart away.

The women at the table looked at him with fear in their eyes as one of them held the crying infant.

"Male or female?" he asked as he took the infant from the woman.

"Female," the woman replied in a shaky voice.

"One life ends and another begins," he said as the infant began to settle down. "She shall be named Aurita after her mother. Feed and clothe her, then bring her to the throne room."

"Yes, My King," they replied as he handed the infant back to the woman.

He had not expected this when he planned the attack on the palace. There had been only light resistance and few deaths. Most of the guards had laid down their weapons including the ones at the front gate. It seemed that they were as discontented with Burkhart's rule as the rest of the people of Brinley. Now Langward knew that the man who had been his sworn enemy must be protected from harm along with his infant daughter. He didn't see the point in putting Burkhart in the dungeon. He had seen the look in the man's eyes; he would die within days in the dungeon. The infant his wife died giving birth to would be his only reason to live. He decided that the village on the western border where he had grown up would be where Burkhart would be sent to raise his daughter, but there would have to be some rules to be followed.

As he left the room, a servant appeared with two of his men. The man carried a bowl of water and a drying cloth. He washed the armbands and ring in the water, along with his hands, before drying them on the cloth.

"I have ordered clean clothes found for you, clothes befitting a king," the servant said. "There will be a bath waiting for you."

He nodded.

"Follow me, please."

Langward wondered at the young man's calm demeanor. Most of the servants had scattered and hid during the fighting. The servant led him to a room with a tub of water. There were several other servants waiting. His men waited outside as the servants undressed and bathed him. They trimmed his hair and beard after he was dried. He had several minor wounds which they cleaned and bandaged before dressing him. They trimmed and buffed his fingernails. He felt a bit uncomfortable with their attention, but knew it was what they felt was expected of them.

As the servant slipped the armband onto his right arm he asked, "Will our queen be arriving soon? We wish to have everything ready for her arrival."

"She is in safe keeping until I send for her," he replied in surprise.

"Very good," the servant said as he led Langward to the throne room. "We will begin cleaning the royal quarters at once."

"No," he said. "You will allow Burkhart to take anything that will fit in one bag before sealing it off as is. I want Queen Aurita's body prepared for burial with all respect due such a noble woman."

"It shall be done immediately, My King," the man said before kneeling before him forehead on the floor with upturned hands.

"Please send in the dungeon master," Langward said as the man stood up.

"At once, My King," the man said and quickly left.

As he sat down on one of the thrones, a woman entered holding a bundle.

"The child, My King," the woman said as she began to kneel.

"Bring her to me," he said.

The woman stood and climbed the steps.

"She has been fed and clothed," the woman said as she handed the infant to him. "We have assembled the things necessary for her care."

He nodded as the door opened again. She removed the bag that had been hanging from her shoulder and handed it to him. As two men brought Burkhart to the bottom of the steps Langward stood. When they released him, he dropped to his belly and lay with palms upturned.

"When I awoke this morning, I was determined to see you dead before nightfall," Langward said and Burkhart did not move. "But now I can see that there is a far different fate awaiting you. Stand on your feet and face your future."

Burkhart slowly rose to his feet. His face bore the same expression of pain and defeat as he met Langward's gaze. He appeared even older than he had earlier as though he had aged ten years in less than an hour.

"You will be sent to live in the very village that I lived in," Langward said as he noticed a change in Burkhart's expression. "I have named your daughter Aurita. There will be conditions you must meet."

"I will do anything you ask of me," Burkhart replied as tears began to stream down his face.

"You must never speak of your past to her. You must not tell her that she is of royal blood. You will be given a small home to live in and a goat to milk. Other than that, you must earn your own keep. She must be cared for and protected. This is your most important responsibility. Her life is your life," Langward said as he carried the infant down the stairs. "Take her now. She shall not be removed from your care for as long as you live. However, when she is a woman, I will choose a husband for her. He will be a man suitable for a woman of noble birth. This much I promise. You may take anything that you want that will fit in one bag. Choose wisely what is important enough to take with you."

He handed the infant and the bag to Burkhart before returning to the throne.

"Take him to the royal quarters and give him a bag," Langward told the guards.

As the men led Burkhart away, a man entered and knelt. Langward could tell the man felt himself to be very important by his smug expression. He remembered this man as Kolis who had attended the military training camp.

"Rise," Langward said.

"I am the dungeon master," he said after he had stood up. "What is your bidding? Am I to keep Burkhart until his execution?"

"No," Langward replied noticing Kolis' obvious dislike for his former king. "Fate has chosen a far worse punishment for him. He will not darken your dungeon. What prisoners do you have?"

"I have ten in all," Kolis replied. "Six men in for displeasing Burkhart, two murderers, and two women."

"Two women?"

"Foreign travelers. One apparently is a fortune teller. Something she said displeased Burkhart and he ordered them thrown in the dungeon," he explained.

"Release everyone except the two murderers," Langward said. "From now on anyone in the dungeon will have to have done something far worse than displease the king."

"It will be done," the man said and left.

The servant entered again and knelt before him. With him were four guards.

"Rise," he said.

"I have found four guards willing to take Burkhart to his new home without harming him," the servant said. "They are men I know are trustworthy. He should be ready to go soon."

"We will need a grave dug. I would prefer it to be as close to the royal quarters as possible."

"There is a small courtyard leading to the palace gardens and the main courtyard," the man replied.

"Perfect," Langward said as he stood up. "After Queen Aurita is buried it is to be sealed off as well."

"Yes, My King," the man answered looking confused. "I have selected some quarters to become the royal quarters, with your approval of course. Would you care to see them now?"

"Yes," he replied. "First get someone to dig the grave."

"I will be right back, My King," the man said and quickly left.

The guards left after receiving instructions on where Burkhart was to be delivered. Langward looked around the elegant room while he waited for the servant. It looked different as he viewed it from the steps in front of the throne instead of when standing guard next to the doors. He almost drew his sword when the door opened. The servant entered and knelt.

"Rise," he said realizing it would take him some time to get used to such formality. "Let's have a look at those quarters."

"Right this way, My King," the man said and led him out the door and up some stairs.

The doors he opened led to a short hall crossed by a longer hall. The longer hall had a door at either end. The short hall opened into a sitting room.

"There are two large bedrooms off the entrance hall and one even larger bedroom through that door," the servant said. "The only direct access for servants is through the private bathing chamber."

"This will do," Langward replied as he looked around the room.

It was elegant without being as lavish as the throne room or the quarters he was having sealed off. The decorations were mostly shades of blue. His wife's favorite color was blue.

"There is a balcony," the man said as he opened a door.

Langward stepped out onto the large balcony. It looked over the palace garden.

"I like it," he said.

"Will Our Queen want any changes to the decoration?" the man asked.

"Probably not," he replied as they left the balcony.

As they left the quarters, a man approached them.

"Burkhart is ready to leave at your leisure, My King," the man said as he knelt.

"Give him enough food for two meals. He may pay his last respects to his wife before he leaves the palace," Langward said. "The grave is being dug and her body prepared."

"Yes, My King," the man said as he rose and left.

"Take me to the courtyard where Queen Aurita will be buried."

The servant led him down stairs and through halls. Langward paid close attention to the path they were taking. He followed the servant out in the palace garden and down a stone path. Soon they came to a tall wall with a door. When they entered, they found three men digging where some of the flagstones had been removed. The grave was almost ready.

"Have the body brought out if it is ready," he said. "And bring out Burkhart."

"Yes, My King," the servant said and quickly left.

He watched in silence as the men dug. Thankfully his wife was not here to see this. He did not want to upset her when she was in such a delicate condition. She would soon give birth to their first born child. He was both excited and anxious about becoming a father. Two women appeared in the doorway leading to the main courtyard. They curtsied.

"We wanted to thank you for freeing us," the older of the two said in the language of the kingdoms to the north.

"My purpose in taking the throne was to right the wrongs that Burkhart had done," Langward replied in the same language as he approached them.

The door leading to the royal quarters opened up and two men carried out the body on a plank. Burkhart was led in through the garden door. He held his daughter close to his chest and did not look up as they stopped near the open grave.

"I know that you loved her," Langward said gently and Burkhart looked up at him. "I have not the power to return her to you, but I wanted you to know that she would be cared for in her death."

Burkhart nodded.

"Say your goodbyes now," Langward said. "Once the grave is filled, this courtyard and the royal quarters will be sealed off. You will not return until your death. Then your place will be beside her."

Burkhart nodded with tears streaming down his face. Langward turned and led the two women out into the main courtyard.

Langward noticed that they were barely more than girls.

6

"Your wife will bear you an heir," the older woman said. "Only by true love can he be named. The lives you spared today will insure the continued reign of your lineage. There will come a day that your blood shall mingle with his and again Burkhart's line will reign, eventually bringing peace and prosperity to many."

"I will remember that," he said. "I do not completely understand, but I will remember."

"In time my words will make sense to you," the woman said. "In time an enemy will become a friend."

"When I entered this courtyard this morning, I thought I was here to kill Burkhart and take the throne," he said. "But when I saw him holding the body of his wife, I knew that no punishment could come close to that. When the infant survived, my heart was softened and I knew that I could not take his life. I know that my greatest challenge lies ahead."

"It is a noble thing you do," the younger of the two women said.

"It can be a difficult thing to rule a nation," the other woman said. "But I see that you and your queen will make changes that will greatly improve this nation and others. Although you will make divisions, it will bring strength and stability to your people."

"We will leave now," the younger woman said.

"Safe journey," he said as he heard the gate open behind him. "You are welcome in Brinley any time you wish to return."

The women went to a waiting wagon as Langward turned to see Burkhart and the four guards behind him. The man was trembling as he clutched the infant to his chest. He knew that Burkhart was in no condition to ride a horse. If he walked, he would collapse if he was not attacked first.

"Bring a coach to take him to his new home," Langward said and one of the men started toward the stables.

While he waited, he considered the words of the fortune teller knowing that saving Burkhart and his daughter was the right thing to do. He only hoped the people of his village would understand as well. Eventually he would also have to explain his decision to his wife. The coach was brought and Burkhart loaded into it with his belongings. Langward watched as the coach left the courtyard. The day had not gone exactly as he had originally planned, but he felt that it had gone as it should have. He felt at peace with himself as he returned to the palace to find the servant waiting for him.

7

"We have a meal prepared for you," the man said.

"Thank you," Langward said as he followed the man to a large dining room. "What is your name?"

"Garman," the servant replied with a smile.

"How is the rest of the palace staff taking the change?" Langward asked as he took the indicated seat at the head of the table. "I want them to realize that I do not intend to make any changes to the palace staff, but if they do not wish to stay they can leave."

"We are all a little relieved to no longer serve Burkhart," Garman replied. "There is some anxiety over what you will expect of us, but so far no one wants to leave. The remaining guards feel the same way."

"Good," he said. "Since I am not accustomed to having servants, I just expect the staff to do whatever is necessary to run the palace."

"Here is your food," Garman said with a smile. "If there is anything at all that you need or want, don't hesitate to ask."

*****

Burkhart was numb from the pain in his heart. He had wished for death with all of his heart, even if it meant his child would be raised by another or even killed. He had feared this Langward, but now wondered at his compassion. He knew nothing of how to earn his own living outside the palace yet he must learn to care for himself and his daughter. He opened the blanket and looked upon his daughter's face for the first time and hoped that he could care for her as she was all he had left. The tears started anew at the thought of her mother's death. This Langward he had so feared understood how much he had loved Aurita and was not afraid to reveal his understanding. He knew that many of the laws he had put in place, Langward would retract. It was his own greed that had brought him to this day.

When the coach stopped and the door was opened he picked up the bags and stepped out. The villagers gathered around complaining that he was there and saying out loud how they hated him and wished him dead. He did not look up as he was led to a door.

"This will be your home," one of the guards said. "The goat will be tied out back. You are not to leave the borders of this village."

"There is nowhere for me to go anyway," he said as he nodded.

He opened the door and went inside. Aurita began to fuss and cry. After finding a bottle of milk for her in one of the bags he fed her until she fell asleep. He laid her on the bed near the wall then looked in the bag to find meat, bread and cheese, Although his stomach was not nearly as empty as his heart, he knew he must eat. She was relying on him to care for her. He ate before lying down beside his daughter to try to sleep.

*****

Burkhart awoke confused as he smelled smoke in the air and heard shouts. The roof of the house was on fire! In a panic he picked up Aurita and the bags before trying to open the door. It would not budge; they were locked in! He kicked at the door until it broke and managed to get out just before the roof fell in only to be faced by an angry mob of people. While none held swords, they held tools as one would hold a weapon. Burkhart ran behind the house to find more people along with the remains of the goat strewn about. He ran as he felt stones pelt him at last finding a bridge over a small stream and crawling under it. There he found a small depression carved out of the bank and cowered in it with his back toward the opening. For the first time in his life he was truly afraid, not so much for himself, but for his daughter.

Chapter 2-Saving an Enemy

Langward had spent a restless night haunted by Burkhart's eyes. He woke early feeling that something was very wrong. He got up and dressed before leaving the room. He found two of his men guarding the door.

Another of his men ran down the hall yelling, "Sir! The house Burkhart was given is on fire! We just got the signal from the border patrol."

"Get me a horse," he said. "Send a coach for my wife and her mother. I want them here where they will be safe."

"At once!" the man replied and left.

His men followed him down the hall to the steps where they found Garman heading toward them.

"Breakfast is not yet," Garman said before Langward cut him off.

"I'll eat later," he said. "I need to take care of an urgent matter. I'll need twenty men to come with me."

"At once, My King," Garman said and ran off.

When he reached the courtyard the men were beginning to assemble. A horse was saddled and waiting for him. He mounted as the last of the men arrived.

"I know that what I am about to request of you may not be something you want to do," he said. "Many of you do not understand why I have allowed Burkhart to live. Death is a kinder fate than to force him to live after he has lost everything dear to him. I now ask you to defend him, knowing that for him life is a worse punishment than death. I must convince my neighbors, friends and family that they must allow him to live among them. I must convince them that they need to teach him what he needs to survive and care for his daughter. Will you do what I ask of you?"

"Long live King Langward!" was the reply.

He turned his horse and urged it to a gallop. The streets were nearly empty as he led the men to the outskirts of town. They galloped through fields and over a small foothill to the village. He could see the people gathered around a bridge over the brook to the west of the village. He was almost to them before anyone took notice of him and the men behind him.

"Where is Burkhart?" he asked in a stern tone.

Blood of Ancient Kings

The crowd split leaving a path open to the bridge.

"Burkhart," he said. "Come out and face me."

The man was muddy and bruised as he climbed up the bank with his infant and belongings in his arms. He laid himself down in front of Langward's horse with the infant in his hands.

"Bring me the child," he said to the man next to him.

The man dismounted and took the infant from Burkhart. He handed her up to Langward. Langward unwrapped the infant and checked her carefully. She seemed uninjured.

"You see before you a broken man," he said and the crowd's murmuring ceased. "His wife died giving birth to this child. I have taken his kingdom from him and expelled him from his palace. He has no home nor will to live other than to care for this child. He probably would prefer to die than to live among you."

Langward paused. He could see that Burkhart would need to be carefully watched for protection, not for escape.

"I have sentenced him to raise this child in this village. He is not to leave the borders of this village until his death. To leave is to face instant death. I will increase the patrols in this area so that they can watch over him as well as our border," he said as he saw their surprised reactions. "I forbid anyone to tell her of her lineage. Someday I might tell her the truth of the matter, but not while he lives. I have entrusted you with an important duty," he said. "Burkhart knows nothing of caring for himself, let alone an infant. He will need to be taught the same skills that your own children are being taught. He does not know how to grow food, nor prepare a meal. He does not know how to maintain a home to shelter himself and his child from cold and storm. I am not asking you to like him, but I am asking you to put aside your hatred of him. The man once known as King Burkhart no longer lives. This man you see before you is not that man."

He let them murmur amongst themselves for a while. At last, silence fell. The Minister stepped forward.

"We will do as you ask," the Minister said. "We have supported you and trust you."

"Help him to build a home for himself and his daughter," Langward said. "Teach him what he needs to know. To your feet, Burkhart."

The man slowly rose to his feet.

11

"Here is your daughter," he said and Burkhart stepped beside his mount. "I will return periodically to check on both of you. Pray that I find her in good condition."

"I live only to raise her and serve you, Noble King," Burkhart said as he met Langward's gaze and took the infant. "You have been far kinder to me than I deserve."

Langward turned his horse and led the men back toward the palace. He had been a little surprised by Burkhart's words, but was careful not to show it knowing that the show of submission, humility and loyalty would help convince the villagers that Burkhart could be trusted to live among them. He could tell from the look in his eyes that Burkhart was sincere in his desire to please him. Langward knew that he would have to frequently check on Burkhart's condition for a while before he could be certain that the villagers would not kill him and his daughter.

As they rode back through town, the streets were busier as people started their day. He could see that people were surprised to see that it was not Burkhart wearing the royal armband and wondered how they would take the change in leadership. Once his wife was safely in the palace, he would need to make a public announcement. Eventually he would have to personally present himself as king. Garman was waiting for them in the courtyard and looked relieved to see him.

"Your breakfast is waiting, My King," Garman said as he knelt before Langward. "Is everything alright?"

"For now," Langward said. "Rise."

Garman led him to the dining hall. As a plate was placed before him the kitchen staff waited near the doorway to see if he liked the food. He smiled after swallowing the first bite of the delicious food.

"Very good," he said aloud. "It has been a while since I have had such a delicious breakfast."

The kitchen staff seemed happy as they shut the door.

"They have been anxious to please you," Garman said. "Two of them had been in the dungeon for angering Burkhart. The other servants have been anxious about pleasing you as well."

"After breakfast, assemble the entire palace staff in the throne room," Langward said. "Perhaps I should let them know that their jobs and freedom are safe."

"I will spread the word at once," Garman said with a smile and quickly left through the kitchen.

Langward was almost finished eating when Garman returned.

"They are assembling, My King," he said as he knelt. "Would you like some clean clothes first?"

Langward thought for a moment before nodding. He realized that if he were to be king he should dress like a king.

Garman smiled and led him back to his quarters. He was soon dressed in clothes finer than he had ever worn. As he looked into the polished shield, the image staring back at him was not one he recognized and he wondered what his wife would think. He followed Garman into the throne room. Everyone knelt as he passed.

He stood in front of the throne and said, "Rise."

Once everyone had stood up, he sat on the throne.

"I know that you are all wondering what to expect from me," he said. "I am not accustomed to being waited on, nor do I know what it takes to run a palace. I trust that you will do your jobs so that I can do the job of ruling Brinley. I promise to not throw anyone into the dungeon without reason. Anyone in the dungeon will have to have broken a law."

As they settled down, He could see the relief on their faces.

"I have sent for my wife, Retanta," he said. "She should arrive before nightfall. I do not want anything said to her about the death of Queen Aurita until after she has delivered the child she now bears. I do not want her to be upset by yesterday's events. In time I will tell her everything."

"When is Queen Retanta due to deliver?" one of the women asked.

He recognized her from yesterday as one of the women who cared for Burkhart's wife.

"Very soon," he said. "It could be any time now. When she delivers, she will need your help."

"We will make certain that she is well cared for," the woman said and the others nodded.

He smiled and nodded before saying, "I plan on making many changes to our laws that should improve everyone's lives. I have always thought that the people should have some say in how they are governed. I also feel that a king cannot know what is best for his kingdom if he doesn't know what his people must do to survive. Until yesterday, I was just a common man, a soldier of Brinley living off the land. I do not mean to forget what that is like. If there is something any of you feel I should know about, do not be afraid to tell me."

He could see that they were pleased with his speech.

"I have things to work on before the day is done," he said. "I will require your assistance, Garman. The rest of you are dismissed."

As the others began to leave, Garman approached and said, "Would you prefer to work in your quarters or your private study?"

"The study," he said as he stood up.

Garman led him behind the throne and to a door. He opened the door revealing a large room with a desk, several chairs and two tables. The walls were lined with shelves of books and a door opposite the one they had come in.

"This will do nicely," he said as he sat down at the desk. "I need a list of all the servants and palace guards and their jobs. Also, if there is anything you feel I should know about any of them, include that as well. Can you write?"

"Of course, My King," he said and opened a drawer. "There is blank paper in this drawer and pens and ink in the one in the center of the desk."

Langward opened the drawer and took out a pen and a bottle of ink. Garman took them along with a piece of paper over to a table. He sat down and began to write. Langward looked in the other drawers to see what they held. He found a large bound book in one of the drawers. Upon opening it he found it to be a book of laws. He settled back and began reading. After a while, he got out a piece of paper and began making notes with the pen and ink that were in an ornate holder on the desk. Many of the laws were very basic and made sense including several that were crossed out with a line through the page. Some of the laws were a little more complicated, but once he read them carefully, he understood them. He flipped through the book until he came to the last page that was written on. The law on that page did not please him at all. It gave the king power to throw anyone in the dungeon without having to give any reason for it. Langward put a line through the page, crossing out the law. He continued to read the laws starting at the back of the book, crossing out those he felt were unnecessary or benefitted the king at the expense of the people.

14

Suddenly, he was startled by Garman clearing his throat. He looked up to find Garman standing in front of the desk.

"The list you requested, My King," Garman said. "You have been busy."

"Yes," he replied as he took the paper from Garman. "I can see that I have a lot of work to do. You are dismissed. Please let me know when supper is ready or my wife arrives."

"As you wish, My King," Garman said with a smile. "This cord rings a bell in the servants' quarters if you need any further assistance."

Langward nodded and went back to his work as Garman left.

*****

Burkhart watched King Langward as he disappeared over the hill. He had felt humiliated lying in the dirt in front of everyone, but understood why King Langward had done it. Hopefully it would work and the villagers would tolerate his presence now. He dared not hope for anything more. He jumped as a hand touched his shoulder. Aurita began to cry.

"I have some food left from breakfast," the minister said as Burkhart turned to face him. "We'll find something for the infant as well."

"Thank you," he said quietly and followed the minister to the small house near the church.

The minister's wife waited for them at the door.

"Let me show you how to change a diaper," she said. "You will need to learn to wash them as well."

She took Aurita from him and went over to the bed that was in the corner of the small house. She laid the infant on the bed and unwrapped her.

"Do you have any diapers?" she asked as she looked up at him.

"I don't know," he admitted as he handed her the bag with the infant's things in it. "They gave me this."

She took everything from the bag and laid it out on the bed.

"These are diapers," she said as she pointed to a stack of neatly folded cloths. "You will need to learn to wash them. You will soon learn that a dirty diaper is not something you will want to have around and they can cause sores on her if you leave them on too long."

She picked up a diaper and unfolded it before folding it in a pattern that resulted in a triangle shape then she undid the piece of metal wire that held the infant's diaper in front and held it up.

"You must be very careful with this," she said. "It is very sharp. Always put your own hand between the infant and the diaper when putting this into the diaper. It must go through all of the layers of cloth or the diaper will fall off and you don't want to poke her with it."

He nodded as he examined the bent wire. He watched as she proceeded to open up the diaper trying to not react as the smell of the diaper reached his nose. She carefully wiped the gooey green stuff from the infant with a corner of the diaper before rolling it into a tight ball. After setting the dirty diaper aside, she placed the wide end of the triangle under the infant and pulled the smaller one up between her legs. She folded the two ends up around the hips and held them in front of the other end. She then took the wire from him and carefully pushed it through the cloth and back up before hooking it on itself.

"After breakfast, I'll show you how to wash the diaper," she said as she wrapped the blanket back around the infant. "What is her name?"

"Aurita," he said as his heart ached again. "After her mother."

"While you eat, I'll feed Aurita," she said.

"Thank you."

He sat down at the table where a bowl of white lumpy stuff sat with a spoon in it. He took a bite of the sticky stuff and found it to be very bland. With difficulty he swallowed and took another bite. It was not the type of food he was used to, but he knew he could not complain. He was lucky to get anything to eat. If this is what the villagers ate for breakfast, he would just have to get used to it. Once he finished, he found the minister's wife with the infant on her shoulder patting the infant's back. He jumped as the infant made a sudden noise.

"An infant needs to be burped after being fed," she said. "They can get air along with the milk. Let me show you how to tie the blanket so you can carry her without using your hands."

He paid close attention as she tied the blanket under one of his arms and up across the opposite shoulder. When she finished, she placed Aurita in the blanket near his chest with her feet under his arm.

"It's a bit awkward until you get used to it," she said. "Now the first thing we need is water."

She picked up a bucket near the door and opened the door. He followed her not knowing where she was going. She led him to the brook that ran through the village.

16

"We get all of our water for washing clothes here," she said. "The water for drinking, cooking and washing dishes comes from the well. We bathe in the river."

She handed him the bucket. Carefully he knelt down and scooped water from the stream. He found the bucket to be heavy as he followed her back to the small house next to the church. She pointed to a tub on a table and he poured the water into the tub. It only filled it a quarter of the way up.

"You'll need another bucket of water for rinsing," she said. "I'll go get the soap."

He returned to the stream and filled the bucket again. His muscles were getting sore by the time he set down the bucket next to the table. She returned with a bucket and drew out a lump of something white, a scoop and the dirty diaper.

"First you get it wet," she said. "When Aurita is older, it will be easier because you can dump the contents into the outhouse."

She pointed to a tiny structure nearby.

"Outhouse?"

"You'll see," she said with a laugh. "You'll be dumping the dirty water there when we are finished."

He nodded as she handed him the soap and put a strange board with a wavy metal piece fastened to it into the tub.

"Unroll the diaper and swish it around a bit," she said.

Although the thought disgusted him, he knew he must learn to do it. He gingerly reached into the water and tugged at the loose corner of the fabric. It began to unroll and the water began to turn green.

"Now, rub some soap on it and put it on the wash board."

He did as he was told.

"Now scrub it," she said.

"Scrub?" he asked, not certain he had heard the term before.

"Rub it up and down on the washboard to clean it. You will have to turn it and then pour scoops of fresh water out of the bucket to rinse it until it is clean. Then we will need to empty the tub."

He followed her instructions and found that the diaper did indeed come clean. She showed him a plug near the bottom of the tub that when removed allowed the water to drain into the bucket she had brought. When he took it to the structure she called an outhouse and opened the door, he found that the outhouse smelled worse than the diaper. He then understood the purpose of the outhouse. Once he had finished emptying the tub, he followed her instructions on wringing the water out of the diaper. Then she took it from him and wrung it again. He was amazed at the amount of water that was still in the diaper.

"The more water you can wring out, the faster it will dry," she said. "I recommend that you wash all of your other dirty clothes before washing the diapers."

Chapter 3 – An Heir is Born

Langward jumped as the door opened unexpectedly. Garman entered and knelt.

"Rise," he said.

"Our Queen is arriving," Garman said as he stood up. "Supper will be ready soon."

Langward stood and said, "Thank you. "Her mother will be with her and will need quarters."

He followed Garman out to the courtyard in time to see the coach pull in. He opened the door to the coach.

"Langward," Retanta's voice said before he heard her draw in a quick breath.

"What's the matter?" he asked as he entered the coach.

"I think the infant is coming," she replied with a pained look on her face. "The pains are much closer together."

"Garman, tell the women to prepare to attend to my wife," Langward said as the man appeared in the doorway. "Supper can wait."

Garman quickly vanished.

"Can you stand long enough to get out of the coach?" he asked.

She nodded and began to slowly rise. He and her mother helped her to the door of the coach. He helped her out of the coach, then picked her up in his arms. She was very heavy as he carried her to the palace door. Garman appeared and led him to a nearby room. He laid her down gently on the table where the women had placed some blankets, kissing her forehead before her mother pushed him out of the room and shut the door. Garman was waiting there for him.

"Do you wish to eat?" he asked. "A snack while you wait? You can have supper later when Our Queen can share your meal."

"I don't want to leave her," Langward replied. "Even though her mother is in with her, I want to stay right here."

"I'll have it brought to you," the man replied. "You can eat right here next to the door."

He nodded and Garman left. The guards who had followed them inside watched as he paced back and forth. He was very anxious about the health of both Retanta and the infant she carried. She had been so very supportive of his quest to rid Brinley of Burkhart's rule. He had known her

19

all of his life. When he left their village to serve in the military, she had cried. He knew then that she loved him as he loved her. It had been a difficult and lonely three years, but he had learned the skills he needed to take the throne while they had been separated. He had learned the language of the kingdoms of the North along with how to read and write in addition to the battle arts. He knew that she might argue, but their son should also serve in the military. He must learn how to live outside the palace so that when he took Langward's place, he would remember the lives and needs of the people.

Garman returned with servants carrying a small table, a chair and some food. He smiled as though to reassure him as Langward sat down. He began to eat even though his thoughts were not of food, but of the birth of his son. The other servants left, but Garman remained. He stood quietly and watched Langward eat. Although he had met the man just yesterday, he liked Garman. He was younger than Langward, but calm and self assured. He knew his job and the other servants obviously respected him.

Suddenly the door opened. Langward stood to face the woman who entered the hall.

"I just wanted you to know that everything is going well and she should deliver within the next hour," the woman said. "She is a strong woman and in good health. Queen Aurita died partially because she was weak and sickly."

"Thank you," he said, feeling relieved.

The woman smiled before going back into the room and closing the door.

"She speaks the truth," Garman said and the guards both nodded. "Queen Aurita spent most of her time in bed after it was discovered she was with child. She was never a very healthy woman."

"I appreciate your efforts to ease my worries," Langward said. "Before the fortune teller left, she said my wife would soon bear me a son. From the rest of what she told me, I know that my son will live and so will my wife."

"She told Burkhart that his enemy's blood would mingle with his own after he had relinquished the throne," Garman said. "That's what angered Burkhart when he threw her and her sister in the dungeon."

"Who else heard what she said?" Langward asked.

"These two guards and myself were the only others present," Garman said and the guards nodded.

"No one else should be told of this," Langward said. "I will tell Retanta part of it, but not everything until much later. Swear to me you will not tell another living soul any of this."

"We swear," the men said in unison after glancing at each other.

"Thank you," he said. "I feel that even though everything has not gone exactly as I planned, everything has gone as it should. This morning I had to rescue Burkhart and his daughter from the villagers I sent him to live with. He demonstrated to my satisfaction that he is eager to obey and please me. I think the villagers will allow him to live among them now, but I will have to check up on him frequently. First thing in the morning I want to meet with General Kannon. Send word to him tonight."

"I'll do that right now," Garman said and quickly left.

Langward paced while he waited for word on the birth of his son. He wondered what Retanta would think of not naming their son. It seemed a very strange thing to do, but at least he would have the title of prince. As he wondered what name his son would eventually bear the door opened and he heard an infant crying.

"Brinley's throne has an heir," the woman said.

Langward hurried past her to Retanta's side. She was sitting in a chair holding their son. Her mother, Kara, stood behind her. She smiled as he knelt beside her reaching out and tenderly stroking the tiny face. He looked up as he heard the door close and found that the women had left them alone. Retanta handed him their son.

"What shall we name our son?" she asked as he met her gaze.

"There was a fortune teller here yesterday. She said that only by true love can our son be named," he replied as Retanta looked confused. "I know that sounds very strange, but I believe we should trust her words. She knew that you would soon deliver and the child would be male. Besides, I love him with or without a name. For now he can be known as Prince."

"I was surprised that you sent for me so soon," she said. "The men who came knelt and called me Queen Retanta. So did the women here."

"You are not only my queen, but Queen of all of Brinley now," he said. "I know that our son will someday sit upon the throne. The fortune teller said that a long reign is insured for our lineage."

21

"I heard rumor that Burkhart still lives and is free," she said with a worried look on her face.

"It is true, but I can guarantee that he will never seek to take the throne from me," he said hoping to reassure her. "He is not exactly free either. I will explain later, but for now you need to recover your strength."

Just then there was a quiet knock on the door.

"Come," he said as he stood.

Garman entered followed by a woman carrying a cushion bearing the armband of the queen. Garman placed the armband on Retanta's right arm before he and the woman knelt before them.

"Rise," he said.

"This is my wife, Stasha," Garman said.

"My Queen," Stasha said. "I humbly request the honor of being your personal servant."

Retanta glanced at Langward and he nodded slightly.

"I would greatly appreciate your services," she replied as the infant in Langward's arms began to cry again. "I believe he is hungry."

"We will go make certain everything is moved to our quarters," Langward said as he handed their son to her. "I'll see you a bit later."

He kissed her lips tenderly before leading Garman out of the room. As they approached the door to the courtyard, it opened and several men entered carrying trunks.

"Bring those and follow us," Langward said.

He was beginning to remember the different hallways from his time as a guard, but it would take time before he would feel confident unescorted. Garman led them to the new royal quarters.

"Set those in the bedroom," Langward said and they obeyed.

The men knelt before leaving.

"Supper is ready when you are ready to eat," Garman said.

"For tonight, I would prefer to eat here," he said. "I'm certain that Retanta will not want to go down to the dining room tonight."

"As you wish, My King," Garman said. "I will go make the proper arrangements. I believe there is a small sedan chair in storage. I doubt Our Queen will wish to climb the stairs for a while. I have had the quarters next door prepared for Lady Kara. Will her husband be joining us as well?"

"He died last year," Langward replied as he shook his head.

"I will go get the sedan chair," Garman said.

Langward nodded as Garman knelt and then left. He went into the bedroom and opened one of the three trunks. It was full of things from their house. He laughed as he found the piece of bark he had painted flowers on that he had given to Retanta in the middle of the cold season when no flowers bloomed. She had acted like it was a real bouquet of flowers he had given her. He had not realized she had kept it. He took it and put it on the bedside table, propped against the wall. He looked through the rest of the stuff briefly before going out onto the balcony.

The fragrance of blossoms greeted him as he looked out over the garden. He could see men working to seal the courtyard to Burkhart's royal quarters. The fresh grave of Queen Aurita had a hastily carved stone at the head of the grave. He knew he must be on guard for any who might still feel loyal to Burkhart. For now he was grateful that Retanta and his son were both safely in the palace where he could watch over them.

He turned as he heard a door open behind him and saw Retanta carried in, seated in a chair carried by two men. Kara followed behind. His wife was dressed in the most beautiful dress he had ever seen. He crossed to her side and offered her his hand as the men set down the chair. She smiled as she took his hand and stood up. The men moved the chair to along the wall before kneeling before them.

"Rise," Langward said.

The men stood and left. As they left, Garman entered, followed by several people carrying serving dishes. The table was soon set and Stasha held the infant while they ate. Garman had left but soon returned with some men carrying a large cradle. It was clean, but showed signs of wear.

"That's not," Langward began, and then paused.

"No, I thought you might prefer this one," Garman answered the unfinished question. "The other remains where it was."

Langward nodded as the men took the cradle into the bedroom. Retanta and Kara gave him a puzzled look, but said nothing. The others left, but Garman remained with Stasha. Retanta looked very tired as she put down her fork and leaned back in the chair.

"Perhaps you should retire for the night, My Dear," he said. "I will be in to join you soon."

"I will assist you, My Queen," Stasha said as she handed the infant to Garman.

"Thank you," Retanta said as she rose to her feet.

Kara went to help as well.

Langward stood and took his son from Garman as the bedroom door shut behind the women.

"Does Our Prince have a name yet?" Garman asked.

"No," Langward said. "Nor will he until he is much older."

"What do you mean, My King?" Garman asked with a concerned look on his face. "Certainly he needs a name."

"According to the fortune teller, only by true love can he be named," Langward said. "Eventually it will be Aurita that will give him his name. Until then, he will be known only as Prince. I know it seems a strange thing to do, but I know it is what must be done. I know it just as certainly as I knew that someday I would take the throne from Burkhart."

"It will be as you command, My King," Garman said. "I feel you should be warned that the dungeon master and his assistant do not understand why Burkhart still lives. They say you are weak."

"Thank you for telling me," he said. "I want four of my own men to guard Retanta at all times until things settle down."

"And four for yourself," Garman added.

"No," he replied. "Only two. I realize that the dungeon master does not recognize me, but he and I have met before in the Military Training Camp. I was the assistant of one of the instructors. I know his every weakness in battle. If I face him, I will face him alone. The only aid I require is to keep his assistant from joining the fight."

"As you command, My King," Garman said looking worried.

Just then Stasha and Kara came out of the bedchamber.

"You are dismissed," Langward said to Garman. "Show Lady Kara to her quarters and tend to her needs."

Garman and Stasha both knelt before leaving. Langward took his son into the bedchamber and laid him gently into the cradle. He covered the infant with the beautiful blanket that was in the cradle before undressing and getting into bed. The infant woke them several times during the night. Langward enjoyed watching his wife and son even though he was still tired at dawn. Retanta still slept as he slipped on some pants and went out into the sitting room.

Langward heard noises coming from the balcony so he quietly crossed to stand against the wall next to the door. He heard men's voices outside. He realized they would be armed, but he did not want to open the bedroom door. There would be no time to call for the guards either. At least they did not know he was waiting for them. He readied himself as the doorknob turned. As the door opened, he saw the dungeon master with his hand on the outer door knob.

As Langward pushed him back out onto the balcony, he said, "What? How?"

"This ends here," Langward said as he shut the door behind him.

"You are too soft to be king," the assistant said.

"You couldn't even kill Burkhart when you had the chance," the dungeon master added with a growl.

"I chose not to kill him," Langward said as the man charged toward him with sword drawn.

He ducked and kicked Kolis in the side. He then spun around and knocked the sword into the air. As the dungeon master sank to his knees, Langward caught the sword in time to deflect the assistant's attack. He was soon able to disarm his attacker and catch the second sword. He held them with a sword point at each man's throat.

"Now, as king, I shouldn't have to explain myself to anyone," Langward said. "But it is obvious you have mistaken my decision to allow Burkhart to live as weakness. What he faces is a torture far greater than any you could inflict upon him in the dungeon. Another thing you do not know is that Burkhart willingly relinquished the throne to me. After the death of his wife, he had no more will to live."

Langward paused to let his words sink in.

"Now I want you to realize that I easily could have killed you both with my bare hands," he said. "As king, I could rightfully execute you for treason."

The dungeon master swallowed noisily and his assistant had sweat pouring down his face.

"Instead, I believe I will give you a day to think about it," he said then paused. "To your feet."

Kolis slowly and carefully stood up.

"Now, to the dungeon," he said watching their eyes widen.

They glanced at each other as they turned around. He poked the dungeon master in the back and the man opened the door. He followed them through the room and out of the quarters into the hall. The six men at the door drew their swords.

"Take them to the dungeon," he said. "Take everything from them except their pants. Put them in separate cells so they cannot speak to each other. They will receive one small meal tonight and then bring them to me tomorrow morning."

As the two men glanced at each other, he could see the guards were struggling to keep straight faces. He handed one of the guards the two swords he held and returned to his quarters to find Retanta in the sitting room.

"What is going on, Langward?" she asked in a worried tone. "I heard a noise and saw you escort two men through the room at sword point."

"Just taking care of a little business," he said as he kissed her forehead. "Nothing you need to worry about."

He took her into his arms and kissed her lips. He could feel her body pressing against his and felt her arms around his neck pulling him closer. Her sweet scent was intoxicating as he kissed her more passionately. She laid her head on his shoulder and sighed. It felt so good to feel her in his arms again. Without her he did not quite feel whole.

"Oh! How I have missed you, My Love," he said with feeling.

"I have been so worried about you," she whispered. "Your messages were so few and far between."

"I could not risk putting you in danger," he said softly as he stroked her silky hair. "I needed to know you were where my enemies would not find you."

Just then there was a quiet tap on the outer door. He released Retanta from his arms and she retreated to the bed chamber.

"Come," he said as the door closed behind her.

Garman and Stasha entered and knelt.

"Rise," he said.

"My King, are you alright?" Garman asked in a worried tone. "I saw the dungeon master and his assistant being escorted by six guards."

"I am fine," he said. "They will be learning what things look like from inside the dungeon cells."

"You are not executing them for treason?" Stasha asked in a surprised tone.

26

"I don't think they need to be executed," he said. "And now they know that the new king of Brinley is a strong king."

He could see the fleeting smile play across Garman's face.

"It is time that I get dressed for the day," he said. "My queen is awake as well."

He opened the bed chamber door to find Retanta looking at the infant sleeping in the cradle.

"A bath is being prepared for you, My King," Garman said. "The royal seamstresses want your measurements this morning so they can make your new wardrobe. They are waiting in the bathing chamber."

Langward nodded and followed Garman back out into the sitting room to a door opposite the bed chamber. Inside there were two men and two women.

"Take your measurements," he said.

They carefully and thoroughly measured him before leaving. The bathing chamber featured a large basin of water built into the floor that was fed by what appeared to be a water fall. The water was warm and soothing as the men washed him. He was finding it difficult to stay awake.

"You did not sleep well, My King?" one asked him as they finished.

"I discovered that newborn infants do not sleep through the night," he said, shaking his head.

"That will pass in time," the other said with a laugh.

Langward scratched his beard and said, "I think I'll shave this off. I never have cared for having a beard."

"We can shave that off, My King," one said. "What about the mustache?"

"That can go too."

He leaned back and let them shave him. Soon he was clean shaven and dressed. As he looked into the polished shield, he saw a king staring back at him.

"Much better," he said quietly to himself. "Much better."

As he left the bathing chamber, two women entered and knelt.

"Rise," he said.

"We have come to attend to Queen Retanta," they said as the bedroom door opened.

Retanta was holding their son as she entered the room. The two women quickly knelt at her feet.

"Rise," she said.

"We have come to attend to you while you bathe," they told her.

She gave Langward a look that he understood all too well. He smiled and nodded realizing it would take her a while to feel comfortable being waited on. She handed him the infant and followed the women into the bathing chamber.

"Would you like your breakfast brought in or will you be eating in the dining hall?" Garman asked.

"Let's give Our Queen a few days before taking her down to the dining hall," he said. "I want a couple of my men stationed out on the balcony for now."

"I will see to it," Garman replied and left.

Langward sat down to wait for Retanta. He wondered what great things his son would do in his lifetime. She came out of the bathing chamber just as their breakfast was brought in. He put the infant in his cradle to sleep while they ate.

After the servants all left Retanta commented, "This will take some getting used to."

"Being queen or being a mother?" he asked with a laugh.

"Both," she said. "It will take some time to be comfortable having someone else bathe and dress me."

"I feel the same way," he replied. "But it is what they expect of us. We will need to remember that to keep being king and queen there are certain things expected of us. I have begun going through Burkhart's changes to Brinley's laws, but I feel the people need some input into the process."

"Yes," she said after swallowing. "We don't want to forget what it was like to live in the village. If we had someone to help us that did not live or work in the palace it might help us remember."

"The fortune teller told me that I would make divisions that would strengthen our nation. Perhaps if we divided the kingdom into sections with one representative from each section."

She nodded and said, "Perhaps we could allow the representatives to be chosen by the people of the section."

He was glad she was here. She had always been able to bring out the best in him and would be a great queen. When he had finished eating, he stood up.

"I have a few things to attend to," he said as he kissed her forehead. "I am having two of my men stationed on the balcony and more at the doors. You will be safe until I return. Hopefully I will soon convince everyone that I am King of Brinley and that I am a strong king. Then we can relax the guard a bit."

"I know," she said. "I want to help you."

"You have already helped me, but for now, you can best help by regaining your strength. There will be time later for the rest."

As Langward left, two of his men entered the room and knelt before Retanta. When they rose they went out onto the balcony. He found Garman waiting for him outside.

"General Kannon will be here soon," Garman said as they walked down the hall.

"Good," he replied. "Are there any diagrams of the palace?"

"I think so."

"I wish to study them so I can get around without needing an escort."

"But your safety."

"I want this palace to be as secure and safe as my own bedchamber," he said cutting Garman short. "That is part of why I put the dungeon master and his assistant in the dungeon for a day. Tomorrow I will release them. I am counting on them to tell everyone exactly what I did and said. I will soon have an announcement ready for the people of Brinley. The same day that the announcement is made, I want to grant audiences to some of Brinley's citizens. I want them to have something to talk about that was not in the official announcement. Word will spread. How long have the two murderers been in the dungeon?"

"About two weeks."

"Any doubts about their guilt?"

"None. There were many witnesses in both cases."

"Good," he said. "We will need to schedule a public execution. I need the people to have no doubts that I am willing to enforce the laws."

"I will tell the executioner."

"No," Langward said as they entered the throne room. "I will personally execute them."

"You never have shied away from trouble," a familiar voice said as they crossed the dais to the throne.

"General Kannon, it's good to see you again," Langward said as the general climbed the steps and saluted.

"It's good to see you in one piece," General Kannon said with a smile. "My favorite colonel is now my king. I had been worried about you. When you vanished I was afraid you had really died but there were so many rumors going around."

"I wanted to tell you the truth, but I knew the only way to protect you was to not tell you anything. I did not want Burkhart to be suspicious of you. I have a new position open if you are interested," he said. "Garman, I do not want to be disturbed until lunch unless something urgent comes up or my wife asks for me."

"Yes, My King," Garman said as he knelt before leaving.

"I heard that Kolis and Maughn thought they could kill you," General Kannon said as Langward opened the door to his private study. "I didn't think they had a chance."

"They are now finding out what it is like to be in the dungeon instead of guarding it," he replied with a laugh. "They also discovered that I don't need any weapons to defeat them."

"There are a lot of strange rumors going about," the general said as they sat down. "And what is the position you mentioned?"

"All the rumors will go away as soon as I announce my kingship to the kingdom. I plan on making many changes in the way Brinley is governed."

"You never said it out loud, but I sensed that you didn't approve of Burkhart's new laws. I heard that Burkhart still lives."

"Queen Aurita died giving birth to his daughter," Langward said. "When I found him, he was holding her in his arms. He offered me the armbands of his own free will. I could see in his eyes that look of utter defeat. He had completely lost his will to live. The man known as King Burkhart died with his wife. What was left is an empty shell of a man. I sent him and his daughter to live in Weston."

"So the rumors are true," General Kannon said in surprise.

"I need you to double the patrols around the village," he said nodding. "I think I have convinced them that they need to allow him to live there, but there still might be trouble."

"You think he will try to take the throne back?"

"No," he said as he shook his head. "I am certain that he will do exactly as I tell him to. Mostly the additional patrols are to insure that the villagers don't kill him and his daughter."

Langward described what happened in the village when he rescued Burkhart from the villagers.

"I would love to see him trying to live outside the palace," General Kannon said as he began to laugh.

"The only thing I am worried about besides the villagers killing him is that he will purposely leave the village in hopes of being killed. I need the patrols to understand that their duty there is mostly show of force. In a couple of days I will check on him again and let him know that I expect him to live long enough to raise his daughter. He will obey me."

"So what is this position you mentioned?"

"I want to make some changes to our system of government," he said. "I think part of why Burkhart was able to make so many laws that benefitted only the king is that there was no one to stop him. I want to have three ministers to help in making laws and ruling the people. I want you to be my Minister of Defense."

General Kannon looked shocked. They sat in silence for a while before anyone spoke.

"I feel that the people need to have some say in the laws and how they are governed. Together we will form a council to govern our people."

"That certainly is a big change," General Kannon said at last. "I think the people will like it. Where did you get the idea?"

When I first disappeared I went east across the mountains. I found a small village being built. Many of the people had burns that were still healing. They told me that they had recently escaped with their lives when a dragon burned their town. They were determined to not belong to any kingdom again so they had a council of elders to create laws and govern the village. Every villager has a chance to voice their opinion before a decision is made by the council."

"I've heard rumors of dragons, but not much about what one is. It sounds dangerous," General Kannon commented with alarm in his voice.

"Apparently they are huge winged beasts that breathe fire. The dragon was killed and they feel safe enough where they are between Brinley and the town they escaped from."

"I'll have the eastern patrols watch the skies as well as the border."

"I agree that we need to keep a watch for dragons invading Brinley. The first thing I have done is to revoke all of Burkhart's self serving laws," he said. "I think from there we will need to review all of the remaining laws and make changes as necessary."

"I'm honored you thought to include me," General Kannon said. "I'll take the position of Minister of Defense."

"Good," he said. "Now I need to choose a Minister of the Interior and a Prime Minister."

Chapter 4-New Beginnings

Burkhart lay down on the ground near the burnt out shell of the tiny house. He had fashioned a crude bed from his meager belongings to keep Aurita off the ground. It had been a very long day and his sore muscles ached. He heard voices and footsteps coming toward him.

"You can't sleep outside like this," one man said as Burkhart sat up to face them.

"Especially with the infant," another said.

"I have nowhere else," he replied with a heavy heart as he fought back tears. "I am not worthy of anywhere else."

The men glanced at each other.

"You can sleep in the empty stall in my barn," one of them said.

"Don't you even have a blanket?" the first man asked.

"Only the cape," he replied, pointing to the cape he had wrapped around Aurita to keep her warm. "This is everything I own."

The men looked at each other again and then back at him.

"I think I can find an extra blanket somewhere," one man said. "It's too early for the horse to need one."

"Thank you," Burkhart said as he picked up Aurita.

He followed the men to the barn. One of the men went to get a blanket while the other two helped him make a bed for Aurita in the empty feed box. They left him in the dark, alone with Aurita and the animals. The dried grasses that were spread out on the floor poked at him while he tried to get comfortable, but at least he had a roof over his head.

The next morning came early. Aurita had awakened hungry several times in the night and had drunk all the milk the minister had given him. He heard voices and squinted at the sudden light as about a dozen men entered the barn.

"Today we start to rebuild your home," one of the men said.

"My wife has offered to tend the infant while you are working," the minister said as Burkhart stood up.

Burkhart was too surprised to do anything but nod. King Langward's efforts in his behalf had succeeded. He followed the men outside of the barn. The minister's wife took Aurita and his belongings from him. He followed them out to the edge of the village but stopped short as they crossed into the forest. A border patrol came galloping up. The minister stepped between Burkhart and the soldiers.

"In order to build a home, he must be allowed to enter the forest unharmed," the minister said. "Will you escort him?"

The three men glanced at each other before nodding.

"Let us signal to approve it with King Langward," one of the men said and turned his horse back toward the border.

They waited for the man to return.

"King Langward replied that all the wood must be gathered today," the man said as he brought his horse to a stop.

"We can do that," one of the men said. "Burkhart can sleep in my barn again tonight."

*****

Langward was pleased with the message Garman had delivered to him. It confirmed that the villagers were trying to help Burkhart instead of trying to kill him.

"Send this reply," Langward said. "All the wood must be gathered today."

"At once, My King," Garman said before he knelt and left.

"What was that all about?" Retanta asked as she came out of the bedchamber holding their son. "I think it's time you told me exactly what you have done with Burkhart."

She handed him their son and sat next to him.

"I didn't want to upset you," he replied. "But now I think you are ready to hear what happened."

He described what had happened when he captured the palace and in the village the following morning. "Without the child, he would have lay down and died on his own. His wife was the one thing he loved more than power."

"I think I understand," she said. "But do you think they'll survive there?"

"I was able to convince the people of Weston that he was no longer King Burkhart, but simply a broken man who's only reason to live was his child," Langward explained. "He even called me 'Noble King' loudly enough for everyone to hear."

Retanta began to laugh.

"He will have to be taught everything about living outside the palace. He doesn't know how to take care of himself, let alone how to care for an infant."

"I'm glad I'm married to such a compassionate man," she said. "But, I would love to see him changing diapers."

Langward began to laugh as well. Garman and some servants brought some breakfast in to them. After breakfast, Langward wrote out a public announcement to inform the people of Brinley that Burkhart was no longer king. Garman took it to have it read in various places around the kingdom, while Langward and General Kannon began to divide the kingdom into districts.

"I think the people will like this," General Kannon said.

"I know they will," he responded. "Hopefully it will work. I have gone through the book of laws and know what ones I want reinstated and what ones should be revoked, but I will give the people some time to elect someone to represent them before creating any new laws. My next task should be to choose the other two ministers."

"I would suggest that Mikan would be a good Prime Minister," General Kannon said. "He and I don't always agree on things, but he is a very wise man. I know he respects you."

"I agree," Langward said with a smile. "It has been a couple of years since I last saw Mikan. I was thinking about Nokar as Minister of the Interior. He always knew everything that was going on."

"Yes, but I doubt he knows you are king yet," the general said with a laugh.

"I'll send for the two of them now," Langward said as he gave the cord a tug.

Garman soon appeared and was sent to summon the men. When they were brought into the study, they were very surprised.

"You're the new king?" Nokar asked. "There have been so many rumors going around."

"I had heard you were dead," Mikan added in a surprised tone. "I also heard Burkhart still lives."

"Burkhart is in Weston learning what hard work it is to live outside the palace. He is not the same man who ruled Brinley. The man known as King Burkhart died with Queen Aurita. Besides, death would have been a kinder fate," Langward replied with a grin.

"Why have you brought us here?" Mikan asked. "The man wouldn't tell us anything."

"I have a position for each of you if you are interested," he replied.

"What type of position?" Nokar asked.

"I am completely changing Brinley's government. Burkhart proved to us that a single man with too much power cannot be trusted. I have decided to form a counsel with three ministers and a voice for the people," Langward said as the men sat in the seats he indicated. "General Kannon has agreed to be Brinley's Minister of Defense. I want to appoint you, Mikan, as Prime Minister and you, Nokar, as Minister of the Interior. We are dividing Brinley into districts and will ask each district to choose a governor to represent them."

The men seemed stunned. General Kannon began to laugh.

"I didn't quite believe it at first either," the general said. "But I believe it will work well."

"I can't believe you thought to ask me," Mikan said at last.

"Actually, General Kannon suggested you for Prime Minister," Langward said.

"You did?" Mikan asked as he looked at General Kannon. "I thought after our last battle of wills you would never speak to me again."

"Just because we don't always agree doesn't mean I don't respect your opinions."

"I have sent around a public announcement to let the people of Brinley know that I am now the king," Langward said as he stood. "I want to grant audiences after lunch, but first I think it's about time to deal with Kolis and Maughn."

He opened the door to find Garman waiting outside.

"Have Kolis and Maughn brought in," he said before heading to the throne.

"At once, My King," Garman said with a smile and quickly left.

"He never used to smile," General Kannon said as the door shut behind Garman.

"I get the feeling that he was glad to be rid of Burkhart," Langward replied.

The doors opened and Kolis and Maughn were escorted in by four men each. They each had a chain and manacles around their wrists. They

36

did not look up as they were brought to the bottom of the steps lying down without prompting. Langward glanced at his ministers to find them grinning. General Kannon seemed especially pleased.

"To your knees," Langward said sternly and the men complied. "I think you two need less responsibility than you have had."

They finally looked up at him.

"General Kannon, do you think you can find a use for these two?" he asked.

"If you think they can be trusted," General Kannon said. "I can always use more patrolmen."

"They should be fine as long as they are stationed separately," Langward said. "They can start right after tomorrow morning. I want them to witness the execution. Do you have anything to say for yourselves?"

"I don't ever want to spend another night in the dungeon," Kolis said. "I'm sorry I doubted you."

"I don't even want to work in the dungeon anymore," Maughn said. "Thank you for giving me the chance to redeem myself, Noble King."

"Take them; give them their clothing and belongings back. They can stay tonight with their families."

The guards took the men away. When the doors closed, they began to laugh.

"I'll remember that for the rest of my life!" Mikan exclaimed.

"Why are you letting them spend the night with their families?" Nokar asked.

"I want them to talk to their families," Langward said. "I want their families to talk to all of their friends and neighbors. What they have to say will go much farther than any announcement I could have made. After lunch I will grant audiences to the public. I know that although careful planning and my sword made me king, public opinion is what will keep me on the throne."

"You always did know how to get what you want," General Kannon said with a laugh.

Garman entered and knelt.

When he stood up he said, "Our Queen has eaten already and is resting. Lady Kara ate with her. Lunch is ready for you and your ministers."

Once they were served, Langward had all of the servants leave and shut the doors.

"Garman seems to know a lot," General Kannon commented as they ate.

"I think he can be trusted," Langward said, realizing the general's concern. "It was Garman that warned me about Kolis and Maughn."

"His wife is Burkhart's cousin," General Kannon said. "He married them about a year ago. It was Burkhart's idea, not theirs."

"I'll have to confront them with it," Langward said. "I want everything very clear and out in the open when it comes to the palace staff."

After lunch, Langward and his ministers returned to the throne room. Once he was seated he nodded and the guards opened the doors. He watched as a crowd of people poured into the room then signaled to Garman who was waiting near the study door.

"I want you to select the order in which the audiences are granted," Langward said as Garman approached. "Do not favor one over another based on wealth or social status."

"Yes, My King," Garman said. "There is one I believe should be heard first."

Langward nodded and Garman went down into the crowd. When he returned to the bottom of the steps he was followed by two women. One of the women was weeping and did not look up. The other had her arm around her and seemed very concerned and protective. They both dropped to their knees before him.

"Rise and state your reason for seeking audience," Langward said, curious as to what had the woman so upset.

"My King," the one began. "We come to plead for the life of one of the men you are going to have executed tomorrow morning."

"One of the men found guilty of killing another?" he asked in surprise.

"The soldiers took him away before we could speak to them," the woman said. "The man he killed attacked his wife. She has done almost nothing but cry since he was taken. This is what she was wearing when she was attacked."

The woman pulled some cloth out of the bag that hung at her side. It was ripped and barely resembled a dress. The story it told made the situation very clear.

"Bring the dress here," Langward said quietly to Garman. "Then have the man brought in."

Garman brought him the dress and quickly left. Langward could see the blood on the dress and knew that a grave mistake had been made by putting the man in the dungeon. He stood and held up the dress for everyone to see.

"This tells far more than any other witness could," he said and the crowd fell silent except for the weeping of the woman. "Any such attack against a woman will not be tolerated. Any man found attacking a woman in such a manner will certainly face the consequences. I am changing our laws for the better of all people and giving the people a voice in any new laws."

There was quite a stir among the crowd as the doors opened again. The man the guards led in was chained at the neck, wrists and ankles. He did not look up as they pushed him to his knees before Langward.

"Remove his bindings," Langward said sternly as he handed the dress to General Kannon.

The guards hesitated only a moment before complying. Langward went down the steps and dropped to one knee in front of the man. He placed a hand on the man's shoulder. The man looked up at him in surprise.

"You will not meet your death by my hand or any other tomorrow," he told the man. "Stand on your feet as a free man."

Langward stood up and the man stood up too.

"Certainly life is a precious thing," Langward said. "Murder cannot be tolerated, but the protection of our homes, our wives, and our children must take precedence. It is clear to me that regardless of witnesses seeing the man die at your hand, what they did not see justifies your reaction. Take your wife home."

"Thank you," the man said with emotion. "My life is yours to command."

"My purpose is to right the wrongs done by Burkhart," Langward said. "I am here to improve Brinley and the lives of its people. I can claim no debt for freeing you. Your wife needs you much more than I do."

The man took his wife into his arms and carried her out followed by the other woman. Langward returned to the throne and sat down.

"Are there any here who wish to speak on behalf of the other man condemned to die?" he asked the stunned crowd.

An old man stepped forward cautiously, knelt then stood. Langward nodded as the man met his eye.

"I am his father," the man said then paused. "His actions shame me. He has always had an evil temper which he doesn't care to control. I know that he must die for his deeds. All I ask for him is a swift end. All I ask for myself is to be allowed to take his body to bury it next to his brother's."

"It is by my hand that he shall die," Langward said and heard gasps around the room. "I promise that his end will be swift. I give permission for you to take his body and do with it as you please."

"Thank you, My King," the man said and knelt at the foot of the steps.

After the man left, the rest of the matters were very minor in comparison, but he gave them the same attention he had afforded the first two matters. Some were almost silly and he had a hard time keeping a straight face, but he knew that regardless of the issue it was him that was being judged by the people. Finally the last matter was settled and the throne room stood empty.

"Supper is ready for you," Garman said as he knelt. "Our Queen ate earlier."

"Thank you," Langward said. "I wish to speak to you just after supper."

"Me?" Garman asked in a surprised tone as he stood up and Langward nodded.

Garman appeared nervous as he led them to the dining room. Once the servants had left and they were alone, Langward began to laugh. Soon the other three men were laughing as well.

"I just couldn't hold that in any longer," he said with a sigh as he finally was able to quit laughing.

"I don't know how you managed to keep such a serious tone in your voice," General Kannon said.

"I just had to keep reminding myself that to them these matters were serious enough to bring before their king," he replied. "I can guarantee that soon everyone in Brinley will hear about the audiences."

"Especially the man you released," Mikan said.

"I'm glad that woman had the courage to bring the truth to my attention," he said as he picked up his fork. "That alone will prove me a good king."

The conversation was light during the meal. Langward was glad that they had accepted their new positions. They would be a great help to him. When the meal was finished, he found Garman waiting for him in the hall. He looked nervous.

"Come," Langward said, not waiting for the man to speak or kneel.

He led Garman to his private study. He sat on the edge of the desk instead of behind it. He could see Garman's hands trembling as he stood before him.

"I learned something interesting about you today," Langward said and watched the man go pale. "I decided I should ask you to confirm the truth about it."

Garman began to sweat.

"I need to know everything about you if I am going to be able to trust you," Langward continued. "There can be no secrets between us."

"I pledge myself entirely to you, My King," Garman said with a trembling voice. "My life is yours."

"Do you love your wife?" Langward asked.

Garman looked like he had been hit.

"Do you love Stasha?" Langward repeated. "I am told that Stasha is Burkhart's cousin and it was his idea that you marry her, not yours."

Garman looked like he was going to collapse or faint.

"Sit down and answer the question," Langward said sternly.

Garman was trembling as he found a chair and sat down. His face was pale and his hands shaking uncontrollably.

"I. . . I. . . We," Garman began, and then cleared his throat. "We have grown closer since we were married."

"Do you love her?" Langward persisted. "Does she love you?"

Garman looked distressed as he said, "We know that we must learn to love each other. The day we were married is the first day we met. I

41

do care for her. I want her to be happy. I have always thought she was beautiful."

"Do you share your bed with her?"

"At first we did not share a bed," Garman said after he swallowed. "But last cold season, she insisted that I sleep in the bed because the floor was too cold. Some mornings I awaken to find my arms around her."

"That is a good start I suppose," Langward said. "Do you kiss her?"

"Not since our wedding," Garman said seeming to relax a little. "I think about it sometimes. I do someday want children, but I don't want to push her into something she doesn't want."

"Have you ever spoken to her about it?"

Garman shook his head. Langward stood and went to the door. Two guards were stationed just outside.

"Bring Garman's wife, Stasha, here," Langward said.

One of the guards quickly left. Langward went back into the study and shut the door. He wondered how best to proceed. He noticed the shelves near the window left an alcove that was not easily noticed from the door.

"Come stand here," Langward said as he approached the spot. "Remain still and silent while I question your wife. You may learn something."

He moved a chair to the center of the room facing the desk as there was a knock at the door. He crossed to the door and opened it. He found Stasha kneeling before him.

"Come in and sit down," Langward said, indicating the chair he had placed.

She obeyed. He sat down on the edge of the desk. He could see Garman peeking out of the alcove.

"I learned something about you and Garman today," he said and noticed her reaction was similar to Garman's. "I was told that you are Burkhart's cousin and that the day you were married was the first time you met Garman."

"Yes, My King," she replied in almost a whisper.

"If you are to serve my wife, I need to know that I can trust you completely," he said. "My wife and son are more important to me than all of Brinley. There can be no secrets between us. I must know everything if I am to trust you and Garman."

"My life and loyalty belong to you, My King," she responded.

"Do you love your husband?" he asked.

"Do I love Garman?" she repeated. "When we were first married, I was frightened, but he has always been very kind and considerate. Over time I have come to love him. Sometimes I awaken in the middle of the night and find his arms around me. Sometimes he says my name in his sleep. Sometimes I kiss him on the forehead and he smiles in his sleep."

Langward noticed Garman's hand go to his forehead.

"What about children?" he asked.

"Before Garman suggested I serve Our Queen, I served in the palace nursery tending children of the palace servants," she said. "I would be very sad by the end of the day."

"Why were you sad?" he pressed her further.

"Because I do want children," she said. "I want Garman's children."

"Have you told Garman?" he asked and she shook her head.

"I've been afraid to."

"What would you tell Garman if you were not afraid?"

She swallowed before saying, "I would tell him that I want him to be my husband in more than name only. I want to bear his children. I would tell him that I love him, but I am afraid that he doesn't love me."

Langward noticed that Garman was looking a little shocked as he stepped out of the alcove. As Garman met his eye, he nodded.

"You shouldn't be afraid," Langward said. "I believe it is what he has wanted to hear."

Stasha stood and turned around to see Garman approaching her.

"I have hoped that you could love me," Garman said before he took her in his arms and kissed her.

"I believe I am going to retire and suggest that you two do the same," Langward said as he went to the door. "Don't stay up too late."

He left the room and shut the door behind him.

"Is everything alright?" one of the guards asked as they followed him across the dais to the doors.

"Everything is just as it should be," he replied. "You may want to have someone wake Garman just before dawn. I will need him tomorrow morning."

The guards began to grin.

"I'll see that it gets done, My King," one of them said as they reached his quarters.

He shook his head as he shut the door behind him. Retanta and his son were both asleep as he got into bed.

Chapter 5 – Reunion and Revelations

When Langward awoke at dawn, Garman was waiting for him in the sitting room. He looked happy, but tired.

"I want to thank you, My King," Garman said. "Burkhart gave me a roommate, but you gave me a wife."

"I just did what needed to be done," Langward said. "Women will not always tell you what they are feeling. She didn't seem angry that you had been in the room the whole time."

"She said that she was very relieved that I had heard her and now knew how she really felt about me," Garman replied as he opened the bathing chamber door.

Soon he was bathed and dressed. The clothes were black except for the designs around the edges of the tunic. Retanta ate breakfast with him before he left to perform the execution.

There was a large crowd assembled in the town square where the platform was set up. As he climbed the stairs, Langward noticed the condemned man's father standing next to the stairs. He placed his hand on the father's shoulder and he gave a brief smile as he met Langward's gaze. The man was brought to kneel before him. He could see that the man was not sorry for the murder he had committed. He understood then the father's request. He knew that had circumstances been different, he could have been the one kneeling before the king waiting for his death. His blade cut cleanly through the man's neck. Four men brought a wooden box onto the platform at his nod. They helped the father place his son's body and head into the box as the crowd began to dissipate.

Garman held his horse as he mounted it. The executed man's father approached and knelt at the horse's feet.

"Rise," Langward said.

"Thank you for keeping your promise," the man said. "The day he killed his brother, I lost them both."

"There was no sense in any other manner of death for him," Langward said. "The look of defiance in his eyes confirmed that. He had enough time in the dungeon to consider his crime, but he still was not repentant. He now faces a higher judge which will show him the error of his actions."

45

The man nodded and returned to the small wagon carrying the box containing the body of his son. Garman followed him back to the palace as the people knelt at his passing. He knew he had gained approval as Brinley's king.

"Burkhart never personally preformed an execution," Garman commented as they entered the palace. "He was never willing to do anything that would dirty his hands."

"He now has no choice in the matter," Langward replied. "He will learn that the life of the common man of Brinley is a dirty one. He will also learn that the waters of the river are very cold to bathe in and there will not be anyone there to dry or dress him."

*****

Burkhart was exhausted by the end of the day. His hands were sore and bloodied. He had not realized what hard work it was cutting wood into the proper pieces to build a house. The men began heading for the river which bordered the village.

"Aren't you coming?" one of the men asked.

"Where are you going?" Burkhart asked, confused.

"To bathe and look for brown burrowers," another replied as he followed them.

A couple of the men were building a fire while the rest were taking off their clothes. He wasn't quite certain what was going on. When the fire was going, those two men began to strip off their clothes. One of them had a strange tool that had a knife like handle, but instead of a blade it had a long, pointed shaft. He heated it in the fire until the shaft was red and white. Then he touched the point to a dark spot on another man's back. Burkhart was amazed to see the dark spot drop to the ground. Another man smashed it with a rock.

"He's got one behind his ear," a man beside him said.

The man heating the tool drew it out of the fire and approached him.

"This might sting a bit," the man said as Burkhart began to back away.

Several men grabbed him and held him. He felt the heat of the tool as it touched his skin. When they released him, he saw something small on the ground begin to scurry away. One of the men smashed it with a rock.

"What was that?" he asked.

"A brown burrower," the man with the tool said. "They can make you sick if you leave them on. They burrow their heads under your skin and suck your blood."

Burkhart felt a bit sick over the explanation. He began to take off his clothes with shaking hands. It took a while for the men to finish removing the brown burrowers from their skin before smashing them. Afterwards they took their clothes and rinsed them in the river. They hung the clothes on bushes before walking into the river. He followed them into the river to discover it was very cold.

He slipped on something slimy under his feet and fell into the water. He felt himself begin to be carried away by the river before he felt someone grab his arm. He gasped for air as they hauled his head above the water. The men were laughing.

"We're going to have to keep a closer watch on you," one of them said. "We wouldn't want you to drown."

"Thank you," he said as he found his footing among the slippery rocks.

He watched them as they dove beneath the water and swam. He was startled as something brushed against his leg and he slipped back into the water with a splash. He found his footing again and stood up before anyone got to him.

"There's something in here," he said as he tried to look beneath the surface of the water. "Something moved against my leg."

"It was a fish, a pincher or just moss," one of them said.

"A pincher?" he asked with concern and began moving toward shore.

One of the men dove down under the water and returned holding something in his hand.

"A pincher," the man said as he approached.

It had lots of legs and a curved tail, but what concerned Burkhart were the two front legs it was waving at him. They both ended in dangerous looking, pointed pairs of claws that opened and closed almost like scissors. Burkhart heard laughter as he scrambled up the bank.

"They're more afraid of you than you are of them," said the man who had hauled him out of the water the first time. "They won't bother you unless you step on them."

"How do you not step on them?" he asked, shaking as a breeze chilled his skin.

"They hide under rocks mostly," the man said. "Just don't put your feet under the edge of the rocks."

"Are you men going to come to dinner or not?" a female voice behind him asked.

Burkhart turned his head to find a woman standing on the other side of the bushes.

"We'll be right there," the man replied as he came to shore.

Burkhart grabbed his damp clothes and pulled them on. He was embarrassed by the thought that she had probably seen him standing there naked.

"Don't worry," the man said quietly as he began dressing. "As long as we're here bathing the women will stay on the other side of the bushes. When they're bathing we stay on the other side of the bushes."

Burkhart nodded as the other men began to get dressed. The man grabbed a small bucket that was nearby and doused the fire with water. He followed them as they went toward the church. There was a large group of people around a couple of tables. Someone handed him a plate and a fork. He watched as the men filed along the table and put food on their plates then followed behind the last man. After filling his plate with food he hadn't seen before he found a place to sit down that was away from the rest and began to eat.

"I'll keep the infant tonight," the minister's wife said as she stood in front of him. "You look too tired to care for her."

"Thank you," he said.

"You had best sleep inside the house tonight," the minister said as he and the man who had helped Burkhart joined her. "It looks like it will be cold tonight. We can't have you getting sick."

"Thank you," he said as he slowly stood up.

He followed them into the small house and held Aurita while the minister's wife washed the dishes.

"She's beautiful," the man said as he sat down next to Burkhart. "My name is Langford. Let's have a look at your hands."

Burkhart held out his left hand palm up.

"Just as I thought," Langford said getting up and retrieving a small box from a chest in the corner of the room.

Once he had sat down, he opened the box and drew out a smaller box made of clay. He opened it and dipped out some of the contents to gently rub onto the palm of Burkhart's hand. Langford then took a strip of cloth and wound it around the hand tying its ends together. Burkhart shifted Aurita to his other arm and allowed Langford to do the same to his right hand.

"You two should get some sleep," the minister's wife said as she took Aurita from him.

"Come on," Langford said as he stood up.

Burkhart followed him across the room and up a ladder through the ceiling of the room. There were two beds that were barely more than a mattress and some blankets in a room too short to stand upright in. Langford laid down on one of the beds and covered himself up. Burkhart gratefully crawled into the other bed and was soon sound asleep.

*****

The week had been a busy one. Langward and his three ministers had completed establishing eight districts and two of them had already chosen governors. This morning he decided it was time to visit his family and check on Burkhart. General Kannon and Garman would go with him. Things had settled down in the palace. There had been a few changes in staff, but very few. He at last felt comfortable enough to leave the palace for more than an hour or two at a time.

They arrived mid-morning and few people paid much attention. Langward went into the church, but it was empty. He felt the same peaceful feeling that he remembered from his childhood memories of the place. As he approached the outer door he heard a familiar voice speaking with one of the guards.

He grinned as he burst through the doors and tackled the man, carrying him to the ground. They wrestled for a few minutes before he pinned his opponent. He released the man and collapsed on his back next to the man as they both burst in to laughter. As their laughter slowed, he opened his eyes to find some very worried looking guards standing beside a confused looking Garman. General Kannon was grinning as he offered them both a hand up. He turned to find Burkhart standing behind him, looking very frightened. Burkhart quickly dropped to his stomach at his feet. Langward noticed the bandages on the upturned hands.

"I see my twin has been taking care of you," he said to Burkhart. "To your feet. I wish to see your hands."

"L. . . Langford is your twin, My King?" Burkhart asked as he rose. "He has been most kind. He has taught me many things that I need to know."

"When did you get home?" Langward asked as he looked at Langford.

"A week ago," he replied as Langward unwrapped one of the bandages from Burkhart's hands. "I have some news and a favor to ask."

"I have some news as well," he replied as he examined the healing blisters. "There's a lot to catch up on, but business first. I want to see how the house is coming along. These will heal nicely."

He replaced the wrapping before leading the way to the house. It was almost complete. In addition to the pile of shingles waiting to be nailed into place, there was an unfinished cradle and a door. He walked into the small home. It had been rebuilt matching his original plan. It was one room just big enough for a bed, a trunk, a table and some chairs. There were some shelves with a couple of pots on them beside the fireplace. There was a ladder leading up to the sleeping loft for the children.

"It looks like it could be finished today," he said as he stepped outside. "I know that you will appreciate it more after building it with your own hands."

"It is far more than I deserve," Burkhart said with his head bowed.

"I was told that he was going to sleep on the ground next to the chimney before someone insisted he sleep in their barn," Langford said. "He's slept in your bed since I got here. He only had one tunic, so I gave him one of your old ones. It wouldn't fit you now anyway."

Langward had a hard time not laughing at the stunned look on Burkhart's face.

"Let's get this finished," he said. "I can't wait to eat lunch. The palace food is good, but it is not Mother's."

Langford laughed as he picked up a hammer. Soon even the guards were helping. Garman handed things to people and Burkhart worked on the cradle. They had the shingles finished before noon. The blacksmith brought the latch and hinges for the door just as they got off the roof. Burkhart finished the cradle as the door was shut for the first time. The cradle was simple, but surprisingly well built.

"All this needs is some decoration," Langward said as he examined it. "I'll do that after lunch. Let's get bathed."

"Mother would be upset if we walked in smelling like this," Langford said with a laugh.

Langward picked up his tunic that he had hung on the hitching post next to the door. Burkhart followed quietly as they went to the river. Soon they were in the water. It was not the warm waters of the palace bath, but it felt good to wash away the sweat. He noticed Burkhart stayed away from the rest as he bathed and Garman stayed on shore.

"He is a changed man," General Kannon commented as he stood beside Langward. "I almost didn't recognize him at first."

"You now understand why there was no need to execute him," Langward said.

"I doubt I would have believed it if I had not seen it for myself," General Kannon said as they walked to the shore. "I can see why you sent him here."

The others followed as they got dressed and walked back to the church. Mother was coming out of the house holding a fussing infant.

"There you are," she said as she hurried to meet them. "She needs a new diaper and to be fed."

Burkhart took the infant from her and went into the house.

"This I've got to see," General Kannon said with a chuckle as Langward hugged Mother.

"It's good to see my two boys together again," Mother said as she led them into the house.

General Kannon stood shaking his head with a grin as he watched Burkhart change the diaper. Then Burkhart prepared a bottle and began feeding Aurita. By the time she was finished, the rest of them had begun to eat. Burkhart tied a blanket over one shoulder and around him in which he cradled the infant before he took a plate of food for himself. He sat on the floor next to the fireplace to eat. Langward was pleased with his progress. When he was finished eating, he stood up and took his plate to the tub of wash water. Before he could wash the plate, Burkhart came over and began washing it for him.

"I want to speak with you for a moment in private," Langward said and Burkhart looked at him in surprise.

*****

"I am yours to command, My King," Burkhart replied wondering what King Langward wanted to say to him.

He had noticed that General Kannon seemed amused by his present situation, but didn't care much. Most of the village seemed to enjoy laughing at him. Some days he still wished for death to take him, but he could not abandon Aurita. He was all she had. If he could not learn to take care of her and himself, they would both die.

Burkhart had been very shocked to discover that it was King Langward's family that had taken him in while his house was being rebuilt. The heart shaped birthmark on King Langward's right shoulder matched the one he had noticed on Langford's left shoulder, so he knew that this was true. But even more shocking was discovering that he had been sleeping in the very bed that King Langward had slept in while growing up and that the tunic he was wearing had belonged to King Langward. He hoped that King Langward would not be angry with him for it.

When he finished washing the dishes, he followed King Langward out of the house and into the church. He was finding it hard to keep his hands steady as he wondered what King Langward had to say to him.

"Sit down," King Langward said as he sat down on the front row of the benches.

Burkhart began to sit on the floor.

"No," the king said. "Here on the bench."

He swallowed the lump in his throat as he carefully sat down on the bench.

"I am pleased with your progress," King Langward said. "I wanted to make certain you understand that I expect you to live long enough to raise your daughter until she is old enough to wed."

"Although I still wish for death, I cannot abandon her," he replied knowing he could not lie to King Langward. "I will not disappoint you."

"I can see that I can trust my family, friends and neighbors to not kill you," he said. "I have increased the patrols in the area. That is as much for your protection as it is for your imprisonment. I consider it in my best interest that Aurita is well cared for. I spoke with the same fortune teller that you did."

Burkhart felt the blood drain from his face as he remembered her words. He still did not understand what she had said.

"I was told that she told you that my blood would mingle with yours," King Langward said as Burkhart began to feel dizzy.

"I am not worthy of such an honor," Burkhart said as he leaned against the bench back. "But if it means that I die at your side in battle, then I will do my best to protect you until my end."

"I believe it means something different," he replied. "She told me that the lives I spared would insure the long reign of my lineage. She also said that one day your line would reign again, bringing peace and prosperity to many."

Burkhart felt a shock run through him. He was not certain that he had heard correctly.

"The day my wife arrived at the palace, she bore me a son."

His heart was pounding in his chest as he began to grasp what King Langward was saying.

"Remember that you cannot tell her any of this," King Langward said. "In time I will instruct you to teach her certain things, things that you both must hide from the villagers. You alone will be able to teach her these things which she will need to know when she sits on the throne at my son's side."

"I will do exactly as you ask," Burkhart said realizing that King Langward had promised her a husband fitting a woman of noble birth. "I will not fail."

"Some of this I will not tell anyone except my queen," King Langward said. "Be certain that you do not either."

"I swear to you that I will not tell anyone," Burkhart replied quickly. "I do not wish to anger you."

King Langward smiled and nodded.

"You will need to learn a trade," he said. "That way you can earn the money you will need to care for Aurita and yourself."

"I am worthless," he responded with a sinking heart. "I am not even fit for manual labor."

"You will find something you are good at," King Langward said. "It might take some time, but you cannot give up on yourself. Aurita will grow quickly and you will find yourself needing to get her new clothes frequently. You will wear out clothes and need new ones. That tunic you are wearing is the only one I did not wear out before I outgrew it."

"I hope you are not angry that I am wearing it," Burkhart said. "I did not know it was yours."

"I'm not angry with you for wearing it, nor for sleeping in my bed," King Langward said with a smile. "It is a sign that the villagers and my family are accepting you. If you are to live the rest of your life in this village, you need to be accepted as a part of the village. We had best get back to the others. I haven't even told my own mother that she has a grandson."

Burkhart followed quietly. He was very surprised that King Langward was so kind to him. It was not something he had expected. Nor had he expected that King Langward's own son would someday be Aurita's husband. The king was apparently happy about Aurita someday becoming Queen of Brinley. He carefully moved the edge of the blanket so he could look at the sleeping infant's face.

*****

"Where did you run off to?" Mother asked as Langward entered the house.

"Just some business to attend to," he said. "I have some news for you. Retanta gave birth to my son."

"We have a grandson?" she asked and he nodded.

She burst into tears as she threw her arms around him. The Minister smiled and patted his shoulder. Although he was not Langward and Langford's father, he had long ago accepted them as his own sons. He had married their mother a few years after their father had been killed in battle. Langward barely remembered his father.

"What is his name?" Mother asked as her tears finally slowed and she released him.

"For now he shall be known by his title alone," Langward said.

"You haven't given him a name?" the Minister asked.

"A fortune teller said that he must be named by his true love," Langward said.

The Minister bowed his head with closed eyes. After a moment he looked up and met Langward's eyes.

"It is as it should be," he said.

"You had some news, too," Langward said as he turned to his brother.

"I'm getting married," Langford said. "I want you at my side at the wedding. We will get married here in the church in a week."

"It's about time," he said with a laugh. "I wouldn't miss your wedding for anything. I think Retanta will be ready for a visit by then as well."

Langward got his paints and brushes out of the box in the sleeping loft. While they talked about the wedding, he painted the cradle. When he was finished, he was pleased with the result. The flowers and vines complimented the shape of the cradle. Although Burkhart did not say anything, Langward noticed his eyes were filling with tears. They left for the palace shortly after the cradle was finished.

*****

Burkhart could not believe that the cradle he had made could be so beautiful. He had not known that King Langward was such a talented artist. The day had been full of surprises for him. He had heard many rumors about this man who was now king, but he now knew most of them to be lies. He had heard that he was cowardly and heartless, but now he understood that the one who was cowardly and heartless was himself. King Langward was a very kind and generous man who obviously cared more for others than himself.

He rocked Aurita in her cradle as he thought about it. He had heard that one of the two murderers had been released from the dungeon. It had been discovered that the man he had killed had attacked his wife. King Langward had personally executed the other. Burkhart himself had never personally executed anyone. The thought had made his stomach churn. Besides learning to survive outside of the palace, he was learning a lot about himself. He was learning that he was not a very likable person. He blew out the candle before lying down in his bed.

Burkhart began to realize that he had lived up to his father's expectations, he was worthless. As he rubbed the scar on his arm that the royal armband had covered he remembered the day he had gotten it. His father had been trying to teach him to write, but Burkhart had spilled the ink. His father was enraged and dragged him by the hair out of his chair before beginning to beat him. He could not remember exactly when during the beating he had gotten the wound, but he remembered the words his father screamed at him; worthless, incompetent, clumsy, stupid, good for nothing idiot. Then Father dragged him to his bedroom to watch as Father put everything he cared about in the fire and forced Burkhart to watch it burn. He wished his mother had been there, but she had died the year before when Burkhart was six years old. After that day, Burkhart learned to hide anything he cared about, especially his love for Aurita.

He had seen the few scars that King Langward bore. All were straight and obviously a result of a battle. He saw that the men of the village looked up to King Langward. Burkhart wished that his father had been a man like King Langward. King Langward's son would grow up knowing he was loved, knowing that his father would be there to help him, not humiliate him. Burkhart realized that what he had done to the people of Brinley was a result of what he had learned from his own father, cruelty and selfishness. Burkhart's heart ached as he rolled over to hide his tears from the infant sleeping in the cradle beside the bed.

Chapter 6 – Langford's Wedding

Langward was excited when he awoke before dawn. Today was Langford's wedding day. Retanta was excited too. She had spent time helping him decide what to give his brother and bride as a wedding gift. At her suggestion, he had painted Langford and himself as boys playing in the river. Garman had found a frame for the picture. They would also give Langford some money. He hardly tasted the breakfast they ate just before leaving the palace. The ornate carriage that was waiting for them was pulled by four white horses. He was surprised by the cheering of the people as they made their way through the streets. Retanta and Kara were talking as they rode toward Weston.

"The people are much happier," General Kannon commented as he brought his horse beside the carriage. "They did not give Burkhart such a welcome."

Langward nodded with a smile. He knew that to keep the throne, he would need to keep the people happy. He was anxious to meet the woman Langford had chosen to be his wife. The village was busy with activity when they arrived at the church. The Minister came out to greet them.

"Your mother has been up since before dawn," he said as Langward helped Retanta from the carriage. "I doubt you'll get to see her until after the wedding. I haven't seen her this excited since the day you got married."

"There's time to visit later," Langward said. "Would you like to meet your grandson?"

"Yes," the Minister said with a smile.

Retanta handed him the infant. He uncovered his face and smiled.

"He is definitely your son," the Minister said with a laugh. "He's got the same expression that you always had when you were asleep and the one hand clenched over his ear. He's beautiful."

He kissed the sleeping infant just as Langford came out of the house. The white clothes made his tanned skin and brown hair look even darker. Langward hugged him and thumped him on the back.

"After today you'll no longer be a free man," he said with a laugh as Retanta gave him a sour look before laughing. "Your wife will keep you out of trouble and close to home."

"That she will," Langford replied with a laugh. "But what sane man would want it any other way?"

"None that I can think of," Langward agreed with a laugh.

"We should get inside," the Minister said as he handed the infant back to Retanta. "It's almost time."

Garman and Stasha followed them inside along with the four guards. Langward noticed that his mother was busy with Burkhart following behind. He was carrying two baskets with flowers in them. The guests were beginning to arrive as the last of the flowers were put in place. He kissed Retanta's hand before he took his place at Langford's side. The Minister smiled as they waited for the crowd to settle down.

Suddenly the doors at the back of the church opened and everyone turned to look. A man led the bride down the aisle between the benches and came to a stop beside Langford. He kissed her cheek before placing her hand in Langford's. Langward was surprised to see that half her face was scarred by a burn, but he was careful to not let his surprise show. He remembered Langford telling him about what a beautiful woman she was. Her hand was bound to Langford's as she smiled up at him.

"I give this woman, Minara of Rockmount to this man, Langford of Weston, that they become husband and wife," the Minister said with a smile. "May joy be with them always and their happiness increase with each passing day."

Langford turned and kissed his bride. They unbound their hands before walking down the aisle together and out the doors. Langward went to Retanta and led her outside with him. Out on the lawn there were tables of gifts and food.

"This is my brother, Langward, his wife, Retanta, and her mother, Kara," Langford said with a smile as they approached. "This is Minara, my wife."

"My King," Minara said. "Langford has told me so much about you."

"You are now my sister. Call me Langward."

"You can call me Retanta," she said as she hugged Minara. "Welcome to the family."

"Langford told me that you had not spoken to him in a couple of years," Minara said. "I was worried that you would not come, especially after I found out that you are now Brinley's king and queen."

"I wouldn't miss this for all of Brinley," Langward said as he hugged her. "I just wanted to protect him. That's why I hadn't spoken to him in so long. I was very surprised and pleased to discover he was finally going to get married."

Burkhart appeared carrying a cradle. He looked nervous as he cautiously approached. He stopped a short distance away.

"What are you doing with that cradle, Burkhart?" Langward asked.

"A gift for your brother, Noble King," he replied as he came closer. "Someday they will have children and will need it."

"Thank you," Langford said as Burkhart put the cradle at his feet.

Burkhart then lay down in front of Langward.

"Rise," Langward said as he noticed Retanta trying to keep a straight face. "That was most thoughtful of you. I noticed that Aurita's cradle was very well made"

Burkhart blushed as he said, "I think I have found something I am good at, My King. Perhaps I will even be able to make some money at it."

"I am pleased," Langward said. "I noticed you were helping our mother with the wedding preparations."

"I have learned much from her," he replied. "She is a most noble lady. I must go now. She asked for help with the food."

Langward nodded and Burkhart quickly left. Garman and Stasha joined them.

"That's not," Minara began then stopped.

"The Burkhart from whom I took the throne," Langward finished for her. "Yes, it is that Burkhart."

"He doesn't act like a king," Minara said. "He almost seemed terrified of you."

"King Burkhart died with his queen," Langward said. "The man you see today is merely a shadow of his former self. He knows his life is mine to command."

"He is not the same man that I served," Garman commented.

"When he speaks of you, he tells of your wisdom, strength and kindness," Langford said. "Once some of the men were laughing about the time you had to be pulled out of the river. Burkhart told them that they could ridicule him all they wanted, but they should never speak ill of you. I do believe he would die defending you. What did you do to him?"

59

"I spared his life and allowed him to raise his daughter," Langward explained.

"Enough serious talk," Retanta said. "Garman, go get our gifts."

Garman was soon back with the gifts.

"It's beautiful," Minara said as she looked at the painting.

"This is way too much," Langford said as he looked into the pouch Langward handed him.

"Keep it," Langward said. "It will give you time to get settled."

They enjoyed visiting for the rest of the afternoon. He learned that Minara had been burned saving her younger sister from a fire when she was just a child. When it was time to leave, they had a hard time getting their son from Langward's mother.

"You must come visit at the palace," Langward told her as he hugged her.

"We will," she replied.

Chapter 7 – First Meeting

Time passed quickly as Langward, Retanta, their ministers and the district governors went through all of Brinley's laws. They changed those that needed to be changed and created new laws. The people of Brinley appeared to be happy with the changes. Langward was too busy to visit Weston very often, but since Langford had been chosen as that district's governor, he got frequent reports on Burkhart and Aurita.

Langward and Retanta's son grew quickly and was a happy child although he did not play with the other children in the palace. He spent a lot of time with his grandmother. He showed an interest in reading at an early age and Langward began teaching him in the evenings before bedtime. There was so much he wanted to teach his son that would prepare him to be king someday.

*****

Burkhart worked hard to grow a few vegetables and build things out of scraps of wood left over from building houses and barns. King Langward had been right about how quickly Aurita grew. Each day she resembled her mother even more. She grew to be a gentle and caring child. The other children in the village shunned her, but she was happy helping in the garden or playing with the goat. She never complained when there was little food to eat. Sometimes she asked why he was sad. At first he did not know what to tell her, but he eventually told her that he missed her mother.

One morning he heard some excitement near the church. He looked over and saw that King Langward was there. Aurita came out of the house to see what the commotion was about.

"Who is that, Father?" she asked.

"That is King Langward," he replied as he put down his tools. "We must go to greet him. When we greet him, we must lie down on the ground and stretch our upturned hands out toward him. We must not move until he tells us to rise."

"Why must we lay in the dirt, Father?" she asked with her head cocked to the side. "Everyone else looks like they are kneeling."

"It is just the way it must be," he replied. "I owe my life and yours to Our Noble King. He may want to ask you some questions and look at you to see that you are healthy. You must do everything that he says. Can you do that for me?"

61

"Alright," she said. "I will do that for you."

"Come," he told her and held out his hand.

She placed her small soft hand in his large rough one and followed him to the church. As they neared where King Langward stood, he turned toward them. Burkhart released her hand and lay out on the ground. He was relieved to see that she had done the same.

"Rise," he heard King Langward say.

He rose to his feet as Aurita did beside him.

"She has grown a lot since I last saw her," King Langward said as he looked at Aurita. "She favors her mother."

"Yes, she does, My King," he said.

"Let me see your hands," King Langward said.

Aurita held out her hands with a very serious expression on her face.

"They are soft and unscarred," he commented as he examined her hands.

"She is a good helper, My King," he said. "But I do not make her do more than a child her age should be expected to do."

"Good. She has clear eyes and a straight back. What about boots?" King Langward said as he met Burkhart's eye. "The cold season will come soon. I see you are barefoot as well."

"She outgrew hers and mine wore out completely," he responded. "I hope to get enough money from the next couple of pieces to pay for new ones. I promise that she will have boots before the weather turns cold."

"You will buy them first thing in the morning," King Langward said as he opened the pouch at his waist. "Along with new capes."

He handed Burkhart five silver coins. Burkhart felt his hands begin to tremble and he felt tears begin to form.

"I am undeserving of such kindness, My King," he said as he tried to keep his voice steady.

King Langward put one hand on his shoulder. He looked up to find the king smiling.

"I just want to make certain that you are able to fulfill your obligation," King Langward said. "I want to inspect your house."

"Of course, My King," Burkhart said as King Langward's mother came out of her house led by a boy about Aurita's age. "Is that your son?"

"Yes," King Langward said as he glanced toward the boy.

"He is a handsome young man," Burkhart said.

"Why don't you stay here, Aurita?" King Langward said. "This is my son. You may call him Prince."

She nodded as King Langward's mother approached with his son. She lay down as she had before.

"Why are you lying down?" the prince asked.

"Because you are the son of the king," she said seriously as she stood back up.

"What is your name?"

"Aurita."

*****

Burkhart followed King Langward to the house. He watched as King Langward checked the garden and inside the house. He came back out and looked up at the roof.

"It is clean and in good repair," he said at last. "The garden looks good as well."

"I'm glad you are pleased," Burkhart said.

"I am pleased with Aurita as well," he said. "What have you been teaching her?"

"Only what the other children in the village learn," Burkhart said.

King Langward nodded and said, "When she is a few years older, I want you to teach her to read and the language of the kingdoms to the North. Make certain she understands that she can not reveal such knowledge to anyone else."

"It shall be exactly as you ask," Burkhart said.

"Good," he replied. "Now what about you? How have you been doing?"

"I am alright," Burkhart said. "I have nothing I can complain about."

"How do the villagers treat you?"

"They mostly ignore me unless they need something built or repaired," he said. "I prefer it that way. Your family has been most kind to us. We have started attending church, but we slip in after everyone else and stay in the back where no one notices us. We leave during the final prayer. I don't want anyone offended by my presence."

"What sort of things is Aurita interested in?" King Langward asked.

"She loves animals," he replied. "A couple of years ago she began learning about healing from your brother, Langford. He told me that she learns quickly and that some day she could become a skilled healer."

"Good," King Langward said. "The healing art is one that is good to know. Encourage her in her learning. You alone can teach her what she will need to know after she is married."

"I will, My King," Burkhart said.

"It is time for me to leave," King Langward said as Aurita and his son came walking down the path.

"Safe journey, My King," Burkhart said.

Aurita took his hand as they watched the king and prince leave.

*****

"What do you think of Aurita?" Langward asked his son as they walked back to the church.

"She knows so much about animals, Father," he replied. "She showed me how to make my horse lay down so I can get on without help."

Langward laughed.

"She seemed almost afraid of me at first," his son said. "She said that her life and that of her father belongs to you, but did not know why. What did she mean by that?"

"I'll tell you when we get home," he replied. "Let's tell your grandmother goodbye."

His son was quiet on the ride home. Langward wondered how much he was ready to know. They went directly to the study off the throne room when they arrived at the palace.

"There are some things that must be kept secret," Langward began as they looked out over the garden together. "This is something that must for now be kept secret from Aurita. You know that before you were born another man was King of Brinley."

"Yes, Father," he replied.

"Aurita's father was that king," Langward said and his son looked up with a surprised expression.

"The man who lay down before you?" he asked. "He did not act like a man who was king."

"Aurita's mother died giving birth to her," Langward said. "After that, Burkhart no longer wished to live. I sent him and Aurita to live in Weston. One of the conditions that I let him live is that he never tell Aurita

64

that he was once king. He can never tell her that she is a princess. Some day when he is dead, I will tell her, but not while he still lives."

His son was silent for a while before asking, "What will happen to her when he dies?"

"She will be taken care of," he replied.

"She said that the other children don't like her," his son said. "She said that you will choose her a husband. What if he doesn't love her?"

"Don't worry about that now," he replied. "For now it is our responsibility to watch over both of them. It is time for supper."

As Langward and Retanta stood out on the balcony after supper she said, "I noticed you took our son to Weston with you."

"I wanted him to meet Aurita," he said. "I know that they are still young, but I thought they should meet."

"What did he think of her?" she asked. "Did you tell him that some day she may be his wife?"

"I did not tell him, but she had mentioned that I would choose her a husband," he replied. "He was concerned that the man I chose as her husband would not love her."

"What did you tell him?"

"To not worry about it for now and that until then it was our responsibility to watch over her and her father."

"Are you going to take him to visit her again?" Retanta asked.

"No," he replied after a moment. "I think that when he is old enough, he should attend the Military Training Camp and become a patrolman. I will have him assigned to guard Weston. I think that while there he should be known by his military rank and not by Prince. Perhaps it will give them both a chance to get to know each other. I don't think either of them needs to be told of their future just yet."

"I hope you know what you are doing," she said. "But I will trust you on this."

He took her into his arms and kissed her gently.

*****

"What did you think about Our Prince?" Burkhart asked Aurita as they sat down to eat supper.

"He is much nicer than the children here in the village," she replied after swallowing. "He asked me what I liked to do."

"Our King was pleased with you," he said. "Someday Our Prince will get married and become king."

"Why do you owe Our King your life and mine?" she asked. "Why did he say that I favored my mother? Did he know her?"

"King Langward and I met the day you were born," he replied. "Your mother died giving birth to you. It was him that named you for your mother."

He paused wondering how to explain it to her satisfaction without revealing forbidden information.

"Before then I worked in the palace," he said. "When King Langward took the throne there were those who wanted rid of some of the palace staff, especially me. King Langward ordered that you and I not be harmed. He sent us here to live. Because of that, my life is his to command."

"Couldn't we just run away, Father?" she asked.

He sighed.

"Before you were born, I was an evil man," he said softly. "I did things that were hurtful to others and most people hate me for it. At the time I did not understand that what I did hurt many people and did not care. From King Langward I have learned much about myself and I am trying to be a better person. King Langward is a very kind and compassionate man. He is a man like I should have been. I must try to make up for what I did to the people of Brinley. That is why King Langward sent us to live here. Here we are both protected and imprisoned. I will not leave this village before my death."

"What will happen to me?" she asked. "Will I have to stay here until I die?"

"King Langward promised that after I am dead you will not have to stay here in the village and you will be taken care of. Before then he has said that I am to teach you things that the rest of the villagers do not know. You can not reveal that you know these things until after I am dead."

"I don't want you to die, Father," she said as her voice quivered with emotion.

"Everyone must eventually die," he replied as a tear ran down his face. "Once I die you will be free of my past and shame. King Langward has promised to explain everything to you. I can only pray that when you learn the whole truth you can find it in your heart to forgive me."

"I love you, Father," she said as she got up and went over to him. "And I always will."

"I love you, too," he said as he hugged her. "I need to take a walk. I will wash the dishes when I return. Go to bed."

She watched him leave before she shut the door.

Burkhart walked toward the church in the fading light. He knew that the coming years would be hard ones for him to bear. He had not meant to cry in front of Aurita, but his heart ached so that he could not help it. He wished that he could sit at his wife's grave, but that was just not possible. He went to the cemetery and found the grave of King Langward's father. Although it was too dark to read the words engraved on the stone, he knew every word by heart. He had been coming to the grave when the burden on his heart was too great. He had found it not long after Langford's wedding.

He sat on the ground with his legs crossed and his head in his hands while he cried. He knew that life was a greater punishment than death could ever be, but as King Langward had said on that first day, this was his fate. He wished for death to take him, yet he could not leave Aurita alone in this world, not until she was much older. King Langward was much kinder to him than he deserved. Occasionally some of the men got drunk and would beat him. Sometimes that was easier to bear than the lonely ache in his heart.

"What are you doing here?" the minister's voice said. "Are you alright?"

Burkhart looked up in surprise to find the minister and his wife standing across the grave from him.

"You are crying," she said. "What's the matter?"

"I'm sorry," he said. "I didn't mean to trespass. Aurita was asking questions about my past and why my life and hers belong to King Langward."

"Why are you at my husband's grave?" she asked.

"I wish I could sit at my wife's grave and speak to her, but the next time I am at her grave it will be to be buried next to her," he replied with a lump in his throat. "I come here sometimes to ease the burden on my heart for a while. He must have been a very wonderful person to have sons as kind and noble as King Langward and Langford."

"He was," she replied.

"We all miss him still," the minister said. "He was my brother."

Burkhart was surprised at the revelation.

"Do you want to come in for a while?" she asked.

"No," he said with a sigh. "I had best get back home."

"You are welcome to come here anytime you want," the minister said. "Langward is right. You are not the same man who sat on Brinley's throne. You work hard and never complain. You give more thought to others than yourself. I have seen you in the back of the church during the sermons. I know that when you leave this world, it will be as an honorable man."

He offered Burkhart a hand and helped him to his feet. He patted Burkhart on the shoulder before letting him leave. Burkhart walked slowly home in the darkness as he thought about his life here in Weston. King Langward had become like a father to Burkhart, an example to follow. In other ways he was the friend that his own father had never allowed him to have. Langford and Minara had become his friends as well. Even if King Langward released him, Burkhart would not leave the village. Weston was his home. This is where he belonged now. When he opened the door he found the dishes and table had been cleaned. Everything was in its place and the house was quiet. He climbed the ladder and found Aurita to be asleep in her bed. He undressed and got into bed.

Chapter 8 – An Injury and New Friends

When Aurita woke up her father was still asleep. He had been so sad last night. She had worried that he would not return. She quietly went out to the outhouse before starting the fire. He was still asleep when she returned from the well with a bucket of water. She got the pot on the hook before pouring in the water. She measured and stirred in the porridge before swinging it over the fire. As the smell of the cooking porridge filled the house, she set the bowls and spoons on the table. Father began to stir.

"Why didn't you wake me?" he asked. "I should be the one making breakfast."

"I'm so sorry I made you sad, Father," she said as he sat up.

"It's not your fault, it's mine," he said as he began to get dressed. "I know that there are many things you are curious about that I have promised not to tell you."

"You promised King Langward?" she asked.

"Yes," he said as he stirred the cooking porridge. "He has always kept his promises to me. I will not break my promises to him."

"Why would he not want me to know about what happened before I was born?" she asked.

"Someday you will understand," he said. "When he tells you of my past, it will all make sense. When I am gone, he will make certain that you are taken care of. You will not have to worry about having enough food or clothing. You will be happy. That he has promised."

"Where did you go last night?" she asked as he dished up the porridge.

"I went to the cemetery by the church," he said as he sat down. "When I am sad, I wish that I could sit at your mother's grave and talk to her. Since that is not possible, I sit by King Langward's father's grave."

She thought about that while they ate. She knew it must be hard for him to raise her alone. Everyone else in the village had a mother and a father who lived with them. Sometimes the fathers went to guard the borders or fight in battle, but they almost always returned. When they didn't the mothers would marry a new husband.

"When you're finished, go get bathed," he said. "I will wash the dishes and then pick you up so that we can go visit the cobbler."

"Yes, Father," she said as she scraped the last of the porridge into her spoon.

Aurita was deep in thought as she went to bathe. Some of the other girls and women were already there. She undressed and slipped into the water away from everyone else. Two of the girls noticed her and came toward her.

"You think you're so special," one of them said in a disgusted tone.

"Asking the king for money just because your father is too stupid and lazy to earn any," the other girl said.

"We didn't ask for any money," she replied as she began to head for shore. "Father earns money selling the things he builds."

"Why did he let the prince play with you instead of us?" one said. "He shouldn't even have to look at someone as ugly and stupid as you."

"King Langward does what he wants," she said. "It is not my place to ask why he does something."

One of the girls pushed her down. She tried to stand up again, but the other girl pushed her back down. As she went down a sharp pain went through her leg. As she tried to get up, her leg was stuck on something that sent more pain through her. She could barely keep her face above the water.

"Is that blood?" one of the girls asked, pointing toward Aurita's leg.

"Let's leave," the other said.

Aurita took a deep breath and ducked beneath the water. She could see a stick coming out of her leg. She felt below it and found the other half of the stick. She got another breath of air before working to break the stick. She almost passed out from the pain before the stick finally broke free of the log it was attached to. She somehow made it to the bank.

"What's the matter, Aurita?" King Langward's mother asked as she approached.

She drew in a quick breath and covered her mouth as Aurita drew her injured leg from the water. She helped Aurita to get dressed and picked her up in her arms. As she went around the bushes, Aurita heard someone running toward them.

"What happened?" Father's worried voice asked.

"Some girls were angry and pushed me," she said as he took her in his arms. "They didn't mean to hurt me."

"Why were they angry?" King Langward's mother asked as the sound of someone on horseback approached.

"They were angry that King Langward gave Father some money for shoes and introduced me to his son," she replied.

"We will send word to Our King at once," a man said as her father turned revealing three patrolmen.

"Don't bother him because of me," she said. "That will just make the girls angrier with me."

"We have to," the man replied. "King Langward gave us strict orders to report anything like this."

He turned his horse and headed toward the hill to the east of the village. The other two followed them to the little house by the church. Langford and the minister were outside when they arrived.

"Bring her inside," Langford said when he looked up.

Aurita was surprised to see the patrolmen follow them into the house.

"It looks like it isn't bleeding much," Langford said after she was placed on a chair. "We will need fresh water from the well, but first let me get my box."

He quickly returned with his box and knelt at her feet. He opened the box and found two leaves of a pain killing herb. He handed them to her and she put them in her mouth. As she chewed on them, she watched Langford. He took three more of the leaves and put them in a small stone bowl. He ground them up with a stone rod before adding a couple of powders that she recognized into the mixture along with just enough water to make a paste. He carefully spread the paste around where the stick was poking out of her leg. While he waited for the paste to numb her leg, he took a knife that one of the patrolmen handed him and carefully cut around the stick until he cut through it.

"Are you ready for me to pull it out?" he asked her.

She grabbed the seat of the chair with both hands before nodding. Even with the numbing paste it still hurt as he quickly pulled out the stick. The wound began to bleed more. Langford caught the blood on a cloth as the other man returned with the water from the well. Langward tossed several more cloths into the water. The man pushed them into the water.

Once they were wet, he wrung them out and handed them one by one to Langford. He put them onto her leg and pressed tightly. After a while, the bleeding slowed. He handed his mother a metal rod with a wooden handle.

"You were smart to not remove it yourself," Langford said. "You could have bled to death."

"I remembered that you told me to never just take out something large that had punctured the skin," she said.

"Good girl," he replied as the third patrolman entered the house.

King Langward's mother returned with the rod glowing red with heat.

"This will hurt," he said.

She nodded as she braced herself for the pain. He carefully inserted the rod into the wound. She could feel the metal searing her skin, but did not cry out. When he removed the rod, there was no more bleeding. He carefully washed the leg with the cold water before bandaging it.

"If it shows no sign of infection tomorrow, I will stitch the wound closed," Langford said.

"Thank you," she said as she finally released her grip on the chair.

"You are very brave," one of the patrolmen said. "When I got an arrow removed from my shoulder, you could have heard me from the next valley."

The other two men grinned and nodded.

"She did not even cry out when it happened," Langford's mother said. "I did not know she was so badly injured until she showed me."

"King Langward is on his way to check on her himself," the third patrolman said.

Aurita wondered why the king would come just because she was injured. Then she remembered the shoes.

"He will be angry that I don't have any shoes yet, Father," she said.

"You're not going to be walking for a couple of days at least," Langford said. "He'll understand."

"We'll just have to wait and see," Father said as he stroked her face.

"You should lie down and put your leg up," Langford said.

"I want to go home," she replied.

"You can sleep in my bed until you are well enough to climb the ladder again," Father said as he picked her up in his arms.

The others followed as he carried her home. He laid her on his bed and propped her leg up with a folded blanket. She laid there and looked at the ceiling while the adults went outside and talked. It seemed like forever before the door opened again. King Langward entered and closed the door behind him.

"Tell me what happened," he said as he pulled a chair over to the bedside. "Everything."

"Yes, Sir," she said before swallowing. "I went to bathe this morning before going to the cobbler's. I was almost done when two girls came over to me. They were angry that you had given Father some money for shoes and introduced me to your son. They said I was stupid and ugly. They thought Father had asked for the money and called him stupid and lazy. I told them that Father didn't ask for the money and that you do what you want to. Then they pushed me. When I tried to get up, they pushed me again. That is when I fell on the stick. It was hidden under the water. They left when they saw the blood. I broke the stick off and crawled to shore. That is when your mother found me."

King Langward frowned.

"Don't be angry with them," she said. "They did not mean to hurt me. They just don't like me."

"Don't you have any friends?" he asked.

"Not my own age," she said. "Your parents, brother and his wife are my friends."

"I'm sorry to hear that," he said. "I wish the situation could be different, but right now it can't be helped. I know that life is difficult for both of you here. I've been told that sometimes the other men beat your father, but you are safer here than anywhere else right now."

"Last night Father said that when he worked in the palace he did many things that hurt other people. He said that he was an evil man before I was born," she said quietly. "He wouldn't tell me anything more because he promised you he wouldn't."

"That's right," King Langward said. "Someday when you are a grown woman I will explain everything to you. Your father is not the same man that he was before you were born. I am giving him a chance to make up for what he did wrong. I have worked hard to undo some of the things he did and I am making certain that no one else can be tempted to do such things again. I have changed some things so that no one, not even I, could do such things."

She thought about that for a moment before saying, "Father was very sad last night. He left for a while and came back after I was asleep. This morning he said that he had sat at your father's grave because he could not sit at my mother's."

"Interesting," King Langward said. "I'm glad you told me. I want you to listen carefully and remember everything I tell you."

She nodded.

"Your father is neither stupid, nor lazy," he said. "Many people have a hard time earning enough money for clothes and shoes. You are neither stupid nor ugly. You are a very smart little girl. You are also beautiful. No matter what anyone else says, remember that. Someday you will be a very beautiful woman."

"I will remember that," she said. "I just hope that whomever you choose as my husband feels that way too. I hope that he can love me in spite of whatever my father has done before I was born."

"I know that he will love you," King Langward said with a smile. "Your husband has already been chosen, but he does not know it. I will give him a chance to get to know you without knowing what I have planned."

"How will I know him?" she asked.

"Don't worry about that," he said. "For now you need to heal. There are many things I want you to learn before then."

"Father said that someday you would have him teach me things that I can not reveal to the villagers," she said.

"What happened this morning is a good example of why some things you are taught must not be revealed to the other villagers," he said.

"I do not want them to be angry over something I know," she said. "I barely speak to anyone anyway. It will not be too hard to not tell them."

"Maybe you are ready to start," he said with a smile. "I will have your father start by teaching you to read. It is something that you can do while you are in bed, but you must not ever do it outside or when someone else can see."

"I promise I won't," she said, wondering what reading meant.

"Good," he said before leaning over and kissing her forehead. "Now anytime that you need help or need me to know something, all you have to do is go to the edge of the village and wait for a patrolman."

"Father said they are here to protect us as well as imprison him," she said seriously.

"That's right," he replied as he stood up. "Most people thought that he should be thrown in the dungeon or executed, but when you survived I knew that I could not rightfully do either. For him this village is a prison of sorts. He will die here but you will not. Just remember that you can get help from the patrolmen if you need it. They will not harm you, but if your father leaves the village he will be killed."

"I understand," she said.

*****

He smiled and left. She would someday make a good queen. He just hoped that she would not become bitter by growing up in such a harsh social environment. Burkhart looked up from his work as he heard the door shut.

"Take care of her," he said. "I will send some things for you, things to help you accomplish what we discussed yesterday. You will understand when you receive them."

"Yes, Noble King," Burkhart replied. "I understand."

"Stay here," Langward said. "I need to speak to the rest of the villagers."

"I am yours to command," he replied. "I will get her shoes as soon as she can stand."

Langward nodded and left followed by the others.

"If ever Aurita goes to the edge of the village and waits, go immediately to find out what she wants or needs. She may have a message for me," he said to the patrolmen. "You will deliver it immediately. Spread the order to the rest of the patrols."

"Yes, My King," they replied in unison and left.

"I'll go assemble the villagers," the Minister said and hurried on ahead.

"She told me that Burkhart was at Father's grave last night," Langward said.

"Yes, the poor man was crying like a child," Mother said. "He said he was there because he could not visit his wife's grave."

75

"He loved his wife very deeply," Langward said. "If it were not for his daughter, he would not have survived more than a few days."

"He said he had come to ease the burden on his heart," she said.

He nodded as he saw the villagers assembling. Someone brought a chair for him to stand on. He waited for them to be quiet.

"This morning Aurita was injured," he said and the crowd began to murmur. "She did not say who exactly was responsible nor did I ask. She did say that they were angry that I had given her father money to buy her shoes with."

He waited for them to quiet down.

"I want to make something very clear," he said. "I know that none of you are too happy about Burkhart living among you. Although he has never mentioned it to me, I know exactly how many times he has been beaten and by how many men. I know who has beaten him more than once. I also know that the children in this village do not play with Aurita. I know that you do not understand my reasons for ordering Burkhart to live here among you or even why he still lives. In time you will understand. Many of you may not be very happy about it, but I do not have to explain any of my reasons to you at this time."

This time they stood in silence as he paused.

"I have not asked you to support Burkhart and Aurita," he said. "That is his responsibility. Nor have I asked you to like either of them. This much I do command, Aurita will not be harmed in any way. She will remain in this village until she is old enough to be wed. At that time I will have her escorted from this village to be wed to a husband which I have selected for her already. Until that time, she is to live as normal of a childhood as possible under the circumstance."

The people were quiet as they waited for him to speak again.

"Remember that you must make even your children understand that the lives of both Burkhart and Aurita belong to me," he said sternly. "I will deal with them as I see fit. If they are to be punished, I will do it personally. If I see fit to give them assistance, it is my right. Any interference in my orders in regards to them will not be tolerated."

He stepped down off the chair and headed toward the church. Two women and two girls caught up with him. The women looked determined and the girls looked pale. He stopped and turned toward them.

"Tell him," one of the women said sternly.

"W . . . we were," one of the girls stuttered.

"We pushed her," the other girl said with a tremor in her voice.

"We didn't mean to hurt her," the first one added.

"We're sorry," the second one said and the first one nodded.

"She is going to need some help while her father is working," he said sternly. "She cannot stand on her leg until it has begun to heal."

"The girls will be happy to help her," one of the women said.

"Won't you," the other added sternly.

Both girls nodded.

"I think that you will find that she is a good person," he said. "She is not here to be punished for her father's past. She is here because she has no one else to take care of her. Thank you for coming forward."

He mounted his horse and led his guards back toward the palace. As he rode he thought about what he had learned. He knew that even though he was satisfied that Burkhart had paid for his past; releasing him would put him and Aurita into greater danger. He also knew that it would not make Burkhart any happier. The fact that he never reported the beatings confirmed that. His son met him in the courtyard.

"Is she alright, Father?" he asked. "She must have been so frightened."

"She is doing fine," Langward replied as he dismounted. "She is a very brave girl. I am told that she didn't cry out even once while they were removing the stick and searing the wound to stop the bleeding. It may be a while before she can walk again though."

"She won't be able to do anything for herself," he said in a serious tone. "Can we send someone to help her?"

"I have already found someone to help her," Langward replied, surprised by his son's thoughtfulness. "It is kind of you to worry about such things. Why don't you help me get some things together to send her? I told her father he can teach her to read as long as no one in the village knows about it."

"Can we send her a toy, too?" he asked. "She said she doesn't have any toys. She doesn't even have a doll."

Langward laughed.

"Of course," he said. "That's a good idea."

*****

Aurita was surprised when her father entered followed by two women and the two girls who had pushed her.

"You have visitors, Aurita," he said.

"They have something to tell you," one of the women said as she nudged one of the girls forward.

"We're sorry you got hurt," the girl said as she looked at the floor.

"I know you didn't mean to hurt me," Aurita replied, surprised by the girl's confession.

"We want to help you until you get better," the other girl said as they both finally looked directly at her. "King Langward said you couldn't walk for a while."

"I'm pretty much stuck in bed," she replied. "If I move around too much or try to walk, it would start bleeding again."

"Does it hurt?" one asked.

"Yes, but it's not too bad when I lie still," Aurita said as she noticed the adults leaving. "What are your names?"

"I am Noka," the taller of the two girls said. "She's Carria."

"Can you sit up?" Carria asked.

"Yes," she said. "I would need to keep my leg up."

The girls helped her to lean against the wall and got her leg propped up. They talked until lunchtime. While Father made lunch, they went home to eat lunch.

"Are you doing alright?" Father asked as they ate. "What were you three doing while I was outside?"

"We were just talking," she replied. "They can be nice if they want to."

"What were you talking about?"

"Mostly about my leg." she said as she shrugged her shoulders.

They were just finishing when the two girls came back. Both of them were holding dolls.

"We thought you might want to play dolls," Noka said. "Where's your doll?"

"I don't have a doll," she replied trying to ignore the lump that was forming in her throat. "Dolls cost money we don't have to spend."

She noticed Father's shoulders sagging and his head bowed as he gathered up the dishes. She was sorry she had said it, but before she could

78

say any more there was a knock at the door. Father opened the door revealing a man carrying a saddlebag and something wrapped in cloth.

"King Langward sent this for you," the man said. "He said you would know what to do with it."

Father took the saddlebags from him and looked into one of the pouches. He nodded to the man. The man walked over to the bed.

"Our Prince sent this for you," he said as he handed the package to Aurita.

She unwrapped the cloth and found it to be a cape. Inside the cape was a doll.

"Please tell him thank you for me," she said as she felt a tear begin to run down her cheek. "Tell him I love the doll."

"I will," the man said.

He nodded to Father as he opened the door to leave. Father put away the clean dishes and went back outside.

"She's beautiful," Carria said.

"I can't believe she's mine," Aurita said softly as she looked at the doll.

The doll's head, hands and feet were carved from wood and painted. The body was soft leather. She had a beautiful dress made from material that was much smoother and softer than the clothes of everyone in the village. She wished there was a gift she could send the prince in return.

They played with their dolls and laughed the rest of the afternoon. Any time she needed something the girls got it for her. They even got Father when she needed him to carry her to the outhouse. She was sad to see them leave when suppertime came.

"It's good to see you smile," Father said. "And I haven't heard you laugh in a very long time."

"They said they wanted to be my friends even after I was well," she said before beginning to eat.

Father seemed happy. After the dishes were washed, Father opened up the saddlebags and brought out something. It was flat and rectangular. He opened it up and she saw lots of lines and dots. Some of the lines were wavy and some were straight.

"This is a book," Father said. "These markings are writing. I am going to teach you to read them. Just remember that you cannot tell anyone that you are doing this."

She nodded. He brought a piece of paper like the ones in the book out of the saddle bags and laid it on the table. Then he took a small bottle and a short stick with a metal end out of the bag. He dipped the metal end of the stick into the black fluid in the bottle and began making the markings on the paper.

"Each of these is a letter and each letter has its own sound," he said. "We will start by learning what sound each letter makes. Once you learn what sounds the letters make, then I can teach you to read the words."

He worked with her until it was getting dark outside. She was beginning to recognize and remember the sounds for some of the letters.

"Why does King Langward want me to know how to read?" she asked as Father prepared a bed for himself on the floor.

He was silent for a moment before he said, "He has a job for you when you are married. To do this job, you will need to know how to read and how to write. You will also need to know the language of the kingdoms to the North. It is a very important job and there is much for me to teach you so you are ready to do it when the time comes."

"I'm sorry I said what I did about not having money for a doll," she said. "I didn't want to make you feel bad. I wish I could do something to help earn money."

"I know you didn't mean to hurt my feelings," Father said as he lay down.

"I know you do everything that you can to take care of me," she said. "I love you, Father."

"I love you, too," he said.

Aurita slept fitfully. The pain in her leg woke her every time she tried to roll over. She kept thinking about what she could do to earn money. Toward dawn she remembered seeing an old woman sitting near the brook weaving baskets from the reeds that grew there. Maybe she could learn to weave baskets and sell them. Noka and Carria arrived shortly after breakfast. Langford and Minara arrived not long afterward. Father watched as Langford unwrapped her leg. He felt it carefully near the wounds.

"No heat," he said. "No more bleeding. I think we can stitch it closed, but it will need to be watched."

"I'll check it once a day and look for heat, pus or unusual color," she said, nodding. "I'll keep it clean, dry and wrapped."

Langford laughed.

"Someday you will make a good healer," he said as he took a jar from his box. "Let's get this numbed."

She noticed that Minara had taken the two girls outside. Langford opened the jar and gently dabbed some of the contents around the edges of the wounds. He took out a small bottle and opened it. He drew out a small curved needle and a tiny spool of fine thread. He measured out a length of thread and cut it with a small knife from the box. He threaded the needle and took out a pair of small pliers.

"Ready?" he asked.

She nodded. She felt the sharp pain as he pushed the needle into her skin. Bit by bit, stitch by stitch he pulled the skin over the wound. At last he had closed the wound on the top of her leg. She lay on her side, facing the wall while he stitched the wound on the back side of her leg.

"That does it," Langford said as he patted her shoulder. "I wish all my patients were as good as you. Most people that I have to stitch up need to be held down."

She rolled over and looked at the stitches. He wrapped it with a clean wrap.

"When the skin begins to seal together, you can start putting some weight on that leg."

"Thank you," she said. "I would like it if you could teach me to be a healer."

"For now, just work on getting back on your feet," Langford said with a smile. "Just don't do anything to rip out your stitches."

"I won't."

*****

Langward smiled as he read the message Garman handed to him.

"What is it?" Retanta asked after the servants delivering breakfast had left.

"Aurita's leg is showing no signs of infection," he replied, noticing his son's interest. "Langford says that she didn't have to be held down and didn't even cry when he stitched it closed. She asked if he would teach her to be a healer."

"She's very brave," Retanta said.

"Aurita wanted me to thank you for sending the doll," Langward said.

"I'm glad she liked the doll we sent to her," his son said. "Maybe when she learns to read I can send a letter to her."

"You could send one now," Langward said. "Her father could help her read it."

After breakfast, they went to the study so the letter could be written. Langward was glad to see his son take an interest in Aurita, but knew it would be another seven or more years before they were old enough to be wed. Many things could happen in that time.

Once his son had gone, he looked over the report General Kannon had sent. Something was up in Mannton to the south. There had been an increase in the number of Mannton's soldiers seen near the border. There had been an uneasy peace between the two kingdoms with occasional skirmishes along the border. He did not want Brinley to be at war, but knew that he must protect the people if necessary.

The rest of the day was busy taking care of various matters and granting audiences. The rest of the week was about the same, so was the rest of the month. His son was learning quickly and sometimes even sat in the throne room to listen to the audiences. Langward was pleased that he took an interest in learning to be king. He got back a report from Weston that Aurita's leg had healed enough to remove the stitches. Her two helpers had turned into friends. Langward was happy to hear that. He wished his son would find some friends of his own. He had discovered that he had been fighting with some of the boys who were teasing him about not having a name.

Chapter 9 – Little Prince No-Name

He was on his way back to the royal quarters when he heard voices around the corner. He felt his muscles tense as he recognized the voices. The two boys never passed up an opportunity to tease him. He wished there was a way to avoid them entirely, but they were just down the hall from the royal quarters. He held his breath as he turned the corner.

"Look," Larkin said. "It's Little Prince No-Name."

"He thinks he's better than the rest of us," Nokar said. "But he doesn't scare me."

He tried to ignore them, but they stepped in front of him. They began pushing him back and forth between them. He began pushing back. They tried to pin him up against the wall. He swung his fist and it connected with Nokar's right eye.

"That's enough!"

Father sounded very angry. Nokar and Larkin ran away around the corner leaving him to face Father's anger. Father frowned as he pointed at him then turned his hand over and gestured him forward. He swallowed as he followed Father into the royal quarters. He stood trying not to shake as Father stared at him with an angry look on his face.

"What am I going to do with you?" Father said at last. "I don't like you fighting. You could have really hurt one of those boys."

"They're bigger and stronger than I am," he replied quietly. "And they are always together. It is more likely that I would be the one getting hurt if I didn't fight back."

"Why don't you get along with anyone your age?" Father asked.

"They tease me about not having a name," he said with a sinking feeling. "They say I think I'm better than they are because I am your son. All of the boys tease me and none of the girls will even speak to me. I think I know how Aurita feels sometimes."

Father sighed and said, "I guess I had better teach you how to beat them without hurting them."

"I wish I had a name," he said quietly.

"I know," Father said as he shook his head. "But it is not my place to give you one."

"It doesn't make any sense," he said. "Everyone else's parents name them. Why can't you?"

"Before you were born a seer told me that only by true love can you be named. When I told your grandfather, he said that is how it should be," Father said. "I can't give you a name because I don't know what that name is. I do know who will eventually give you that name, but I can't tell you."

"And I know it will do me no good to ask who that is," he said bitterly. "I won't ask ever again."

He had asked Mother about why he didn't have a name, but she wouldn't tell him any more than Father had.

*****

Aurita's leg was sore from working in the garden when she went down to the river. She sat on the bank and let the cold water numb her legs. She found some small twigs floating in the water nearby and found them to be easy to bend without breaking. That must be how they could be woven into a basket. From the angle of the sun, she knew that soon the men would be coming to bathe in the river. She picked up her boots and began to walk home.

People had been much nicer to her and her father since she had gotten injured. Father was able to sell more of the things he made. One man even took some to the city to sell and brought back more money than they had expected. Still, she wanted to learn to weave baskets to sell. The old woman who had woven baskets had died and no one else seemed to know how. Somehow she would learn. She had been practicing with the long grass and discovered that she needed an odd number of starting sticks or it wouldn't come out right.

She was deep in thought as she heard Father's voice ask, "What's the matter?"

"Nothing," she said. "I was just thinking about the old woman who used to weave baskets."

"The one that died?"

"Yes," she replied as she watched him smooth out the wood he was building into a chair. "Now no one in the village weaves baskets."

"You're up to something," he said with a laugh. "I saw you weaving grass yesterday."

"I just thought that if I could weave baskets, we could sell them too," she replied.

"You shouldn't be worried about money at your age. We have enough from the things I sell," he said. "But if you really want to learn to weave baskets, I will help you sell them."

"Thank you, Father," she said as she kissed his cheek.

She went inside to get the bucket. She had been worried that he might not want her to weave baskets. She went to the well to get water. The weather was getting cooler. She soon would need to start wearing a cape outside. The cape that she got with her doll was very soft and very warm. It also had a hood. It was dyed a bright dark blue with maroon patterns along the edges. She returned with a full bucket of water as Father was putting his tools away for night. After supper she helped wash the dishes before climbing the ladder up to where she slept. She changed into her night gown before lying down in bed.

She awoke early to the sound of thunder. She quickly got dressed and climbed down the ladder. She got her cape from the hook near the door before she slipped outside. On the way back from the outhouse, she got an armload of firewood. Father was still asleep so she quietly got the fire rekindled. She got the bucket and went to get water. It was beginning to rain as she made her way to the well. She put the hood up on her cape as the rain began to come down harder. When she got back home and took off the cape, she noticed that other than scattered drops of water, the cape was dry, in spite of the downpour she had been in. Father woke up as she began making breakfast.

"You shouldn't be out in the rain," he said. "I could have gone to the well."

"My cape kept me dry, Father," she said. "It doesn't seem to soak up the rain like my old one did."

Once he was dressed he went over and examined the cape closely. Suddenly he laughed.

"This cape cost more money than I made all last year," he said. "The wool comes from a rare type of sheep. Last I knew there was only one man who owned those sheep in all of Brinley. It is waterproof even after being dyed. It rarely gets dirty because there isn't much that will stick to it."

Aurita was stunned. Why would King Langward send such an expensive cape as a wrapping for a doll? She would have to ask next time he came to the village. Even though they were essentially his prisoners, he did not treat them as such.

"What are you thinking about?" Father asked as he dished up the porridge.

"We are King Langward's prisoners," she said and Father nodded. "Yet he does not treat us like prisoners. Other than we cannot leave the village, we are free to do whatever we want. It doesn't make sense."

"King Langward is a very wise, kind and noble person," Father said. "Even though he could have rightfully killed me, he did not. When we first met, he looked into my eyes and saw right into my very soul. He allowed me to see your mother buried before sending us to Weston. He had ordered her to be prepared for burial as a noble woman."

Aurita sat silently as he paused. She could see that the memory was a painful one.

"We were nearly killed by the villagers that first night," he continued. He paused again. She was beginning to understand, but felt there was a lot more that he was not telling her.

"When King Langward first looked into my eyes, he instantly knew the truth about me," Father said. "He understood that a part of me died with your mother. He knew that the only reason for me to live was to raise you. He could see that without you I would die."

"Our King has been most kind to me," she said at last. "When my leg was injured he asked what had happened. He seemed genuinely interested in what I had to say. When I said that the girls didn't mean to hurt me and that I didn't want them to be in trouble because of me, he didn't even ask for their names. Then, just before he left, he kissed me on my forehead."

"I think he loves you as he would his own daughter," Father said with a smile. "Let's eat so that we can gather some reeds for you to learn to weave with. In this weather I can't work outside anyway."

"It would be nice if we had enough room inside like the blacksmith does, even just a roof to keep the rain off."

"That it would," he said. "That's a great idea. Perhaps we can build a roof on poles. It wouldn't take as much wood or labor to do that."

They spent the morning gathering reeds by the brook. By lunchtime they had a large pile of them. After lunch, she began to try to weave a basket. By using the washtub, she was able to keep the reeds wet.

Her first attempt was misshapen and tipped over, but she learned a lot. Her next basket was much better. After supper they worked on her reading.

By morning the skies had cleared. Father talked to Langford and the minister about building a roof to shelter him while he worked. They walked over to the house and discussed it. Some of the other men noticed and joined in. By lunchtime half of the men in town were there. Not long after lunch, some men dragged the first log next to the house. She worked on her weaving while she watched her father and the men saw the logs into pieces and the pieces into boards.

For the next several days the stacks of wood and boards got taller. They brought some logs that were very straight and smaller around than the others and put them to one side. By the time they began to actually build, she had made several baskets that she was quite pleased with. Before going home for the night, one of the men even bought one of the baskets from her.

"I'm very proud of you," Father said. "Those are very good baskets."

"Look," she said as she held out her hand with the money in it. "I even sold one of them already."

It took another week for the men to get the building ready to put the shingles on. She was surprised to discover the building was more than twice the size of the house. It even had a fireplace. It did not connect to the house, but was next to it. By the time the shingles were on it and the door hung, she had sold three more baskets. It had a wooden floor instead of a dirt one like their house had. It also had windows that could be propped open by sticks or latched shut. The day after the building was completed; Aurita and Father moved his tools and wood into the building along with her reeds. Father purchased six lamps to hang from the walls to light it when the windows were shut.

"Some of the men asked if this was our new house," he said as they hung the last lamp. "But I told them that our house was big enough for what we needed."

"I like our home just the way it is. This gives us room to put the things we are ready to sell until they are sold. The house would be much too small for both of us to work in anyway."

"Langford asked if we would mind putting in a bed in the corner near the fireplace," Father said. "That way if he needed to watch over someone who was sick or injured he wouldn't need to take them to his house or stay in their house."

"He would get tired," she said as an idea came to her. "Why don't we build two beds, along with a table and two chairs? We could even gather scraps of cloth to make divider curtains around the beds."

"I like it," he replied as he laughed. "It would also give you a chance to learn to be a healer."

By the time they had built the furniture and made the curtains, it was the Month of First Snow. Aurita enjoyed weaving the baskets, but found time to play with Noka and Carria as well. They had helped her to dye reeds different colors for a basket to send as a gift to the Prince.

Chapter 10 – Practicing New Skills

The Prince frowned. He didn't understand why Father wouldn't take him to Weston to stay the night. He watched as the gate shut behind Father. He wanted to see Aurita again. He hadn't seen her since the day before her leg got injured and that was four years ago. He had wanted to ask her to teach him how to train his new horse. The horse sometimes tried to buck him off. Father would not explain, but just said that, for now, he did not want him to see Aurita. At least Father let him write her a letter about it. He went back in the palace.

The other children in the palace acted nervous around him or they would tease him about not having a real name like they did. Larkin and Nokar both still went out of their way to tease him. Father had shown him a few things so that he would be able to fight back without actually hurting them. He never told Father, but he had enjoyed seeing Nokar with a swollen black eye.

He went to his room and closed the door. He got out some paper and began to draw, but nothing came out right. Father could draw anything he wanted to and paint it as well, but he could not draw the simplest things. Grandmother told him that eventually he would find something he could do better than Father could. He enjoyed spending time with Grandmother but she had been sick a lot lately. Father had promised that when the cold season was over he would become General Kannon's assistant. But he would first have to train his horse. He was still shorter than most of the palace guards, but he had grown a lot in the last three years. He would not be able to do more than run errands for General Kannon for another year before he was old enough to actually begin to learn the battle arts at the Military Training Camp.

He flopped down on his bed. He picked up the beautiful basket on the night stand. Aurita had made it for him. She had been learning to become a healer. He always wondered what she would think when she found out that she was the one with the royal blood, not him. He wondered who Father had chosen to be her husband. Every time he asked, Father refused to tell him. Mother wouldn't say either. He sighed and put the basket back on the night stand.

He went to Father's study and began reading the book of laws again. Someday he would be king and need to know the laws. He had been learning to speak the language of the kingdoms to the North as well as read and write it. It was very different from their language. Even the letters were written differently than those used in Brinley. Sometimes he got frustrated, but he had gotten better at it. He read until suppertime.

*****

Aurita was finishing up a basket while Father made supper. She was startled by a knock on the door. She opened the door and snow swirled in blown by the strong wind. A man and a woman stood there. Suddenly the woman's face contorted and she moaned as if in pain.

"Please," the man said with a worried, frightened tone. "Can you tell us where to find a midwife or a healer? We stopped for the night, but I think she is going to have the infant tonight."

"You are in the right place," she said. "Bring her in. There's a bed behind those curtains by the fireplace."

She helped the man get the woman to the bed. While the man took the woman's cape and helped her to lie down, Aurita got several of the large cloths from the cupboard.

"Go to the little house next door," she told the man. "Tell my father to get Langford to come right away."

The man nodded and left as she began to prepare for the birthing.

*****

Burkhart was surprised by the knock at the door. He opened it to find a very worried looking man. As the man looked up, his expression turned to one of shock.

"Y . . . you're," the man stuttered. "You were."

"My name is Burkhart," he said nodding. "The only title I now hold is that of father."

"But, why?" the man asked, still confused. "Don't you want?"

"No," he replied shaking his head. "King Burkhart died with Queen Aurita. I gave the throne to King Langward of my own free will. King Langward ordered that no one but him can tell my daughter of my past. Please don't tell her. When she is grown and wed I will at last be released from my obligations and can petition Our Noble King for release from this world that I may rest next to my wife."

The man blinked then said, "Wife, my wife is going to give birth. The girl told me to ask you to get Langford right away."

"Get yourself some soup," he said as he pointed to the pot over the fire then to the bowls on the table. "I'll be back soon."

He put on his cape as he closed the door behind him. The icy wind took his breath from him and the snow blinded him as the made his way to the bridge. He went as quickly as possible through the deepening snow before arriving at Langford's house. He knocked at the door.

"Burkhart," Minara said as she opened the door wider. "What brings you out in the storm?"

"There's a woman ready to give birth," he said. "Aurita is caring for her now, but asked for Langford to come."

*****

Aurita made the woman as comfortable as possible. She could tell that the infant might not wait for Langford to arrive. Suddenly the head began to show.

"One more push," she told the woman.

Soon the head was completely out, but it was a little blue. She noticed the cord around its neck.

"Relax and don't push for a moment," she told the woman in as calm a voice as she could.

She knew she had to get the cord off the infant's neck. She turned the infant so one shoulder was up and the cord loosened a bit. She carefully got her fingers around it and gently pulled it up over the infant's head.

"Now one more big push," she said and the infant slipped out into her hands.

She laid it on the bed while she tied two pieces of string tightly around the cord with a space between them. She cut the cord with a pair of scissors then tied the end left on the infant into a single knot near its belly. She turned the infant on its stomach along her left arm and patted the infant's back. As she heard the door open behind her, the infant began to cry. She breathed a sigh of relief and began to dry off the infant.

"It looks like I'm too late," Langford's voice said behind her soon after the door opened again.

91

"The cord was around his neck, but everything's fine now," she said as she handed him the infant. "We need to finish. You need to give me one more push."

She pulled firmly on the cord as the woman pushed and the afterbirth came out. She dumped it in a bucket before rolling up the bloody cloths. She gently cleaned the woman up and helped her change into a clean nightgown. She helped the woman back into the cleaned up bed and covered her up. She could hear men's voices behind the curtains over the infant's cries.

"Thank you," the woman said. "I didn't know a girl so young could be a midwife."

"I've watched and even helped before, but this is the first time I've done it alone," she replied. "I'll get your husband and infant. You need time alone with your family."

She went around the curtains and was surprised to find King Langward standing next to the woman's husband. She began to get down on the floor.

"Don't," King Langward said and she looked up at him. "Go get cleaned up. Your father has your supper waiting for you."

"Thank you, My King," she said before hurrying out the door.

*****

She had grown a lot since he had last seen her. He gestured for the man to go to his wife. As he drew Langford to the other end of the room, he heard the man begin to explain to the woman just exactly who Aurita was.

"She delivered the infant all by herself," Langford said with a note of pride in his voice. "And it wasn't a simple birth either."

"She hasn't delivered one before?" Langward asked. "I thought she was a bit young to be a midwife."

"She's helped, but never delivered one on her own," Langford replied. "She is a very mature young woman for her age. She is very calm and doesn't easily panic. She has the ability to calm a patient while performing her work. I'm glad we put the two beds in here. She has been able to learn a lot."

The man came out and approached them.

"My wife wants to speak to Burkhart," he said.

92

"I'll go get him," Langward said. "I want to speak to Aurita in private."

He noticed her cape hanging by the door and took it with him. The storm was beginning to subside. He tapped on the door. Burkhart opened it with a surprised look on his face.

"You need not knock, My King," he said. "Everything that is mine is yours."

"The woman wants to speak to you for a moment," Langward said. "I wish to speak to Aurita."

*****

Burkhart wondered what the woman had to say to him. He nodded and put on his cape. He went inside the shop and saw the man look out from around the curtains. He gestured Burkhart forward. He hesitantly went around the curtain to where the woman was in bed.

"I wanted to thank you," she said. "Your daughter saved my infant's life."

"I do not need to be thanked," he said. "It is our wise and compassionate king who should be thanked. It was he that preserved both my life and hers."

"But it is you who has raised her," the woman said. "You are not the same man who caused much suffering among the people of Brinley. You have changed. We would like to name our son after you."

*****

Aurita came down from the sleeping loft.

"I wanted you to know how proud I am of you," Langward said as she looked at him in surprise. "No other girl your age would have been able to do what you just did."

"Father taught me that we must give back to the people what we can," she said. "That we must be in service of others regardless of how they treat us."

Langward smiled. Burkhart was doing an excellent job as a father.

"My son sent you a letter," he said as he handed it to her. "I will not be returning to the palace until tomorrow."

"I can have a reply written by then," she said. "I had hoped he would come with you some time. It has been so long since I have seen him. I barely remember what he looks like."

"Someday you'll understand why I do not bring him," Langward said.

"I wonder if the woman would like some soup," she said as she dished up a bowl.

"Let's take it to her," he replied and placed her cape around her shoulders.

As they entered the shop they heard Burkhart say, "I do not deserve such an honor. May I suggest that you name your son after Our King's father instead? His name was Lawrence."

"I think our mother would be honored if your son was named after our father," they heard Langford say as they approached the curtains.

"Perhaps we should ask King Langward," the man said.

"I would be very pleased if you named your son after Father," Langward said as he and Aurita came around the curtain. "Burkhart was most thoughtful to suggest it."

"Would you like some soup?" Aurita asked as she approached the bed.

"Yes, please," the woman said with a smile.

Aurita handed her the bowl of soup.

"We wanted to thank you for helping deliver our son," the man said.

"Infants are so amazing," she commented. "They are so tiny and helpless, yet at the same time they are strong."

"It is hard to believe that something so tiny and frail has the power to save a man's life," Burkhart commented quietly.

Langward rested his hand on Burkhart's shoulder and he looked over to meet his gaze.

"I wanted to talk with you, My Friend," he told Burkhart. "In private."

Burkhart nodded and allowed himself to be guided to the door. He followed quietly to the house. Once inside, Langward gestured to a chair. Burkhart obediently sat down.

"You are a very good father to Aurita," Langward said as he sat down. "She is turning out to be a very fine young woman."

Burkhart looked relieved.

"She mentioned that she had hoped I would bring my son for a visit," he said. "My son was very disappointed that I did not bring him."

"Why didn't you?" Burkhart asked. "If they are to be married, shouldn't they spend time with each other?"

"You know how if you tell a child to do one thing they will do just the opposite?" he said and Burkhart nodded. "I felt that it would be best to allow them to communicate through letters, but not let them see each other for a while. I want them to decide that they want to get married."

"By true love can he be named," Burkhart said, nodding.

"Exactly. My plan is that when the cold season ends, I will have my son become General Kannon's assistant. After a year, he will be old enough to train for the military. A couple of years later, I will have him assigned to patrol duty around this village. At that time he will not be known as Prince but only by his military rank. I will have him teach her to ride a horse, but I will forbid him to tell her who he is."

Burkhart began to laugh and said, "They're certain to fall in love."

"I will have him deliver a message to you so that you will recognize him," Langward said. "I will also tell him that he needs to take special care to protect and watch over her, but I will not tell him that she will be his wife. If I know my son, eventually he will ask to marry her even though I have told him I have already chosen her husband."

"I remember that my father did not want me to marry Aurita," Burkhart said. "That alone made her more attractive to me."

"Exactly my thoughts," Langward said and they both began to laugh.

The fortune teller had been right, Burkhart was now his friend. They stopped laughing suddenly as Aurita opened the door. She looked at her father and then him with a puzzled look on her face. It was all he could do to not laugh again.

"I'm going to eat and go to bed," she said as she hung her cape up.

"I'll walk with you to the church," Burkhart said as Langward stood up.

*****

Aurita watched the two leave. She wondered what was so funny. She dished up her bowl of soup and sat down at the table. They were up to something, that much she was certain of, but what? She opened up the letter from the Prince and read it while she ate.

'Dear Aurita,' the letter began. 'I had hoped Father would bring me to Weston with him so I could see you in person. It has been much too long since I last saw you. I had hoped to ask for your help in training my new horse, but Father refused to bring me and would not say why.'

She wondered why he would not tell his own son why he would not let him come to Weston.

'I frequently wonder what you are doing and if you think about me at all.'

That surprised her. Why should he wonder if she thought about him? Certainly the prince would have many friends.

'What I needed to ask you is how to get my horse to stop bucking. He sometimes tosses his head and then turns sharply before galloping toward home. He gets the bit upturned so that pulling on the reins does no good at all. I hope that you can give me some advice on this. I don't want to ask anyone around the palace, because they have laughed when I have problems controlling my horse.'

She was startled by the door opening. Father entered and hung up his cape.

"I thought you would be through eating by now," he said.

"Our Prince sent me a letter," she said. "I was just reading it. King Langward wants me to have a reply ready before he leaves tomorrow."

"Get to bed," he said. "You can write your reply in the morning."

She folded up the letter as Father took her empty bowl. She climbed up and got ready for bed. She lay in bed for a while thinking about the letter and the events of the day.

*****

The prince was brushing his horse when his father returned from Weston.

"Here's the reply to your letter," Father said as he handed him a folded piece of paper.

He tucked it into his pouch before he finished brushing his horse. Once he had put the horse in its stall, he hurried up to his room. He locked the door behind him and sat down at the desk to read the letter.

'Dear Prince,' Aurita wrote. 'I had been hoping to see you again as well. Your father would not say why he had not brought you, only that I would understand some day. Yesterday I helped a woman deliver an infant.

It was kind of scary at first, but soon I was too busy to think about being scared. They named the infant Lawrence after your grandfather.'

He was quite surprised about her delivering an infant. It was not something he had guessed she would know how to do.

'Your Uncle Langford has been teaching me to be a healer. I really enjoy being able to help people, but seeing a new infant being born is better than anything else.'

He smiled at her obvious enthusiasm. He was glad she was doing something she enjoyed. He had always worried that she would be sad because she couldn't leave the village.

'I'm sorry to hear that people laugh at you because of your horse misbehaving. That isn't very nice. I hate to be laughed at. Your horse might be bucking because there is a problem with the saddle or saddle blanket. You need to be careful about checking them for even small slivers or burrs. You wouldn't like to carry around something heavy if there was a sliver or burr on your back.'

He smiled at her description. He hadn't ever thought about it in that way.

'When you are riding, you need to not let the reins be too loose. Don't pull on his mouth, but don't give him enough slack to toss up the bit. One of the patrol men had a horse that did that. It ran away with him a couple of times before I noticed the reins were so loose the horse could toss up the bit easily. After I got a chance to tell him what I had noticed, he hasn't had any more problems. His patrol and the others were laughing at him. He hated it, but it did look kind of funny. I try not to laugh out loud when something like that happens. I don't want to make anyone feel bad. I know how I feel when people do or say something that makes me feel bad.'

He was glad she understood. He felt frustrated and lonely a lot of the time. He was looking forward to being General Kannon's assistant. Father said that then he would have a military title to use instead of just being called Prince. He hated not having a name. He had tried to think about what name he would like to have, but nothing sounded quite right.

He jumped as the door knob jiggled followed by someone knocking on the door. He quickly folded the letter and put it back in his pouch before unlocking the door to find his father and mother were standing there.

"It's time for supper," Mother said.

"Give me a chance to wash up," he said. "I'll be right there."

*****

Langward and Retanta headed toward the dining hall.

"Did you read her letter to him?" Retanta asked him.

"Of course," he replied. "I do believe the plan is working. Keeping them apart is encouraging their interest in each other."

"It's amazing to think she delivered that woman's infant all by herself," Retanta said as they arrived at the dining hall.

"She is a very clever girl. Langford said that she doesn't panic easily. From her letter, I can tell that she is very aware of other people's feelings. When the time comes, she will do her job perfectly even if she knows nothing about it."

"I hope you are right," she said as their son entered.

"I have complete faith that I am," he replied as the servants began to dish up their food.

Their son seemed deep in thought. He didn't say much during the meal and excused himself as soon as he had finished eating. When they returned to their quarters, he was already locked in his room. Langward worried about that. He wondered if it meant that he felt vulnerable. He needed to learn to feel strong and confident about himself and those around him. He would learn much of that at the Military Training Camp.

The next morning, Langward awoke early, but his son was already gone. He asked Garman who told him his son had already eaten and gone out to the stables. Directly after breakfast, Langward went out to find him. He was carefully looking over his saddle blanket and picking something out of it.

"What are you doing?" he asked as he sat down on the bench next to his son.

"I realized that this got put on the stall gate where the horse had been chewing on the wood. Aurita said there might be a problem with the saddle blanket that was making him buck. It's full of slivers."

"That makes sense," Langward said chuckling a little. "I never would have thought of that."

"I'm almost done. Can we go for a ride?"

"Sure."

Langward went to get his horse ready, but as soon as he got the horse led out of the stall, a man showed up with the saddle and bridle. He went back to find his son saddling his horse. Soon they were ready and mounted up. They rode around inside the palace walls for a while. He was pleased when his son's horse seemed to be behaving perfectly. Even when they went out into the streets of the town, the horse didn't give him any trouble. It tossed its head but was unable to run away from him.

"I'm pleased," Langward said as they waited for the palace gate to be opened for them. "I've never seen that horse behave so well for you."

"Aurita knew just what to do even though she has never seen the horse," he replied. "I want to do something to thank her. Maybe give her a gift."

"What would you like to give her?" Langward asked and his son shrugged his shoulders. "Let me know when you figure it out."

Langward wondered what he would come up with. He spent a lot of time locked in his room or in Langward's study reading the book of laws. Perhaps it would be best to not wait until the cold season was over to send him to the Military Training Camp.

The next day at lunch Langward noticed that his son was very deep in thought. He was barely eating.

"What's on your mind, Son?" he asked.

"You've been so quiet lately," Retanta added.

"The people in Weston bathe in the river," he said, speaking at last. "Isn't it too cold to be bathing in icy water?"

Langward had not expected that response.

"One gets used to it," he said. "During the coldest time people sometimes just use a wet cloth instead of getting into the river."

"Wouldn't the healer need something large to hold water in case someone needed to be bathed to clean their wounds?"

"Langford dug a hole in the ground and lined it with smooth flat stones so it would hold water long enough to bathe a person," he replied.

"That's hardly cleaner than the river."

"I suppose so," he replied wondering where this was all leading.

"Could I send a bath tub to Aurita?" he asked. "Then she could use it for her work as a healer as well as bathe herself in it."

Langward struggled not to laugh as Retanta said, "I think that is a lovely idea."

Their son smiled and said, "Can I take it to her myself?"

Retanta glanced at Langward with a worried expression.

"We need to talk, Son," he said with a sigh.

Langward led his son to the study, but was not quite certain how to begin. He needed to be able to satisfy his curiosity without telling him everything.

"You once asked what if the man chosen to be Aurita's husband could not love her," Langward began.

The prince said nothing but nodded.

"I have known people whose parents had chosen their husband or wife. It used to be quite common. Most of them were lucky if they eventually became friends. Some of them never even have any children," he said, then paused again.

He could tell that his son was beginning to understand.

"I want to make certain that Aurita and her husband are more than just friends. I want to allow them to fall in love."

*****

"How can you do that?" he asked, speaking for the first time.

Father didn't speak for a few minutes. He knew that Father was trying to avoid telling him everything.

"There are still a few years before she will be old enough to wed," Father said. "I will have her husband assigned to the village as a patrolman. I want the two to have a chance to meet on their own. As she gets older I will encourage more direct interaction between her and the patrols. If the fortune teller is correct, that will be all that is necessary."

He thought about it for a while. He knew that all of the patrolmen knew that her father had been king of Brinley. He had learned what an evil king Burkhart had been. Yet the time that he saw Burkhart, he knew that what Father had said about him being changed was correct. Still, he was worried that some men may not be able to accept that. He wondered what all this had to do with him not seeing Aurita.

"I still don't understand why you won't let me see Aurita," he finally said.

"There is more that the fortune teller told me than what I can reveal to you now," Father said with a sigh. "I know that you have questions, but all I can ask is that you will be patient. By the time you are ready to be told, you will already have all the answers you have been looking for."

"Including my name?" he asked. "I hate not having a real name."

"I know, Son," Father said. "I promise that when I tell you everything you will have a real name."

"What about while I am at the Military Training Camp?" he asked. "I don't want the men there to treat me the way the children in the palace have."

"While you are there, you will have a military title," Father said. "There are so many men there that most of the time only a title is used instead of a name anyway. At some point the men there may figure out who you are, but you don't have to tell them if you don't want to."

"I am looking forward to going into the military," he said. "You have said that it was there that you learned many of the things you needed to become king. I want to be able to learn those things too."

"You have learned a lot already," Father said. "I do want you to learn how to live outside the palace too. It is a whole different world outside the palace. You need to understand how the people live so that you can make their lives better. Burkhart did not understand what it was like to live outside the palace. He did not know what it was like to go hungry because there was not enough food. He did not know how to make his own food; it was always brought to him prepared. He did not know what it was like to wear the same clothes or boots until they were wearing out. Right now, you are kind of like Burkhart. I want you to learn these things for yourself. While you are in the military, you will be paid and will have to take care of yourself. You will have to pay for the things that you need. You will be given a cape and several tunics to wear but will have to pay for any new pants or boots. That way you will understand the lives of the people of Brinley."

The next morning Father took a large bath tub out to Weston and gave it to Aurita. She sent back a note thanking him for his thoughtfulness. He worked with his horse to train it. Soon it would come to him when he whistled and obeyed his lightest touch while he was riding it.

Chapter 11 – General Kannon's New Assistant

Within a couple of months, Langward felt his son was ready to become General Kannon's assistant. He made certain that he had exactly what the other men at the Military Training Camp had in the way of clothing. He would start out as a Private just like everyone else. General Kannon seemed happy when he came to the palace to pick up the Prince.

"I've been looking forward to having an assistant that can actually read and write," the general said. "My last assistant could barely read. You will be a big help to me."

"I will certainly try, Sir," he replied. "I have been looking forward to this."

"I can't believe my little boy is so grown up already," Mother said as she wiped a tear from her eye.

"I'm certain that you'll do well" Grandmother said as she hugged him.

"I'm proud of you, Son," Father said. "Now one thing I want you to remember, in assisting General Kannon, you may have the opportunity to visit Weston. If you do, under no circumstance are you to tell any of the villagers who you are. In part this is for your own safety. I don't want anyone from Mannton or anywhere else figuring out who you are either. I especially forbid you to tell Aurita who you are. If you write to her as my son, you will not reveal to her that you are now in the military."

He was surprised at that request.

"I know you don't understand right now, but in time you will," Father said. "General Kannon will make certain that you obey my wishes. He will make certain that only those who need to know who you are will know and recognize you. When you are ready, you will be assigned to a patrol. At that time only the senior member of your patrol will know exactly who you are."

"It's time to go," General Kannon said.

He quickly hugged Grandmother, Father, and then Mother. Mother was crying as he picked up his saddlebags and bedroll. He followed General Kannon out to the courtyard. His horse was saddled and waiting next to General Kannon's. He secured his belongings before mounting and following the general out of the palace wall. People glanced up as they passed, but went back to what they were doing. They did not recognize him without his armband. Father had made him leave it behind. Now he was just another soldier in Brinley's army.

General Kannon took him to the barracks to drop off his belongings. It was a large building with three floors. Each floor was simply a large open room with a fireplace at each end. There were beds stacked two high lining the walls. He hoped he would be able to find which bed was his.

"All the new men start on the top floor in the center," General Kannon explained. "As you are here longer and progress in rank, you will move closer to one of the fireplaces or to a lower floor."

He nodded and began counting the beds between his and the door. The rest of the morning was spent in General Kannon's office. He was given pen, ink and paper and told to make twenty copies of orders that General Kannon wrote out. By the third time through he had the orders memorized. When he finished it was nearly noon.

General Kannon took him to another very large building that had a line of men standing at the door.

"Follow the line in and get your meal," the General said. "Eat quickly and return to my office."

"Yes, Sir," he replied before stepping in line behind the last man.

Before long there were more men behind him. Once they were in the building, the man in front of him glanced back and saw him. He nudged the man in front of him.

"They're getting younger this year," the first man said. "I hope we don't have to change this one's diapers."

"General Kannon thinks I am old enough to be here," he replied to the comment. "I am capable of taking care of myself."

That made the man angry. The man tried to punch him, but he was able to dodge the blow. When the man tried to punch him in the face, he grabbed the man's fist with his right hand and twisted as he dodged the blow. He soon had the man's arm twisted behind his back. The man's companion drew a knife and raised it. He grabbed the man's wrist with his left hand. The man was stronger than he was so he rubbed his thumb across the bone in a way he knew would hurt. The man dropped the knife and it fell to the floor. A man in a captain's tunic got up from his table and came over.

"What is going on?" he asked in a stern tone.

He released the men before quickly saluting.

"Just getting acquainted, Sir," he said quickly. "They thought they may have to take care of me."

"They were obviously mistaken. What's your name, Private?" the captain said, then paused. "You're. . ."

"New here, Sir" he said quickly, realizing he had seen this man before. "It's my first day."

The man looked a little surprised.

"Father was a patrolman for a while," he said. "He told me that here name and age don't matter, only rank and experience."

"He's right," the captain said. "Get your meal and sit with me."

"Yes, Sir," he replied.

The two men were staring at him. He picked up the knife and handed it to its owner.

"The cook is waiting to serve your meals," he said and nodded toward the table where the food was.

The men turned and got their meals. He did not recognize what was put on his plate, but knew that if he wanted to eat, this is what he would have to eat. He went to the captain's table and sat where the man indicated.

"I didn't think I'd see you here," the captain said softly so only he could hear.

"I realized you recognized me," he replied quietly. "I am to be known only by rank now. I am not to tell anyone who I am. General Kannon will tell those who need to know. That is Father's order and we both know that no one disobeys my father."

"You handled yourself well," the captain said.

"Father taught me a few things," he replied. "And I don't always get along with the others my age at home. I learned to control my anger and use it to my advantage. It will be several years yet before I gain what they already have."

"Is that why you don't get along with them?" the captain asked.

"They delighted in teasing me about that," he replied.

"So how did you wind up here? I thought it would be too great a risk."

"Father felt it necessary for me to learn what I could not at home," he replied and the man nodded. "For now I am General Kannon's assistant. I should eat quickly and get back to his office."

When he finished eating the bland food, the captain followed him out of the building. He wondered why the captain seemed to be walking with him. General Kannon arrived just as they did.

"I need a word with you, General," the captain said.

"Wait out here, Private," General Kannon said.

He stood patiently outside the door as he had seen the palace guard do. It seemed like forever before the door opened. He was motioned inside.

"Your father was right about you," General Kannon said. "He did not think you could get through your first day without fighting with someone. He said you seem to like to fight."

He felt a sinking feeling in the pit of his stomach.

"It's not exactly that I like to fight," he replied trying to keep his voice steady. "Only that I don't go out of my way to avoid a fight."

The two men began to laugh.

"Captain Rowand told me what happened," General Kannon said. "He said that you handled the situation quite well. You will soon learn when to back away from a fight and when to start a fight."

"Yes, Sir," he replied trying to not sound too relieved.

"Captain Rowand teaches wrestling and hand to hand combat skills," General Kannon said. "I want you to attend his class that starts in an hour. That will give me time to notify your father, but I think he will approve."

"Yes, Sir," he replied.

"Besides, you got enough done this morning that I really don't have anything else for you to do right now," General Kannon said. "I will expect you back here directly after breakfast. You may go with Captain Rowand now."

As he followed the captain out of General Kannon's office, he wondered what his father would think about him starting training already. He had thought he would have to wait another year. Obviously Captain Rowand and General Kannon thought he was ready to start training. He waited patiently for the hour to pass. When the men started to assemble, he noticed that the two men from lunch were in the class. Suddenly this was not looking like such a good idea.

Captain Rowand paired him with another young man that was not much larger than him. It soon became apparent that this was a beginning class since most of the things covered, Father had already taught him. He was able to pin his opponent a couple of times before he was the one pinned. He was surprised as the young man offered him a hand up.

"You're good," the young man said as they walked toward the dining hall.

"Father taught me a few things," he said. "He was a patrolman for a while."

"My name's Kennar," the young man said. "What's yours?"

"Just call me Private," he replied hoping Kennar wouldn't press him further. "Father bet me I couldn't get through to patrolman before telling anyone who I am."

Kennar just shrugged his shoulders as they stepped in line. He breathed a sigh of relief. He hadn't exactly told a lie, yet he hadn't exactly told the truth either.

"That's a strange thing to bet," Kennar said as they entered the building.

"I think he would rather me get through on my own abilities rather than on his reputation," he replied realizing that much was probably true as well.

He would have to send Father a letter explaining it. He would do that in the morning. He was surprised when the two men from lunch sat next to them.

"We're sorry about what we said earlier," one of them said. "We were watching you during class."

"You are obviously quite capable of taking care of yourself," the other added. "We've been in the class for half a year, yet you seemed to know most of what we had already learned."

"We were certain that we would get into trouble when Captain Rowand came over," the first one said. "We were very surprised that you did not ask to have us punished for attacking you."

"I know it will take a while for everyone to get used to me because I am smaller and younger than everyone here," he replied. "I knew it wouldn't be easy."

"I'm Monau and this is Kon," the first one said. "What is your name?"

"You're just going to have to call me by my rank," he replied. "I'm not telling anyone who I am until I become a patrolman."

"I was amazed that Captain Rowand was not angry with you for not telling him your name," Kon said. "How did you manage that?"

"Actually, my father and General Kannon are good friends," he said. "General Kannon knows all about why I don't want to tell anyone who I am. After Captain Rowand spoke to General Kannon, no more was said."

"I heard rumor that you are General Kannon's assistant," Monau said. "And that you can read and write."

"My father heard General Kannon needed a new assistant, one that could read and write," he said. "Father has always wanted me to be in the military, so he had taught me to read and write several years ago."

"You will probably know everything before anyone else around here," Kon said. "We Privates are always the last to know. Do you think you could let us know what is up?"

"Sorry," he said shaking his head. "I'm sworn to secrecy. Besides, if my father found out, I would really be in trouble. Trust me; no one wants Father angry at them."

Once they finished eating, they went to the barracks. He discovered that the men were in the beds next to his. Kennar slept in the bed below his. As he went to sleep, he was happy to at last have some friends.

*****

Langward was glad when lunch time came. The day's meeting had been mostly routine. Retanta was waiting for them in the dining hall. He kissed her hand before they sat down.

"Your son sent this for you," General Kannon said as he handed a folded paper to him.

'Dear Father and Mother,' the note began. 'I just wanted you to know that I am happy here. I have made three friends already. I thought I had best tell you that when people ask for my name I am telling them that you bet me that I couldn't make patrolman before telling anyone my name. If they press me further, I tell them that you would rather I get through training on my own abilities, not your reputation. They seem satisfied with that answer.'

Langward stifled a laugh at that revelation. His son was a clever young man to think of such an explanation.

'I saw Captain Rowand yesterday and he recognized me. He had me sit next to him and I explained the situation to him, but in a way that no one overhearing our conversation would understand. I finished all my work for General Kannon in the morning, so he had me join Captain Rowand's class on wrestling and hand to hand combat. I am excited to be learning things already. I will send any future letters with General Kannon. With all my love, your son.'

"What is it, Langward?" Retanta asked.

"I'll read it to you later," he said. "Thank you for bringing this, General Kannon. I'm pleased."

"I thought you would be," the General replied.

They granted audiences until suppertime. After the meal, they retired to their chambers and he read the letter to Retanta.

"I don't know whether to be relieved or frightened," she said as he finished. "I didn't think he would be doing any training yet. He is so young. I am glad he has at last made some friends."

"It is time for him to grow up and become a man, Retanta," Kara said.

"I think this will be very good for him," he replied. "I have been so worried about him spending so much time locked in his room."

"I know," she replied. "I've noticed the way he has been treated by the other children, yet he never complains."

"I think he will be a good king when it is his turn to sit on the throne," he said. "I know that he has worried about Aurita's husband not loving her. I think that he will be a very kind and loving husband for her."

"I've caught him holding the basket she made him and turning it in his hands as though he were deep in thought," she said. "I just hope that she will fall in love with him as well."

"Only in time will we know," he replied.

Chapter 12 – Delivering a Message to Weston

He awoke in the barracks before the bugler arrived to wake them. He put a couple of pieces of wood on the fire. In the last year, he had moved from the center of the top floor to the end. The first bed that became available on the second floor would be his. He had outgrown three sizes of tunics as he grew taller and his shoulders broadened. He had been training with the sword for three months now. Most of the men seemed to like him and were not bothered by his refusal to give them his name. General Kannon had given him even more responsibilities. He had even been sent as a messenger to the king of Burton.

Just yesterday he had been advanced in rank to corporal. As far as he knew, he was the youngest corporal ever in Brinley's army. He dressed quickly while the other men slept. General Kannon said that today they would be going somewhere to deliver a message. He was puzzled by the general's vague explanation of where they were going. It must be something very important.

He passed the bugler on the way out the door. He went to the pasture where the horses were kept and whistled. His horse came quickly to the gate. He soon had it saddled and bridled. He then went to get General Kannon's horse ready. By the time the horse was ready, General Kannon arrived.

"I didn't expect you to be here yet," the general said. "You must have gotten up early."

"I just couldn't sleep any longer," he said as the general mounted.

"Good. I didn't want to have to wait for you."

He followed General Kannon through part of the town before they turned toward Weston. He was quite surprised. He did not think he would be allowed to visit Weston ever again. They stopped on the crest of the hill overlooking Weston.

"Now, I must remind you of your promises to your father," General Kannon said as he stopped his horse beside the general's.

"I am not to reveal my identity to anyone, especially not Aurita," he replied, nodding.

"Good," General Kannon said before starting down the slope.

The people looked up from their work briefly as they passed, but took no further notice of them. It was about an hour before lunchtime. He was getting hungry since he had skipped breakfast. He was very surprised when they stopped in front of Burkhart's house. There was a building beside the house that was much larger than the house. He tied their horses and followed General Kannon into the building.

"General Kannon," Burkhart said as he looked up from his work. "I didn't expect a visit from you."

"It's been a long time," General Kannon replied. "But what is past is past."

"Yes, yet the shadow of it haunts me still," Burkhart replied. "What brings you here?"

"A message from King Langward."

"Certainly you've not been reduced to being a mere messenger," Burkhart said as he took the scroll from General Kannon.

"Read it," the general said with a laugh. "You'll understand then."

While Burkhart read, he kept glancing up. He laughed before going over to the fireplace and putting the scroll in the small fire.

"I see you have a new assistant," Burkhart said. "Is he doing well?"

He felt uncomfortable as Burkhart looked him over very closely, yet spoke as though he were not there.

"He is doing quite well," General Kannon replied. "I'm certain he is destined for greater things."

Just then the door opened and a very beautiful young woman entered the room. She went behind a curtain at the back of the room. He felt a hand under his chin closing his mouth and felt his face turn red.

"Tell Our Noble King that all appears to be progressing as promised," Burkhart said in a serious tone.

He felt confused and embarrassed as the woman returned.

"I'll have lunch ready soon, Father," the woman said.

"Aurita, this is General Kannon," Burkhart said and Aurita curtsied. "The corporal is his assistant."

He bowed to her and she blushed slightly.

"It's a pleasure to meet you," she said. "Would you like to stay for lunch? I made extra today."

"We would enjoy that," General Kannon replied. "Corporal, stake the horses out to graze."

"Yes, Sir," he replied and quickly left.

*****

Aurita was puzzled by the corporal's actions. None of the other soldiers had ever bowed to her. He seemed nervous about something.

"Why did he bow to me?" she asked as she looked at Father.

"That is what a true gentleman should do when he greets a young lady," Father replied. "He seemed to find you attractive. What did you think about him?"

She began to blush. She had definitely liked the looks of him. She had gone behind the curtains and straightened the empty bed to compose herself.

"That reaction says more than any words could," General Kannon said, causing her to blush even more.

"Why don't you go out and help him stake out the horses," Father said. "He knows King Langward's rules. You will be safe with him."

She quickly left. She heard laughter just as she shut the door behind her. She looked up to find the corporal staring at her as he held the reins of the two horses. One of them nudged his shoulder making him stumble forward a step.

She swallowed and said, "I know a good place to stake out the horses."

"Where?"

She led the way toward the bridge over the brook. When she glanced at him, he was looking at her. He quickly looked down at the path.

"You certainly don't talk much," she said.

"I. . . I," he began then blushed. "I just have never spoken to a young woman as beautiful as you are. I don't know what to say."

"You probably don't get to see many women at all while in the military," she said. "I'm not that pretty."

"What makes you say that?" he asked in a surprised tone.

"That's what the young men around here say," she said with a lump in her throat. "But it doesn't matter anyway. King Langward has already chosen a husband for me. I don't have to be pretty to get a husband. I don't even get a choice in the matter."

111

"They've been lying to you," he replied. "I've had to take messages to a lot of places for General Kannon and even King Langward. You are the most beautiful young woman I have seen."

She stopped and looked at him. He had a very serious look on his face. He was either telling the truth or was very good at lying.

"I know how you feel about having your husband chosen for you," he said. "My parents have chosen a wife for me. I've never even met her. I know that I must find a way to love her and I pray that your husband can do the same for you."

She was surprised. He was very serious.

"You are different than anyone I have ever met," she said at last as she began walking again. "The villagers mostly ignore us unless they are injured or want to purchase something. The patrolmen watch over us, but I am somewhat afraid of them. They are polite, but some obviously don't like Father at all."

"I know what you mean," he said. "Most of the children I grew up with were cruel and mean. They didn't like me and teased me a lot. I like to spend time by myself mostly."

"I can't understand why people can be mean like that," she replied.

She felt kind of sorry for him, but in a way it made her feel better to know that she was not the only one who felt that way.

"Here we are," she said as she stopped at the edge of the meadow. "I can't go any further. This is the border of the village. If Father or I step outside the border, the patrolmen would kill us."

He looked at her, and then nodded before leading the horses further out. He took something out of the saddlebags and stuck them into the ground. He tied the horses to them before loosening the girth straps on the saddles. He rubbed the darker horse's forehead before returning to her.

She turned around as she heard voices behind her. Her heart froze as she saw two of the meanest young men in town approach.

"Why don't you just leave?" one of them said. "I'm tired of all the rules we have to remember because you and your father are here."

"You are a burden to our village," the other said. "I was hoping you would starve to death last winter."

One of them approached her, but the corporal stepped between them.

They laughed. Both were larger and stronger than the corporal, but he stood his ground. One of them charged at him. Before she realized what happened, the man was laying on his back on the ground. Suddenly the other was on his back as well. She heard hoof beats behind her.

"These two again," one of the patrolmen said in a disgusted tone. "Good work, Corporal."

"No one should speak that way to a woman," the corporal replied.

"Take her home," the patrolman said. "We'll take care of these two. They have been warned. Now they will have some time to think about it in the dungeon."

"What's so special about her?" one of the young men said as he rose to his feet.

"King Langward has ordered her protected," the patrolman responded. "That's all we need to know."

The corporal touched her arm, and then led her back home.

"Thank you," she said as they crossed the bridge. "I don't even know your name."

"You don't need to," he said. "Just call me Corporal. When I finish training and get assigned to a patrol, I hope I get stationed here."

"I hope so too," she said and noticed he smiled at her response.

Father and General Kannon were waiting outside for them when they returned. Soon they were seated at the tiny table. The corporal was watching her, but would glance down when she looked at him. He seemed to enjoy the simple vegetable soup she had made. He was very handsome and his smile made her heart beat faster. General Kannon spoke to Father as though speaking to an old friend. The corporal also seemed very comfortable speaking to Father. She had just finished eating when there was a pounding at the door. Father opened the door.

"We need a healer!" the man at the door exclaimed. "His leg was crushed."

Aurita quickly ran out the door to find three more men carrying another into the shop. Father grabbed a bucket and went for water as she cut the man's pant leg open to examine the wound. It was very badly damaged. Someone had already tightened a belt around his leg above the wound. She opened the chest of tools and medicines and drew out a flask. She poured some over her hands before pouring some over the man's leg just below the belt.

As she glanced up, she saw the corporal watching her. She put him out of her mind and got out her knife. She began to cut into the wound and found the bones were crushed into splinters. The leg would have to be cut off. The man was still unconscious. She looked up to see a terrified looking woman staring at the leg.

"You are his wife?" Aurita asked and the woman nodded. "The leg is too badly damaged. It would never heal. If I don't cut it off, he might even die."

The woman nodded before bursting into tears. Some of the men took her back around the curtain. Father heated the water over the fire. She looked up to find General Kannon and the corporal still there.

"We need to tie him down," she said and Father took the thick leather straps from the shelf. "I need him kept still."

The man moaned and opened his eyes.

"I need you to drink something," she said as she drew out a second flask. "It will dull the pain."

"Why are you tying me down?" the man asked.

"Drink this," she said as she pressed the opening to his lips.

He began to drink.

"Your leg is too damaged to save," she said. "If I am to save your life I must remove the leg."

"My wife," he said. "How will?"

"She already knows."

As Aurita picked up the knife again, General Kannon and the corporal sat down on either side of the bed and held down the man's legs. The man screamed as she began to cut away the damaged leg. He had passed out again before she took the small saw Father had cleaned in the boiling water. She sawed off the jagged end of the bones before folding the flesh over the bottom of the bones. Most of the remaining skin was too short to pull over the end. She looked over at the leg. Even the shank of his boot had been shredded, but the foot was intact.

"Father, take off his boot," she said. "I need the skin from his foot to cover the wound."

He hesitated. She could see the fright in his eyes.

"Hold this leg," the corporal said. "I'll do it."

*****

114

They switched places. He took the knife from his belt and cut down the shank to the sole on both sides, then cut around the heel and was able to pull the foot out.

"Wash it with this," Aurita said as she handed him a flask.

He did as he was told then held the foot sole up.

"That part is already cushioned," she said softly as if to herself.

She cut away the large callused part just behind the toes and began to stitch it to the bottom of the severed leg. He could tell that Burkhart was trying to not look at what she was doing. His face looked like he was ill. When she finished her stitching, she removed the belt from his leg slowly before bandaging the leg. She then placed her instruments in the pot of water. She took the bloodied cloths from the bed and wrapped the leg in one of them. Burkhart and General Kannon removed the straps and covered the man with a blanket. She washed her hands and found a clean cloth to wrap the leg in. Burkhart began washing the instruments with trembling hands. She placed the leg on a small table under the shelves. He washed his hands as she had while she stood looking at the man's face.

"You saved his life," he said and she looked at him.

"It is now up to him," she said.

He followed her out to where the other men waited with the man's wife. He was shocked to see Father standing there as well, but tried not to show it. He joined her on his knees at Father's feet.

"Rise," he heard Father say.

They stood up.

"How is her husband?" he asked.

"He is sleeping. I had to take off his leg below the knee, but Father can make him something to help him walk," she said. "It will take a month or so for the leg to heal properly, but he should be able to get around on crutches in a week or so."

"Thank you," the woman said with tears in her eyes. "May I see him?"

"Yes," Aurita said. "He needs your love and support to heal now. I have wrapped the leg for burial. If you do not want to take care of it, I will get it buried for you."

The woman nodded and went to see her husband.

"You don't look so well, Burkhart," Father said.

115

He turned to see General Kannon supporting Burkhart as they came around the curtain.

"My daughter is strong enough to deal with things such as that," Burkhart replied. "But I am not. The corporal was able to do what I could not."

"I need to go wash this dress," Aurita said.

"Don't you have another?" Father asked.

"It ripped this morning when I was gathering reeds," she answered.

"Corporal, take this and buy her a new dress," Father said and handed him some coins.

"At once, My King," he replied.

"I want to go bathe," she said and pointed to the river. "I will stay in the water until you have placed the new dress next to the old one and gone back around the bushes."

While he walked to the tailor's shop, he wondered why his father was there. When he entered the shop the man working near the back looked up.

"May I help you?" the man asked.

"Our King sent me to purchase a dress for Aurita," he said.

The man thought about it for a moment before saying, "I think that I have three dresses that would fit her. Let me get them."

He soon had three dresses laid out on the table. There was a tan dress, a dark brown dress and a sky blue dress.

"The blue one," he said after looking at each of them.

He soon had the man paid and was on his way to the river. He walked around the bushes and placed the folded dress next to the one she had been wearing. It was wet, but clean. He went back around the bushes without looking out at the river. He stood with his back toward the river. It was a while before he heard a movement behind him. He jumped as someone touched his arm.

He saw the look on Aurita's face and said, "Are you alright?"

She shook her head.

He put his arm around her back and led her back to her house. She hung the wet dress across the hitching rail before leaning against it with both hands. Her hair hung down and covered her face, but he could hear that her breath was labored. The door of the shop opened and his father stepped out followed by General Kannon and Burkhart. He placed his hand on her back and patted gently.

"Let it out," he said softly. "I doubt many people could do what you just did. I don't think anyone could without having it affect them."

She suddenly turned and buried her face against his shoulder. As the prince put his arms around her he looked up in shock to find the three men grinning. They quietly went inside the house. She was trembling as she cried so he held her tightly to him.

Although he was worried about her, but he was also worried about what his father would have to say. He had always liked her, but now it was a bit more than that and he had to admit to himself that he liked the feel of her body pressed against his own, but he didn't dare admit it to anyone else, especially his father. He did not know how long he stood there while she cried, but at last her tears began to slow.

"I want to help people, not hurt them," she whispered hoarsely. "I can still hear him screaming."

"Without your help, he would have died," he replied softly. "I will remember his screams for a long time. I know that if Brinley goes to war, I will see injuries even worse than his. Father and General Kannon have told me that sometimes it is kinder to kill an injured man than leave him to suffer until he dies. I know that someday I may face that choice and can only hope that I can face it as bravely as you have."

She looked up at him. He released her from his arms and gently wiped the tears from her face.

"Thank you," she said. "I don't know if I could have gotten through this without your help."

"Are you ready to go inside now?" he asked. "Your father is in the house with Our King and General Kannon."

She just nodded. He gently led her into the house. The three men were sitting at the table talking. They had quit talking as the door opened. Burkhart stood and hugged Aurita.

"I am so proud of you," he said softly to her.

The prince could tell she was beginning to cry again.

"I'm very proud of you as well," his father said as he stood up, approached where she was standing and put his hand on her shoulder.

"I only want to help people," she said softly as tears ran down her face. "I want people to like me."

117

"I promise that someday many people will not only like you, but they will love you," his father said. "I also promise you that your husband will love you."

Tears were streaming down her face as his father kissed her forehead, then hugged her before saying,

"You need some rest. We will be just outside if you need us."

She looked a little stunned as she nodded.

"Lie down on my bed," Burkhart said.

He led her over to the bed and she sat down on the edge.

They left the house. Burkhart brought out chairs for them to sit on.

"I am told that you were of great assistance to Aurita while she worked on the man, Corporal," Father said. "General Kannon told me that you did not hesitate nor turn your head."

"I know that I will see other injuries far worse and must be able to deal with it," he replied. "Someday I will face similar decisions and must be prepared to make them."

"I am very pleased with your progress in training," Father said. "I heard that tomorrow you begin to make your own sword."

"Yes, Sir," he replied.

"Perhaps when it is complete you might be ready to take a few guard shifts at the palace," Father said.

"It would be an honor to do so," he replied knowing he must act as though he was talking to his king, not his father.

"After today I believe he is ready," General Kannon said. "He is very good with the sword. He makes decisions quickly after gaining the facts. For the most part he makes the same decisions that I have made."

"Excellent," Father said.

"He has shown himself to be a true gentleman to my daughter," Burkhart said. "That is something no other man has done. I know that he can be trusted."

"I heard from one of the patrols that he took on two men that were harassing Aurita," Father said. "He stayed calm and was able to put both of them on the ground before they could touch her."

He was beginning to wonder what was going on. They were acting rather strangely.

"I should check on our horses," he said. "With your permission of course."

"Good idea, Corporal," General Kannon said.

He was glad to leave. He did not enjoy being the center of that kind of attention. He was not certain why they were making such an obvious effort to praise him. He found the horses where he had left them. His horse nuzzled him. He rubbed the horse's forehead while he thought about it.

*****

"I'm glad you sent him today," Burkhart said. "He certainly has changed since I last saw him. I'm certain that she did not recognize him."

Langward had to agree with that. She did not seem to realize that he was the Prince and not just another soldier.

"You should have seen them when she walked into the shop," General Kannon said. "I had to close his mouth because it was hanging open. And I know that she went behind the curtains because she found him attractive."

"Most definitely," Burkhart said.

"Good," he said. "This is exactly what I was hoping for. I have known for a while that his interest in her was more than just politeness. They have been corresponding fairly regularly for years. I'm glad that he looks more like Retanta's mother than me. I knew that if she knew who he was, she would not dare fall in love with him."

"You are right," Burkhart said. "She talks about him a lot, but when she does she always ends by saying that he would marry some princess."

"I only hope that someday they will understand the reason for our deception," Langward said as they watched him walk over the bridge. "Burkhart, I do not want him to discover that you know his identity if possible."

"I agree," Burkhart said.

The shop door opened and one of the men stepped out.

"He's awake and wants to talk to Aurita," the man said.

*****

"Why don't you go see if she's awake, Corporal," Burkhart said as he approached the house.

"Yes, Sir," he replied.

He was certain they had been talking about him. He opened the door quietly and stepped inside. She was lying on the bed facing the wall.

"Aurita," he said softly as he approached the bed.

He could hear her quietly crying.

"The man is awake and is asking to speak to you," he said as he sat on the edge of the bed.

"I'm not certain I can face him," she said softly. "I was going to ask someone else to check the bandages while he heals."

"I know you're afraid of him being angry," he said as he softly stoked her hair. "I'll go with you if you want me to."

She rolled over on her back and looked at him.

"You would?" she asked.

"Of course I would," he said as he took her hand and softly kissed it. "I'll stay as long as you need me to."

"What about General Kannon?" she asked. "Won't he need you? I don't want to make anyone upset."

"I don't think he'll mind," he replied. "In fact your father doesn't seem to mind either."

"What about King Langward? You know he has chosen my husband already."

"I know that, but he didn't seem bothered when he saw you crying on my shoulder."

She blushed and sat up.

"Don't be embarrassed," he said.

"I want you to know that I really liked the feel of your arms around me," she said, but didn't meet his gaze. "But I don't want to get you in trouble."

"Is that why you were crying just now?" he asked in surprise.

She nodded, but did not look up.

"I have to admit that I liked it too, but I would not dare admit that to anyone besides you."

She finally looked into his eyes. He softly brushed the hair back off her face.

"Come on," he said. "I'll be right there with you."

He stood up and offered her his hand. She smiled as she took it and stood up. They went outside and met the man waiting for them. He dared not look toward Father and the other two men as Aurita led him by the hand into the shop. The woman was sitting on the edge of the bed holding her husband's hand. He looked up and smiled as he saw them.

"I wanted to thank you," he said. "My wife said that I may be able to walk again with something your father can make."

"Yes," she said. "A man came through the village last year that wore a wooden leg. It was cracked and Father made him a new one. I'm certain that he could make one for you as well."

"I don't know how we can ever repay you," he said as the woman turned to face them.

"Don't worry about that," she said. "It is more important to me to know that I saved your life. I was worried that you would be angry that I had to put you through so much pain."

"It's a little painful if I move, but nothing compared to how it was before," the man said.

"Let me give you something for the pain," she said as she at last released his hand.

"I remember seeing you," the man said to him as Aurita opened a jar on the shelf. "You were holding down my leg."

"Yes," he said.

"I could not even look at it myself, yet you could," he said. "Thank you for helping her."

"I did what needed to be done," he said. "I know that as a soldier I will see much worse some day."

"Your parents must by very proud to have such a fine young man as their son," the woman said.

He could feel himself blush as Aurita handed the man two leaves of a pain killing herb.

"You need to rest," she said as he chewed on the leaves. "You can stay here until you are ready to get around on crutches."

"May I stay with him tonight?" the woman asked.

"Of course," Aurita said. "That is why there are two beds, so someone could stay to watch over someone who is injured."

He followed Aurita out from behind the curtains and out the door.

"Are you feeling better?" Burkhart asked as he hugged Aurita.

"Yes," she said. "He wasn't even angry with me for putting him through so much pain. He thanked the corporal for helping."

121

"I want to thank you too," Burkhart said as he extended a hand toward him.

He shook the hand that Burkhart offered.

"I need to start supper, Father," Aurita said and Burkhart nodded.

Once she had shut the door behind her, Burkhart said, "You have done what I could not. While she was working on that man, it was all I could do to keep from passing out. Also, you were able to comfort her when she was upset."

"I was only worried about her," he replied feeling a bit embarrassed.

"You have been told of my past and know you cannot tell her about it?" Burkhart asked and he nodded. "Yet you do not seem to fault her for the evil I have done."

"I see no reason to," he replied. "I can see that you are not the man that you were before her birth. From what I have been told and what I have seen today, I know that you feel true sorrow for your past deeds. You have not blamed others for your current situation."

"Do you also know that regardless of what anyone says King Langward did not exactly capture the throne in combat?" Burkhart said. "I want you to know that when I first saw him, I gave the throne to him willingly. In fact I gave it to him without him asking for it."

"I had been told as much," he said nodding. "I have been told that you have sworn complete obedience and loyalty to King Langward."

"You have been correctly informed," Burkhart said. "I also swear my future loyalty and obedience to his son and heir. I can only hope that he will treat me as King Langward and you have, as a man with dignity. It is far better than everyone else thinks I deserve."

"I'm certain that he will not disappoint you," he said in surprise. "I know him to be kind and considerate of others."

Burkhart smiled. He noticed that Father was smiling as well. Father nodded as he caught his eye.

"We cannot stay any longer," Father said. "I need General Kannon and his assistant back at the palace."

"Why don't you go tell Aurita," Burkhart said. "I think it best you don't leave without telling her, Corporal."

He nodded and entered the house. She looked up from the vegetables she was cutting.

"We are leaving now," he said. "Will you be alright?"

"Yes," she replied as she put down the knife. "I will miss you though."

"I will miss you as well," he replied with a smile.

He took her hand in his and kissed it before he left. He followed Father and General Kannon to where the horses were staked out. There were four guards waiting for them. He quickly tightened the girth straps before holding General Kannon's horse for him to mount. Soon he was mounted and followed behind. He could not keep himself from smiling as he thought about holding Aurita in his arms. He could still remember the smell of her hair. When they reached the palace gate, he realized that he could not exactly remember what route they had taken to get there. He knew he had to put her out of his mind and pay attention to what he was doing. They dismounted in the courtyard and he followed Father and General Kannon inside. Father led them to his private study and closed the doors behind them.

"You seemed lost in thought on the way here, Son," Father said and he felt his cheeks turn bright red.

The two men began to laugh.

"I can't help it," he said.

"We know exactly how you feel," General Kannon said.

"Father, I know that you have chosen her a husband already," he said. "I know that regardless of my feelings for her, she will be married to the man of your choosing. I just wish I knew who that was so I could tell him how lucky he is."

"I haven't told him that she will be his wife," Father replied. "I have not told more than a select few people. I hope that you can understand why."

"It doesn't make a lot of sense right now, but I'm certain you have your reasons," he said. "I'm just relieved that you are not angry at me for what I did today."

"You did exactly what needed to be done," Father said. "I am very pleased with you. Aurita does not know what it is like to be treated like a lady. She only knows what it is like to be shunned and hated. Today she learned that not everyone will treat her as the villagers have."

"I got the feeling that Burkhart knew that I was your son," he said. "And that he did not mind when he saw me holding his daughter in my arms. He seemed pleased, not angry."

"He is pleased to see that there is someone who genuinely cares about Aurita instead of caring because they have been ordered to," Father explained. "He has been worried about how to convince her that not everyone will hate her because of him."

There was a tap on the door.

"Come," Father said.

Garman entered and knelt.

"Rise," Father said.

"Supper is ready and our queen is waiting for you in the dining hall," Garman said as he rose to his feet. "Lady Kara took her supper in her room again. Will you be staying General Kannon?"

"My assistant and I would be pleased to stay for supper," General Kannon replied.

Garman looked at him for the first time. His eyes widened in surprise.

"I am General Kannon's assistant," he said. "That is all anyone needs to know."

Garman glanced at Father who nodded and said, "My reasons will become clear eventually, but for now he is to be known only by his military rank."

"It is probably safer that no one knows otherwise," Garman commented as he opened the door.

He followed behind General Kannon and his father to the dining hall. Mother was waiting for them. There were servants placing food and additional settings on the table. Garman sent them into the kitchen as soon as they were finished. When the door shut behind the servants, Mother drew him into her arms and hugged him tight.

"You've grown so much," she said.

"I've missed you too, Mother," he replied as he patted her back.

"You look happy," she said as she released him at last.

"I have enjoyed serving in the military," he said. "It is hard sometimes to not reveal my identity to others, but I have friends now who really don't care that I won't tell them a name."

"I'm glad to hear that," she said as they sat down. "I know you did not have many friends here."

"I really didn't have any that were my age," he replied.

"He has really grown up," Father said. "He is turning out to be a fine young man and gentleman."

They discussed the day's events while they ate. By the time he got back to the barracks, he fell into bed, asleep before his head was on the pillow.

Chapter 13 – Gifts and Letters

Morning came early, but he still was ready for inspection. Kon, Monau and Kennar met him for breakfast.

"We thought you would be back for supper at least," Kennar said as they waited in line.

"We went to Weston to deliver a message," he replied.

"Did you see old Burkhart?" Kon asked with disgust. "And his daughter?"

"Actually, yes," he replied realizing he would have to be careful about what he said.

"Are they as horrible as everyone says they are?" Monau asked.

"No," he replied and shrugged his shoulders. "Burkhart builds things out of wood. He's surprisingly good at it. Aurita weaves very nice baskets. Her soup is certainly better than anything they serve here."

"You weren't afraid of being poisoned by them?" Kennar asked.

"If General Kannon trusted them enough to eat it, I couldn't argue," he replied shaking his head.

They sat down in the corner of the room.

"Why did you stay so long?" Kon asked.

"A man was brought that had an injured leg," he explained. "Aurita had to take off his leg just below the knee. General Kannon and I helped to hold the man down."

"She knows how to do that?" Monau asked. "Is she a healer?"

"Yes," he said.

"She is probably so hard hearted that such a thing would be easy for her," Kon commented.

"Actually, once Aurita had finished and gotten cleaned up, she broke down and cried," he said. "She was really upset by the man's screaming before he passed out. Aurita said she wants to help people not hurt them."

They sat in silence for a while, not even eating. He knew that he could not change everyone's opinion of Burkhart and Aurita, but it wouldn't hurt for people to know how much Burkhart had changed.

"What does she look like?" Kennar asked.

"She is very beautiful actually," he said knowing the rumors about her being ugly.

"I think you like her," Monau said and laughed.

"If you had seen her, you would know that I can't help but at least like her looks," he replied laughing.

Three men came over and sat next to them. One of them looked at him closely and nudged his neighbor with his elbow.

The man looked up at him then said, "You were in Weston yesterday, Corporal."

"Yes, Sergeant," he replied.

"You were the one who captured those two we put in the dungeon yesterday for harassing Aurita," the other said.

"Yes, Sir," he replied.

"Is Aurita as ugly as everyone says she is?" Kon asked. "The corporal says she is beautiful."

"Very beautiful," the sergeant replied. "And very kind. She sometimes brought us fresh vegetables in exchange for some meat. She was always very pleasant to talk to and to look at."

"The corporal helped her cut a man's leg off," Kon said.

"There's been talk about that going around," one of the men replied. "You certainly are in the middle of things, aren't you?"

"I suppose so," he said.

"What happened to the man?" the sergeant asked.

"She was able to get the bleeding stopped and sewed the bottom of his foot to what was left of his leg," he replied. "His leg was too messed up and there wasn't enough skin to cover the wound. Later, when he regained consciousness, he thanked her. Burkhart will carve him a wooden leg so he can walk when the end of his leg heals up."

"Someone said they were going to advance you to sergeant," one of the men said.

"I doubt it," he replied. "I just made corporal. I've got to get going. The sword master is expecting me first thing this morning."

As he walked across the camp to the blacksmith, he thought about the conversation. He wasn't certain he liked being that well known while he was here. He certainly didn't want to get any special treatment either. Some had already thought he was getting special treatment by being allowed to train and advance while still so young.

"You're General Kannon's assistant?" the blacksmith asked. "They're usually older."

"Don't let his age fool you," the sword master said as he came out of the shop. "He's earned his rank."

"Well, take off your tunic and grab an apron," the blacksmith said.

He began to remove his tunic. As he hung it on the hook by the leather aprons, he heard a gasp behind him.

"I've only seen a birthmark like that once," the blacksmith said.

"My father attended here before becoming a patrolman," he said.

"Then you're . . ." the man trailed off and the sword master looked confused.

"Here to learn the things I can't at home," he replied quickly. "Rank and ability matter here, not name or age."

The man blinked then nodded. The sword master looked from the blacksmith to him and back.

"General Kannon can tell you all you need to know," he said to the sword master before following the blacksmith back to the forge.

The blacksmith showed him how to heat and work the metal. Soon he was on his own coaxing the metal into a sword. The hand guard and the hilt gave him the most trouble, but by suppertime he was at last satisfied and ready to sharpen it. He swung it to check the balance and found it suited him. After he had sharpened it, the blacksmith showed him how to heat the metal then cool it rapidly to strengthen the metal. He then tested it again to check the balance.

"Now all you need is a scabbard," General Kannon's voice said behind him. "And you need to remember to keep that birthmark covered."

"Yes, Sir," he replied as he saluted the general.

"I've had several people say you deserve the rank of sergeant," General Kannon said.

"I just made corporal," he replied. "Most will think it is too soon or will be suspicious."

"That is why you will work very hard for the next six months to make certain everyone knows you have earned the rank of sergeant," the general said with a grin.

"Yes, Sir," he replied feeling very relieved. "I don't want to draw undue attention to myself."

"Go wash up and get your tunic back on then."

Blood of Ancient Kings

As he approached the back of the shop, the blacksmith came out and saw him. He could see the man begin to bend his knees.

"Please don't," he said. "It would be too dangerous for me if anyone knew I was here. I am to be known by rank alone, not by any title or name."

The man seemed confused, like he didn't quite know what to do.

"Forget who I am," he said. "Just treat me like everyone else here. I like it that way. I am happy here."

The blacksmith nodded at last. He washed his face, hands and arms before putting his tunic back on. He was admiring his new sword when he heard footsteps behind him. He turned to see his father approach with a couple of guards. He quickly knelt with the sword across his open palms and was soon joined by the blacksmith. He felt the sword being taken from his hands.

"Rise," he heard Father say at last.

Father was closely examining the sword. He balanced the sword on one finger near the hand guard.

"Excellent workmanship, Corporal," he said as he offered him the sword, hilt first.

"Thank you, My King," he replied.

"It seems you are quite the center of attention since yesterday," Father said.

"I did not seek such attention, My King," he replied. "What I did yesterday was no more than anyone else would have done."

"But it was," Father replied. "Many would have turned their backs saying it was not their problem and therefore not their obligation to help. You have proven yourself in a manner that most people never do and I am pleased. I know it is too soon since your last rank advancement to make you a sergeant, so instead I present you with this scabbard as a token of Brinley's appreciation for your service."

His hand trembled as he took the scabbard that Father offered him. He knew it was from Father's first sword.

"Thank you," he said as he sheathed the sword then buckled the belt around his waist. "I will treasure it always."

"It seems that I am not the only one to offer thanks in the form of a gift," Father said before handing him a pouch. "The pouch is from the

129

man who was injured. What is inside is from someone else. That can wait until after you eat supper."

"Yes, Sir," he replied as he put the pouch on his belt and buckled the belt again.

"You are dismissed," Father said.

He looked Father in the eye and nodded before heading back toward the dining hall. He was very surprised that Father had given him the scabbard. He knew Father must be very proud of him even though he could not say it out loud. He wondered what was in the pouch, but his stomach rumbled as the smell of the food finally reached him. Kennar, Kon and Monau were in line not far ahead of him. He joined them after he got his food. He put his tray on the table before sitting down. The sword was awkward to sit down with, but he knew he would eventually get used to it.

"You made a scabbard too?" Kon asked.

"No," he replied. "Apparently news has reached even Our King. He gave this to me instead of advancing my rank. General Kannon said it will be at least six months before he would consider me for sergeant."

"What about the pouch?" Kennar asked. "I've never seen one like it."

"The injured man sent it," he replied.

"A bed opened up on the second floor today," Monau said. "We've already moved your things down."

"You didn't need to do that, but thank you," he said before he began to eat.

The conversation was light as they ate. He was anxious to get to the barracks to see what was in the pouch. The pouch was not plain like most he had seen, it was decorated with beadwork along the edges. The beadwork was in a popular pattern of squares, rectangles, and triangles. After supper, they headed toward the barracks. It was dark inside, but they lit the small lantern mounted to the wall between the beds. He opened the pouch and looked inside.

"What is it?" Kon asked.

"I don't know," he said. "But it is not from the same man who sent the pouch."

He first drew out a small scroll. He broke the plain wax seal and unrolled it. There were two pages.

'I greatly appreciate you helping Aurita,' the letter began without greeting. 'I know that you have made quite an impression upon her. She is happier than I have seen her in a long time. I know you must realize how she suffers because of my punishment. You have shown her a glimpse of the world that lies beyond this village and given her hope. You are welcome in our home always, for I know that in your hands she is safe. With great appreciation, Burkhart.'

He looked up from the letter to find three eager faces watching him.

"So, what does it say?" Kennar asked.

"Who is it from?" Monau asked.

"Burkhart sent it," he said. "I'll read it to you."

When he finished, Kon said, "That certainly doesn't sound like the man who lost the throne to King Langward in battle. I heard he was a real tyrant."

"He was," he replied. "But King Langward did not take the throne in battle exactly. Burkhart himself said that he gave the throne to King Langward of his own free will before King Langward even asked for it."

They sat in silence for a while before he put the letter down and looked at the second page.

'Dear Corporal,' the letter began. 'I only wish I had more than just a military rank to put with the face that I see every time I close my eyes. You showed me there is someone in this world that knows my father's past and can see beyond it. Yesterday your presence gave me the strength I needed to save that man's life. Whenever I am sad I will remember the feel of your arms around me and I will be happy again. I can only pray that King Langward will allow me to see you again. With all my love, Aurita.'

His hand trembled slightly as he read the last line. He knew there was no hiding it from Father, but he hoped Father would not be angry with him. But then again, perhaps if she could love him, she could learn to love the man Father had chosen to be her husband.

"What's the matter?" Kenner asked. "You are shaking."

"King Langward has ordered that no man not of his choosing can touch Aurita. He has chosen a husband for her," he said trying to keep his voice steady. "Yesterday, when she broke down and cried, I patted her on the back. Before I knew what she was doing, she had turned and leaned

131

against me. I put my arms around her and held her while she cried. He seemed pleased when he saw me standing there with her in my arms, but now..."

He trailed off.

"What?" Monau asked.

He read them the letter. They all seemed very shocked.

"I know that I must now tell King Langward and even let him read this letter," he said. "I also must admit that I love her. I know that I must obey his order no matter how I feel about her. I may never see her again."

The very thought distressed him. He rolled the letters up with trembling hands and placed them on the bed. He took the pouch off the belt and something fell out onto the bed. He picked it up and found it to be a ring carved from a dark wood.

"A ring?" Kon asked. "Did Aurita send it?"

"No," he said. "Burkhart carved it. Yesterday he appeared to approve of my interest in his daughter, not that he would have any choice in who her husband would be."

"Put it on," Monau said.

It fit perfectly on the third finger of his right hand. He then looked into the pouch again. He found there was a piece of folded cloth. As he drew it out, he could see that it was the same color as the torn dress he had seen hanging on a hook near the door in Burkhart's house. As he brought it out closer to the light, he saw something shiny along the edges. There was something stitched in shiny, smooth black thread along the edge. As he moved it more, it became clear that it was lettering.

'I send this that you might keep it next to your heart. My heart is yours even though I know I must marry the man chosen for me.'

He raised it to his nose and smelled her sweet scent on it.

"That has to be from Aurita," Kon said.

"Your smile gives it away," Kennar said and laughed as he blushed.

"That stitching is not regular thread," Monau said. "My mother says that young women in love often send a handkerchief to the man they love. The handkerchief is stitched with their own hair."

The other men had begun to come in to go to bed. He hung his sword from the hook on the bedpost as he had seen other men do. He got undressed and laid down in bed. Although he was tired from the day at the blacksmith, he could not sleep. There was too much to think about. He remembered Father saying that it took him three tries to make his first sword. Yet Father had praised his workmanship in front of others, and then the gifts. He wondered why Father had not read the letters already. He knew that when he had written to Aurita in the past, Father had read every letter to and from Aurita. He wished he had a chance to talk to Father as they had in the past, alone in the study where no one could overhear them.

When they were awakened, he felt as though he had not slept at all. He dressed before putting the handkerchief in the pocket of his tunic. While his friends laughed and talked at breakfast, he was silent. He hurried to General Kannon's office, hoping for some work that would take his mind off the letters in the pouch at his waist. He was surprised to find two palace guards waiting outside General Kannon's office. They opened the door for him without speaking.

"There you are," Father said.

"Yes, Sir," he replied and quickly knelt.

When he rose to his feet, he pulled the letters out of his pouch and handed them to Father.

"These are yours," Father said.

"Yes, but you should read them," he replied.

He waited nervously while Father read the letters. Then he pulled the handkerchief out.

"Read the stitching along the edge," he said. "I admit that I feel the same way although I know that your orders must be followed."

Father read the stitching before handing it to General Kannon to read. Father's face was expressionless as he waited for General Kannon to finish. General Kannon looked up at Father with one eyebrow raised.

"Anything else?" Father asked as he turned to face him.

"Just this ring that Burkhart carved."

He removed the ring and handed it to Father.

"Go out and wait in the hall," Father said in a stern tone.

"Yes, Sir," he said with a sinking feeling.

He waited in the hall facing the door. Although the guards did not look directly at him, he felt as though they were staring at him. He knew he must be in serious trouble, but he could not avoid it. It would be best to just take the punishment and get it over as quickly as possible.

He jumped as the door opened. Father pointed at him then turned his hand over and beckoned him forward with the same finger. He swallowed the hard lump in his throat before entering the office. Father shut the door firmly making him jump again.

"There are certain things that for now must be kept from you," Father said after staring at him for what seemed like an hour. "You are still too young even though you have grown up a lot since coming here."

He stood silently waiting to find out what his punishment would be.

"You are obedient, loyal and trustworthy," Father continued. "I appreciate your honesty in this matter. I know this is very difficult for you to understand right now because of what I have not told you, but I want you to continue on exactly as things have been."

He could not believe what he was hearing.

"I know that I cannot control your feelings with orders," Father said. "Nor can I control hers. I have worried that she would not allow herself to love anyone, so I am glad that you have opened her heart to love. I have also worried about you. I want you to learn to love as well. I would not be the man I am without the love of my wife. Now, you are to reply as honestly as possible to both these letters and have the replies sent by messenger to Weston before noon. You are to wear this on your hand and keep this in your pocket next to your heart as she meant it to be."

"Yes, Sir," he said in shock as he took the items from his father.

"I want you to know this," Father said. "I have told Burkhart exactly who Aurita's husband will be. He has met this man and approves of my choice. He also knows that I will not marry them until I am certain they are both ready. I want to give them a chance to get to know each other before they are married. Ideally they will petition for the union before I reveal to them my plans."

"Yes, Sir," he said feeling a little relieved. "I love her enough to want to see her happy regardless of who she marries."

"I also want you to write a letter to your father. He needs to know what is in your heart."

"Yes, Sir," he replied. "I want him to know what is in my heart."

"I will not forbid you to see Aurita," Father said as he stood up. "In fact after today you will be the designated messenger to Weston unless you are unavailable. We will be inspecting the camp. I expect you within two hours at the wrestling class. Bring the letters with you."

"I will be there, Sir," he replied as General Kannon stood up.

They both left, shutting the door behind them. As he crossed the room to his desk, his knees felt weak. He felt very confused by what had just occurred. Not only was he not going to be punished, he was ordered to do what to him was a reward. He could not understand why Father was not angry. Certainly Father would not have appointed him the exclusive messenger to Weston if he were angry. He shook his head and took out some paper.

'My Dearest Aurita,' he began to write, and then paused.

He sat silently for a few minutes as he considered the wisdom of such a greeting. He decided to leave it since Father had emphasized he reply as honestly as possible and that was honestly how he felt.

'I keep the handkerchief you sent in my pocket over my heart. When I smelled your scent upon it I remembered how good it felt to hold you in my arms. I want you to know that I love you with all of my heart. I could never love another woman as I love you. While I am in the Military, my life is not my own, but that will not last forever. I have been told that I will be visiting Weston in the future to bring messages. My heart is glad to know that I will see you again. I wish I could give you my name, but I am bound by an oath to not reveal it to anyone. With all my love.'

He paused wondering what he could put in place of a name. Certainly his military rank was a bit cold.

'Your Corporal,' he finished with a sigh.

He put the letter aside and began the one to Burkhart.

'Dear Burkhart,' he began the letter. 'I thank you for your kind words and for the ring you sent. I have been told that I will have the opportunity in the future to deliver messages to Weston. I look forward to seeing you and Aurita again. Although I know that King Langward has chosen a husband for her, I want you to know that I will always love her. I could never do anything to hurt her. I will not disobey King Langward's orders regarding her future. I have spoken to Our King and have admitted to him my love for Aurita. He told me that he wants things to continue exactly as they have been. As you are her father, I also will not disobey your will in this matter.'

He put the letter aside and drew out a third piece of paper. He knew the letter to his Father might be the hardest, but he was glad Father had requested it. With a sigh he began the letter, but soon he found the words coming more quickly than he could write. He told Father how he loved Aurita and how confused he felt about it. He also wrote about how confused his father's orders had left him. He thanked him for not being angry and for not punishing him. He also thanked him for his praise about the sword. He concluded by telling his father how much he liked it here and about the friends he had made.

When he was finished he sat back in his chair for a moment considering the three letters. He began rolling up the letter to his father when he realized there was nothing he wanted to change. He sealed it with wax followed by the other two. He wrote the appropriate name on each of the ones for Weston. He gathered them up and hurried out to the wrestling class. He found Father and General Kannon watching as the men wrestled. Kon pinned Kennar just as he reached the edge of the class. Monau soon joined them.

"Where have you been?" Monau asked.

"King Langward and General Kannon were in deep discussion when they passed by," Kon said. "They were discussing Burkhart, Aurita and, I think, you."

"We couldn't hear much besides the names," Kennar added. "They were talking funny."

"Funny like this?" he asked in the language of the kingdoms to the North.

"Yeah," Kon said. "You showed King Langward the letters, didn't you?"

"Yes, but instead of being punished, I was ordered to write responses to the letters," he said. "And now I will be going to Weston every time a message is sent there."

"It doesn't make sense," Kennar said as Father noticed him.

The four of them quickly knelt as Father approached.

"Rise," he heard Father say. "So, are these men your friends, Corporal?"

"Yes, Sir," he replied. "Corporal Kon, Corporal Monau, and Corporal Kennar."

Each bowed in turn.

"Can they be trusted?" Father asked in the language of the kingdoms to the North.

"Yes," he replied in the same language. "They know that certain things must not be repeated. They do not know who I truly am though."

"Good," Father said. "Choose one of them to deliver your letters."

"Yes, Sir," he replied. "Here is the other one."

He handed the letter to Father who put it in his pouch. Father and General Kannon turned around and left.

"What was that all about?" Kennar asked.

"I didn't know you knew another language," Monau said.

"I must choose one of you to deliver the letters to Weston," he said.

"I know where Weston is," Kon said. "It is just over the hill from my home."

"Burkhart's house is on the far side of the brook that runs next to the village," he said. "There is the shop and the smaller house. Check inside the shop first."

"Have you chosen your messenger?" Captain Rowand asked as he approached. "And he knows the orders in respect to Weston?"

"Corporal Kon has agreed to take it," he replied as he saluted. "I'll make certain he knows the orders, Sir."

"Once he has explained the orders then get on your way, Corporal Kon," the captain said.

*****

Aurita had been gathering reeds when Carria and Noka approached with another girl. She tied the bundle of reeds and laid it on the ground as they neared her.

"You are the one who saved Father when he crushed his leg," the girl said and Aurita nodded. "I wanted to thank you myself. I don't know if I could handle seeing him die."

"I know what you mean," she replied. "My father is all I have in this world. I don't know what I would do if he died."

"Barna wanted to know if she could see her father," Noka said.

"Certainly," Aurita replied as she saw a lone soldier approaching.

He drew his horse to a stop as he reached them.

"Do you know where I can find Aurita and Burkhart?" he asked.

"I am Aurita, Corporal," she replied. "What is your name? Have you brought a message for Father?"

"The corporal was correct," he said after nodding.

"Correct about what?" she asked. "What corporal?"

"General Kannon's assistant," he replied as he dismounted. "I can't tell you his name because he won't tell me either. He just said he had a wager with his father that he wouldn't tell anyone his name until he made patrolman. He thinks you are the most beautiful woman he's ever seen."

"So that's it," she said as she felt herself blush.

"I heard him say your name in his sleep last night," Corporal Kon said which caused her blush to deepen.

"Father is in the shop along with Barna's father," Aurita said as she picked up the bundle of reeds to hide her embarrassment.

"The corporal asked me to speak to the man you saved yesterday," Corporal Kon said. "My father lost a leg and a hand in battle long ago. He thought the man might want to hear about how he has healed."

She was surprised to find out that the corporal had been dreaming about her. She led the group to the shop. Corporal Kon was a lot younger than the other messengers, but a little older than the corporal. He opened the door and held it while everyone came in. She noticed Corporal Kon glancing at Barna. Father looked up from his work.

"I have a couple of messages for you," Corporal Kon said.

He opened his pouch and pulled out two scrolls. He offered them to Father who examined them. He glanced up at her and back at one of the scrolls before looking at her again.

"Do you know who they are from?" Father asked.

"From General Kannon's assistant," Corporal Kon replied. "He also asked me to speak to Barna's father."

She could see the grin begin at the corners of Father's mouth as he nodded.

"Right this way," she said as she wondered what the messages said.

Obviously one of them was addressed to her. She led the small group around the curtain.

"Barna," the man said as he saw his daughter.

"I had to see for myself that you are alright, Father," she replied as she crossed to his side. "From what the men said I doubted they were telling the truth about how you were doing."

"I'm just a bit weak still," he said as he held her hand. "But I'll be just fine thanks to Aurita."

"I couldn't do it alone," she said. "General Kannon, his assistant and Father helped."

"For that I am grateful," he replied.

"Corporal Kon said he had a message for you from the general's assistant," Aurita said.

The man turned to look at the corporal.

"He wanted me to tell you that he was very surprised by your gift," he said. "And that he thanks you for it. It is a very fine pouch. Where did you get it?"

"Barna and my wife sewed the beadwork on it," the man said and Barna blushed slightly. "They wanted to thank the corporal for his help."

Corporal Kon smiled and nodded.

"He also wanted me to tell you about my father. When my father came home from battle, he was severely injured," Corporal Kon said. "He had lost a leg and a hand. For a while we didn't know if he would live or die. Eventually he got better. He has a wooden leg now and gets along just fine. Losing his hand hasn't slowed him down either. He has two bakers working for him, but he is still up every morning before dawn mixing and kneading the dough for bread."

Aurita left them talking and went to see what messages the corporal had sent.

Father silently handed her the unopened scroll. He seemed pleased about something. She opened the scroll and read it quickly. She felt her heart beating quicker at his words. She was happy that he would be allowed to return to Weston. She quickly handed the scroll back to Father as she heard someone coming from behind the curtain. Corporal Kon came out and began looking at the finished baskets.

"You wove these?" he asked as he looked up. "The corporal was talking about the baskets you weave."

"Yes," she said. "He talks about me? Are you his friend?"

"My mother has always wanted a basket like this," he said as he nodded. "Are these for sale?"

"Yes," she said. "But since you are one of the corporal's friends, you can have any one you want for free."

She heard Father chuckle softly behind her as he picked up one of the larger baskets.

"It's too big for you to just give it away," Corporal Kon said. "I should pay you something for it."

"Trust me," she said. "Bringing the messages was payment enough."

"You," he began, but stopped as she put a finger to her lips and nodded.

She motioned him outside. She shut the door softly behind them.

"King Langward doesn't want the villagers to know that I can read and write," she said softly. "They hate us enough already. The two with Barna are my only friends. I will prepare a response to send back to the corporal before you leave."

"I understand," he said. "I had heard a lot of lies about you and your father before I met the corporal. I can see that everything he has said has been the truth. He never has cared if his opinion differed from everyone else."

"How long have you known him?" she asked hoping to learn more.

"Just over a year," Corporal Kon said. "I met him the first day that he arrived at Military Training Camp. Monau and I thought he was too young and began to tease him. He stood up for himself. I'm certain that General Kannon knows who he is, but he won't tell anyone else."

"Not even me," she said with a sigh. "King Langward has some strict rules about me. He has chosen my husband for me and no other man can touch me, yet he was not the least bit angry with the corporal."

"The corporal mentioned that, but he doesn't know who you will marry either," he replied. "I guess if the two of you are lucky, maybe he is the one chosen to be your husband."

"I can only pray that you are right," she said as the door opened and Father stepped out.

"Don't say a word about it to him, please. He was worried enough about it."

Corporal Kon nodded as Barna came out followed by Carria and Noka. Barna seemed a little white.

"Are you alright?" Corporal Kon asked with concern as he went to Barna.

She just shook her head. Aurita watched Corporal Kon reach out and gently wipe away a tear that had begun to run down Barna's face.

"Your father will recover in time," Corporal Kon said gently.

"It's just so scary to see him like this," she said in a trembling voice. "Mother came home yesterday and was crying. I had to come see him for myself."

"It's alright to be scared," he said as he stepped closer and drew her into his arms.

Aurita smiled as she went inside the house. Noka and Carria were patting Barna on the back while Corporal Kon held her in his arms. Father was inside getting out the pen and paper.

"I'm quite impressed with General Kannon's assistant," he said. "Someone like him would be a very good husband for a young woman."

"I wish I could just marry him, Father," she said as she sat down at the table. "But we must obey King Langward. I'm just relieved that King Langward is not angry with him. I can hardly wait until he comes to Weston again."

*****

"I'm looking forward to seeing him again as well," Burkhart said as his daughter began to write.

He was pleased with how King Langward was handling this. He could see that as promised, Aurita and the prince were beginning to fall in love. He realized that the very fact that they thought they were not to love each other actually was pushing them together instead of apart. He would have to give them plenty of time alone when the prince came to visit. He knew that the prince would not dare do anything he shouldn't. He could trust the prince alone with his daughter.

Life was hard here in Weston for him, but no one beat him up anymore and Burkhart knew it was far better than being in the dungeon. He was doing what he could to prepare Aurita for her future as queen of Brinley. He was looking forward to the day she would marry. He knew that he would at last be free, even if only through death. King Langward had become a friend to him. One of the few he had.

He stirred the pot of soup. He had been thinking again of his wife. He dreamed of her at night. Aurita looked very much like her mother. At times it pained him so to look at her and remember her mother. Sometimes he lay awake at night unable to get rid of the painful memories. He had relived that awful day many times in his dreams. He had hoped that time would fade the memory, but he still remembered every detail.

*****

Langward returned to the palace in a good mood. He was very pleased with his son. The prince had proven himself to be a man of honor. He was not expecting to be able to read the letters sent by Burkhart and Aurita, yet his son had insisted on it. He did not have to show him the writing on the handkerchief either, but he revealed it anyway. He was pleased at his son's honesty.

"You look happy," Retanta said as she met him in the courtyard.

"I am," he said before kissing her lips. "Come inside. I need to talk to you."

He took her up to the study knowing that the thick doors would prevent anyone from overhearing them.

"Our son is falling in love with Aurita," he said with a smile. "And she is falling in love with him."

"I'm so glad," Retanta said. "I have been worried about that."

"I believe he thought he would be punished because he held her in his arms as she cried," he said remembering the letter in his pouch. "He could not hide his surprise and relief when I told him that things should continue as they are. I appointed him to be the exclusive messenger to Weston."

"Your parents should like that," she said.

"I met his friends today. I have heard much about them. They are very loyal to him."

"It's good to know he finally has friends," Retanta said. "He would fight all the time or spend his days locked in his room. I had been so worried when he went to be General Kannon's assistant, but now I see it is the best thing we could have done."

"He will make a good king," he replied as he drew the letter out of the pouch and broke the seal.

As he read through the letter, he could tell that his son was confused and concerned about falling in love with Aurita. He wished he dared tell his son that he would be Aurita's husband, but for now things needed to stay as they were. They were both still too young to marry. He knew that with time all things would change.

Chapter 14 – Death and Burial

Langward was very pleased with his son's progress. For the last year he had worked very hard. Langward made certain that he was regularly sent to Weston with messages. Mostly the sole purpose of the messages was to give his son a chance to spend time with Aurita. He also had his son stand guard in the throne room at least once a week.

Lady Kara had taken ill during the cold season and never completely recovered. Langward suspected that some of her illness was due to loneliness.

"We need to talk," Langford said as he quietly shut the door to Lady Kara's room.

Langward nodded and led him to the study. He suspected he already knew what Langford was going to say. Lady Kara had been very ill. He knew it was only a matter of time before she died. Retanta had spent a lot of time with her.

"She is dying," Langford said. "You had best send for your son, Dornor, Katia and their children."

"I sent word about an hour ago for General Kannon to bring my son," Langward replied nodding. "I sent two guards and a coach for the others the day before yesterday."

There was a knock at the door. Langward opened it to find his son, General Kannon and two nervous looking privates.

"Stay here," he said, pointing to the privates.

His son looked worried as he turned around after shutting the door.

"Your grandmother is dying, Son," Langward said. "She won't live much longer. I knew you would want to see her before she dies."

His son nodded, but was silent. Langward could see his jaw muscles tighten and his hands clenched in fists. This would be very difficult for him. Langward opened the door. Garman was waiting with the privates.

"Take these men down to the kitchen and get them something to eat," Langward said. "Prepare provisions for several days for them and the sergeant."

"Come with me please," Garman said and led the two away.

Langward led the others to Lady Kara's room. He opened the door and peeked in. Retanta and Kara were talking.

"Is that my grandson?" Lady Kara asked as they approached the bed. "He's so tall."

*****

"It's me, Grandmother," he replied unable to control the tremor in his voice.

"I know you will miss me, but it is time for me to go," she replied as she gripped his hand tighter. "I will be watching over you."

"I know," he replied as he felt the tears running down his face. "I don't want you to die. I wish you could stay."

"My dear boy," Grandmother said. "You have other friends now and a bright future waiting for you. No one lives forever. I wanted you to know that I am so proud of you."

He heard the door open behind him. He turned to see Uncle Dornor and Aunt Katia enter followed by his cousins. He kissed Grandmother's cheek softly before moving away from the bed. He watched as the others gathered around the bed. He didn't know his cousins very well. They almost never came to visit. He felt a hand on his shoulder and looked to see Father looking at him with a concerned expression on his face.

"I'll be alright," he said softly in the language of the northern kingdoms.

"I want you to take the two privates with you to Nordam to arrange for her burial and headstone," Father replied in the same language. "You can wait until she has died before leaving."

"I would prefer to leave now," he replied.

"Take this with you," Father said and removed his signet ring. "You may not need it, but if there are any questions that you are acting in my behalf, show this."

"I will," he replied as Father handed him the ring.

"Wait for us at Nordam," Father said. "Do the privates know who you are?"

"I don't think they have been told," he said. "One of them is General Kannon's grandson. The other is his friend."

"Take care of them," Father said as he led him out into the hall. "Garman should have your provisions ready by now."

145

He went and washed his face before he was ready to leave on his journey. He found Garman and the two privates in the kitchens.

"It's time to go," he said as the privates looked up at him.

"There's food ready if you wish to eat before leaving," Garman said.

"I'm not hungry," he replied.

"I've had your provisions packed on a horse," Garman said as he nodded. "Safe journey."

He nodded in return before leading the Privates out to the courtyard.

"Where are we going, Sergeant?" Private Adamok asked.

"Nordam."

"Gran. . . General Kannon wouldn't tell us anything," Private Caddaric added. "He wouldn't even tell us your name."

"It's not important," he replied, trying not to growl.

He would have preferred to take this trip alone, but he knew he would just have to put up with them. He led them out of the palace wall and through the city. He was relieved to get away from everyone as they reached the outskirts of the city. It would take half a day to reach Nordam.

They rode in silence until just after noon. His empty stomach finally took his attention away from his empty heart. He stopped at a small clearing beside the road. There was a ring of rocks where someone had built a fire before.

"It's time for lunch," he said as he dismounted.

"I thought he'd never stop," he heard one of them mutter under his breath as he approached the pack horse.

He found some meat and his favorite cheese along with bread and fruit. Everything was divided into individual portions. He handed each of the privates their food and sat on a rock next to a tree. They sat across the clearing eyeing him nervously and whispering to each other. It would be a long trip, especially if he couldn't get along with them.

"I suppose I should tell you what's going on," he said after he finished his lunch. "We are going to Nordam so I can make the arrangements for Queen Retanta's mother to be buried. She is dying."

"That doesn't explain the way you are acting," Private Adamok said. "One would think it was your own grandmother who was dying."

"My grandmother did die," he replied. "I got word of it while we were at the palace."

"Oh," Private Adamok said with a surprised look on his face.

He got up and secured the pack before mounting up. The two men scrambled to get mounted. They were silent during the ride to Nordam. He led them straight to the minister's house near the church. The minister and his wife were working in the small garden next to the house.

"Can I help you?" the minister asked as he noticed them.

"I have been sent by King Langward to arrange for the burial of Lady Kara," he said after he dismounted.

"Your face is almost familiar," the minister said. "Do I know you?"

"I have been to Nordam before," he replied. "Perhaps we should talk in private. Stay here, Privates. I will return shortly."

The minister led him into the house.

"What is your name, Sergeant?" the minister asked as he sat at the small table.

"I have none I can give you at this time," he replied. "Just call me by rank."

"That's a strange thing to say," the minister commented.

"It is by King Langward's order," he said. "Until he arrives, my voice is his voice. He sent this with me in case there were those who doubted my authority."

He pulled the signet ring out of his pouch and the minister drew in a quick breath.

"I would have thought he would have sent someone with a higher rank," the minister said. "But I will not question his reasons for sending you."

"Nor will I," he said. "My men and I will need a place to stay for a couple of days. I will receive word when King Langward's family leaves the palace."

"You and your men are welcome to stay here," the minister said as he stood up. "I should go get some men to dig the grave."

"I will help," he said. "We also need her headstone carved."

"There is no need for you to help," the minister said in surprise.

"It is what I want to do," he said.

147

The minister stared at him for a minute before saying, "You look a lot like Lady Kara, enough to be related to her."

"I am her grandson," he said realizing it would only be a matter of time before the minister realized who he was.

"That would make you," the minister said, then stopped.

"It is for my own safety that I am to be known by rank alone," he said nodding. "While I serve in the military I must not do or say anything that would reveal my identity. That is why I was sent to arrange the burial. It is the only way to explain my presence without arousing suspicion. Even the two privates do not know who I am."

"I will keep your secret," the minister said. "I will ask my wife to do the same."

"Thank you."

He was grateful the minister understood. It would help make the next couple of days bearable. The minister gave him a shovel and showed him to where Grandmother would be buried next to Grandfather.

"Do we have to dig the grave ourselves?" Private Caddaric asked.

"I don't expect you to help dig the grave," he replied. "The minister went to get some men to do it."

"Then why are you digging?" Private Adamok asked.

"Because I feel like it," he replied. "We will be staying with the minister. Go take care of the horses, and then you are free to do whatever you want. Watch for the signal from the palace that King Langward is on his way."

"Yes, Sergeant," they replied.

It wasn't long before a couple of men came to help him dig. By the time the grave was finished, he was sore and tired. He went to the pond that was fed by the brook and found the two privates talking and watching the horses graze. He took off his belt and placed the handkerchief Aurita gave him in the pouch before getting into the water. It felt good to wash away the dirt and the cold water soothed his aching muscles. When he was finished he took his belt and pouch over to where the men were sitting with the horses.

"Why didn't you take off your clothes to bathe?" Private Adamok asked.

"They were dirty too," he replied, hoping they wouldn't press the matter further. "Give me my saddlebags. I've got some dry clothes packed in them."

Private Caddaric handed him the bags. He quickly changed his clothes with his back against a bush. As he was finishing the village men came to bathe. He laid his clothes across a branch to dry.

"Sergeant," Private Caddaric said. "There's the signal."

He looked toward the border to see a flash of light.

'Leaving palace. Prepare for arrival in morning,' the signal said.

He slipped the metal signal mirror from the belt buckle and sent an acknowledgment in reply.

"Bring your things," he said as he picked up his wet clothes and saddle bags.

They quickly followed him to the minister's house.

"I can hang those to dry," the minister's wife said as she took the wet clothes from him.

"King Langward and his family will be arriving in the morning," he said as the minister came out of the door.

"Supper is almost ready," the minister's wife said as her husband nodded.

"Thank you," he replied.

Soon they were crowded around the small table. Although the privates weren't talking, he could tell that they still did not quite trust him. He knew he must find a way to gain their trust. After supper they were shown to the barn. They began to spread straw to cushion them as they slept.

"I know you two don't quite trust me," he said as he finished rolling out his bed roll. "I know I haven't given you any reason to trust me."

They both looked very surprised as they glanced at each other.

"It's mostly that you act kind of strange," Private Adamok said. "We sat near you and your friends at supper a few days ago. You were the only one that they called by rank, not name."

"I made a bet with my father that I wouldn't tell anyone who I am until I make patrolman," he said. "He was a patrolman. He doesn't want me to rely on his reputation to make it through training. General Kannon and a few of the instructors know who I am, but no one else does."

"That explains some of it," Private Caddaric said. "But what about bathing in your clothes?"

"I have a birthmark that would give away my identity," he said. "Even if you do figure out who I really am, you would not be able to admit it to anyone. That is by King Langward's order."

"King Langward knows who you are?" Private Adamok asked.

"Would I be carrying this if he didn't?" he asked as he pulled the signet ring from his pouch.

They both shook their heads.

"I do get extra duties like this because I am General Kannon's assistant, not because of who I am. I have proven myself trustworthy in his eyes and in the eyes of Our King. I have worked hard to earn my rank because I became a private about a year younger than you were when you did," he said. "I know that if I disobeyed General Kannon or King Langward I would spend time in the dungeon. There will come a day that I will no longer hide my identity. I look forward to the day that I can give people my name when they ask for it."

"You seem sad about it," Private Adamok said.

"That I sometimes cannot hide," he replied with a sigh. "When you learn who I really am you will understand. Take my advice; you must make your own place in this world regardless of who you are related to. I'm going to take a walk. Get some sleep."

"Yes, Sergeant," they replied.

He doused the lantern before he went outside and began to walk toward the cemetery. The minster came out of his house and began walking toward him. The sun was just setting.

"The stone is ready if you wish to see it," the minister said.

He nodded. The minster led him to the grave. The stone was nearby.

"It looks good," he said after examining it. "I'm certain King Langward and Queen Retanta will be pleased."

"It must be very difficult for you to do this," the minister said. "Especially considering what you must not reveal."

"Actually being in the military has given me a certain freedom that I did not have before," he replied. "For the first time in my life I have friends who don't care who I am or what my name is. I am learning many things that I would not at home. At home she was my only friend besides my parents."

The minister shook his head.

"I have been watching you today," the minister said. "I could see that you were trying to bury your emotions. You know you will eventually have to let yourself grieve."

"I know," he said with a sigh. "I had hoped to take this trip alone, but I think I understand why the privates were sent with me. Although they do not know it, they are here to watch over me so that I don't do anything that I shouldn't. I wish I could spend some time alone to get through this, but I probably wouldn't eat or sleep if I didn't have to take care of them."

The minister laughed and said, "Our King is a wise man. He seems to know you well."

"That he does," he replied. "I should get some sleep. Tomorrow will be a long day."

The next morning he was up with the dawn. The two privates still slept as he rolled up his bed roll. He sat down and leaned against a post as he watched them sleep. The prince knew that eventually he would be responsible for more than just these two men but, for every man, woman and child in Brinley. He knew that he was being tested.

"Didn't you sleep, Sergeant?" Private Adamok asked.

The question brought his attention back to the present.

"Yes," he replied. "I'm just used to getting up very early."

The minister came in to milk the cow.

"I was afraid I would wake you," he said. "But I see that you are an early riser."

"It comes with the job," he replied. "Sometimes I must leave before dawn to deliver a message."

The minister just laughed as he began to milk the cow. He was glad the minister knew who he was. Soon the privates had rolled up their bed rolls and changed into fresh clothing. He knew that Father would be arriving shortly after breakfast. The simple porridge and fruit tasted good. He thanked the minister's wife before leaving the house. He found a spot where he could watch the road. The privates followed him. Soon he saw the flash of light reflecting off of metal.

He responded and waited for the message.

'Is all prepared?'

'All is ready for your arrival,' he replied.

He turned around to find the privates looking at him.

"Go tell the minister to assemble the villagers," he said. "Our King and his family will arrive within the next half hour."

"Yes, Sergeant," they replied and left.

He thought about the conversation with the minister he had the night before. He knew that his Father loved him. He also knew that regardless of the current situation, if he gave General Kannon a direct order, General Kannon would follow it. He knew that General Kannon had chosen his grandson and friend to accompany him because General Kannon trusted him. He heard the villagers begin to assemble after a while. He turned back toward the road to see Father and General Kannon leading the carriages. They would enter the village within a few minutes. He hurried to where the villagers were assembling and found the two privates.

"Come with me," he said. "We must be ready to greet them. I see you have both been given swords to carry on the trip. When we kneel, you must lay the sword across your open palms while kneeling on one knee. Do not move until we are told to rise. Then we will lead the procession to the grave."

"Yes, Sergeant," they replied as they followed him through the crowd.

They reached the edge of the village just as Father and General Kannon came around the bend in the road. He knelt with his sword across his palms and was relieved to see the privates had done the same. He saw the horses' hooves stop right in front of him.

"Rise," he heard Father say.

He stood and sheathed the sword. He turned and led the procession to the cemetery. He waited patiently while they dismounted and helped the women from the carriage. As the men assembled to carry the coffin, he noticed that there were only five.

"Sergeant," Father said. "You will assist us."

"It is a great honor to do so, My King," he replied as he took the empty place.

He had not expected to participate. He hoped that no one else would notice what the minister had, but most people only saw the uniform and not a face. He stood quietly to one side after the coffin had been lowered into the ground. The two privates stood with him. He could see that Mother and Aunt Katia were very sad. Father stood with his arm around Mother while she cried. He wished he dared hug Mother and tell her how he felt. He was relieved when the crowd began to leave. General Kannon had stayed at Father's side, not paying any attention to them. The minister's wife invited Mother and Aunt Katia to sit in the house. Father and General Kannon were talking quietly as some men began to fill in the grave.

"A word with you, Sergeant," Father said.

He left the privates to join Father and General Kannon.

"How are you doing?" Father asked in the language of the northern kingdoms.

"A little better," he replied. "I know in time I must let myself grieve, but I knew that I must do my duty first. I understand why you sent the privates with me. Thank you for sending them."

"I have some messages for Weston," Father said. "But first you had best speak to your mother. She has been very worried about you."

"I have been worried about her," he replied. "The minister figured out who I am. He promised that he and his wife would not reveal my secret to anyone."

"Good," Father said. "Go talk to your mother. I will send these two to join you shortly."

"Yes, My King," he replied in Brinley's language. "I will do so at once."

Father nodded before saying, "Come here, Privates."

They looked nervous as he passed them. It was hard to not run to the house. When he knocked on the door the minister's wife opened it.

"Come in, Sergeant," she said.

Aunt Katia looked surprised as Mother hugged him. He hugged her tightly and patted her back.

"It was so hard to not admit you are my son," Mother said with a tremor in her voice.

"I wanted so much to hug you when I saw you crying," he replied. "I know I must eventually let myself grieve. I wish I were returning to the palace with you, but Father is sending me to deliver messages in Weston first."

"Are you going to be alright?" she asked as she finally released him.

"Yes," he said. "I'll take my time in Weston. I'll probably talk to Grandfather about all this."

"You had best get going," she said as she hugged him again.

"I thought you seemed familiar," Aunt Katia said as she spoke to him for the first time.

"For now I am just a soldier in the military," he said. "For now no one can know who I am, not even my own friends. I must leave now. Thank you for your hospitality."

"I was very surprised to find out that we had royalty sleeping in our barn," the minister's wife said.

He smiled at her as he opened the door and left. He found the two privates waiting nearby with the saddled and packed horses. The message pouch was hanging from his saddle. They were oddly silent as they mounted up and left the village. After an hour they stopped for lunch.

"You two are awfully quiet," he commented as he sat down to eat.

"King Langward asked us about how you acted and how you had treated us," Private Caddaric said.

"He seemed worried about you," Private Adamok said. "When we mentioned that you had told us that your grandmother had died, he said he himself had given you the news."

"Yes," he replied, surprised at what they had said.

"It's sad you didn't even get to visit your family," Private Adamok said. "I guess the prince must feel the same way."

He just nodded.

"Do you know where the prince is?" Private Caddaric asked. "Nobody has seen him for the last few years. No one seems to know where he is."

"I've been told he was sent away to study," he replied, wording his response carefully. "There are certain things he needs to learn to be king that he cannot learn living in the palace."

"We told King Langward that you mentioned getting put in the dungeon if you disobeyed him or General Kannon," Private Adamok said. "He confirmed that was true but seemed surprised that you had mentioned it."

"With trust comes responsibility, the greater the trust, the more severe the punishment for breaking that trust," he said. "I know that King Langward does what is best for Brinley. I know that if I disagree with him,

154

I am able to tell him so. I know that it is not my place to tell him what to do or what not to do, but I know that because I have gained his trust, he respects my opinion."

"You are very comfortable around King Langward and his family," Private Adamok said. "You seem more comfortable around them than around other people."

"I've done a lot of guard duty in the palace mostly in the throne room," he replied. "When I am around other people, I worry about them finding out who I am."

The two glanced at each other before Private Caddaric said, "Even if we find out who you are, we won't tell anyone."

"We swear," Private Adamok added.

After they finished eating, they continued on their way. It was nearing nightfall when they finally reached a clearing along the side of the path. They ate in silence after setting up camp for the night.

"One of us should keep watch," he said as they finished eating. "If we each take a shift we can all get enough sleep."

"Why aren't we taking the regular road?" Private Adamok asked.

"I really don't care to have any company," he said. "When we get to Weston I will be spending some time with the minister there. He is a friend of mine. It may be a day or two before I am ready to return to the military training camp."

"What about us?" Private Adamok asked.

"I'll make certain you have a place to stay," he replied. "I've gotten General Kannon's permission."

"I heard that there are special orders in respect to Weston," Private Caddaric said.

"Yes," he said. "Burkhart and his daughter live there."

"The former king?" Private Adamok asked in a surprised tone.

"Yes. He cannot leave the village until his death. If he tries to leave he will be killed. His daughter, Aurita, is to be protected at all costs. She is not to be told that her father was once King of Brinley," he replied. "I will take the first watch."

"I'll take the second watch," Private Caddaric said.

As he kept watch he thought about the last few days. He began feeling the sadness over the death of Grandmother. He had been very grateful to be able to participate in the burial. It had helped to ease the pain of losing her.

Chapter 15 – Of the Future and Mourning

The next morning they continued their journey. It was almost noon when they came across a large meadow. He knew the main road was on the other side of the meadow. He wasn't surprised to see a wagon with two women cooking over a fire. The younger of the two looked up and saw them as they were passing through the meadow.

"I was beginning to think you weren't coming," she said in the language of the northern kingdoms.

He looked around but didn't see anyone else.

"We have been waiting for you, Prince of Brinley," she said as she walked toward them.

His heart froze at her words.

"What is she saying?" Private Caddaric asked.

"I have no idea," Private Adamok said.

"Come join us for lunch," she said. "I have something to tell you. Just as I foresaw your birth, I have foreseen your future and that of your descendants."

"She's inviting us to share lunch with them," he said as he dismounted.

They glanced at each other before dismounting. He followed the young woman back to the fire.

"My name is Riva," she said. "I know that you have not yet been given a name."

The other woman handed them plates that she had put some food on. They ate in silence for a while. He was curious what this woman knew. He wasn't certain how someone so young could have foreseen his birth, yet she knew too much to be lying.

"There are questions that you have that I cannot answer for you," the young woman said. "I know that you are in mourning and somewhat uncertain of your future."

He nodded not quite knowing how to respond.

"You are feeling pain and sorrow," she said. "You must experience sorrow so that you will know joy and pain that you will know pleasure. In time you will learn the whole of what I have seen. I cannot tell you all of it for it is best for you to learn it for yourself."

"I have learned to not press for answers concerning my future," he replied.

"I can tell you that the birthmark you bear will be passed to your descendants. You must tell your queen that when all seems lost, the birthmark will reveal your true heir," she said to his surprise. "It will be hidden and the search will be difficult, but she should not give up hope. She will live to see your true heir, but you will not."

"I won't live to see my children born?" he asked.

"You shall have two sons," she said. "Just as you hid your treatment at the hands of others, they shall hide things from you. It will be hard to let them make their own way in this world, but it is what must be done. There is a high price to be paid for the peace and prosperity that your true heir will bring to Brinley and many others. Just as you shall risk your own life to protect others, so shall your true heir. Although your true heir will be unparalleled with the sword, your true heir will bring peace to many kingdoms without drawing blood."

"I will remember what you have told me," he said.

"I know that the time before your marriage will be difficult and confusing," she continued. "You will learn many important things before you are wed. My purpose in speaking with you today is to give you hope for the future. Your life is worth living. Your contributions in life are vital to the future of this world."

He nodded as he thought about what she had said.

"What did she say?" Private Adamok asked.

"It was about my future," he said.

"Just as these two have come to trust and rely on you, in time you will come to trust and rely on them," she said. "It is time for you to continue your journey. Just remember that the changes your father made to the governing of Brinley will insure Brinley's future."

"Thank you," he said. "I needed someone to give me hope."

"Farewell, Prince of Brinley," she said.

"It's time for us to go," he said as he stood up.

The two privates followed him to the horses and mounted up. They spent another night in the forest before reaching Weston. He was comforted by the familiar sights. He paused to check the messenger's pouch that had been sent with him. There was the usual message for Burkhart along with one for his Grandfather and another for him. This surprised him. He led the men to Burkhart's house. He found that no one was home. This concerned him. He mounted his horse and led them to the church. There were some men coming from the churchyard. One of them was Barna's father.

"So you made sergeant," he said. "It's good to see you again."

"Have you seen Burkhart?" he asked.

"He and Aurita are still eating," the man said. "Almost everyone else has finished and left."

"Thank you," he replied.

He led them around to the yard near the house. There he found some scattered tables and a few people eating. He suddenly didn't feel like talking to anyone.

"Can you do something for me?" he asked as they dismounted.

"What is it?" Private Adamok asked.

"See the man in the dark grey tunic eating with the beautiful young woman?" he asked and they nodded. "Deliver this one to him. He is Burkhart. The woman is his daughter, Aurita. There is one last thing you should know before speaking to them. It is by King Langward's order that no man touches her that is not of his choosing."

The two glanced at each other and nodded.

"Deliver this one to the Minister," he said handing them the other message. "I will be in the church."

"Who is the last one for?" they asked.

"Me," he said before he turned and left.

The church was quiet. He found a seat near the front with good light and sat down. He broke the seal and unrolled the small scroll.

'My Dearest Son,' the message began. 'I know how alone you must feel right now. I'm sorry that the situation could not have been different, but I feel that things must remain as they are for now. Stay for a couple of days in Weston. I asked General Kannon to send two privates with you to give you a distraction from your sorrow because I suspected you would take your grandmother's death very hard. When I saw your reaction to the news, I knew I was right. Remember that we love you, Father.'

He felt the tears as they began to roll silently down his face. The scroll dropped to the floor as he put his head in his hands.

*****

Burkhart looked up at the sound of someone clearing their throat. The young private looked nervous. He was holding a scroll.

"May I help you?" he asked.

"Are you Burkhart?" the private asked.

"Yes," he replied.

"This is for you," the private said. "The sergeant asked me to deliver it for him."

"Thank you," he said as he took the scroll. "There is still food if you are hungry. Is the sergeant here?"

"Yes, but I don't think he is hungry right now," the private replied. "He went straight into the church."

This puzzled Burkhart. He broke the seal and opened the scroll.

'Burkhart,' it began. 'I wanted you to know that Queen Retanta's mother has died. Our son took the news very hard. Although he showed no signs of grieving at the burial, I know that his grandmother was the only friend he had before joining the military. You understand the pain he is feeling. I know he will need support from those who care about him. Your friend, King Langward.'

He looked up in surprise.

"What is it, Father?" Aurita said in a worried tone.

"Our friend, the sergeant, needs our help," he said as he stood up and put the scroll in his pouch.

He led her away from the tables and to the door of the church.

"His grandmother has died, but he has not been able to grieve because of his duties in the military," he said as he saw the minister and his wife hurrying toward them. "Our Noble King asked that we do what we can to comfort him as he grieves."

"You got the same message?" the minister asked.

"The private who delivered the message to me said that the sergeant went in the church," Burkhart replied, nodding.

"Perhaps I should go talk to him first," the minister said.

"I'll go start cleaning up," Burkhart replied.

"I'll help you, Father," Aurita said.

They went back to the tables and began to clear away the empty dishes. The minister's wife began washing the dishes with Aurita's help while Burkhart began to take the tables and benches apart to be stored. He could see the private who delivered the message to him and another private watching him closely. The other one looked almost familiar. He began to stack the tables and benches in the storage shed. He was surprised when the two privates began to help him. Soon all the tables and benches were put away.

"Thank you," he said as he shut the door to the shed.

"My grandfather told us about how you had changed," the familiar looking one said.

"I am grateful that Our Noble King has insured that my mistakes can not be repeated," Burkhart replied. "I now do everything I can to repay my debt, yet I am still haunted by my past. You look familiar somehow."

"My grandfather is General Kannon," the private replied.

"That explains it."

As they came around the corner of the house, they saw the minister coming out of the church. He looked very worried. Aurita looked frightened as she joined them.

"We must not leave him alone for more than a few minutes at a time," the minister said. "I think you should talk to him next, Burkhart. You will understand his pain more than any of us."

Burkhart nodded. He knew how hard it was to grieve for someone so close. He quietly entered the church. He could hear the prince as he cried. He went to sit next to him.

"King Langward's message said your grandmother had died," Burkhart said as he put his hand on the Prince's shoulder. "He said that the two of you were very close."

The prince just nodded.

"Our King is worried about you and so am I," Burkhart said.

The prince did not respond.

"When I first arrived in Weston, I was numb from the pain in my heart," he said softly. "After my house was finally finished, I cried myself to sleep for a whole month. Eventually I couldn't even cry. Over the years I have become accustomed to the pain. I cannot tell you how to feel or how to grieve. I can only tell you that I understand what it is like to lose someone you love deeply. I know that she can never be replaced, but I can promise that there will be others that you love just as deeply."

The prince continued to cry. Burkhart wasn't certain what to do except just sit there with him. It was a very long time before he seemed to be calming down. Burkhart patted his back and handed him a handkerchief.

"Thank you for understanding," the prince said at last without looking up.

"Whether you know it or not, your friendship has been a great comfort to me," Burkhart said. "Aurita will be very worried about you by now."

"I don't want anyone to see me like this," he responded as Burkhart saw a movement out of the corner of his eye.

He looked up to see Aurita coming toward them. He could see that she was crying.

"I don't care what you look like," she said with a tremor in her voice. "I only care about how you feel."

The prince looked up at her and she threw her arms around his neck. Burkhart quietly left.

*****

"I didn't want to worry you," he whispered as he felt Aurita trembling in his arms.

"I love you too much to not worry," she said. "I don't want you to be so sad."

"I'm feeling a bit better now," he said. "Your father and the minister helped, but I know it will take me a couple of days before I will be ready to report back to General Kannon."

"Will you be going home to see your family?" she asked.

"It just isn't possible right now," he said with a sigh. "I will be spending a couple of days here. It is the only other place I would want to be. I'm grateful King Langward sent me here and told me to stay for a couple of days."

"It's strange that he isn't allowing you to go home," she said as she finally released him.

"It's difficult to explain, but I think I understand his reasons," he replied. "I know he is doing what he feels is best."

"Everyone is so worried about you," she said. "Even the privates you brought with you."

"One of them is General Kannon's grandson," he said as he retrieved the scroll from the floor. "I think they were sent to keep watch over me."

"I have noticed that both King Langward and General Kannon care about you very much," she replied as he put the scroll in his pouch. "The minister and his wife seem to feel the same way. I know that Father and I both love and care about you."

"It comforts me to know that," he said. "It is the first time I have allowed myself to begin to grieve."

*****

Burkhart was very relieved as the church doors opened. The prince looked very tired. He noticed that the two privates seemed relieved as well. The minister's wife hugged the Prince and patted his back.

"I've still got some food left if you are hungry," she said as she released him.

"I think I could eat a little," the prince replied.

"It must be so hard to not be able to visit with your family," the minister's wife said.

"King Langward needed me to make the burial arrangements for Lady Kara," the prince said. "He even had me participate in the burial. It helped to ease my pain to think that I was participating in my own grandmother's burial."

"She will always be with you in your heart," Burkhart said as he noticed the minister's reaction.

"The privates and I will need a place to stay for a couple of days," the prince said.

"There are the two beds in the shop," Burkhart said. "I just finished another one for an order. They can wait a couple of days before I deliver it. I'll get these two settled in while you eat."

*****

He followed Grandmother to the house and sat down at the table. She set a plate of food in front of him. Grandfather came in and shut the door behind him.

"I was surprised by what you said about participating in the burial," Grandfather said. "I don't think Burkhart or Aurita noticed, but you must be more careful about what you say."

"I spend so much time hiding who I am," he said. "It's like lying to everyone. I don't want to be lying about anything else. When I am able to reveal who I am, I do not want people to wonder what else I have lied

163

about. I want them to realize that I have always told the truth about everything else."

"I know this is hard for you," Grandfather said. "But I also know that someday you will be a good leader for our people."

"I should be going now," he said as he finished eating. "Thank you."

He hugged Grandmother and kissed her cheek before hugging Grandfather.

"Do you want me to walk with you?" Grandfather asked.

"No, I'll be fine."

The sun was beginning to set as he made his way across the village. The villagers smiled and waved to him as he passed them. It made him feel as though he were at home. When he reached Burkhart and Aurita's shop, she was just coming out of the shop. She ran to him and hugged him.

"I'll be alright," he said as he held her tightly to him. "I'll see you in the morning."

"I'll make a big breakfast for you," she said before she kissed him on the cheek.

She released him and went quickly into the house. His hand went to his cheek where she had kissed him.

"My daughter loves you, you know."

Burkhart's comment startled him. He felt himself blush.

"I know," he replied. "I love her."

"You look very tired," Burkhart said. "Come get some sleep."

He followed Burkhart into the shop. He was surprised to see a bed roll laid out on the floor in addition to the three beds. The two privates seemed a bit nervous.

"You don't need to sleep in here on the floor," he said.

"I'll admit I want to keep a closer watch on you," Burkhart replied. "I'm certain that both General Kannon and King Langward would be very angry if anything happened to you."

"I think I should talk to these two alone for a moment," he said in the language of the northern kingdoms. "They need to know they can trust you."

Burkhart nodded and left.

"I want you to understand something," he said. "I trust Burkhart completely and so does King Langward. Burkhart has sworn complete loyalty and obedience to King Langward. He knows his life belongs to King Langward. He knows he remains alive solely to raise his daughter and serve King Langward."

They both looked a little calmer but still unsure.

"I know that you have heard all the rumors about him," he said. "He is a changed man. Because you are in my charge and I serve both General Kannon and King Langward, Burkhart would die defending you from harm. I have no doubt of that."

"I trust you," Private Caddaric said.

"So do I," Private Adamok added.

"Get some sleep," he said as he opened the door.

He nodded at Burkhart's questioning look. Burkhart came in and laid down on the bedroll. His dreams were jumbled and troubled. He awakened several times during the night. Each time he woke and sat up, Burkhart did as well. Burkhart's concern comforted him. He was still tired in the morning. He awoke to find the two privates watching him.

"You must not have slept well, Sergeant," Private Adamok said. "You still look tired."

"No, I didn't sleep very well," he replied as he noticed Burkhart was gone. "Where is Burkhart?"

"He asked that we watch over you while he helped Aurita fix breakfast," Private Caddaric said. "He seemed very worried about you. From what I've been told, King Burkhart did not care about anyone except himself. You were right about him being changed."

"There was one person he cared about more than himself," he replied as he got out of bed. "He loved his wife more than anyone knew. She was sickly and died giving birth to Aurita."

There was a knock at the door. He opened it to find Aurita standing there. She flung her arms around his neck and hugged him. He put his arms around her and held her tightly.

"I'll be alright," he told her softly.

"I've been so worried, I hardly slept," she said.

"It's just been hard since I haven't been able to visit my family because of my duties," he said. "But I chose to be in the military knowing that my duty must come before everything else."

"Breakfast is ready if you are hungry," she said as she finally released him from her arms.

The conversation over breakfast was light. The two privates seemed less nervous. They were just finishing when there was a knock at the door. Burkhart opened the door and suddenly lay down on the ground. Aurita joined her father as he and the privates stood up. They knelt with their swords across their palms.

"Rise," he heard Father's voice say. "We are not here on official business. We just wanted to check up on the sergeant."

"I am doing better, My King," he responded after sheathing his sword.

"You look a bit more relaxed, but tired," General Kannon said.

"Come walk with us, Sergeant," Father said.

The two privates looked confused. He signaled for them to remain as he exited the house. The guards stayed by the house as they began to walk toward the river. They walked in silence for a while before anything was said.

"Your mother has been very worried about you," Father said. "She insisted we come to check on you."

"Yesterday was very rough," he admitted. "But I finally had the chance to let myself grieve. I wanted to thank you for letting me participate in the burial. It was not something I was expecting."

"I knew that if I were the one to ask you to participate, there would be no questions," Father said. "I also knew that you needed to participate."

"You did a good job of hiding your feelings," General Kannon commented. "I got a report that none of the patrols saw you on the road between Nordam and Weston."

"We didn't take the road," he replied. "I didn't want any extra company. We did encounter two women though."

Father looked at him. He knew the look in Father's eyes. He would have to tell him everything.

"The younger one called to me in the language of the northern kingdoms," he said. "She said they were expecting us. She knew exactly who I was. After we ate lunch with them she spoke to me for a few minutes."

"Have you ever seen her before?" Father asked in an alarmed tone.

"Never," he said. "She mentioned that she had foreseen my birth."

"What else did she tell you?" Father asked.

"She told me some things about my future," he said. "She said that I would come to rely upon the privates just as they were now relying on me. She also told me something about my wife and children."

Father glanced at General Kannon with a worried expression on his face. He began explaining what the fortune teller had said about his true heir.

"Did she say who your wife would be?" Father asked.

The question surprised him.

"No," he replied. "She said that the time before my marriage would be confusing and difficult for me. She also said that I must know sorrow that I might know joy and pain that I might know pleasure."

Father was silent for a while. He wondered what he was thinking.

"I want you to write down everything she told you," Father said. "Seal it with wax and the imprint of your ring. Do not show it to anyone and do not tell anyone. I will take it with me and put it in the desk in the study. I have a feeling that you may have spoken to the same woman that spoke to me before you were born."

"She said there were things she knew that were best for me to learn on my own," he said. "She knew I did not have a name."

Father nodded and said, "Stay here tonight and return to the training camp in the morning. I'll schedule you to guard duty for tomorrow afternoon. You can stay at the palace until the next morning."

"Thank you," he said as they turned back toward Burkhart's house. "I'm glad you came. I was hoping to talk to you about all of this."

"I thought as much," Father said as he patted him on the shoulder.

"Also, Aurita has been worried about me," he said. "Last night she kissed me on the cheek."

Father nodded then glanced at General Kannon. Father's face was expressionless, but he saw a hint of a grin on General Kannon's face.

When they reached the house, the two privates were standing there watching for them. They looked relieved to see them return. Aurita came out of the shop as they approached.

"How are you doing, Aurita?" Father asked.

"I am well, My King," she replied. "I have been worried about the sergeant though."

"We all have been," Father replied. "I am leaving him in your care for another day. Why don't you two go for a walk?"

"Thank you, My King," Aurita said as she took his hand. "His visits are always infrequent and too brief."

"Sergeant, when you return from your walk complete the task I have assigned you and deliver it to the Minister's house," Father said. "I will be waiting there for you."

He heard Father chuckle as they walked toward the river. They walked in silence for a while.

"I wish I could come more often," he said as they sat down on a fallen tree. "I miss you when we are apart."

"I miss you as well," she said. "I sometimes lay awake at night trying to imagine what you are doing. I try to imagine what your family is like. I wish I could meet them."

"I tell them everything about you," he said.

"What was your grandmother like?" she asked. "I've always wondered what it would be like to have a mother and grandparents."

"She was a wonderful lady and my best friend," he replied. "She loved to be outdoors and we would take long walks together."

"You look sad," she said. "I didn't mean to make you sad."

"It's alright," he said as he kissed her hand. "I was just thinking about how much she was like you. I have been told what my future holds for me. I wish I knew what your future holds for you. King Langward has told me that you will be loved and well cared for but won't tell me anymore than that."

"He won't tell me either, but I think Father knows," she said. "What were you told about your future?"

"Unfortunately it isn't anything I am allowed to tell you," he said with a sigh. "I told King Langward and he forbade me to tell anyone at all."

"That seems strange," she said. "It isn't bad is it?"

"It's both good and bad," he said. "It did give me some hope."

She leaned against him and put her head on his shoulder. He put his arm around her and pulled her closer to him. It felt good to feel her body pressed against his. They sat for a while watching the river.

"I wish you could tell me your name," she said as she sat up straight.

"There is nothing I want more than to hear you say my name," he replied. "It is just not possible right now."

"I want to show you something," she said.

He followed her toward where the brook met the river. There was a small stand of trees with low branches growing a short distance from the river. She ducked under the branches on the riverside and disappeared. He ducked under the branches and was surprised to find a hollowed out place beneath the branches. She was sitting on the ground leaning back against a smooth stone. He sat down opposite her.

"I found this when I was quite young," she said. "I would come here to be alone and when I wanted to hide from the other children."

"I've been told that they weren't very nice to you," he replied remembering the time he spent locked in his room. "I heard that your leg was injured, but the girls who caused the injury became your friends."

She nodded as she straightened her leg. He could see the scar on her leg. He reached out and softly traced the scar with his fingers. He looked up at her and she smiled.

"The stick went all the way through to the other side," she said. "Langford told me that most people have to be held down to have such a wound treated. One of the patrolmen that sent word to King Langward said when he had an arrow removed from his shoulder he screamed very loudly, but I did not even make a sound. I even watched while Langford stitched it up."

"You are so very brave," he said.

"You too are very brave, and so very kind," she said. "You are so different than anyone else I have met. The patrolmen are nice to me, nicer than most of the villagers, but with you it is different. Where they seem afraid to even touch my hand, you are not. Your touch is gentle and your smile is genuine. You are not afraid to be seen holding my hand."

"I have no reason to fear," he replied with a smile. "I have told King Langward about every contact I have with you. Each time he has told me that he wants things to continue as they are. I don't understand why, but I will not question it. I was expecting to be punished for holding you in my arms when you were upset, but instead I was rewarded by being appointed designated messenger to Weston. I also know that if I disobey King Langward's wishes, he will put me in the dungeon."

"Our King seems to care a great deal about you," she said. "I don't think he would put you in the dungeon. He treats you more like a son than a soldier, but then I have noticed that he is kind to everyone."

"Trust me," he said. "If the prince broke a law or disobeyed King Langward, even he would be put in the dungeon."

*****

"You really believe that," she said in surprise.

"I'm certain that if you asked him he would confirm it," he replied.

"Let's go see if he is still here," she said and got up.

He followed her back to her house. She was surprised at his certainty. King Langward was getting ready to mount his horse.

"Back so soon?" King Langward asked as he saw them.

"I had a question for you," she said.

"What is it?"

"The sergeant said that if he disobeyed you that you would put him in the dungeon," she said. "He also believes that you would put your own son in the dungeon if he broke a law or disobeyed you."

"That is correct," King Langward said. "I too must obey the law even though I am king. My son cannot be exempt from punishment for breaking a law. When he is king, I would expect to be put in the dungeon if I broke a law. If we can not obey the law, how can we expect the people of Brinley to obey the law? Laws that are unfair need to be changed or revoked by the counsel."

"You have said that no man not of your choosing may touch me," she said and King Langward nodded. "The sergeant said that he had expected to be punished after he held me in his arms, but instead was rewarded. Is he to be my husband?"

King Langward was silent for a moment before saying, "Neither the man who is to be your husband, nor you are quite ready to be married yet. In time you will understand why I am handling this the way I am. I hope that you will see that although I will have created opportunity, I have not, nor do I mean to make certain choices for you. I can give orders in regards to you and your future, but I cannot order you to love the man I have chosen for you."

She was relieved to hear him say it out loud.

"Your father also knows who has been chosen to be your husband," King Langward continued. "He knows that the man is kind and honest. I know this is difficult and frustrating for you, but I feel that to handle it in any other way would be wrong. The man I have chosen as your husband does not know you will be his wife. For now, do not worry about it. The sergeant knows my orders in regards to you and I trust he will not disobey them. Take good care of him."

She watched as King Langward mounted and rode off. Although he had confirmed what the sergeant had said, King Langward's words had left her even more confused than she was before. She could see that the sergeant was a bit confused as well.

*****

"I need some paper, pen and ink," he said.

"I think Father has some," she replied.

Burkhart was in the shop. He looked surprised to see them, as did the two privates who were watching him work.

"The sergeant wanted to know if you had some paper, pen and ink he could use," Aurita said.

"It's in the house," Burkhart said. "Why don't you get those baskets finished for that order, Aurita?"

He signaled for the privates to stay. He followed Burkhart into the house. Burkhart opened a chest and began to take things out of it. At last he brought a pen and bottle of ink to the table along with some paper.

"Take what you need." Burkhart said. "I have learned to make paper from the sawdust in the shop."

"Thank you," he said. "What King Langward asked me to write he ordered that I reveal to no one. He asked that I seal it."

"I'll be just outside the door if you need me," Burkhart said as he drew a yellow wax stick out of the box.

He brought a lit candle to the table before leaving. Burkhart shut the door behind him. As he wrote, he tried to remember the exact words the woman had used. It was easier to remember it in the language she had used, so that is what he wrote it in. He was relieved to at last finish it. He rolled it and carefully sealed it with the wax before imprinting the wax with his ring. It was the first time he had imprinted a wax seal, but he had seen Father do it many times. He sat in silence for a moment before taking

171

another sheet of paper. He wrote a letter to his mother telling her that he was feeling better and would be alright. As he folded and sealed the letter, he realized how difficult this must be for her. He knew that she loved him very much and worried about him. He would be glad to see her in person again, but he was happy to have more time to spend with Aurita.

He blew out the candle before picking up the scroll and the letter. True to his word, Burkhart was standing patiently by the door when he opened it. Burkhart smiled and patted him on the shoulder.

"I'll walk with you to the Minister's house," Burkhart said.

"Thank you," he replied. "I wanted you to know that I appreciate your obvious concern for me."

"I have very few friends in this world," Burkhart said. "You treat me as a friend, with dignity and respect. I can only hope that I am worthy in your eyes of such treatment."

"You are, My Friend," he replied in surprise. "I too have very few friends. Most of them do not even know who I am. King Langward and General Kannon are my superiors, yet they treat me more as a friend. There are very few people outside of my family that know my identity."

"It must be very difficult for you," Burkhart said. "I know how hard it is for me to hide my past from Aurita."

"Sometimes I feel as though I am living a lie," he said. "I feel as though when I am able to tell others who I am, they will not trust me because of that."

"I have noticed that you are very honest when dealing with others," Burkhart said. "I know it is a difficult thing for you to do, but I know you to be a trustworthy person regardless of your true identity."

They arrived at the Minister's house as Father and General Kannon came out of the door.

"Here is what you requested of me," he said as he held out the scroll. "I also wrote a letter to my mother."

"I will see that she gets it," Father said with a smile. "Now go and spend the day with Aurita. I know that is what you would prefer to do over anything else."

"You know me well, My King," he said. "I will cheerfully obey your command."

He heard Father chuckle as he and Burkhart left. The way that Father dealt with his relationship with Aurita confused him. He knew that

Father had chosen her husband, yet he did not know of any other man that was allowed such close contact with her.

"Does something trouble you?" Burkhart asked as they reached the bridge over the brook.

"I just don't understand why I am allowed such close contact with Aurita," he replied as he stopped in the middle of the bridge. "I even told King Langward that Aurita had kissed me on the cheek. He did not even say a word. I will not disobey his orders, especially where it involves Aurita. I know it must be hard for you to know that you have no say in her future."

"King Langward has told me his plans for her future, but I am not allowed to share that information with anyone," Burkhart said. "My heart is at peace with his decisions in regard to her future. He is a much wiser man than I ever could be and I trust him implicitly. It is my duty to prepare her as best I can for that future. I do understand why you are allowed such close contact with Aurita. I agree completely with King Langward's decisions and actions in that matter. Even if it were not by his wishes, it would be by my wishes."

He looked Burkhart in the eyes. The man was completely serious, but happy about what he had said. He patted Burkhart on the shoulder and smiled. He felt a little better about the situation, but still confused. He spent the afternoon with Aurita. It was nice to know he did not have to leave until morning. When he left the next morning, the two privates seemed glad to leave. Burkhart had given him a message for King Langward.

"May we ask you something, Sergeant?" Private Adamok said.

"What is it?" he replied, curious about what they may want.

"You seem more comfortable in Weston than anywhere else we have seen you including at the training camp," Private Adamok said. "It is almost like you were born there."

"I was not born in Weston, nor have I ever lived there," he said with a laugh. "But I suppose it feels like home more than anywhere else right now. King Langward has appointed me as the designated messenger to Weston, so I get to go there a lot. Sometimes I am even allowed to take one of my friends."

When they reached the training camp, it was time for lunch. He invited the two privates to sit with him and his friends for lunch.

"We heard about your grandmother dying," Kennar said after the introductions were made.

"I'll miss her," he said. "But I know she is now with my grandfather. He died before I was born."

"Tonight you'll have to tell us everything," Kon said.

"I can't tonight," he replied. "I have guard duty at the palace throne room."

"So do we," Monau said. "We were all very surprised when General Kannon told us."

After lunch they prepared to go to the palace. He was glad that the palace guard had special uniforms since all of his were dirty from the trip. When they relieved the throne room guard, he saw Mother enter. She smiled and nodded. He nodded ever so slightly back. He listened carefully to every audience. He was standing so he could watch Father without moving. He was amazed at Father's serious expression during some of the audiences. He was having trouble not bursting out in laughter. It was all he could do to stand still.

There was one audience that resulted in a man being condemned to death for murder. He paid close attention to how Father coaxed the truth out of the man. He and Kennar escorted the man to the dungeon.

"I had no idea standing guard could be so interesting," Kennar commented as they were returning to the throne room. "Some of it was quite funny. The only thing that kept me from laughing was that no one else was laughing."

"I have the same problem," he said as they reached the throne room doors.

General Kannon arrived as the audiences were completed. He was surprised when he and his friends were invited to eat with his parents and General Kannon. His friends looked very nervous as they followed his parents down the hall.

'Don't worry,' he signaled to them as they walked. 'They are people just like you and me.'

The three nodded, but still seemed unsure. The conversation between General Kannon and his parents was light. They asked occasional questions of him or one of his friends. Mostly they just listened. Once supper was finished, he led his friends down to the guard's quarters. They sat down and talked while he washed his uniforms.

"That was very strange," Kon commented. "It was kind of like being at home when company came over for dinner."

"King Langward grew up in Weston," he said. "Queen Retanta did too, but her family moved to Nordam when King Langward went into the military. He once told me that part of why he formed the counsel is so he can remember what it was like to be a commoner."

"I was surprised how interested he seemed in us," Monau said.

"So was I," Kennar said. "I noticed Queen Retanta was as well."

"I suppose because I work for General Kannon and sometimes work closely with King Langward as well, they wanted to know more about my friends," he said. "I have learned a lot from King Langward and Queen Retanta."

"I noticed that she participated in the audiences as much as he did," Monau said.

"I have seen how they share equally in ruling Brinley," he replied as he hung up the last tunic. "We should get some sleep. Morning comes early around here."

The next morning they were assigned to guard Mother as she went into the city to purchase some things. He was surprised, but happy to spend time with her even if he couldn't admit to being her son. They went from shop to shop as she purchased things which she had them carry to the carriage. He noticed that she purchased four very nice leather belts with bronze buckles. The belts were marked with the pattern of triangles, rectangles and squares popular in Brinley. When they finally returned to the palace around lunchtime, they carried Mother's purchases up to the Royal Suite. She presented them each with one of the belts before dismissing them.

"I can't believe Queen Retanta actually bought these for us," Kennar said. "I've never had a belt this nice before."

"Neither have I," Monau said.

"She is one of the nicest people I've ever met," Kon said.

"Where did you get those belts?" a voice asked as they turned the corner.

They looked up to find Father standing in front of them. They were quickly on their knees.

"Rise and answer the question," Father said.

175

"Queen Retanta purchased them today," he replied. "She gave them to us after we had delivered her purchases to the Royal Quarters."

His friends nodded. Father held out his hand. He laid the belt across Father's hand. Father examined it closely then nodded before handing it back to him.

"Remember to keep them clean and oiled," Father said. "They will last a very long time if properly cared for."

"We will," he replied. "Thank you."

"No," Father said. "Thank you for escorting Queen Retanta today. You may return to the training camp now."

They stepped aside and Father went around the corner. They got halfway down the hall when they heard laughter behind them. He grinned as he recognized his father's laughter.

"What's so funny?" Monau whispered.

"King Langward sometimes has a strange sense of humor," he replied. "He once told me that everyone expects the king to be serious, so he has to wait and laugh about things later. I'm certain we were assigned to Queen Retanta today because he wanted to test us."

"Did we pass?" Monau asked.

"Apparently so," he replied with a laugh.

As they returned to the training camp, they talked about his trip. They were amazed that he was invited to participate in Lady Kara's burial. He knew they would be even more amazed if he told them that she was his grandmother. When night came, he was glad to be sleeping in the barracks again.

*****

"I like our son's friends," Retanta said as they prepared for bed. "They were very polite and helpful."

"I thought you might like the chance to meet them," Langward said with a laugh. "I saw the belts you bought for them. I've been quite impressed with them myself. I found out from Major Rowland that Sergeant Kon and Sergeant Monau gave our son some trouble on his first day at camp, but he handled the situation well and they became his friends that same day."

"It's good to see him getting along so well with them," she said. "I know how the children in the palace treated him. He never complained, but I know he was not very happy. Even though I worry about him, I can see that having him join the military was one of the best things we could have done."

"I worry about him too," Langward said. "But I know that he is learning what he needs to know when he is king."

Chapter 16 – Birthday Surprises

He yawned as he gathered the papers up off his desk and put them in the drawer. Although still serving as General Kannon's assistant, he had been progressing along with Kennar, Kon, and Monau during the last two years, but that meant extra study which took up time. He became a captain almost a year ago. He also took every message to Weston and picked up any when told to. About once a week he joined the palace guard. Father stationed him in the throne room to stand guard while audiences were held. A month ago he had been given the book of laws to copy after the audiences were over with. He did not understand why he needed to include even the crossed out laws as he made twelve copies of the book, but did not question Father's orders. He appreciated the opportunity to study the laws again.

He shut the door and locked it behind him. It was dark as he made his way across the camp to the barracks as the last of the sunset faded. He yawned again as he entered the barracks. He checked the fire before getting into bed. He thought about the laws that he had copied. He had seen the crossed out ones that had been Burkhart's. He was beginning to understand exactly why everyone hated Burkhart so much.

He awoke to the sound of the bugler. He reported to General Kannon's office as soon as he had finished breakfast. General Kannon was not at his office yet. He sat down and got out the work he had not finished the night before. He was just completing it as the general entered.

"If you have finished those copies of the laws, you can take one set to Weston and deliver it to Burkhart," General Kannon said. "Stay the night. It looks like you need a day off."

"Yes," he replied. "Thank you, Sir."

"I know how hard you have been working, Captain," the General said. "Trust me; you'll be glad you are used to it when you take your father's place."

"He has said the same," he replied as he finished placing the last page into the delivery pouch. "But I know Mother has been worried about me."

"Although he hasn't said it, I know your father is too," General Kannon responded as he approached the desk. "When you return you can start training for patrol duty."

He laid something on the desk next to the pouch.

"You'll need to change before leaving, Major," General Kannon said with a grin.

He picked up the folded cloth and found it to be a Major's tunic. He looked up at General Kannon in shock.

"You've more than earned it," the General said. "There's two more on your bed. Take Major Kon with you. He's been a bit off lately. I overheard him talking about Barna again yesterday."

"He'll appreciate that," he replied. "He's been thinking about her a lot. I'll bet he marries her once he makes patrolman."

"I guess that means I had best station him near Weston," General Kannon said with a laugh. "What about those other two you hang out with? Want to take them along also?"

"Noka and Carria were asking about them last time I was in Weston," he replied. "I hardly got a moment away from them until I told them everything I could think of about Major Kennar and Major Monau."

The General just laughed and said, "I've already told them to get packed. I suspect you won't have to pack; they'll have done it for you. Get going."

"Yes, Sir," he replied as he fastened his belt around the new tunic.

He grabbed the pouch and left the office. He couldn't help but run across camp to the barracks. Kon, Monau and Kennar were coming out the door when he reached the barracks.

"It looks good on you," Kennar said as he tossed a bedroll at him.

"I certainly wasn't expecting it," he replied with a grin as he took his saddle bags from Monau. "I'm glad we can all go this time. I won't have to answer a bunch of questions about everything you three have been up to."

They laughed as they started out for the horse pasture. He had his horse saddled and ready by the time they were beginning to saddle theirs. He was glad to have his own horse and not have to catch one of the camp's horses for every trip. They were soon on their way. They talked and laughed as they made their way toward Weston. When they reached the top of the hill, they paused for a moment.

"You know, this is really a beautiful village," Kon said. "Perhaps someday I'll make my home here."

"With Barna," he finished for Kon.

The others laughed as Kon began to blush.

"If General Kannon knows how you feel about Barna, everyone in camp must know," he said as they started down the hill. "Just don't forget the rules."

"I still don't understand the reason for some of the rules," Kennar said.

"I don't either," he replied. "But since it is King Langward's order, there must be some reason. I'm guessing that once Burkhart dies and Aurita is told the truth about his past, the rules will make sense. Until then I'm just grateful to get to see her once in a while."

"You are so in love with her," Monau said, laughing at him. "You know that she must marry whomever King Langward has chosen for her."

"I know that," he replied with a sinking feeling. "It tears me up inside to know that. It is very confusing and difficult to know that I love her, but can't have her as my wife. I can't even begin to explain how embarrassing it is to have to report every detail of every contact with her to King Langward."

"Last time I was here, Barna's father caught me kissing her," Kon said. "I was so embarrassed when he confronted me with it, but when I told him that I love her he smiled. I explained to him that when I make patrolman, I will ask to be assigned near Weston. He gave me permission to ask her to marry me, but the final decision would be hers."

"Have you told your parents?" Kennar asked.

"Actually, they were visiting at the time," Kon said. "My father had been with Barna's when I got caught kissing her."

"You are so lucky," Monau said with a sigh. "I'm still not certain if Carria's parents like me or not. I think her father hates me."

"I'll meet you at Aurita's shop later," Kon said as he turned toward Barna's house.

As he turned back toward the road, he noticed a man entering the graveyard behind the church. His shoulders drooped and his head was bowed. He walked slowly as he made his way across to sit at a particular grave. He realized it must be Burkhart when he noticed that the grave was that of Father's father.

"I've got to stop here first," he told Kennar and Monau. "I'll meet you later."

They nodded as he turned his horse toward the graveyard. He dismounted and laid the reins over the fence rail. He patted the horse before entering the graveyard. As he neared the grave, he could hear Burkhart's labored breathing. He gently rested his hand on the man's shoulder and he looked up.

"What's the matter?" he asked as he knelt down beside Burkhart.

"I got word from the patrols that you would be bringing me the copy of the book of laws," Burkhart replied. "I know that you are the one King Langward had copy them. You have now seen all of the wicked, greedy laws I forced upon Brinley's people."

"Yes," he replied understanding the problem. "I now fully understand the people's hatred of you. I also know within my heart that you are not the same man that wrote those laws. I know that it is very difficult to convince people that you have changed. I know that some people hate Aurita for what you have done and the rules placed upon this village because you two are here."

"I have worried about what you would think of me once you knew the whole truth," Burkhart said. "I have also worried that your feelings for Aurita would change as well."

"King Langward once told me that part of what happened is that you had too much power," he responded. "The reason that he formed the council is so that no one person, including the king, could ever have that much power again. He said that when one person has too much power they are tempted to abuse it, using it for their own benefit without thought for who it would hurt. No man can be expected to forever resist such temptation, not even him."

"You are a wiser man than I," Burkhart replied. "I know that you have benefitted from the time you have spent with Our Noble King. No matter what you do with your life, I know that it will be something you need not be ashamed of. I can only pray that the man chosen as Aurita's husband will be as understanding and forgiving as you are."

"I pray for that as well," he said. "It tears me up inside when I think about her marrying someone who cannot find it in his heart to forgive her for your past."

"I know that you feel that way," Burkhart said. "I have seen it in your eyes. It hurts you to know that she must marry someone chosen for her instead of someone she loves."

"There are some things that cannot be changed," he replied with a sigh. "Unfortunately that is one of them. King Langward has promised that the man she marries will love her and I trust him. I hope that she can learn to love him as she loves me."

"I appreciate your openness about your feelings for her," Burkhart said.

"It is difficult sometimes, but I know that it must not be hidden," he responded. "I tell King Langward everything that happens between us knowing that he has the power and authority to keep me from seeing her. I see no point in not sharing the same information with you. Regardless of anything else, you are her father."

"Yes," Burkhart said as he stood up. "It is my blood that flows in her veins, but in regards to her future, it is King Langward who is her father, I have forfeited that right to him long ago."

He stood up and looked Burkhart in the eyes. He could see the conflicting emotions he was feeling. He felt sorry for Burkhart. Father had once told him that if Aurita had not lived, Burkhart would have lay down and died on his own. He knew that this was true. He put his hand on Burkhart's shoulder and Burkhart smiled at him.

"I should get back to the shop before Aurita worries about me," Burkhart said. "She will be very happy to see you."

"I'll be very happy to see her," he replied. "I even brought her a small birthday gift. I bought it weeks ago not knowing I would be seeing her on her birthday."

"That will make her happy," Burkhart said as he began leading his horse toward Burkhart's shop. "But I know one thing that would make her even happier."

He looked at Burkhart and found he had a strange grin on his face.

"I overheard her talking to her friends not long ago. Apparently all of them have been kissed by your friends," Burkhart said and he nodded remembering similar conversations with his friends. "She was kind of quiet but they did not notice. Later I found her crying. I didn't have to ask her what the matter was. I know that she desperately wants you to kiss her lips instead of her hand."

His heart skipped a beat for he wanted to kiss her more than anything, but had not dared.

"I know that if you do, you will feel the need to tell King Langward what you have done," Burkhart continued. "I'm certain that you would get into more trouble because you made her unhappy by not kissing her than you would by kissing her."

His heart was pounding and the reins he was gripping were almost cutting into his hand. He could not believe he was hearing Aurita's father tell him he should kiss her on the lips. He had heard of fathers being angry that a man had kissed their daughter, but never that a father told a man to kiss his daughter. By the time they reached the shop, he was almost feeling dizzy. He dropped the reins as Burkhart went into the shop, closing the door behind him. He fumbled with the buckle on the saddle bags and once he had opened it, was grateful to discover they had packed the present on top. His hand was shaking as he gently picked up the box containing the beautiful earrings. Although he knew she would say they were too fancy for her or she might sell them for the money, he didn't care. He just wanted her to know how beautiful he thought she was.

He took a deep breath before opening the door. Burkhart was working on a chair, while Aurita was bent over placing more reeds in the tub of water. When she looked up at him, his heart skipped a beat. Before he knew what had happened, she had flung her arms around his neck and was hugging him.

"I've missed you too," he managed to say in a steady voice.

He felt the box being taken from his hand. He glanced up and Burkhart nodded to him. He drew her into his arms until she was pressed closely against his body. He kissed her hair and she suddenly looked up at him. As their eyes met, he suddenly didn't care that her father was standing there watching them. He leaned down and found her lips with his. As their lips parted he gasped for breath as his heart hammered in his chest. He could feel her gasping as well. He suddenly didn't know why he had waited so long. He felt her hand creeping up the back of his neck as he leaned down and kissed her again, this time with even more passion. He was barely aware of hearing a chuckle and the door shut.

*****

Burkhart chuckled to himself as he went into the house to start lunch. King Langward's plan was working perfectly. The prince had done exactly as he had hoped. Although he knew it would still take time for the prince to get the courage to ask his father to marry Aurita, it was an eventuality. He had known that the prince would take his suggestion to kiss Aurita. His silence had betrayed his willingness to Burkhart. It was good to feel so happy.

*****

"You should have seen his expression when I told him to take a copy to Burkhart," General Kannon said as he put the book of laws and the copies on the table. "I watched him run across camp toward the barracks."

Langward laughed. His son had told him weeks ago that he had purchased a birthday gift for Aurita. He and General Kannon had planned this so that he would be in Weston on her birthday so he could deliver his present to her.

"I caught his friends coming out of breakfast and told them about the trip," the General continued. "They were all very excited when I handed them his new Major's tunics and told them to pack for him."

"Perfect," Langward said as he began to laugh again.

"He changed into the one I gave him right there in the office," the General said with a laugh. "He left the Captain's tunic laying crumpled on the desk before dashing out the door."

"I sent a message to Burkhart a week ago telling him what we had planned," Langward confessed. "I suggested that if there were some way to convince him to kiss her that he should do it when my son arrived. Burkhart replied that he knew the perfect way to do it."

General Kannon collapsed on a chair in a fit of laughter. They were laughing as the other members of the council entered the room. Most of the things they went over were routine, but then they covered the reports of increased activity along the western border. Usually trouble came from Mannton in the south, but this was the first time Okiah had showed signs of aggression.

*****

Aurita could feel herself trembling as he held her in his arms. His chest rose and fell as he breathed and she could hear his heart beating even faster than hers was. She had not expected him to kiss her on the lips. She knew that he was completely obedient to King Langward and reported everything to him. She prayed that he would not get in trouble for kissing her, yet at the same time it was what she had wanted with all her heart. It was obvious that he had wanted it too. He had kissed her like a thirsty man

184

drinks water, as though his very life depended upon it. She wondered if this was his last visit and the thought made her sad.

"You're trembling," he said softly. "Are you alright?"

"This isn't your last visit, is it?" she asked as a knot began to form in her throat.

"Not as far as I know," he replied. "I know you must be worried that King Langward will not let me visit again after I tell him I kissed you."

She just nodded.

"I worry about the same thing, but we both know it is better to tell him than try to hide it," he said. "Your father thought King Langward might be more forgiving if I kissed you and made you happy than if I didn't and you were unhappy. I must admit that I have wanted to kiss your lips since the first day General Kannon brought me to Weston."

"You have?" she asked in surprise as she looked up into his eyes.

"Yes," he whispered before he leaned down and kissed her again.

She felt she could stand there forever in his arms kissing him. His kiss had awakened something deep within her that she had been trying to deny. She loved him with all of her heart and did not want to marry anyone else. She wanted to be his wife and bear his children. She didn't care that she didn't know his name. By the time he broke off the kiss, she was beginning to get dizzy. As her head fell to his chest, the door opened.

"Aren't you two going to have some lunch?" Father's voice asked. "You can kiss more later."

Her face was hot with embarrassment as he released her from his arms. She glanced up to see how red his face was. She heard Father laughing quietly as he led them into the house. She had not heard Father laugh in a long time. As they sat down to eat, she noticed that his tunic was different. No longer was it the tunic of a captain, but of a major.

"You made major?" she asked. "When?"

"Just this morning before I was sent to Weston," he replied with a grin. "I was also told to stay the night. When I went to pack for the trip, I found that Kennar, Monau and Kon had packed for me and were coming as well."

"Oh, the girls will be so happy!" she exclaimed. "They can talk of little else."

"The men talk about the girls all the time," he admitted with a smile. "I think Kon wants to settle down in Weston."

"Barna has been so mixed up," she said with a laugh as Father began dishing up the meal for them. "One day she is happy saying she just knows he will marry her, the next she is crying because he hasn't asked her yet."

The major laughed as he picked up his fork. She watched him as they ate. His shoulders were broader and he was taller than she remembered. She would never forget his face and his smile for as long as she lived. After they finished eating, Father got a small box off the mantle and handed it to the major with a smile. He nodded and smiled back. Father went to the trunk in the corner of the room and took out something.

"I brought you a gift for your birthday," he said with a smile as he handed her the box.

"You remembered my birthday?" she asked as there was a knock on the door.

He nodded as Father opened the door and she saw Barna and Major Kon at the door.

"Have you given them to her yet?" Major Kon asked.

"She hasn't opened the box yet," he replied. "Maybe we should go outside so everyone can see."

He offered her his hand and led her outside. Father followed. Noka, Major Kennar, Carria and Major Monau were waiting outside for them. As they watched, she opened the small wooden box. She dropped the lid as she saw the beautiful earrings that were nestled in the box. They had the light blue gems that mostly nobility and royalty wore because they were very rare along with diamonds. She had seen Queen Retanta wearing a bracelet once and asked Father about it. He told her what the gems on the bracelet were and how much they cost. She was shocked to think that the major had spent so much money for a pair of earrings.

She looked up at him in shock. He smiled at her as he reached into the box and drew out one of the earrings. He carefully put it on her ear before getting the other one out. Once he had put the second earring on her he stepped back for the others to see. They were talking excitedly, but her attention was on the major as he stood there smiling at her.

"Absolutely perfect," he said and she could think of no reply.

She dropped the box and flung herself into his arms. She kissed him as he had kissed her, with all of the passion she felt for him.

"I take it you like them," he said as she stepped back.

"I love them, but they are much too expensive," she said. "I can't keep them. You must have spent two whole month's salary on them."

"Four months actually, and worth every bit of it," he said with a smile. "Keep them, sell them, I don't care. All I wanted was to see them on you just once."

She glanced at Father who looked very happy.

"They'll look very nice with the dress I bought for you," her father said as he held it up for her to see.

Suddenly she was surrounded by her friends who were talking all at the same time. She couldn't believe what he had just said. He had spent four whole months' salary on the earrings knowing she might sell them. She decided she would keep them. They had enough money for what little they needed. Even if she never wore them again she would keep them because they were from him.

*****

As he watched her and her friends, Kon elbowed him in the ribs.

"Finally got up the nerve to kiss her, didn't you?" Kon said and the others laughed as he felt himself blush. "We could tell as you walked out the door."

"Something about the stupid grin on your face gave it away," Kennar said with a laugh.

"You know, Burkhart looks happier than I have ever seen him," Monau said. "He really seemed to like seeing you two kissing."

He drew them a little farther away from Burkhart and the women.

"Actually he mentioned that she had been crying because I hadn't kissed her," he admitted. "Then he suggested that I might get into more trouble for making her unhappy than for kissing her."

"Too bad you aren't the one she will marry," Kon said. "Maybe you should ask King Langward anyway."

"Maybe someday," he said. "I know that there have been rumors about Okiah wanting to invade Brinley. We may all be patrolmen sooner than later if all the experienced men are needed for battle."

"You had best learn fast then," Monau said. "I've heard the same rumors."

"If we're lucky, we'll be assigned here," Kennar said.

"Do you think the General will let you become a patrolman?" Kon asked.

"I guess we'll just have to see when the time comes," he replied as he wondered what he would be doing if there were a war. "He told me I would start training for patrol when I get back to camp."

After Aurita changed into her new dress, they all went for a walk down by the river. They found a place to sit and talk for a while. Aurita seemed happy and smiled whenever she looked at him. They had been there for a few hours when they heard the sound of galloping horses. He was surprised to see Father and General Kannon approach. He quickly stood up. They and their guards slowed their horses as they turned toward the group. He quickly knelt with his sword held up on outstretched palms and was soon joined by the other three men.

"Rise," he heard Father say.

The men sheathed their swords as they stood up. Father and General Kannon had dismounted. He felt a hand in his and found Aurita at his side.

"What have we here?" Father said as he looked directly at her. "Did the major give you those earrings, Aurita?"

"Yes, My King," she replied as he swallowed hard.

"There is something else different about you besides what you are wearing," Father said. "You look happier than I have ever seen you before."

"I am happy, My King," she replied.

"The major looks different as well," General Kannon said.

"Now that you mention it, he does," Father said as he looked at him. "Something has happened. Do you care to tell me, Major?"

"This morning I kissed Aurita for the first time, My King," he replied, careful to keep his voice steady. "Her father mentioned that she had been unhappy because I hadn't kissed her. He said that she had been a bit sad since all of her friends had been kissed, yet she had not."

Father frowned, but there was something in his eyes that contradicted the frown.

"You know that I alone will choose her husband," Father said sternly. "You know that no man is to touch her that is not of my choosing."

"Yes, My King," he replied. "I will not kiss her again if that is your will. My sword and my life are yours to command."

"In the past I have ordered you to protect her and make certain that she has what she needs," Father said. "I have also told you that I wish her to live as normal of a life as possible under the circumstances."

"Yes, My King," he replied. "I take that duty very seriously. I have no desire to disobey your orders."

"How do you feel about the major kissing you, Aurita?" Father asked and her hand began to tremble.

"I like it very much, My King," she replied. "I have often dreamed about him kissing me, yet I will not disobey your orders even if it means I shall never kiss him again."

He felt a shock run through him at that revelation. Father glanced at General Kannon.

"How does your father feel about you kissing the major?" Father asked.

"I haven't ever seen him look as happy as he was after watching the major kiss me," she replied.

"You kissed her right in front of her father?" Father asked sternly.

"I know that her life belongs to you as does mine, yet he is her father by blood," he replied. "I do not want my interactions with her to be secret from him anymore than they are from you, My King. I will not do anything that need be hidden from anyone including her father."

"You would kiss her right here in front of me, Major?" Father asked.

"Yes, Sir," he replied.

"Do it," Father said.

He could see the surprise in her eyes as he turned toward her. He gently stroked her cheek as he drew closer to her. He drew her into his arms and kissed her. As their lips met he did not care who was watching, he was not ashamed of loving her. He saw her smile before she rested her head on his shoulder. He knew she was not ashamed of loving him either.

"That would explain it," he heard Father say.

He looked up to see General Kannon nodding.

"He reminds me of his father," General Kannon said. "He never went out of his way to avoid trouble either."

"What shall we do with these four?" Father asked.

"I suppose they will want to be assigned near Weston when they become patrolmen," General Kannon replied. "It might be simpler to assign them to guard Weston than anywhere else."

"I agree. You three will be assigned to patrol Weston as soon as your training is complete. What about your assistant?" Father asked. "Shall we assign him to guard Weston as well?"

"I suppose I will eventually have to find a new assistant anyway," General Kannon replied.

He was shocked. He never expected to be allowed to return after Father's reaction. Now they were going to assign him to patrol Weston. Aurita looked up at him in surprise.

"I suppose we should get to the original reason for my visit," Father said and gestured with his hand.

One of the guards came forward leading a beautiful brown horse wearing a side saddle.

"Aurita, as a birthday present, I have brought this horse so that the major can teach you to ride," Father said. "Since you will not remain forever in this village, you will have the opportunity to ride horses once you leave here. Since it is by my order that you are restricted to this village, it is my responsibility to provide you a means to learn what you must know once you leave."

"Thank you, My King," she responded. "And thank you for not punishing the major for kissing me."

"When is your birthday, Major?" Father asked.

"Tomorrow, My King," he replied knowing that Father could not admit to knowing the date.

"You and the others can stay until two days after your birthday," Father said.

"Isn't that the same day your son was born, My King?" Aurita asked.

"Yes," Father replied. "It is."

"Please let him know that I hope his birthday is a happy one," Aurita said.

"I'm certain he will be pleased that you remembered his birthday," Father said. "I want a word with you in private, Major."

"Yes, Sir," he replied and stepped forward.

Father led him away from the group.

"I didn't want her to know that I actually expected you to kiss her," Father said softly in the language of the kingdoms to the north.

"Why didn't you tell me?" he asked.

"I didn't want you to feel forced into it," Father replied. "Part of why the four of you will soon be assigned to patrols here is that I feel that the trouble to the west will not go away. I know that the four of you can be trusted to guard and protect this village. I cannot explain it entirely, but it is vitally important that Aurita is safe from harm. Any attack against her is to be considered an attack against me since she is under my protection. Do not forget that."

"I will not," he replied. "And thank you for allowing me to stay here for my birthday. I couldn't ask for a better gift."

"I thought as much," Father said. "How did Burkhart react when you kissed Aurita in front of him?"

"He seemed happy about it," he replied. "My friends even noticed that he seemed happier than they had ever seen him."

"Good," Father said. "Do your friends know who you are?"

"I have not told them," he replied. "Nor have they asked."

"It might be best that they know and get used to the idea before you are assigned to patrol here," Father said to his surprise. "I want you to tell them before you return to the training camp."

"What about Burkhart?" he asked. "Sometimes he says things that make me wonder if he knows."

"I have told him everything he needs to know," Father replied. "I will go speak to him before returning to the palace. Take care and I will see you in a few days."

He returned to the group and the guard holding the horse handed him the reins. He noticed that General Kannon was grinning as he mounted his horse. The rest of the group seemed stunned.

"I can't believe you did that," Kon said. "I wouldn't have dared."

The rest echoed the same.

"Our King is a fair and understanding man," he said. "I know that if I am to be allowed to continue seeing Aurita, nothing can be secret. I knew that from the very beginning. By admitting everything to him, I have proven to him that I can be trusted."

"Trying for a palace job after being a patrolman?" Kennar asked. "You know you would have to tell him your name."

"It's a possibility," he replied knowing they would be very shocked when they learned the truth of the matter. "And King Langward already knows exactly who I am. I doubt I would be here in Weston if he did not."

"I'm just glad that you are here to spend my birthday and yours with me," Aurita said as she looked up into his eyes.

He leaned down and kissed her again.

*****

"He has no fear," General Kannon said with a chuckle. "When he takes his father's place, he will do well."

"Of that I have no doubt," Langward replied with a grin. "I expected he would obey when I asked him to kiss her, but I didn't expect more than a quick kiss."

"That was certainly more than a quick kiss," General Kannon replied. "But he has always tried to exceed what was expected of him."

They found Burkhart working in the shop. They closed the door with the guards on the outside. Burkhart was quickly on the floor before him, yet he was smiling instead of his usual serious expression.

"Rise, my friend," Langward said and Burkhart got to his feet. "I see that you are in a good mood today."

"Yes, My King," Burkhart replied. "Your son took my suggestion without hesitation, although he looked shocked that I was telling him to kiss my daughter."

Langward laughed then said, "When I said that Aurita seemed very happy and asked what had happened, he admitted to kissing her in front of you. I then ordered him to kiss her in front of me."

"What happened?" Burkhart asked with obvious interest.

"He kissed her without hesitation," Langward replied with a grin.

"And from the length of the kiss, he obviously didn't care who was watching," General Kannon added.

"Your plan is working perfectly," Burkhart said. "I had been worried about what he would think of me after reading the book of laws, but he told me that although he understood why the people hate me, he could see I was not the same man who wrote those selfish, evil laws. It took some of the burden from my heart to know that he does not hold my past against my daughter."

"I'm glad to hear that," Langward said. "I wanted you to know that there is trouble to the west. It is fairly minor so far, but I am worried that before long it will become much more. My son and his three friends will be assigned to patrols around Weston. I have told him to reveal his identity to his friends while he is here. He asked if you knew, but I told him only that you knew everything that you needed to know."

"I will watch what I say to him," Burkhart replied.

"I have told him he may stay another couple of days," Langward said. "How have you been doing?"

"I am well," Burkhart replied. "We have enough money to care for our needs."

"Good," he said. "I feel that as soon as the trouble to the west dies down, they might be ready to be married."

"I know how happy that will make Aurita," Burkhart said. "Once she is married I only ask one thing."

"What is that?" Langward asked.

"That you release me from this world and let me rest beside my wife," he replied with a tremor in his voice.

He was very surprised at the request, yet he could see that Burkhart was very serious.

"It is the only thing that I want other than to see Aurita happy," Burkhart said. "Yet if you feel that I must remain alive, I will obey without question."

"By the time the day comes, I will have an answer for you, My Friend," Langward said as he put his hand on Burkhart's shoulder. "I promise you this, if I decide to grant your request, it will be by my hand and no other."

"Thank you," Burkhart said. "Some nights I dream of my wife calling to me. My heart wants to go to her, but I know that I am bound to remain until my daughter is married."

"No one lives forever," Langward said. "The time will come for you to answer your wife's call. Until then I know that you will continue as you have. I know that I cannot order you to be happy, but I do not want you to be miserable either."

"I know," Burkhart replied. "Both of you have been most kind to me. It has made my life bearable to know that you do not hate me."

As they left, Langward was worried about Burkhart. He had not expected the request Burkhart had made. He had hoped that Burkhart had gotten past wanting to die. If the day came that Aurita and his son were married and Burkhart asked again, he would grant the request, but there would not be any witnesses to the execution. He owed Burkhart that much.

"What's the matter, Son?"

The Minister's words brought his mind back to the present. He drew his horse to a stop.

"I need to talk to you for a moment," Langward said as he dismounted.

"I'll wait with the guards," General Kannon said. "Take your time."

"Thanks," he replied as he followed the minister into the church.

They went to the small office at the back of the chapel. He sat down in a chair and the Minister closed the door. He looked older than Langward had remembered him to be as he sat down at the desk.

"What troubles you, Langward?" he asked.

"I just spoke to Burkhart," he began. "My son has fallen in love with Aurita and she with him. It has been something I had worried about knowing that someday they would be married but not being able to tell them. Burkhart was happy to see that they were in love."

"But what is bothering you?"

"It may be a while before I can marry them because there is trouble in the west that may lead to war with Okiah," he replied. "When I mentioned to Burkhart that I wouldn't marry them until the trouble is settled, he asked me something."

He tried to think of a way to explain it.

"What did he ask you?" the Minister inquired. "He has seldom asked anything of anyone."

"He said that in his dreams his wife calls to him," Langward said watching the Minister's eyebrows raise. "He asked that once his daughter is married that I release him from this world that he might answer his wife's call."

"Release him from this world?" the Minister repeated as though he didn't hear it right.

"He wants to die," Langward said. "He wanted to die the day his wife died, but I would not execute him."

The Minister leaned back in his chair and closed his eyes. Langward knew that the man who had raised him as his own would be able to counsel him as no one else could. Several minutes passed before the Minister spoke again.

"What was your reply?" the Minister asked.

"That when the day came, I would have an answer for him," he replied. "I also told him that if I decided to grant his request that it would be by my hand and no other."

Again the Minister's eyebrows raised in surprise.

"I have come to consider Burkhart my friend," he explained. "If he is to die by my order, then I want to make certain that he dies with dignity in a swift and painless manner. I do not want him to die by the hand of a man who hates him. I can only pray that if I do take his life, his daughter can find it in her heart to forgive me."

The Minister stared at him for several minutes before saying, "I do not feel it will come to that. Something tells me that although he will hear your son promise to marry Aurita, he will not see them wed."

"I had already decided that if he asked after their wedding, I would grant his request," he replied. "I would do it in private with no witnesses although I would not hide from anyone what my intentions were."

"You will not have to bear that burden," the Minister said. "He will die the death of an honorable man in service to Brinley."

"That makes me feel better," Langward said as he finally relaxed a bit. "I thought I should mention to you that my son will be in Weston until the day after his birthday. His three friends are here with him. I have asked him to reveal to them his true identity. I still do not want anyone else to know, especially not Aurita."

"Why do you hide this from her?" the Minister asked.

"Because she would not dare think of loving him if she knew the truth right now," he replied. "She is still adjusting to the idea that I am not angry with him for kissing her. She will learn the truth before they are wed."

The Minister shook his head and laughed.

"You had best see your mother for a few minutes before you leave," he said as he stood up.

Langward followed him out of the church to find his son and three friends outside. The young women were nowhere in sight. He decided that he might as well admit to them that their friend was his son.

"You four, come with me," he said and they followed him to the door of the house.

They stopped short at the door.

"Come in," he said. "I have something to tell you."

His son caught his eye with a questioning look.

"You didn't tell me you were coming, Son," Mother said as she put down the spoon she had been stirring the pot over the fire with.

"I didn't have time to once I decided to come, Mother," he replied as he hugged her. "I thought you might like to meet my son's friends."

He turned around to find the men looking confused, surprised and almost frightened. It was hard not to laugh.

"This is Major Kon, Major Monau, and Major Kennar," he said as he indicated each in turn.

"This . . . ," Major Kon began.

"You're. . . You're?" Major Kennar asked looking at his son.

"No . . . ," Major Monau added.

Mother burst out laughing and he joined in as he put his hand on his son's shoulder.

"The reason I haven't given anyone my name is that I don't have one," his son said.

"I had heard that the prince had no name," Major Kon said. "But I didn't believe it."

"The reason he hasn't been allowed to tell anyone his identity is for his safety," Langward said. "I need your promise not to tell anyone, especially not anyone who might tell Aurita who he is."

The men looked at each other and nodded.

"We swear," the three said in unison.

"I still can hardly believe it," Major Monau said shaking his head.

"Show them your birthmark, Son," he said as he removed his tunic and turned around.

"They're the same," one of them exclaimed.

"No wonder you seldom take off your tunic," another said.

He turned around and put his tunic back on.

"You've grown since I last saw you," Langward's mother said as she hugged the prince. "You look happy."

"I am happy, Grandmother," he replied. "Father has assigned us to patrol Weston once we become patrolmen."

"I'll enjoy being able to see you more often," she said. "I got you something for your birthday."

She went to the trunk in the corner and got something out. When she returned she held a small book and a long narrow wooden box.

"There are ink and a pen in the box," she said. "It's a journal for you. I tried to get something that wouldn't take up too much room in your saddlebags."

"Thank you, Grandmother," he said as he hugged her.

"Go on now and find your women," Langward said.

"They were going to fix us some supper," Major Kon said.

"We were going to find some flowers for them," Major Kennar added and Langward laughed as they left.

"I'm so glad he has friends now. He looks so happy," Mother said. "I had been so worried about him."

"We all have," he replied. "But part of why he is so happy is that he kissed Aurita today. I'm certain he is still confused about why I am not angry and have assigned him to Weston."

"So you are still going to marry the two of them?" she asked as Langford entered.

"What's up with your son?" Langford asked. "I've never seen him smiling quite like that. He looks like you did the day Retanta said she would marry you."

"He kissed Aurita," Langward replied with a laugh. "I noticed the same thing about Aurita when I brought the horse for her to learn to ride. He admitted to kissing her in front of her father. I asked him if he would kiss her in front of me and he did."

Langford began to laugh.

"It was obvious that neither one cared who watched them kiss," he continued as Mother and the Minister joined in on the laughter. "It's just a matter of time before he asks me if he can marry her."

"If she doesn't ask first," Langford said. "I just saw her and her friends. They were very excited and she looked happier than the rest of them. I noticed she was wearing some expensive looking earrings."

"My son spent four months of wages on those earrings," Langward explained with pride. "I can't wait to tell Retanta."

Chapter 17 – Haunted by His Past

When the door closed behind King Langward and General Kannon, Burkhart sat down and put his face in his hands. He was not accustomed to such sudden changes in emotion. His heart ached for his wife. Although it made him happy to see the prince kissing Aurita, it reminded him of kissing his wife. He at last knew that the prince would love and care for Aurita as she deserved to be. And he knew that it was by the prince's choice, not anyone else's. Although he had a lot of work to do, he felt all numb and achy inside. He did not know how long he sat and silently cried.

"What's the matter, Father?"

He jumped at Aurita's question. He had not heard the door open.

"You're crying," she said as she knelt at his side.

He looked down at her beautiful face that was so much like her mother's and his heart ached with the thought of it.

"You look so much like your mother," he said in a whisper. "I miss her so much."

"I sometimes hear you crying in the night," she said as she took his hand in hers. "You call out my name, but I realize that it is my mother that you are calling out to."

"She calls to me in my dreams," he admitted. "Once you are married, I hope to be allowed to rest next to her. I don't want you to grieve for me. Just remember that I will be where my heart wants to be. I love you very much, but soon it will no longer be my job to care for you. You will have a husband who will love and care for you. You will have a long and happy life. You will be free of the burden of my past and my shame."

"How can I be happy without you?" she asked as her hand began to tremble.

"Your mother and I will be watching over you," he replied as he drew out the key that was hanging on a cord around his neck. "We will always be with you in your heart. When I am gone, take this key. There is a box under everything in my chest next to the bed. Do not open it until King Langward has spoken to you."

"What is in it, Father?" she asked.

"When I was sent here, I was allowed to bring with me what would fit in one sack," he said. "There were very few things that I cared to

V.J.O. Gardner

bring. I think you will understand when you see what is in the box. I have left a letter of explanation for you as well, but you must not read it until King Langward has told you the full truth of my past."

"Is it really that terrible?" she asked.

"I'm ashamed to admit that it really is," he said. "I have met and spoken with the man you will marry. He knows the full truth of my past, yet he has forgiven me for it. He will not be afraid or ashamed to say that his wife is my daughter."

"Who is he?" she asked. "Do I know him?"

"I can tell you no more. I have promised King Langward that I would not. I can tell you that he does not know that he will be your husband. King Langward knows that he cannot order you to love the man he has chosen. He is hoping that in time, you and this man will love each other and ask to get married. That way he will know that you will be loved and happy."

"It is all so confusing," she said with a sigh. "I was so worried that King Langward would be angry with me and the major, especially when he ordered the major to kiss me while he was watching. I was afraid, but the major was not. Then after we had kissed, he told the major and his friends that they would be assigned to patrol Weston."

"I'm glad to hear that. I like the major," he said.

"I found out that the major's birthday is the same as the prince's birthday," she said. "I don't even know what to give him. He spent a lot of money on these earrings. I can't believe he spent four months wages on them."

"I don't think he cares what you get him for his birthday," he said. "I think he only cares that you are happy."

The door opened again and the prince looked in. He came in and shut the door behind him. He drew over a stool to sit next to Burkhart.

"What is the matter?" he asked.

"I miss my wife," he said with a sigh. "Aurita looks so very much like her. When I saw you kissing her it reminded me of kissing my wife."

"I'm sorry," the prince replied as he put his hand on Burkhart's shoulder. "I did not mean to stir up old memories for you."

"It is not your fault," he said as he met the prince's gaze. "It could not be helped. There will soon come the day that Aurita will be married and I will ask for release from this world. King Langward has promised

200

that if he grants my request, it will be by his own hand. It is a comfort to know that I will meet my end at his hand."

"King Langward has told me much about you," the prince said. "I know that there are no words of comfort that will ease your pain. I do want you to know that no matter who it is that will marry Aurita; I will make certain he knows I will be watching. I will not tolerate it if he does anything that will make her unhappy."

"Thank you, My Friend," Burkhart replied. "That alone comforts me more than you could know. You two should go be with your friends."

"Are you certain you will be alright?" Aurita asked.

"Yes," he replied and tried to smile. "Even though it reminds me of the past, it makes me happy to see the two of you kiss. I have worried so that no one could see beyond my past to love you."

She smiled and kissed his cheek as she stood up. The prince patted his shoulder before rising to his feet. Burkhart was grateful for his kindness. He had worried that the prince would kneel as Aurita had, but that would have made him feel very uncomfortable since it should be him on the ground at the prince's feet.

*****

Aurita was quiet as the major closed the door behind them. He turned and looked into her eyes. He stroked her face softly with a look of concern in his eyes. She buried her face into his shoulder as she felt the first tears coming. She had not known that looking at her could cause Father such pain. She did not want him to die, but knew there was no way to stop him if that was what he was determined to do. He had always tried to hide his loneliness from her.

"I don't want him to die either," the major said softly to her.

She looked up into his eyes and he leaned down to kiss her lips. His kiss was tender and his arms comforting. She wished she could just marry him even if he wouldn't tell her his name.

"Are you ready to join the others?" he asked. "They are waiting for us."

She nodded, not trusting her voice. He led her by the hand to near where the brook joined the river. The other three couples were talking as a small animal cooked over the fire. They talked while they waited for the food to cook. It felt good to sit with the major's arm around her, but it felt even better to know that he would not get in trouble for it.

They were just finishing eating when Carria's father showed up. He looked angry.

"Here you are, sitting around in the dark with this man," he said in an angry tone.

"We were just eating supper," Carria replied as Major Monau stood up. "We just finished."

Major Monau offered her his hand and helped her to stand up.

"Sir," Major Monau said. "I realize that you don't like me very much, but I do need to speak with you."

"You're right," her father responded. "I don't like you at all. You have kissed my daughter and who knows what else."

"I have kissed and held her hand," Major Monau responded. "I have kissed her lips and held her in my arms, but nothing else. I have done nothing that she needs to be ashamed of, nor anything that I would not do in front of you. I could never do anything to hurt her in any way because I love her."

Carria's father seemed surprised by this confession.

"I wanted to find out where I would be assigned as patrolman before speaking to you about this," Major Monau continued. "But just today King Langward himself assigned the four of us to patrol Weston when our training is completed. I did not want to make her decide between staying here with you and her mother and moving to where I was assigned. I love her very much and I beg your permission to ask for her hand in marriage."

Major Monau's voice was calm, but Aurita noticed his hand was shaking.

Carria's father looked stunned as he turned to look at Carria.

"What do you know of this?" he asked her.

"It is what I have been hoping for, Father," she replied. "I was beginning to think he didn't love me. I love him."

He was silent as he looked from one to the other. Carria's mother approached, but stopped short as she looked between the man and their daughter.

"What is going on?" Carria's mother asked.

"This man claims to love our daughter," he responded. "He wants to marry her. I'm not certain I trust him."

"I saw him kiss her the last time he was in Weston," her mother replied as she came to stand next to her husband. "He did not force her to kiss him."

"Has he ever forced you to do anything?" Carria's father asked.

"No, Father," she replied. "I wanted him to kiss me. In fact he has only kissed me twice."

"You said you would not do anything that you would not do in front of me," the father said. "What about children?"

"After she is my wife that would be for her to decide," Major Monau replied. "I will not force her to do something she does not want to. I do want children, but I will respect her decision."

The father looked at his wife who was smiling. Carria stepped beside Major Monau and put her hand in his.

"I suppose if you are to be my son, I should get to know you better," the man said with a sigh.

"I won't be leaving for a few days," Major Monau said. "I could spend the next two days with you and your family, but I will not spend the night in your house. I will sleep out here with my companions."

"I will see you first thing in the morning then," the father said. "Kiss him good night and then it is time to come home, Carria."

*****

He chuckled softly as he watched Carria throw her arms around Monau's neck and kiss him. Carria smiled before leaving with her parents.

"I think it is time we escort the women home," he said as he stood up. "We will go as a group."

"I'll stay and watch the fire," Monau said as he sat down.

They dropped off Noka and then Barna before turning toward Aurita's home. They were just passing the small tavern, when several men came out carrying something large.

"Where are you taking me?" asked an almost familiar voice. "Aren't you going to beat me?"

"We don't want any trouble with King Langward," one of the men replied. "You need to just go home."

"Father?" Aurita said and ran over to where the men had set down their burden. "What's the matter with you?"

"He's drunk," one man said.

203

"He only had one drink, but it is the first I've seen him drink since arriving in Weston," another said.

"He keeps insisting we beat him," a third said.

He sighed. Although the men seemed confused by Burkhart's actions, he knew exactly why he was acting this way.

"Kon, Kennar, take him home," he said. "I'll be right behind you."

They tried to lift Burkhart, but he was too heavy for them to lift.

He whistled and soon heard a horse galloping up behind him. He stroked the horse's nose before flipping the reins over his neck. He led the horse over next to Burkhart and gave it the command to lie down. He heard Aurita gasp as the horse laid down beside Burkhart. He would have to think of a way to explain why he knew how to make the horse lay down. He helped Kon and Kennar get Burkhart laid across the horse's back before getting the horse to stand back up.

He watched them disappear in the darkness before saying, "Burkhart wanted you to beat him because he feels guilty for his past. Also he is still grieving for his wife. Physical pain may be easier to bear than the pain he feels in his heart."

"I remember seeing him smile once as we beat him," one of the men said. "But what made him come looking for us to beat him today?"

"He knew that I had been making copies of the book of laws," he replied. "I'm not certain why he cares what I think of him other than he wants to know that someone who knows his past can love Aurita anyway. When I arrived this morning, I found him in the cemetery. He was worried about what I would have to say about all of the evil laws he had made when he was in power."

"You have read his laws and still do not hate him?" one asked. "You do not know what it was like to live under his rule."

"I have studied Brinley's history," he said. "Although I was not yet alive, I have been told of the suffering and hardships the people endured at his hand. I do hate King Burkhart, yet I cannot hate the man who asked you to beat him tonight. Although it is the same body, I believe that he is not the same man. King Burkhart would not have been allowed to live, but this man is of little consequence."

"You speak like King Langward does," one of the men said. "You said something about loving Aurita. Are you to be her husband? You would have Burkhart as a father-in-law."

"I do not know who will be her husband," he answered honestly. "I do love her enough to marry her and I don't care that Burkhart would be my father-in-law. King Langward has specifically told me that part of my duties includes watching over and protecting Aurita and Burkhart. I had best go help them get him into bed."

He left the men standing in the dark in front of the tavern. He had been surprised that they had compared him to his father. It did make him feel good. He was worried about Burkhart though. He was glad he would be in Weston for a few more days. Perhaps it would be best if he suggested that Kon and Kennar spent time with their potential fathers-in-law which would leave him time to keep an eye on Burkhart.

He found them standing in front of the door trying to decide what to do. He heard Burkhart snoring.

"I don't think we can lift him even with the major's help," he heard Kon say.

"The floor is dirt," Aurita's voice said. "If we moved the table, the horse might be able to get beside the bed and we could drop him off onto the bed."

"Are you certain you want a horse in your house?" Kennar asked as Aurita looked up to see him approach. "It might get spooked."

"I think the horse will be just fine," he said. "Let's get the table moved."

They soon had the table and chairs moved into a corner opposite the bed. With difficulty they turned Burkhart and positioned him so he was laying face down backwards on the horse with his legs hung down on either side of the horse's neck. He led the horse slowly through the wide doorway and into the tiny room. The horse stood calmly next to the bed as they pushed Burkhart off onto the bed. After he took the horse back out, he returned to find Aurita pulling off Burkhart's boots.

"I'll take care of him," he said.

"Where did you learn to get your horse to lie down like that?" she asked as he pulled off the second boot.

"I have done some guard duty at the palace," he said as he began unfastening Burkhart's tunic. "The prince helped me train the horse."

"I haven't seen him in so long," she said as she pulled a chair over and sat down. "What is he like? Did he ever mention me?"

He rolled Burkhart onto his side to hide his smile.

"He is nice," he replied as he began to take off Burkhart's tunic. "He asked what you looked like now. He has a basket you wove for him on the night stand next to his bed."

"What does he keep in it?" she asked in a surprised tone.

"Apparently he doesn't keep anything in it," he answered as he finally got the tunic off of Burkhart. "He likes to sit or lie on his bed and hold it. He turns it around in his hands looking at the interwoven colors and thinking about you."

"You're teasing me."

"No," he said. "Honest. That is exactly what he does."

She was silent for a moment as he covered Burkhart up.

"I wonder why Father is acting so strangely."

"I think I understand," he replied. "He knows that I know everything about his past. He knows that I know all about what evil he did before your birth. He was worried that I would hate him and not be able to love you because of his past."

"You know his past?" she asked. "Will you tell me?"

"I have sworn to King Langward that I will not."

"Why doesn't he want me to know?" she asked with a note of distress in her voice.

He knelt at her feet before taking her hands in his and kissing them.

"King Langward knows that you and your father have no other family. He does not want you to hate your own father. He knows that your father would not survive more than a day or two without your love. He also knows that you need your father right now. Once your father has died, King Langward will tell you the whole truth."

"What if King Langward dies first?" she asked with a tremor in her voice.

"Then the task falls to me," he replied honestly. "I will have Kon and Kennar go with Barna and Noka for the next two days. They should be getting to know their future families anyway. I will spend my time here. I will not leave Weston until I am certain that your father will not do this again."

"What about when you leave?" she asked. "I don't want to be without you."

"I don't want to leave either," he replied as his heart leapt. "I will finish my training as quickly as possible. There is some trouble to the west that King Langward fears will not be resolved without going to battle. That is why we have been assigned to patrol here when we finish training. He knows that we will protect this village no matter what the cost."

"Do you have to go tonight?" she asked. "Can't you stay here?"

"It would not be right," he replied as he stood up. "Your father should not wake until late morning. I will be down where we ate supper. It is not far if you need me and I will be back shortly after dawn."

She stood up and looked into his eyes. He softly stroked her face before he turned and left. He closed the door softly behind him and sighed.

"What?" Kon asked as he picked up the horse's reins.

"It's hard to love someone enough to die for her knowing someone else will be her husband," he replied, glad for the darkness as they made their way toward camp. "I think the two of you should spend time with Barna and Noka's families for the next two days. I have a feeling that I should stay close to Burkhart in case he tries something else."

When they arrived in camp, Monau was putting more wood on the fire.

"It's about time you guys showed up," Monau said. "Your horse ran off all of the sudden."

"I whistled for him," he replied as he tied the horse for night. "Burkhart was at the tavern and drunk. We had to take him home and he was too heavy to carry. I'll have to make some of General Kannon's special hangover cure in the morning."

They began rolling out their bed rolls for night.

Once they had lain down, he heard Kon ask, "What was it like growing up in the palace?"

After a moment's thought he said, "It is a bit like living in the barracks, no privacy and someone else always telling me what to do, eat and wear. The children of the palace staff always teased me and picked fights with me because I have no name."

"I always thought it would be great to be a prince," Kon said. "That doesn't sound like much fun at all."

"Why are you in the military?" Kennar asked. "Isn't it too dangerous?"

"Father said he wanted me to learn what it was like outside the palace," he answered. "When I become king I need to remember what life is like for the people of Brinley. The reason I can't tell anyone who I am is that if no one knows who I am, no one will intentionally try to kill me."

"I bet there is a lot to learn to become king," Monau said.

"I learned to read when I was five or six," he said. "I learned the language of the northern kingdoms when I was about eight. I was studying most of the time. Now when you guys get a day off to visit your families, I get to stand guard in the throne room during audiences. If I am lucky I get to eat a meal with my parents."

"Suddenly, spending time with Carria's father doesn't sound so bad," Monau commented.

"Get some sleep, dawn comes early," he replied.

As he drifted off to sleep, he thought about how nice it was to finally have someone who knew who he was to talk to about everything.

Chapter 18 – A Hangover and Learning to Ride

Aurita had the hardest time getting to sleep. She had always liked the prince, but never realized that he must like her too. She was surprised by the major's comments. She had no idea that he would know the prince. When she was young, she had dreamed about marrying the prince and becoming queen, but had never told anyone. She knew she loved the major, but also knew it didn't matter who she loved. King Langward had chosen her husband long ago.

She was still tired in the morning when dawn came. She had just gotten dressed when there was a soft tap at the door. She hurried down the ladder and opened the door. The major smiled as she let him in.

"You look tired," he said as he kissed her hand. "If you show me where things are, I'll make breakfast."

She showed him where everything was. He took the bucket to get water while she went to the outhouse. It wasn't long before he returned and got the porridge on to cook. Father was still snoring loudly. She set the table with two bowls and spoons. When they sat down to eat, he held her chair out for her. She wasn't used to such treatment. They had just finished eating when Father finally started to stir.

"Oh," he groaned as he sat up in bed.

He held his head in both hands. His expression was one of pain.

"You really shouldn't drink," the major said as he pulled a small flask out of his pouch. "This should take away some of the pain."

Father drank the contents of the flask.

"What was that?" he asked. "It was bitter."

"General Kannon's special hangover cure," the major replied as he helped Father to stand. "Come have some breakfast."

"First, I need to go to the outhouse," Father said.

Father looked very unsteady on his feet. The major put one of Father's arms over his shoulders and helped Father outside. She had just finished washing the bowls and dishing up Father's breakfast when they returned. Father looked a little better as he sat down to eat. She wished she knew why Father was acting so strangely. She felt like the major knew a lot more than he was willing to tell her. Perhaps someday she would understand.

Once she had washed Father's bowl and spoon, she said, "I've got to go work on my baskets. There're a couple of special orders I need to complete today."

*****

Burkhart watched Aurita leave. He knew she was unhappy because of him. The prince stayed with him. He did not understand why the prince was so patient with him and his foolishness.

"Thank you," he said to the prince. "I don't remember anything last night after being sat down in the road in front of the tavern. I know you must have brought me home."

"King Langward told me that one of my duties was to watch over you and Aurita," the prince replied. "I am to protect you two and make certain that you have what you cannot provide for yourself because you are not allowed outside the village."

"Yet, you seem to take it a little more personally than that. I know that you love Aurita very much. I can see it when the two of you are together. She loves you too."

"I know that," the prince replied. "But, both of our fates were decided long ago. I know that King Langward assigned this duty to me because he knew I would take it personally."

"Would you marry her if you could?" Burkhart asked even though he suspected he knew the answer already.

"Yes," the prince replied without hesitation. "I would marry her today if I could. But I will not disobey King Langward. There has been trouble to the west and rumors of war. You cannot do anything stupid like last night. Even though you have no sword, I know that you would be able to defend her if necessary. I cannot always be guarding her. King Langward has ordered the patrols to protect her from harm, but there is only so much they can do."

"I know," he said with a sigh. "I have heard the same rumors of war and it worries me to be so close to it. When I first heard of this man who wanted to take the throne from me, I heard that he was cowardly and heartless. After I gave him the throne, I soon learned that the one who was cowardly and heartless was me. Just as I would die protecting my daughter, I would die protecting King Langward and his son. Not only did King

210

Langward give me my life, he helped me to see the truth about myself. I owe him a great debt; one that can never possibly be repaid, not even with my own blood. Although it is the blood of our ancient kings that flows in my veins, it is worth less than the dust that mars King Langward's boots."

"Come on," the prince said. "You had best not let Aurita hear you say things like that. You are her father and I know she loves you. I think that is part of why King Langward has ordered your past hidden from her until after your death. Are you going to work in the shop today?"

"I would prefer to go back to bed," he said as he stood up. "But Aurita will worry. I have a couple of chairs that need to be rubbed with sand until they are smooth and then oiled. I think I can do that without making my head hurt any worse. I don't know how my father could stand to drink as much as he did."

"What was your father like?" the prince asked as he opened the door.

"He ignored me most of the time. Then when he would drink, he would beat me and call me worthless. I don't think I ever did anything right in his eyes. I was his second son. My older brother died shortly after I was born," Burkhart said with a sigh. "One day my father was very drunk and started to beat me. I finally couldn't take any more. I pushed him away hard and he fell, hitting his head against the wall. I left the room and went to my own. When they found him he was dead and I took his place. Last night was the first time I had ever gotten drunk."

"That explains a lot," the prince said as he turned the knob on the shop door.

He sat down on his stool to begin his work. He was grateful for the understanding and concern the prince showed for him. He was also very grateful that the prince would be Aurita's husband someday. She was worthy of the prophesy that his blood would mingle with King Langward's even if he was not.

*****

"I was beginning to wonder about you two," Aurita said as the major sat in a chair near her. "I've just about finished this one and the other won't take too long. I'll need to deliver them."

"Once they're delivered, do you want to learn to ride a horse?" the major asked.

"I still don't understand why I need to learn now," she replied. "But I've always wanted to try riding a horse."

"I'm not certain either, but if King Langward has ordered it, I will teach you," he replied with a smile.

He watched her as she wove the baskets. He seemed very interested even though she could not understand why he could be interested in baskets. Father quietly worked on two chairs he had finished yesterday. He looked terrible and she wished he would just go back to bed. She wondered what had brought it on. She had been frightened to hear him ask to be beaten. She just couldn't understand why he would desire such a thing. The major had been very calm about the whole thing. He had dealt with the village men and with how to get Father home as though he had done such things before. Even though she loved him, much about him was a mystery to her.

"What's the matter?" the major asked and she looked up suddenly.

He looked sincerely concerned.

"Just thinking," she said as she finished the basket.

"You were frowning," he said as he picked up the other basket and stood up.

"Just worried," she said. "Father, you should be in bed. I'll be back to fix lunch."

"Just worry about you and the major," Father replied as he put down the oily rag. "I'm really not hungry. I can fix myself something simple if I get hungry. You shouldn't burden yourself worrying about a foolish old man. Go have some fun with your friends."

She gently kissed his cheek before picking up the second basket and leaving the shop. The major smiled at her as they turned toward the village. They soon had the baskets delivered and were turning toward where the horses had been left the night before when the minister approached.

"There you are," he said. "I've dropped off some lunch to your father, Aurita. My wife wanted me to see if you two would like to have lunch with us."

She glanced at the major who smiled and nodded slightly.

"We would love to," she replied. "Thank you for taking lunch to Father. He's not feeling well today."

"I heard about what happened last night," the minister said as they walked toward his house.

She felt herself begin to blush.

"It's actually a bit surprising that he hadn't done such a thing sooner," the minister said.

"I just don't know why he would do such a thing," she said as she shook her head.

"He told me that his father used to get drunk and beat him," the major said. "I think he has been thinking about the past a lot lately. He misses your mother terribly."

"I know it has been very difficult for him to raise me alone," she said quietly.

"He has done very well considering that when he arrived here he couldn't even take care of himself," the minister said as they reached the house by the church. "He didn't even know what a diaper was; let alone how to change one. But I know that the last thing he wanted to do then was to disappoint King Langward."

Aurita thought about that as they ate. The conversation was light and she was surprised at how comfortable the major was with the minister and his wife. It was almost like he had known them all of his life. She knew that wasn't likely since they were King Langward's parents. After they ate the major took her around to the cemetery to a particular grave stone.

"Did you know that the minister is her second husband?" he asked. "This man was her first husband and the father of King Langward and his brother Langford. The minister is his brother."

"I think I remember Father saying something about that a long time ago," she replied.

"I wanted to tell you something about how King Langward became king," he said. "You may not understand why it is very important for you to know and believe this, but in time you will."

She looked into his eyes and saw that he was very serious. She knew that he would not lie to her. If there was something he was not allowed to tell her, he would say so. She nodded.

"King Langward did invade and capture the palace," the major began. "There were a few deaths among the palace guard, but most laid down their swords without a fight. When the former king saw King

Langward, he knelt down before him with the royal armbands held up to him. There was no force involved. The former king gave the throne to King Langward of his own free will and decision. Although he took the palace by force, the throne was given to him without him asking or demanding it."

She wondered why it would be important for her to know this. The major was the first person ever to speak to her about the former king of Brinley.

"What happened to the former king?" she asked doubting she would get an answer.

"At that time his fate was sealed," the major said. "You will learn of his fate when King Langward has decided the time is right for you to know. I know you hate having things hidden from you, but I do understand why it must be this way. I also know that King Langward always keeps his promises. He has never lied to me. I know that he has kept things secret from me, but it is because I asked a question and he told me it was not something he was willing to tell me at the time. He has promised that in time you will be told everything and I know he will keep that promise."

"I am always surprised by how comfortable you are around King Langward and his family," she said as they began walking again. "I remember the first time we met. You did not seem bothered by who my father was. I was certain that you had to know about his past since no one is allowed contact with us without being told who Father is and what they can and cannot say around me. And yesterday you kissed me in front of King Langward without any hesitation even though you could have been in a lot of trouble. You did not seem the least bit nervous."

"I actually was a little nervous," he admitted. "But I knew that I would be in more trouble if I didn't obey him. I keep no secrets from King Langward, especially when it concerns my contact with you. I even showed him this and what you embroidered on it."

He pulled the handkerchief she had sent to him out of the tunic pocket that was over his heart. She didn't know what to say. The major was a very brave man indeed if he could show such a thing to King Langward. She knew that nobody wanted to make King Langward angry. She had been told that he had personally executed one man. He was a very large and powerful man physically, but he left no doubts that he was strong in other ways as well. Everyone respected him.

"Are you alright?" the major's worried voice broke into her thoughts.

She looked up and found they were at the edge of the village near where the horses were staked out to graze.

"Just thinking," she said.

"About?"

"About how brave you are to be able to tell King Langward that you love me even though you could be in a lot of trouble," she replied. "And how you are not ashamed to let others see you kiss me."

"There's nothing to be ashamed of," he replied, his smile betraying the serious tone in his voice. "I would never do anything that either one of us need to be ashamed of. I know that I must accept King Langward's decisions about your future and who you will marry. I know that if asked, I will stand at his side at your wedding and not protest."

"You would do that?" she asked in surprise.

"Even though my heart would be breaking because I want to be the one your hand is bound to in marriage," he replied without hesitation.

She could not believe what he was saying. He wanted her to be his wife, yet he would sacrifice his own happiness for her. He was a man who, like King Langward, had an inner strength that was so much more important than any physical strength. She finally understood why King Langward had chosen him to teach her some of what she would need to know. He could be trusted to do exactly as ordered and she would be completely safe with him.

"I'll go get the horses," he said.

She watched him walk across the field to the horses. She knew she was in love with him. She knew that if the choice was hers that she would choose him as her husband even though she didn't know anything about his family or even his name. It didn't matter to her.

He was very patient with her as she learned to mount and dismount. It was an awkward process and she even fell once, but he caught her in his arms. When she looked up into his eyes, he was smiling at her. By the time he actually let her stay on the horse, her legs and arms were getting sore. He mounted his horse and showed her how to guide the horse using the reins. He showed her how he used his heels to make his horse go faster. Since both her feet were on the same side, there was a long stick bound in leather with a loop at one end for her to use on the right side of the horse. They walked the horses around the edge of the village and back to her house. By the time they arrived, it was nearing suppertime.

"You're doing well," he told her as he tied the horses to the hitching rail near the shop. "If you like, we'll do it again tomorrow. I'll see if I can get permission to let you ride in the field."

"I would like that," she said as they walked toward the house. "I have really enjoyed spending the entire day with you."

He paused at the door and smiled at her.

"I have too," he replied as he opened the door.

Father was inside and had the table set for supper. He looked like he felt much better.

"How was your ride?" he asked as he began dishing up the food. "I saw you riding when I went to get water."

"I liked it," she said. "The major said we can do it again tomorrow."

"You look better than you did this morning," the major commented as he held her chair for her.

"I feel better," he said. "I'm sorry I put you to so much worry and trouble."

"Just don't do it again," the major said. "You even had those men confused and worried about you. I understood last night part of why you had done it and I explained that to them."

"You are much too kind to a foolish old man," Father said.

There wasn't much talking during supper. She knew that even though they were speaking out loud in front of her, there was even more that they weren't saying. They seemed to understand each other even when their conversation left her completely confused. Once they had finished eating, the major drew her into his arms and kissed her tenderly before leaving. Father was doing dishes when she climbed the ladder and got ready for bed.

*****

When the prince reached their camp, he found his friends talking about their day. He sat down and quietly listened.

"I think he had me doing every dirty job there was to do on a farm," Monau said. "I'm glad I brought a change of clothes. I had to wash the other ones because they smelled so bad."

216

"Noka's father had me on the roof putting on new shingles. My hands are full of slivers," Kennar said. "I even caught him laughing at me once."

"Barna's father said that Noka's parents have been very curious about you," Kon said. "I also heard that Carria's mother likes you, Monau, but her father might take a while. His father-in-law hates him."

"That explains a lot," Monau said. "I just hope he won't hate me. That would make Carria miserable."

"You're awfully quiet," Kennar commented. "I saw you teaching Aurita to ride today."

"She needs some practice, but she's doing well," he replied.

"How's Burkhart?" Kon asked.

"His head hurt really badly this morning," he replied and the others laughed a little. "I don't think he'll ever try that again."

"I still don't get why he wanted them to beat him," Monau said.

"He said his father used to ignore him except when he drank. Then he would beat Burkhart. He says the physical pain is easier to endure than the pain in his heart from missing his wife. One of the village men commented that he once saw Burkhart smile as they were beating him."

"That's sad," Kon said. "I never thought I would feel sorry for Burkhart."

"Me either," the other two echoed.

The prince explained about how Burkhart gave the throne to his father.

"You are right about him not being the same man who sat on Brinley's throne and caused such suffering among the people," Kennar said. "Even though many of the villagers still hate him for his past, they do admit he is a changed man."

"Let's get some sleep," he said. "You'll probably need it."

217

Chapter 19 – Threat from the West

He woke early the next morning while the others were still snoring. He got up and rolled up his bed roll. When he looked up, he saw Carria's father standing not far away. The man gestured for him to come over to him. He was curious about why he wanted to talk to him.

"How long have you known Major Monau?" the man asked quietly.

"A few years now," he replied. "I met him the day I arrived at the military training camp."

"I've noticed that the others seem to respect you and I saw you talking alone to King Langward," the man said. "I heard that you were General Kannon's assistant."

"Yes, Sir," he replied. "But King Langward has seen fit to give me a special task from time to time."

"I suppose if King Langward and General Kannon trust you, I should be able to," Carria's father said. "If I ask you something, will you tell me the truth, everything I need to know?"

"I will not lie to you," he replied, wondering what the man would ask him. "I will tell you everything I can."

"What kind of man is Major Monau? Can I trust him enough to allow him to marry my daughter?" the man said. "I gave him all of the worst jobs I could think of yesterday and he did everything without a word of complaint. Even though I haven't wanted to, I have to admire his determination."

"He knows you don't like him," he replied. "But he loves Carria enough to try to change your opinion of him. His sister and her friend brought him a birthday gift last month. I could tell that the friend liked him, but he practically ignored her. In fact, she got angry because he was telling his sister all about Carria. He didn't even notice. He wanted his sister to tell their parents all about her. I know that he will do anything and everything you ask of him without question. If you tell him to never see her again he will obey, but it will be with a broken heart. From what Aurita tells me, I'm guessing that Carria would be quite unhappy as well."

"When he left last night, she was practically in tears," the man said quietly. "She was angry with me for what I had forced Major Monau to do. I heard her cry herself to sleep."

"I think you should know that part of why the four of us will be assigned here is because King Langward knows that we each have a reason to guard this village with our very lives. For Monau that reason is Carria, her mother and even you. I have heard that you had a difficult time with your wife's father when you decided to marry her. I know that this must be a very difficult situation for you."

The man looked surprised as he said, "You are right. I hadn't even thought about it in that way. I'm doing to him just what my father-in-law did to me. I've barely spoken to him in the last ten years. Before that we fought every time we saw each other. Although she seldom mentions it, I know my wife wants to see her parents again but she doesn't want me to fight with him."

"I cannot tell you what to do," he said. "But if you will give him a chance, I think you two could become friends. I do know that it may be some time before Monau is able to marry anyone because of his commitment to Brinley's military, yet I doubt his feelings for her will change. It is alright if you are not ready to make a final decision about your daughter right now."

"Thank you for talking to me," the man said. "Please don't tell him I talked to you."

"There are many secrets I am asked to keep," he replied. "I will not tell him."

"I had best get back home before my wife realizes I'm gone."

He watched the man as he walked away and then shook his head. He picked up a few sticks of wood and put them on the coals of last night's fire. He had just gotten the fire going again when the others began to stir. Monau groaned as he rolled onto his side and sat up.

"Sore?" he asked.

"Worse than my first week of training," Monau replied. "I thought I would be used to such physical effort."

"I suppose that doing work around a farm is not quite the same as wrestling and swordplay," he said with a laugh as Kon and Kennar sat up.

"My hands seem swollen," Kennar said as he held them palm up and looked at them.

"Let's go see if Aurita is up yet," the prince said. "She must know what to do about slivers."

"I'd best get over to Carria's house," Monau said as he stood up slowly. "I'm certain that I'm in for another day of hard labor."

He stretched before he rolled up his bedroll and left. Kon was rolling up Kennar's bedroll when they left for Aurita's house. They met her halfway to the well.

"I'll get the water for you if you will take a look at the slivers in his hands," he said after kissing her forehead.

Kennar held up his hands for her to see.

"Why didn't you come to me last night?" she asked. "Now they're infected. Come on."

As she led Kennar back to the shop, he took the bucket and headed toward the well. While he was drawing the water, he saw Monau's sister enter the tailor's shop with a patrolman. He suddenly had an idea. It might help if Carria's father met Monau's family. He left the bucket of water next to the door and went into the tailor's shop.

"You're Monau's friend," Sarriah said as she saw him.

"Yes," he replied. "I wanted to see if you could do something for him without telling him I requested it."

"What?" she asked.

"He spent all day yesterday doing all of the dirtiest jobs Carria's father could think of just to get her father to like him," he said. "If your parents could meet Carria's parents, it might help."

"They're meeting us here any time now," she replied as she glanced at the patrolman, who grinned. "We're getting our wedding clothes ordered. As much as I try, I still can't sew well enough for making wedding clothes. I haven't even told Monau yet."

"Congratulations," he said. "I'll let you tell him. I could arrange for lunch at the churchyard. You could bring your parents. I'll invite Monau and suggest he bring Carria and her parents."

"That sounds like fun," she said and the patrolman nodded. "I'd like to see him engaged to be married."

"I'll see you around noon," he said as he left the shop.

He was excited as he carried the bucket of water back to Aurita's home. He found Burkhart still asleep as he quietly left the bucket just inside the door. He went into the shop and found Aurita still pulling slivers out of Kennar's hands.

"You've got to be more careful when you handle split wood," she was telling him. "Or wear gloves."

Kennar just nodded as Aurita looked up.

"I saw Monau's sister at the tailor's shop. She's getting married soon," he said as he sat down beside Kennar. "I thought that we could all have lunch at the churchyard. I've invited her and her parents. I want Monau's parents to meet Carria's parents. It might help him get her father to like him."

"That sounds like a good idea," Kennar said before drawing a quick breath as Aurita pulled out a long sliver.

"I don't think Father will be up to it," Aurita said. "He didn't sleep well last night."

"We could bring him some food," he replied. "I'm going to go invite the others and ask the minister's wife if we can have lunch there."

"Do you think she'll mind?" Aurita asked as he stood up.

"No," he said as Kennar glanced at him. "I think she'll enjoy it. I left the water just inside the door of your house."

He kissed her on the forehead before leaving. He hurried to find Kon and Barna. When he arrived at Barna's house, he was surprised to find Kon's parents there.

"You look happy," Kon said. "What's up?"

"Monau's parents are here at the village," he replied. "I think that Carria's parents should meet them. We could all have lunch at the churchyard."

"I put a large pig on to cook," Barna's mother said. "I was just thinking it would be too large for just the six of us."

"Great," he replied. "I'll see you about noon then."

He found Noka at the well drawing water.

"Have you seen Kennar?" she asked.

"He's having Aurita pull all the slivers out of his hands," he replied with a laugh. "He should have borrowed some gloves."

"Father was a bit worried about that last night," she said. "I think he likes Kennar."

"I'm organizing a lunch over at the churchyard," he said. "Would you and your parents like to come? Barna's mother is cooking a pig."

"Mother made several pies last night," Noka said. "She cooks when she is happy and excited. She told me she loves Kennar. I wish I had met his parents."

"Before he met you, he would talk about them a lot," he replied. "Then he would get sad. His brother just got married and is moving to live near her parents."

"That means he'll own the house in town," she said. "It's awfully large for just him."

"But just perfect for a family," he said and laughed as she blushed bright red. "I'll see you around noon."

He was glad that Noka's parents liked Kennar. He stopped at Grandmother's house to ask her. She was out back washing clothes.

"Good morning," she said when she looked up.

"I was wondering if I could have a lunch here in the church yard," he said. "I've got the chance to let Monau's parents meet Carria's."

"Carria's father has looked angry the last couple of days," Grandmother said.

"Yesterday he gave Monau every dirty, difficult job he could think of," he replied with a laugh. "Monau is hoping to get Carria's father to not hate him so he did everything he was asked without complaining."

"I accidentally made a double batch of bread yesterday," Grandmother said. "I was wondering what to do with the extra. I'll expect you just before noon."

"Thanks," he replied.

Now all he had to do was convince Carria's father to come to the lunch. He hurried down the path that led to his farm. As he approached, he saw Monau carrying two buckets into the barn. He heard voices as he reached the barn.

"This horse looks awfully small to pull a plow or wagon," he heard Monau say.

"I received it in trade for some wheat," Carria's father answered. "It tried to kick the cart to pieces when I tried to hitch it up the first time. I guess it's only good for riding so it's pretty much worthless to me."

"When I finish my training in a month, I'll need a horse of my own," Monau said as he entered the barn. "Would you sell him to me? I'll pay you a fair price for him."

"You could discuss the price over lunch at the churchyard," he said and the two turned to look at him. "There'll be roasted pig, pies and bread."

"At the churchyard? Are the minister and his wife going to be there?" Carria's father asked.

"I've invited them," he replied surprised at the question. "She's providing the bread."

"What about vegetables?" Carria's father asked. "How many are coming?"

"Nobody's offered to bring any yet," he replied. "But I'm certain we'll have vegetables. There should be about twenty two in all."

"Go tell my wife how many are coming so she and Carria can get them cooking," the man said. "Come on, Monau. We've got some vegetables to pick."

He saw Monau flash him a smile before he followed Carria's father out the other end of the barn. He was hoping that meant they were getting along a bit better today. He went to the house and knocked on the door. It was one of the few in the village that had more than one bedroom instead of a sleeping loft. Carria answered the door.

"Good morning," she said, looking surprised as her mother appeared behind her.

"I've come to invite you to lunch at the churchyard," he said. "Your father and Monau are picking some vegetables to be cooked."

"How many people are coming?" Carria's mother asked.

"Twenty two in all if everyone comes," he replied.

"I'm surprised my husband agreed to come and offered vegetables," she said. "But he has been acting strangely today. I'm just glad he's not scowling anymore every time he sees Monau."

"That's good," he replied. "Don't tell your husband or Monau, but his parents are here in the village today. They're coming to the lunch. I thought it might be good for your husband to meet them."

"I've always wanted to meet them," Carria said.

"So have I," her mother said. "They raised a fine young man."

"I'll see you about noon then," he said with a smile.

He was very happy as he returned to Aurita's shop. Kennar was just coming out with his hands all wrapped up.

"It doesn't look like you'll be doing much work today," he said as Kennar looked up from his hands. "Noka was asking about you."

"Aurita said I just need to keep on the bandages for a couple of hours until the medicine soaks in," Kennar replied. "Did you get everyone invited?"

"Yes," he said. "Carria's mother said her husband had been acting very strangely today and was surprised that he not only agreed to come, but offered to bring vegetables."

"It ought to be an interesting day," Kennar replied. "I'll see you about noon."

He went into the shop and found Burkhart at work and Aurita putting things away.

"How are you feeling today?" he asked as he sat down next to Burkhart.

"Better," he replied. "I wanted to thank you again for being so kind to me."

"I know how difficult it is for you," he said. "I understand what it is like when those who should be your friends dislike you. Before I joined the military, I really didn't have any friends besides my grandmother. I spent a lot of time by myself or fighting."

Burkhart looked very surprised.

"Aurita told me about the lunch at the churchyard," he said. "I will go help set up for it, but I don't think I'll stay around to eat. This should be a happy time for your friends. I don't want anyone to feel uncomfortable because of me."

He patted Burkhart on the shoulder before following Aurita outside.

"He's still a bit sad," she said. "I'm worried about him."

"So am I," he said. "But I think he would get worse if he thought he was making you unhappy."

"Could we go riding this morning?" she said. "I think he needs some time alone."

"Sure."

*****

Langward read the message again. He chuckled to himself. He knew there must be so much more than what was said in the brief message sent by the Minister. He also suspected that his son had started the whole

224

thing. Perhaps he should take Retanta and General Kannon for a visit to Weston today. Retanta was very excited by the idea.

"It's been too long since I've seen our son," she said before she mounted her horse.

"I'm guessing that there's a lot that the message didn't say," General Kannon said.

"I'm certain of it," he replied with a laugh as they started out.

They arrived in Weston well before noon. He found Burkhart and the Minister busily arranging tables.

"I didn't expect to see you today," the Minister said as he hugged him.

"After reading the message, we had to come," he replied as the Minister hugged Retanta.

"I'll take the horses around back," one of the guards said and left leading the horses.

"I don't want them to know we've come," Langward said. "We can wait in the house."

"It's too busy in there," he replied. "Wait in the church."

*****

He and Aurita were the first to arrive. They were immediately handed dishes to be set out. Soon the others were arriving. The roasted pig smelled incredibly good. Carria and her mother arrived without her father and Monau. They looked worried.

"What's wrong?" he asked Carria's mother.

"My husband said he would be here soon and would bring Monau with him," the mother replied. "I don't know what has gotten into him."

"He did ask me to not tell Monau, but did not ask me to not tell anyone else," he said. "He came and asked me some things about Monau early this morning before the others were awake. Something I said made him realize that he was doing to Monau exactly what your father did to him."

"That would explain why he's acted so strangely today," she said. "The only work he's had Monau do is pick and clean the vegetables. He even told him to take Carria for a walk."

"Well, I guess we'll find out soon enough," he said as he saw the two men coming toward the church. "Here they come."

225

Carria's father was carrying a bag and appeared deep in conversation with Monau. When they got closer, Monau noticed his parents.

"Mother? Father?" Monau asked. "What are you doing here?"

"Sarriah is getting married soon," his mother said as she hugged him.

"Danau?" Carria's father asked in a surprised tone. "Is that really you? Monau is your son?"

"Rocar," Monau's father responded as he shook Carria's father's hand. "So this is where you ran off to. Monau has told us so much about Carria, but wouldn't say much about her parents."

"I've been giving him a rough time," Rocar responded. "I think we need to talk. Why don't we step inside the church for some privacy?"

Monau looked very confused.

"I didn't know your parents knew Carria's," he said.

"Neither did I," Monau replied in a worried tone. "Her father has been acting very strange today. He actually smiled at me. He has never done that before."

*****

Langward looked up as the door opened and two men entered.

"We didn't know anyone," one man said and stopped.

They both dropped to their knees after glancing at each other.

"Rise," Langward said after controlling his urge to laugh. "You are welcome here."

"We had no idea you were in here, My King." one of the men said.

"That was intentional," he replied trying not to smile. "What's in the sack?"

"That's what I wanted to speak to Danau about, My King," the man responded. "His son has expressed an interest in my daughter which she obviously returns. I found her finishing this last month. When I took it away from her, she cried for several days straight. Now I'm glad I didn't destroy it like I threatened to."

He pulled a white tunic out of the bag.

"How do you feel about this, Danau?" Langward asked.

226

"If Rocar isn't opposed to the union, neither am I," the other man replied. "I know Monau didn't want to propose to her until he knew where he would be stationed on patrol duty though."

"I just assigned him and his three friends to patrol Weston," Langward replied as he watched Danau begin to smile. "How far is Major Monau in his training, General?"

"Nearly completed," General Kannon responded. "I was preparing to assign him to a patrol for a week's trial."

"Perfect," Langward replied. "Since everyone seems to be here, why don't we have the wedding today after lunch?"

Both men glanced at each other and nodded.

"I'll inform the Minister and my mother," Langward said. "It might be fun to surprise everyone else. Let's go see if lunch is ready yet."

"You have a strange sense of humor, dear," Retanta said as they stood up. "But that's one of the things I love about you."

When they stepped outside, there were several gasps as everyone dropped to their knees.

"Rise," Langward said. "We're here unofficially today visiting my parents. There's little need for such formality."

"There should be enough to feed everyone," Mother said with a smile before she hugged him. "I'm glad you came."

He saw Burkhart begin to leave as Mother hugged Retanta. He walked toward Burkhart, who stopped.

"What's the matter?" he asked as he saw the look on Burkhart's face.

The man looked older than he had just a few days ago.

"I have been very foolish, My King," he replied. "I have made Aurita unhappy and worried because of my stupidity."

He drew Burkhart a little farther away and said, "Tell me what you did."

As Burkhart explained, he began to understand why Burkhart seemed to have aged years in a few short days. He knew that Burkhart would not last many more years regardless of anything he did.

"Like me, you are just a man," he said when Burkhart had finished. "Men do stupid things at times, especially when things seem hopeless to them."

227

"But you are more than just a man," Burkhart said. "You are so much wiser than I could ever be."

"I've done my fair share of stupid things," he replied. "But I learned from them. I know that this is very hard for you, but you must not leave Aurita alone in this world just yet. You need to protect her. I fear that we will be in war before many more days. You are the only one who can keep her safe right now."

"Your son told me the same thing," Burkhart said quietly. "Although he was quite stern in his admonition, he has been most kind to me. I told him some things that you should hear, but the memories are as painful as the day of Aurita's birth."

"I'll ask him later," Langward said. "Come and eat. We're going to have a wedding later. Mother might need your help."

"Yes, My King," Burkhart said. "I will help in any way I can."

He found his mother and the Minister talking to Barna and Kon's parents.

"We know that Kon might have to be gone for another month before being stationed here, but we thought perhaps they should get married now," Barna's father was saying.

"I don't think he'll need to be gone that long," Langward said and they looked at him in surprise. "That would make two weddings today."

"Who else?" Mother asked.

"Major Monau and Carria," he replied.

"What about Major Kennar and Noka?" a man asked. "I'm beginning to wonder why he hasn't asked me for her hand already."

"Three weddings then," the Minister said with a laugh.

"Let's not tell the couples until we are ready to have the weddings," Langward said.

"I know where Noka has the wedding clothes she made hidden," the man said. "I could go get them.

"I'll get the ones Barna made," her mother said.

"Let's have lunch then," Langward said. "We'll have the weddings afterward."

He joined Retanta at the table. General Kannon sat next to him with Burkhart. Retanta was talking to Aurita and their son who were sitting across the table from General Kannon. The food was good and everyone seemed to be having a good time. He was glad to see that even Burkhart was smiling a bit. Their son was telling them about his friends wanting to marry Aurita's friends. Langward chuckled to himself as he thought about how surprised the men would be very soon. After the plates had been cleared away their son went over to talk to his friends. Before long he saw Mother approaching with Rocar.

"Everything's ready," she said. "The women can get dressed in the house."

"I'll take the men over to my house," Rocar said. "My wife has started asking questions."

"Go let her in on our secret," Langward said as Retanta and his son approached with General Kannon.

"Kon, Kennar and Monau are all beginning to wonder what is going on," his son said quietly in the language of the northern kingdoms. "Monau is very worried."

"Their parents and I have decided they should get married today," he replied causing General Kannon to begin to laugh and his son look surprised. "It seems Carria's and Monau's fathers are friends."

"Carria's father spoke to me privately about Monau this morning," his son said. "I was still surprised to see him talking to Monau like they were old friends when they showed up for lunch."

"Come on," he said with a laugh as a patrolman handed him a small scroll. "Let's help get the men over to Carria's house to get ready for their weddings. Later you can tell me what Burkhart told you. He said it was a painful thing to discuss with anyone."

*****

His mother went to with the women to help get the brides ready while the prince followed his father and General Kannon. He was relieved to hear that Carria's father had finally decided to allow Monau to marry her. The prince was happy for his friends and hoped they would be happy when they finally discovered what was going on. They approached where his friends were talking and looking worried. They all quickly knelt.

"Rise," Father said in a stern tone. "I have a task for you three. Follow me."

He was having a hard time keeping a straight face as the three looked almost frightened. They fell into place with him behind Father and General Kannon and followed to Carria's house. When they paused to knock on the door, he glanced at Monau who looked pale. The door opened and they followed Father inside. General Kannon shut the door behind them. They found the women's fathers waiting for them with Monau and Kon's fathers.

"The task I have for you is one that is strictly voluntary," Father said seriously. "It is something you will each have to choose for yourself. If you agree to this, you will be making a lifetime commitment. Each of these men, General Kannon and I have made this same commitment. Although I cannot speak for the others, I know that I have never regretted making the commitment."

Father paused and the others echoed his sentiment. His friends were very confused.

"You three will have a unique opportunity to share this experience with each other," Father continued. "General Kannon's assistant has told me what close friends you are and I felt that you are ready for this commitment. You will all be permanently assigned to Weston within a week or two. General Kannon's assistant will join you shortly although he will not yet be ready to make this commitment. Do you have any questions?"

The three glanced over at him and he nodded.

"I have a question," Kennar said after swallowing noisily. "I see that the fathers of Noka, Carria and Barna are here along with the fathers of Major Kon and Major Monau. If I am correct, the only one missing is my father, who is dead."

"You are correct," Father replied.

"We three and General Kannon's assistant are the only ones present who are not married," Kennar said.

"You are correct," Father said as Kon and Monau stared with open mouths.

Father nodded and the fathers of the women each held out a stack of white cloth.

"I'd be proud to have you as my son," Carria's father said as Monau took the stack of cloth from him. "I'm sorry that I have been so rough on you. I spoke to the major here this morning before you were awake. He answered my questions and made me realize that I was treating you as my father-in-law treated me. I found out from your father that my wife's father has come to regret the way he treated me. I don't want that to happen to me."

When Monau looked over at him, he grinned and nodded.

"Kon," Barna's father said. "When I lost my leg, I did not know how I would take care of my family. I don't know what hurt worse, the pain in my leg or the pain in my heart that first night. You introduced me to your father who showed me that I could still stand on two legs and take care of my family. You comforted Barna and helped her see that I would recover. Since that day, I have considered you my son. Today, everyone else will too."

"I knew how hard it was at first for Father when he lost his leg and hand," Kon said as he took the stack of cloth. "And Barna was so beautiful even when she was crying, I loved her from the moment I first saw her."

"I wish I had met your father, Kennar," Noka's father said. "I know he is very proud of you. I am proud to have you as my son."

He could see a tear in the corner of Kennar's eye as he took the stack of cloth.

"If you three don't hurry, your brides will be ready before you are," Father said with a laugh. "That is if you want to get married today."

The three began to quickly change their clothes. It seemed strange to see them all in white instead of the grey green of a major's uniform.

"Why didn't you tell us?" they asked as they left the house.

"I just found out myself," he replied with a laugh.

"I wish you were getting married too," Kennar said.

"So do I," he replied with a sigh. "But I'll just have to wait."

They went inside the church and stood in front of the pews. People were beginning to gather and sit down.

"I can't believe this is really happening," Monau whispered. "After yesterday, I didn't think I'd ever get to see Carria again, yet here I stand ready to marry her. I don't know what you said to him, but thank you, Major."

"I know that any of you would do the same for me," he replied with a grin.

The people suddenly fell silent and they turned to see the three women being led in by their fathers. He stepped back a bit and watched as the fathers placed their daughter's hand in that of her soon to be husband. He smiled as their hands were bound together as the mothers wrapped them with cloth strips. He found himself wondering what his own wedding

231

would be like. It was certain to be held in the palace. Grandfather performed the ceremony and smiled as the couples kissed. He glanced at the parents to see that even Carria's father looked very happy.

The prince noticed Burkhart and Aurita standing in the back of the church near the door. Burkhart looked very solemn and knew that weddings would be very painful for him to witness. He wondered if Burkhart would live to see his daughter married. Aurita looked very pale and her smile seemed forced. He knew that if it were possible that she would be standing with her friends and her hand would be bound to his. The prince felt as though someone had stabbed him in the heart at that thought. He felt a hand on his shoulder and looked up to see Grandfather's concerned face.

"I know," Grandfather said quietly. "I know."

It somehow comforted him to know that Grandfather knew how he felt. He followed the crowd as they exited the church. When they got outside, Burkhart looked panicked. He reached Burkhart the same time Father did.

"When we got outside, Aurita began to cry and walked off quickly," Burkhart said in a worried tone. "I got caught in the crowd and now she's gone."

Father looked over at him and nodded. He took off at a run toward Aurita's house. He heard a scream just as he reached the corner of a house. He turned the corner to see Aurita on the ground with a man on top of her. He felt his blood boiling in his veins as he ran over to them. He grabbed the man's tunic and a fistful of hair, pulling him off of her. He threw the man to the ground and drew his sword. He had the point at the man's throat as he heard someone coming. He glanced up to see Father come around the corner followed by General Kannon and Burkhart.

"She is under the protection of King Langward," he said, surprised at the growl in his voice. "Any attack on her is considered an attack on him which is treason. The penalty for that is death, same as the penalty for the attack on her as a woman."

"Why should you or anyone else care what happens to her?" the man asked. "She is the worthless offspring of an evil tyrant."

He pressed his sword point firmly against the man's throat before he said anything more.

232

"She is not worthless," he replied as he felt his blood boiling. "I am assigned to protect her, a duty which I hold sacred. I willingly defend her unto my own death. My life is in the hands of King Langward as is hers. I will obey his command without hesitation even if I die in his service."

He didn't care if the man knew how he felt, but he did care that Aurita did. A crowd had begun to gather. He could hear Aurita's sobbing behind him.

"The Major is correct about the law. You have attacked a woman intending to take her honor from her. Also since she is under my protection your actions could be viewed as an attack on me," Father said sternly. "The penalty for both is death."

"Laws you made," the man grumbled.

"Laws that were made and voted on by the council," General Kannon said.

"You would execute this man at my command, Major?" he heard Father ask.

"Yes, My King," he replied without moving his eyes from the man's face.

"Do it," Father said and the man's face lost all color.

He moved his sword and with a swift stroke, cut off the man's head. As he watched the blood drip from his sword he heard Burkhart comforting Aurita. He knelt before Father with the bloody sword laid across his palms.

"Take her home," he heard Father say. "You have served Brinley well today, Major. I am very proud of this young man. He has been able to see past what Burkhart did long ago and does not hold Aurita responsible for it. He is also able to obey orders without hesitation or question. This is not because he cannot think for himself, but because he knows the law and makes choices and decisions based on that law. This young man will someday lead many. I know his parents are very proud of him and feel very lucky to have a man such as him as their son."

He was amazed at Father's praise in front of so many people. He could see that Mother was also proud of him as she brushed a tear from her cheek. The crowd murmured amongst themselves before quieting down.

"There has been trouble to the west," Father said. "Just before the weddings I received word that Okiah's army is massing on the other side of the river. It is with the help of men like the Major here that Brinley will defend herself from invasion. I feel a special bond with this village since I grew up here. I know that most here are farmers, not soldiers, but there is something that you can do during war. The men that will defend Brinley and this village will need food. Two of the best healers in Brinley live in this village. Soldiers who are wounded will need their care to heal. I do not expect you to fight, but only to do what you can to help those who fight."

He could see the people nodding.

"This man needs to be buried," Father said.

Several men stepped forward to lift the body and head. He felt himself begin to tremble as he finally realized that he had indeed taken a man's life.

"Let's go check on Aurita," Father said as he laid a hand on his shoulder.

He just nodded and began walking toward Aurita's house. He began to realize that he had wanted to kill the man even if it was with his bare hands. He had never before felt such anger. He knew that he had wanted Aurita for himself, like a wild animal fighting for a mate. As they began to cross the bridge over the brook, he stopped.

"Go on ahead, Retanta," Father said. "I think she'll respond best to a woman right now."

He turned and watched the water as it flowed toward the river. The water reminded him of the blood that had flowed from the man's neck. His stomach was in a knot and his heart ached.

"Taking a man's life should not be an easy thing to do, Son," Father said softly as he felt Father's hand on his shoulder.

"That's the problem," he replied with a tremor in his voice. "I would have killed him even without a sword."

They stood in silence for a while. He knew that he must admit what was in his heart and why he had been so angry.

"I know that you have chosen a husband for Aurita," he began as he fought to not choke on his words. "I also know that I must marry the woman you have chosen as my wife, but it will always be Aurita that I love. I meant every word I said."

"I know you did. I know that you want her for yourself, and I know that she wants you," Father said in a surprisingly gentle tone. "I wish that circumstances were different right now. If not for the war, there would have been more than three weddings today."

He turned and looked at Father. His expression was very serious.

"In time I hope you can forgive me," Father said. "I hope you will be able to see why I have handled things the way I have. I am confident that when the time comes for you to take the throne, you will rule wisely. I know that this is very difficult for you, but I promise that when the conflict with Okiah is over, I will tell you everything. I will keep no more secrets."

He nodded, not trusting his voice. They both turned as Mother approached.

"She's asking for you, Son," Mother said. "She won't even talk to me or her father."

"I know this won't be easy for you," Father said. "But it is very important that you are the one to comfort her. I know this doesn't make sense right now, but it will later."

He left Mother and Father standing on the bridge. He paused with his hand on the doorknob to collect himself. He knew he must be strong for her. He opened the door and stepped in. Burkhart looked very worried and frightened. He did not see Aurita as he looked around.

"She's up there," Burkhart said.

He patted Burkhart's shoulder and went over to the ladder near Burkhart's bed. He drew in a deep breath before beginning to climb. He could hear her sobbing in the darkness of the sleeping loft. The mattress was empty and he heard sounds back in a corner farthest from the ladder.

"It's me, Aurita," he said softly. "I'll stay right here and not come any closer unless you ask me to."

His eyes were beginning to adjust to the darkness as he sat with his legs hanging down the hole. He heard some shuffling and her pale face appeared to his left. He had never seen her this frightened.

"D . . . did you mean what you said?" she asked with a tremor in her voice.

"Every word of it," he replied.

"Y . . . you would die for me?"

"Without hesitation."

"Y . . . you must have family and responsibilities beyond protecting me," she said. "I am not worth your life."

"But you are to me," he replied. "Although I have family and must take on a lot of responsibility when my father is ready for me to take his place, I would give all of it up for you."

"You never speak of your family or your life beyond protecting me," she said. "You're not ashamed of it are you?"

"No," he replied trying to think of how to explain it.

"I'm tired of things being hidden from me," she said. "I wish I could leave this place and live somewhere that no one knew who I was so that no one would hate me. That man said that since I was so much trouble for the village, I should serve the men of the village. I don't know what he meant."

He felt his blood boiling again because he knew exactly what the man meant.

"You owe no man that, not even your husband," he said, trying to keep his voice calm. "What he wanted from you is yours alone to freely give. If you do not love your husband, he should not try to take it by force. If he does, I will kill him just as I killed the man who attacked you today."

"You would do that?"

"Even if it meant I must die," he replied without hesitation. "I cannot hide the fact that what that man tried to take, I want with all of my very soul, but I will not take it by force. I love you too much to ever hurt you."

"What about the woman who will be your wife?" she asked in a whisper.

"Certain circumstances require that I do marry and produce children," he said with a sinking heart. "I must do what I must do, but not until you are married and happy. Not even King Langward can command me to do otherwise."

"You would disobey him for my sake?" she asked in a whisper.

"Yes."

She was silent for a very long time. He heard quiet voices in the room below. His emotions were all jumbled up inside him. He dared not touch her knowing how much he wanted her. He was finding it very difficult to not hate Father right now.

"I should have stayed with Father," she said quietly as she crept closer to him. "But my heart ached so. I wanted to be standing there with my hand bound to yours."

His heart pounded in his chest as he felt her brush against him. He had wanted the same thing.

"I want you as my wife," he whispered. "I have wanted that since General Kannon first brought me to Weston."

"I want to be held in your arms," she said as she sat next to him.

He carefully put his arms around her. She leaned against him and began to cry again. He lost track of time as he held her in his arms. He knew it might be the very last time he was allowed to hold her. He could feel her trembling as she cried. He could smell food cooking but even though he felt hungry, the smell of her was more attractive to him.

"Are you two going to come have some soup?" Father's voice asked.

"I don't want anyone else to see me," she whispered. "I don't want them to think I am ugly."

"You are not ugly," he replied. "The only ones here are your father, King Langward, Queen Retanta, and me. You are very beautiful to us and we all love you very much no matter what you look like."

She pulled back and looked into his eyes. He took the handkerchief from his pocket and gently wiped the tears from her face before putting it back.

"Come on," he said. "You go down first and I'll follow you."

She finally nodded before going down the ladder. When he reached the bottom of the ladder, he saw that Mother was hugging Aurita.

"It will be a long night for her," Father said softly as he placed his hand on his shoulder. "You must do what you can to restore her self confidence tonight. We go to war at dawn."

He nodded as he felt his chest tighten around his heart.

"My wife will return to the palace tonight under cover of darkness and heavily guarded," Father continued. "You will be under Colonel Rowand's command."

"I will not fail you," he replied before they went to sit at the table.

Everyone was silent as they ate crowded around the tiny table. Aurita did not look up as she slowly ate. Father and Mother exchanged worried glances. He was glad that even Mother seemed very concerned for Aurita. He just wished she were returning to the palace with Mother instead of staying here, but he knew her skills as a healer would be needed.

When they finished, Burkhart silently gathered the dishes and began to wash them.

"It's time to go, Retanta," Father said gently.

As Mother turned toward the door, she glanced at him, smiled and nodded. He knew she was telling him that she loved him. It was what she did when she could not reveal that he was her son. He smiled and nodded back. He noticed Aurita was crying again.

He pulled a chair over next to her and sat down.

"I don't want you to go to war," she whispered hoarsely. "I want you to stay here with me."

"I know," he said. "But I must protect you, which means protecting Brinley. It is my sworn duty. I wish that you could be farther away, but you are needed here. You are a skilled healer."

"I know," she said with a sigh. "How can I heal men when I am afraid of them?"

"You have a lock on the door," he said and she nodded. "They will be in the shop. You can lock yourself in here when you sleep. Your father will not allow anyone to harm you."

"Can you stay here tonight?" she asked as she finally met his eye.

"Yes, but I must leave at dawn," he replied. "You must know that you are always in my thoughts. I will do everything I can to stay alive."

"I know," she said. "I know."

Burkhart was busy at his bed and seemed to not hear what they were saying. He suddenly turned around and stepped aside. He had piled things in the corner between the head of the bed and the wall.

"Come here and sit on the bed," he said. "You can lean against this while you hold her in your arms. I know that it is the only way either one of you might get some rest tonight. I will sleep on the floor."

"As will I," Father said as he shut the door quietly behind him.

He felt stunned and confused as he pulled off his boots before getting onto the bed. He sat down and leaned against the stack of clothing, pillows and blankets. Aurita sat down next to him. He stroked her cheek softly before taking her and turning her to lie across his lap. She shifted a bit in his arms until she was comfortable. He watched Father and Burkhart fix beds on the floor. It felt very strange to think he was spending the entire night in a bed with Aurita while his father and hers slept on the floor beside the bed.

"We must all have our sleep," he told her softly. "Dream of me."

"I almost always dream of you," she replied. "Kiss me goodnight."

He leaned down and tenderly kissed her lips. He felt her hand on his neck as she returned his kiss. He watched her in the dying firelight as her eyes drooped and finally closed. Her body relaxed against him and her breathing slowed.

Chapter 20 – Anger and Responsibility

Langward awoke at dawn to find everyone asleep. He smiled at the sight of his son holding Aurita in his arms while they slept. There was a faint smile on his lips. He wished that there was a way to avoid war, but he just couldn't see any.

He put more wood on the fire and put some water on to heat. Burkhart began to stir. He looked confused as he sat up. Langward put one finger to his lips before pointing to their children. Burkhart turned back toward him and smiled.

"As soon as this war is over, I will tell them," he said in a whisper.

"I know they will both be very relieved," Burkhart replied softly before getting a sack of porridge off the shelf. "I just hope she can find it in her heart to forgive me."

"That's why I won't let anyone else tell her," he replied. "She need not spend the rest of her life hating her father for something that he has repented of."

"Thank you," Burkhart replied. "I am forever in your debt. You and your son have been so very kind to me even though I do not deserve it. Until I got to know you, I did not know what it was to have a friend."

"I have found that everyone deserves a chance to redeem themselves," he replied as he saw his son begin to stir. "They're beginning to wake."

His son smiled as he looked at Aurita asleep in his arms. Langward knew it would be a difficult goodbye. He kissed her softly on the forehead and she began to stir. He was so gentle and loving with her. He would make a kind and loving husband.

"Breakfast is almost ready," Burkhart said as he set the table.

By the time Aurita had returned from the outhouse and his son had left, Langward was dishing up the porridge. When he returned they sat down and ate in silence. He could see that Aurita was fighting back tears. When they finished, his son kissed Aurita goodbye and went outside.

"I don't want him to go," she said softly.

"I know," Langward replied. "But it is something he must do. In time, you will understand. I have done everything I can to insure his safety under the circumstances. I promise you will see him again."

She smiled softly.

"Take care and keep yourself safe as well," Burkhart said.

"I will, My Friend," he replied before leaving.

He found his son fussing with the saddlebags and bed roll on his waiting horse. Langward put his hand on his shoulder but he did not turn around.

"Leaving your mother to join the military was the hardest thing I ever did," he said quietly. "I know that you love her. When this is all over, I will tell you everything. It will be time for you to learn the full truth. I promise your life is worth living."

"I love her, Father," he said softly. "I want her for my wife, yet I know that I must obey you."

"I know," he replied. "I can promise you that you will love your wife very deeply. Aurita will have a very kind and loving husband which she will love. She will be well cared for and never want for anything."

They mounted and turned toward the south. Four guards joined them.

"What was it that Burkhart told you?" Langward asked as they reached the edge of the village. "He said it was a painful memory for him."

"His father used to drink a lot and would beat him. His father hated him and called him worthless," he replied. "One day he couldn't take anymore and pushed his father away. His father hit his head on the wall and when he was found he was dead."

"That does explain a few things," Langward said as they approached where General Kannon and Colonel Rowand were waiting for them. "Report."

"Our scouts have confirmed the message you received," General Kannon said. "Our army arrived late last night. They are smaller in number than we are, but the forest could hide many men."

"Are our troops ready?" he asked.

"And awaiting your orders," General Kannon replied.

"Give these two a chance to join Colonel Rowand's men before giving the order," he replied. "I want to make the first strike."

He watched his son ride off without looking back. He knew that he was angry with him, but it could not be helped right now.

"I've never seen him like this," General Kannon said quietly. "You don't think he'll do something stupid and get himself killed, do you?"

"I hope not," Langward replied. "I have been giving him hints lately, but I don't think he gets it yet. I practically told him this morning. I hope I said enough to give him the will to live. He's very angry with me right now and I hope when he learns the truth he will forgive me."

"In time we will know," the general replied. "Let's just get this war settled first. I made certain Colonel Rowand understands that he must be kept out of the main battle as long as possible."

"Good," he replied as he saw a movement in the distance. "There's word that they've joined the troops."

He signaled back for the attack to begin. He wanted to draw them out before engaging in a full scale battle. He dreaded knowing that some of Brinley's men would not return home, but that was the nature of war.

*****

"Our assignment is to make certain no one gets around the main battle," Colonel Rowand explained as they turned north. "You will lead a unit of twenty men."

"So I will be kept from the main battle," he said bitterly. "Father is determined to protect me by keeping things from me."

"You are Brinley's future," Colonel Rowand replied. "I can tell that you are very angry with him, but don't go getting yourself killed just to get back at him. Brinley needs you. I personally picked the men you will lead, but have not told them who you are. I told them that I was told you were to be known only by your rank."

He rode silently until they reached the unit. He was glad to see Sergeant Caddaric and Corporal Adamok along with a few other familiar faces. He knew Colonel Rowand was right. He hoped they would see some of the battle anyway. For the next few weeks, they caught a few of the Okiahns trying to get across the border, but drove them back. There were a few minor injuries, but none of his men got killed.

At first most his men were not too certain of his leadership, but soon they began to trust him. Most of them were older than he was. Sergeant Caddaric and Corporal Adamok both stayed very close to him. He noticed that Sergeant Caddaric was very skilled and knowledgeable in combat while Corporal Adamok was more reserved. Yet, when there was a disagreement amongst the men it was Corporal Adamok who was able to settle the disputes without his intervention. He also seemed very knowledgeable about the past politics between Brinley and its neighbors. He was unafraid to express his opinions in that regard even when they differed from those of the other men. He appreciated their assistance and their companionship.

The unit eventually became more unified and efficient. General Kannon had sent a package and a scroll sealed with his father's signet ring to him with a scout. When he opened the scroll he found it to be a decree advancing him to Colonel.

"What is it Major? Sergeant Caddaric asked and he handed him the scroll.

His eyes widened as he read the scroll.

"I've seen one of these before but it had a name," Sergeant Caddaric commented quietly.

"If it were for anyone else there would be a name," he replied as he opened the package to find three colonel's tunics.

"I'll tell the men."

It had been two long months since he had last seen Aurita and he thought of her often even though he tried not to. Many evenings, the men would talk about their wives or girlfriends. He would go over the maps and try to not listen to what they were saying. Such talk reminded him of how he felt about Aurita and having to watch her marry someone else. Another popular topic was rumors of large fire breathing beasts that flew in the skies to the east. The rest of the men seemed terrified by the idea that such a beast lived so close to Brinley. One of the men swore he had actually seen one at dusk when on patrol on the eastern border. This evening the topic over supper was again the women they had left behind. He took his plate over to his tent and began looking over the maps that he had long ago memorized.

"May I have a word with you, Colonel?"

He looked up at the man. He was one of the oldest in the unit. He looked worried.

"What is it, Major?" he replied.

"Perhaps it would be best to discuss this in private," Major Fyodor said.

He stood up and led the way to a more private spot away from the campfire.

"What did you want to discuss?" he asked.

"I have noticed that you eat with everyone else unless we begin discussing our wives," Major Fyodor said. "At first it seemed you wanted to study the maps, but you must have them memorized by now. Is anything wrong?"

He knew he could not hide how he felt forever.

"My life is not quite as simple as most men's," he said. "Certain circumstances dictate my future and who I must marry. The woman who will become my wife was chosen long ago, almost before I was born. There is a woman that I have come to love with all of my heart. I would give my life to preserve hers, yet I cannot ever hope for her to be my wife. There are certain other complications that I am not allowed to reveal that make some of the discussions over supper difficult for me to listen to. I do not mean to be rude and I know it is not fair to forbid those topics because of my feelings."

"That explains a lot," Major Fyodor said. "We all have wondered why it was ordered that you be known by rank alone. From what you just said I gather that it is safer for you if no one knows who you are."

"Soon after this war is over, it will be time for me to face my future and all that goes with it," he said. "At that time my identity will no longer be a secret, yet I know that at that time I will not have to worry about who knows and who doesn't."

"It isn't something you are ashamed of, is it?"

"No," he replied in surprise. "It is just the way it must be for now. When you learn my identity, you will understand. Just so you don't wonder, when I first started at the military training camp, it was as a private like everyone else. I trained along with everyone else to earn my rank. Until this war I was General Kannon's assistant, but that did not get me any preferential treatment. Instead, it meant that I had to work twice as hard as everyone else."

"Some of us were a bit worried about your age at first," Major Fyodor said with a laugh. "But we soon realized that you had earned your rank. No one here doubts that. Caddaric and Adamok vouched for your abilities and trustworthiness. I'll try to keep the conversations over supper on a lighter subject. Some of the other men get a bit out of sorts after talking about the women they left behind."

"Thanks," he replied.

They returned to the camp to find the men not on watch preparing to go to sleep. He was not wanting to sleep quite yet, so he sat by the tiny fire that had died down to coals and wondered what Aurita was doing. When this war was over he would ask his father to let him marry Aurita. He knew he would not be able to marry anyone else. The question was how exactly to convince Father that Aurita should be his wife. Before he knew it the moon was directly overhead.

"Colonel," a corporal said in a whisper as he knelt next to him. "There is light and movement in the trees across the meadow."

"Wake the men," he replied quietly. "They will not pass."

Soon the men were awake and assembled. He led them along the edge of the meadow just inside the tree line. They took no torches, using the moonlight to guide their steps. As they approached the lights, he heard men's voices speaking in the language of the north.

"What are they saying?" one of the men whispered to him. "Do you understand that gibberish?"

"Yes," he whispered. "Maybe we can find out something useful."

"We've lost a lot of men, My King," one of the men said. "We had no idea they were that well trained."

"That's no excuse," another man said angrily. "We've known for years they planned to invade. They increased their men along our border to threaten us."

He realized they were talking about Weston.

"We may be small, but we will not tolerate this hostility," the angry man continued. "We must kill their king."

He knew they must be stopped. If his men could take this camp, they would have their king.

"Take your men to the main battle," their king said.

"That will leave you with only ten guards," the first man said.

"They don't know I'm here," the king said. "I will be safe. I'll move down to the bend in the river. The bank is steep and tall, they won't be able to attack me there."

He signaled his men to retreat back to camp. They reached the camp just in time to cover the last of the coals before the enemy's king passed with his guards on the way to the bend in the river.

"We're cut off," one of the men whispered.

"We'll attack at dawn," he replied. "There will be ten men and their king. If we are successful, we can end this war. They said we are better trained than they are. They are losing many men in battle. Get some rest, dawn comes soon."

He tried to rest but was too nervous to sleep as he waited for the dawn. He knew that what he was doing could be very dangerous, but it would insure Brinley's victory. As the sky began to lighten with the coming dawn, he woke the men.

"We'll take the horses as close as we can before advancing on foot," he said. "If we can surprise them, we should be able to take them without much trouble. It would be best if we can capture the camp without killing anyone. I will capture their king while you take the rest of the camp."

They left the horses just out of sight of the enemy's camp. They crept through the trees and brush until they were at the edge of the camp. The men spread out in a line across the edge of the camp to cut off any escape. There were men preparing breakfast. While they watched, a man who was dressed in fine robes and a crown came out of a tent and walked toward the point overlooking the river. He signaled the attack.

There were many shouts and confusion as they captured the enemy. He went straight to their king and soon had him at sword point.

"Brinley does not start fights, but we will finish them," he said calmly in the language of the kingdoms of the north.

"A king should not be captured by a lying colonel," the king replied in an angry tone.

"Perhaps my other title is more suited to the situation," he replied. "I am the son of King Langward and heir to his throne."

"I don't believe you," the king replied and spit at him.

"You probably wouldn't believe that the reason Brinley increased patrols along this border was because it is where the man who was King Burkhart has lived since he gave the throne to King Langward. To leave the village seals his death," he said.

"I had heard that Burkhart still lived," the king replied in a surprised tone as someone shouted.

He saw a movement out of the corner of his eye as someone shouted, "Father!"

The sudden impact drove him and his attacker off the steep bank into the river. He broke the man's hold on his neck just before they surfaced. He gulped in air as the water pushed him down again. He was pummeled against rocks before surfacing again. He could see the other man floating face down near him. He was in pain as he fought to catch the man and turn him on his back. The water battered against him as he fought to gain the shore. He was just about spent as the water finally pushed him the right direction. He gave one last push against the rocks under his feet before pulling the man to shore and collapsing next to him.

*****

Langward was surprised at the signal he just received. The enemy's king had been captured. He and General Kannon approached the river to speak to the patrolman who had signaled when two men washed up onto the bank of the river. His heart froze as he saw the ring on one of the men's hands. It was his son!

"Pull them out of the river quickly!" he ordered as he leapt from his horse.

He checked to find his son was still alive, but looked very battered. The other man lived as well. From his clothes he could see that the man was one of the enemy, but did not wear a soldier's uniform. His clothes showed he was probably Okiah's prince. They were both unconscious.

"Now there's a story I'd like to hear," General Kannon said as he knelt beside Langward.

"Yes," he replied as the guards picked them up. "Take them to Aurita. Post a guard. This man is their prince. He is to be well treated, but he is now our prisoner."

"Where is their captured king?" he asked the patrolman, who had joined them.

"Almost at the northern border of Brinley," the man replied. "I'll lead you there."

When they arrived, Brinley's soldiers had the king sitting on a rock under guard. His guards were tied to trees. The king had his head in his hands and did not move as Langward dismounted and approached.

"Your son is alive," he said and the man looked up in surprise. "As is mine."

"So he wasn't lying," the king said as he stood up. "And my misjudgment of your intent has led us to a needless war."

"So it seems," Langward said. "It's not too late to put things right. Can you signal your armies to stand down?"

"Yes," the king replied. "Release that man and I will give him the orders to take to my general."

They untied the man the king had pointed to. Soon the king had written out his orders. Langward read over his shoulder as he wrote it out. It simply said that the war was over and to withdraw. As the king sealed the orders, Langward went to the point overlooking the river. He signaled for his troops to withdraw to the east side of the river and received a confirmation signal.

"Do you need writing materials to give your orders?" the king asked.

"The signal has been given," he replied shaking his head. "My troops will soon begin withdrawing to the east side of the river."

"Your son said that the increase in patrols was to guard your predecessor," the king said. "I had heard that you took the throne by force, but had let Burkhart live."

"I did take the palace by force," he replied. "But Burkhart gave the throne to me. He lost all will to live that day because his wife died giving birth to his daughter. The child lived and the two have been in the village ever since. He has realized the harm he had done to the people of Brinley and is a changed man. At this point the patrols are more for their protection than anything else."

"You are different than I had imagined you," the king said. "Can our kingdoms live in peace?"

"Yes," Langward said with a smile. "I believe they can."

*****

Aurita was horrified as she realized who one of the injured men was. He wore a colonel's tunic instead of a major's, but it was him.

"This one is our prisoner," one of the guards said. "He is their prince. King Langward ordered him well treated, and well guarded."

"Put him over there and the colonel in this one," she said as she indicated the two beds closest to the fireplace. "They'll both need dry clothing. Call for Langford, he went home to eat."

Chapter 21 – Treaty and Change

The voice was persistent as it intruded into his clouded thoughts. He felt movement against his skin that was punctuated by pain. When he was finally left alone, he ached all over. He had no concept of how much time had passed until his head began to clear. The ache had subsided to be replaced by pressure on his left arm, shoulder and chest. He tried to put his right arm on his chest to move whatever was there, but his hand found what felt like hair. His head ached as he tried to think what it could be. He drifted off into sleep again not knowing where he was or why.

He slowly opened his eyes. Most of the pain and ache were gone, but he didn't recognize where he was. He heard quiet voices talking not far away in front of him. He turned his head and saw a fireplace flanked by shelves and small tables. Something about it was familiar.

"It's about time you rejoined the living," a familiar voice said as Kennar's face came into view.

"Where am I?" he asked.

"Aurita and Burkhart's shop," Kennar replied. "Well, it's hardly a shop anymore now that it is filled with the wounded."

"How long?" he began to ask.

"Since you washed up out of the river where the brook feeds into it," Kon said as he stepped into view. "Aurita's been sleeping with her ear and one hand on your chest. She says it is to make certain you still live, but I'm certain there's more to it than that. Burkhart just shakes his head and grins."

"My father," he began, and then stopped.

"You washed up right at his feet," Kennar said. "Along with him."

He lifted his head enough to see a man lying in the opposite bed. Four guards stood around the bed. The man was asleep.

"Who?" he asked, not quite remembering how he had gotten into the river.

"Their prince," Kon said. "He is quite angry and won't speak to anyone. King Langward and his father are busy writing out a peace treaty. We caught him trying to get to you. You've got some bruises on your neck that I'll bet match his hands."

"I had their king at sword point," he said as he finally remembered. "He attacked me and we both went into the river. He was trying to choke me. When I got free and surfaced, I found him floating face down. I remember dragging him ashore, but nothing after that."

"If anyone else told that story, I'd say they were lying," Kon said. "But I believe every word of it coming from you. No one else I know of would save the man who tried to kill him."

"Except your father maybe," Kennar added.

He laughed, but it was painful.

"Aurita should be here any minute to give you your morning bath," Kon said with a grin. "She'll be glad to see you awake. You've been asleep for five days."

"Bath?" he asked.

"She uses a basin of water and a cloth to wash you," Kennar said. "She's quite thorough, but you're the only one around here that gets anything more than their wounds cleaned."

They laughed as he began to blush.

"By the way," Kon said. "She's been calling you Brook."

"She said since you wouldn't tell her your name, she would give you one herself," Kennar said.

"I think I'll pretend to be asleep while she's bathing me," he said as he heard the door open.

They quickly moved to stand at the foot of the bed and he closed his eyes. He tried to relax as he heard soft noises next to him. Soon he felt a warm, soft cloth washing his face. It was hard not to wince at the pain when she ran the cloth across a sore spot. He felt the covers being pulled back and soon felt his arms and chest being washed. It felt very good to him in spite of the occasional pain. Suddenly he felt himself being sat up and held in her arms as she washed his back.

"I wish you would just wake up, Brook," he heard her say softly. "It hurts me to see you like this."

"And if I woke up would you kiss me?" he asked softly and she jumped.

"Oh, Brook!" she exclaimed as she pulled back. "Were you awake the whole time I was bathing you?"

"And enjoying every minute of it," he replied with a smile. "I like my new name."

"I got tired of calling you by rank," she said. "You've had me so worried."

"I'm sorry," he replied as he brushed the hair from her face. "I've worried about how you've been doing. I've missed you so much."

He leaned forward and tenderly kissed her lips.

"Are you hungry?" she asked. "I've got some porridge ready."

"I'll have a little," he replied. "Am I allowed to get out of bed?"

"Only if you take it easy," she replied as she picked up the basin of water.

"I promise," he said.

She left and he uncovered his legs and swung them off the bed.

"Let us help," Kennar said as he and Kon both came over to that side of the bed.

He allowed them to put an arm over each of their shoulders and stand him up.

"I want to talk to the prince privately," he said. "Do any of the men here know the language of the northern kingdoms?"

"I don't think so," Kon replied.

"Good," he said as they helped him walk over to the other bed.

One of the guards brought a chair. The prince was awake and scowled at him. He was tied down to the bed. He sat down on the chair.

"I know you probably thought I was going to kill your father," he said in the language of the kingdoms of the north. "I just wanted to talk to him without getting myself killed."

"You lie," the prince growled and tried to spit at him. "I wish I had killed you."

"My unit found your camp and I overheard him talk about Brinley threatening your kingdom with the increased patrols along the border," he replied calmly. "The reason for the patrols has nothing to do with your kingdom. King Langward's predecessor, King Burkhart lives in this village with his daughter. He will not leave this village alive. That is the reason for the increased patrols."

"I can't trust you," the prince said and spit again.

"The woman who just left is Burkhart's daughter. It is forbidden for anyone to tell her who Burkhart was before coming to this village," he said. "It is also forbidden for anyone to tell her who I am. Only King Langward is to reveal it to her."

"You kissed her," the prince said in surprise. "Why would she let you kiss her if she doesn't know who you are?"

"She knows me only by my military rank," he replied. "I think part of why she cannot know who I am and who her father was has a lot to do with the fact that when I take my father's place I will get what should rightfully be hers. I am King Langward's son."

"You're. . ," the prince began and then stopped.

"I would have done the same thing you did if I thought someone was trying to kill my father," he replied nodding. "I think you must have hit your head or something, because you were floating face down. I turned you over and pulled you with me to shore. I could not blame you for attacking me."

"I suppose I must believe you even without any proof," the prince replied.

"If you can do it quietly, ask my two friends," he said as he motioned them over. "They know who I am."

"Ready to go back to bed?" Kennar asked.

"He has a question to ask you," he replied. "Answer him with the truth. He is only trying to confirm what I have already told him."

Kennar and Kon looked confused.

"Guards, leave us for a moment," he said.

"We're under direct orders to not leave until someone takes our place," one of the men said.

"Then plug your ears," he said. "Or I'll report your uncooperative attitude to King Langward."

The men shrugged their shoulders before putting their hands over their ears.

"Is this man King Langward's son?" the prince asked quietly in Brinley's language.

"Yes," Kon answered and Kennar nodded.

"Does he lie?" he asked.

"Never," they replied in unison.

"If we have asked something he could not tell us, he just says that he is not allowed to reveal it," Kennar said. "If he says he saved you from the river after you tried to kill him, then that is what happened."

"I believe you," the prince said after a few moments.

He signaled for the guards to unplug their ears.

"Where is my father?" the prince asked.

"Negotiating a peace treaty with King Langward," Kon said. "I was on guard there yesterday. It was like they were old friends, not enemies. I'll send word that you're both awake now. I'm certain they'll come right away."

"Untie him," he said.

"I promise I won't try to kill anyone," the prince said.

"What is your name?" he asked.

"Onan," the prince replied as he rubbed his wrists.

Aurita came in followed by two men with trays.

"What is he doing untied?" she asked when she saw Prince Onan sitting up.

"Aurita, this is Prince Onan of Okiah," he said. "He thought that I wanted to kill his father. I have explained that I only wanted to explain the extra patrols along the western border without being killed myself."

"Then Father and I are the cause of this whole war?" she asked with a tremor in her voice.

"Don't blame yourself," he said.

"Father should have sent an emissary to find out the truth instead of just assuming Brinley was threatening to attack," Prince Onan said. "It seems we are both too impulsive. I am sorry that I tried to kill Colonel Brook."

One of the men with the trays approached and set the tray down on a table along the wall.

He saluted and Brook recognized him as one of his men. He returned the salute.

"It's good to see you out of bed, Sir," the man said. "She's been calling you Brook. Is that really your name?"

"It is now," he said with a smile and the man looked confused. "You'll understand later."

The man and Kennar helped him back into bed. The porridge tasted good to him. Just as he finished, he heard the door open again. His father smiled as he came around the curtain.

"It's about time you quit sleeping, Colonel," Father said. "King Anar has been anxious to speak to you."

"I'll be back to duty as soon as possible, My King," he replied.

"Maybe by tomorrow Colonel Brook will be ready to sit in on meetings as long as he doesn't overtire himself," Aurita said.

He noticed Father's smile widening at her words. Prince Onan's father was talking to him. He soon came over and stood by Father.

"King Langward tells me you are one of his bravest and cleverest soldiers, Colonel," King Anar said.

"I have learned most of what I know from King Langward and General Kannon," he replied.

"Your bravery has saved two kingdoms and my son," King Anar replied with a smile. "For that I am in your debt."

"I can claim no debt for doing my duty," he said in surprise. "As for your son, I knew he attacked me because he did not know that I had no intent of killing you. I know that I would do the same in his situation."

He noticed Father's smile.

"When I saw him floating face down, I realized that I could not let him die," he continued. "I know that you do not wish to lose your son any more than King Langward would want to lose his son."

"King Langward has told me what your future holds for you," King Anar said. "You are everything anyone could want for that."

He glanced at Father who nodded with a smile. He did not have a response for such praise. It made him feel good to hear that Father felt that way.

"May I have just a moment of your time, My King?" he asked. "Then I feel I should rest some more."

"Of course, Colonel," he replied. "Guards, you are not needed inside anymore, but I want this building well guarded."

The guards left. Aurita kissed him on the cheek before taking the empty bowls and leaving. Father pulled a chair over to beside the bed.

"I know you've been very angry with me," Father said quietly in the language of the northern kingdoms.

"I shouldn't have been," he replied. "I have thought a lot about it and I realized that I must trust you. You have never lied to me and you have always done what was best for me."

"It will all be over soon and you will know everything," Father replied. "I can only hope that you can understand why I have handled things the way I have and forgive me for it. I noticed that she has given you a name."

"I like it," he replied nodding. "It feels good to have a name at last."

"I'll send word to your mother," Father said as he stood up. "She'll be happy. Now get some rest. We'll need both of you tomorrow."

*****

"I must admire your courage for allowing him to join the military," King Anar said as they walked back toward the church. "It must be difficult for you."

"Yet it has been the best thing I could have done," Langward replied. "I decided that if only a select few knew his true identity that it would be safer for him. I am very proud of him."

"You should be," King Anar said. "Your son will be a good king. He captured my camp without injuring any of my men. Already he has made peace with my son. Most men would not forgive another for trying to kill them."

"I'm glad that you want our sons to participate in the treaty," Langward said. "Soon my son will be married and it will be time for him to sit on Brinley's throne. At that time I will have to keep my promises to Burkhart."

"You do not owe him anything," King Anar said in a surprised tone. "To allow him to live and raise his daughter is far kinder than I would have been. What promises have you made to him?"

"Once his daughter is married, he has asked to be released to join his wife," Langward said as they entered the church.

"But she is dead, isn't she?"

"Yes," he replied with a sigh. "I have promised that he shall die by my hand and no other. I will miss him though."

"I would think you would be glad to be rid of him," King Anar said as they sat down at the table.

"For most of the people of Brinley that would be true," he replied. "But King Burkhart died when Queen Aurita died. What was left behind is not the same man. He has come to regret his evil deeds. He has learned the hard life lived by most of Brinley's people. He has come to be a friend."

"You and your son are rare men indeed," King Anar said shaking his head.

*****

256

Blood of Ancient Kings

Brook awoke to a clap of thunder. It was early morning, but he was no longer tired. Yesterday had been a good day. He and Prince Onan had spent a lot of time talking while Aurita was busy with the other injured. He had been surprised to see that the same men who had beaten Burkhart were now working beside him and speaking to him as friends would. He could hear the wind blowing and the rain beating on the roof. One of his men smiled at him and saluted before putting more wood on the fire.

He thought about his new name. He remembered that there was a particular reason that his parents had not given him a name, but he couldn't quite remember why. He didn't care what his parents thought; he would keep the name that Aurita had given him. He remembered how good it had felt as she washed him. Her hands were very soft and gentle as she caressed his chest with the wet cloth. He sighed and smiled at the memory. He only wished he could make her his wife.

One of his men brought fresh clothes for him and Prince Onan. They changed as soon as they had finished breakfast. They dashed from the door to the waiting coach in the pouring rain.

"Do you know where we're going?" Prince Onan asked.

"Probably the church," he replied. "It will be good to see Grandmother and Grandfather again."

"Aurita is a beautiful woman. I can see that she loves you," Prince Onan said. "Will she be your queen?"

"I can only hope," he replied. "I can't think of anything I want more than that."

They arrived at the church and were escorted inside. When the guards had left, Father hugged him.

"It's so good to see you on your feet, Son," Father said. "We wanted to involve the two of you since it will be up to you to uphold the treaty when you are kings."

The rest of the morning was spent going over the points of the treaty. They signed the treaty just before lunch. Grandmother was very glad to see him when they went to the house for lunch. She just about wouldn't let him go when she hugged him. Even Grandfather hugged him and thumped him on the back. The food was very good. It seemed like he hadn't had such a delicious meal in quite a while.

They were on their way back to the church when they saw Burkhart coming toward them. They turned and walked toward him. Suddenly there was a loud crack in the tree above them. Burkhart ran and pushed Father and King Anar back. Burkhart looked up just in time for the branch to fall on him. Brook and his father rushed to Burkhart's side to find a part of a branch had gone right through his chest and there was bleeding around the branch. As Burkhart breathed there were bubbles forming a pink froth on top of the blood.

"Burkhart! Lie still" Father said then turned to one of the guards. "Go bring Aurita here immediately."

"Hold on," Brook said. "She'll be here soon."

Brook took a hold of Burkhart's hand.

"There are some things I wanted you to know before I die," Burkhart said in a rasping voice. "Although your father forbade it, every time I see you, in my heart I lay at your feet, My Prince."

"I suspected you knew who I was," he said as he patted Burkhart's hand.

"I have known since General Kannon brought you that first time," Burkhart replied. "You have been a true friend to me and to Aurita. I know the love you feel for her, for it is the same love that I hold for her mother. I could never ask for anyone else to be my son. She is your responsibility now. When I am gone, your father will explain everything to you and Aurita. I have left you a letter in the box that is opened with the key around my neck. Make certain she takes it from my body before I am laid to rest."

"I will," he replied as he heard the hoof beats of a horse approach. "I will miss you, My Friend."

"Father!" Aurita said as she knelt beside him. "Oh!"

"Do not mourn for me, Aurita," Burkhart said as he took her hand in his. "I am going to be with your mother at last."

"But I don't want you to go, Father," Aurita said as she began to cry.

Brook put his arm around her shoulders.

"It is time," Burkhart responded. "I have fulfilled my obligations and kept my promises. I know that you will be happy and well cared for. King Langward was the one who handed you to me when you were born and now I give you back to him. He is now your father."

"How can I be happy without you?" she asked.

"When King Langward explains things to you, what he will say will put everything in place for you," Burkhart said. "He has promised that you shall never want for anything and your husband will love you as I love your mother. I know this to be true. Your mother and I will be watching over you."

"I love you, Father," Aurita sobbed.

Brook turned her and put his other arm around her. She buried her face into his shoulder and cried.

"My King," Burkhart said and Father came closer. "I ask now that you release me that I might answer my wife's call."

"You have kept your promises and I shall keep mine," Father said. "I shall miss you, My Friend."

"You, your family, Brook and General Kannon have all been true friends to me," Burkhart said. "I did not know what a friend was nor the value of friendship before you sent me here. I die a happy man."

"You die an honorable man, Burkhart," Father said. "I release you. You have paid your debt."

Burkhart smiled briefly before his chest stopped moving and he relaxed. Father stood and spoke to one of the guards. Brook held Aurita in his arms while she cried. He had known that she would take her father's death very hard.

"He wanted to make certain you took the key," he said softly to her.

"I don't want to look at him," she responded.

"I will get it for you," he said as he released her from his arms.

He helped her to her feet. While Father hugged her and patted her back, he gently took the key from around Burkhart's neck. He closed Burkhart's eyes as some soldiers began to lift the branch from his body. He then placed the key around her neck. She buried her face against his shoulder and began crying again. He glanced up to see King Anar and Prince Onan looking on with stunned looks on their faces. The soldiers took Burkhart's body and placed it in a wagon. They covered the body with a blanket.

"Where are they taking him?" King Anar asked.

"To be buried next to his wife," Father said. "It is what I promised him."

"When you first introduced me to him I could not believe that it was really him," King Anar said. "I have heard that you are the best king Brinley has ever had. I believe this to be true. I know that your son will carry on your legacy."

"When I first looked into Burkhart's eyes, I knew that he was not the same man," Father said as he led the others toward the church.

Brook stood holding Aurita until he began to feel rain falling on him.

"We need to go inside now," he said gently. "It's starting to rain again."

"I don't care," she sobbed. "I want Father. Where have they taken him?"

"Let's go ask King Langward," he said realizing that she wasn't thinking straight.

He left his arm around her as he led her into the church. Father was talking quietly to General Kannon. Aurita began to kneel, but Father took her hand and lifted her back up.

"Aurita," he said. "You are never again to kneel or lay before me."

She looked up at him in surprise.

"I'll give you a few days to take care of things here and prepare to leave," he continued. "Colonel Brook will stay in Weston to help and comfort you. He will accompany you when you leave Weston."

"Where is Father?" she asked as though she did not fully understand what he had said.

"Long ago I promised him that when he died he would be buried next to your mother," Father replied. "You need some time to adjust to your father's death before you will be ready to learn the truth about his past and your future. I will take you to his grave once you have left Weston."

"I don't understand," she said as he felt her begin to tremble. "Father said that now you are my father."

"He spoke the truth," Father said. "When you are ready I will explain it to you. Don't worry about figuring it out right now. What is important right now is that you know that Retanta and I love you as our own. We always have and we always will."

Tears were streaming down her face.

"You need to rest," Father said gently.

He put his arm around her and led her to a lounge in Grandfather's office. Brook followed, but hesitated at the door.

Father looked him in the eye and said, "Do you remember what I told you the day before we went to war?"

He nodded.

"It applies today as well," Father said.

He sat down at the tall end of the lounge and soon Aurita was laying on the lounge across his lap. He held her in his arms and gently wiped the tears from her cheeks. He still did not understand why it was so important that he be the one to comfort her.

*****

Langward shut the door quietly behind him. King Anar and Prince Onan looked puzzled.

"She is not his wife, yet you allow him alone with her," King Anar said.

"He has been told that I have chosen her husband and his wife. He knows that no man may touch her that is not of my choosing. He will not disobey," Langward explained, and then smiled. "What neither of them has figured out yet is that within a week they will be married to each other. I have hidden his identity from her because she would not dare love him if she had known he was the prince."

"He told me this morning that the only thing he wished was for her to be his wife," Prince Onan said with a grin. "She has not kept her feelings for him hidden either. It was obvious that she wants him."

"I know," Langward said. "Burkhart has long known that my son would marry his daughter. A fortune teller told us both that our blood would be mingled some day. When she told me my wife would bear me a son, I knew what that meant."

"We should be returning home," King Anar said. "Take care of both of them."

"You are welcome to visit Brinley any time," Langward said as he nodded.

"Please thank Prince Brook for saving me even though I tried to kill him," Prince Onan said. "And thank Aurita for treating my wounds. She too saved my life."

"I will," Langward said.

*****

Aurita woke slowly. Her heart ached and she felt all empty inside. Brook had told her that Father had pushed King Langward and King Anar out of the way of the branch that had killed him. Brook had not left her side since Father's death. He had prepared supper for her and washed the dishes. Her friends had come to visit and offer their condolences. Even many of the villagers had come by, some even bringing small gifts or food. Various soldiers came and left. Brook spoke briefly and quietly with each of them before they left. She climbed down the ladder to find Brook putting wood on the fire.

"How are you feeling this morning?" he asked.

"Empty," she replied as she sat down at the table. "I don't know what I am going to do now."

"I know that King Langward will take care of you now," he said. "He promised your father that you would not want for anything."

"What did Father mean when he said that King Langward was now my father?" she asked.

"I'm not certain," Brook said as he put a kettle of water over the fire. "Your father said that you were my responsibility now. What little King Langward has told me seems to agree with that. There is something else that I can't quite remember, but I know it is somehow important now."

"I guess we'll find out very soon," she said, puzzled by his words. "I wonder what is in the box, but I promised that I would not open it until after King Langward had explained everything."

"Your father said there was a letter in there for me," he said as he reached for two bowls. "He didn't say what else there was."

They ate breakfast in silence. Langford came to tend to the few wounded that were still in the shop. He had hugged her when he saw her, but said nothing. Brook helped her to wash the dirty bedding. He smiled at her when she looked at him and never complained although she was certain he had never had to wash such things before. He carried bucket after bucket of water for her without being asked. She was grateful for his presence.

"Would you like to go for a walk?" he asked as they hung up the last blanket to dry.

"Shouldn't you take a rest?" she asked.

"I'm alright," he said. "I would rather not just sit around."

She nodded and he took her hand in his. He led her along the brook until it met the river. He looked closely at the swirling water where the brook fed into the river. She knew this must be near where he was pulled out of the river. She stood silently waiting for him to speak.

"The water is very rough and wild here," he finally commented.

"Some said it was amazing that the two of you survived," she replied. "People have died in this section of the river."

"For a while I did not know if I was still alive," he admitted as he turned to face her. "I ached all over and I heard your voice, but did not understand your words."

"When they brought you in, you looked dead," she replied as he put his arms around her. "It frightened me so to see you like that."

"It's all over now, and I will not leave you," he said with a tremor in his voice.

She looked up and he kissed her lips. It was not like the tender kiss he had given her yesterday. This kiss was passionate and demanding. The kiss promised what she dared not admit she wanted with all of her heart. He held her tightly to him and she listened to his heart pound inside his chest. She knew how difficult it must be for him to be so near her and alone with her without trying to make her his wife. She knew that she wanted to be his wife and no one else's.

Chapter 22 - Leaving Weston

The last couple of days had been very strange. The last of the wounded had finally gone home. Brook had helped her to clean the shop and wash all of the bedding. He had held her when she cried and sat with her until she fell asleep. She did not know where he slept because he was always awake before she was. He cooked all of the meals and washed the dishes. Today they were going to clean the house and pack up her belongings.

She laid Father's things out on the bed and began folding up his clothes. She had never noticed that he had so few belongings. She had found the box in the bottom of the chest along with an infant's blanket and a tiny dress. These sat undisturbed on the corner of the table. She did not quite know what to do with Father's clothes. Brook helped her to pack her belongings into the trunk. When she found her doll, she felt the tears begin to well up again. Brook smiled as she held it close to her chest. He put his arms around her and kissed her on her forehead. He had been strangely quiet today. Even quieter than he had been the last several days. She felt very anxious for some reason. They had just placed the box and infant things into the trunk when there was a knock at the door.

"King Langward has ordered us to take you to the palace," the guard at the door said when she opened it.

She nodded and opened the door wider. Two men came in and took the trunk. She took one last look around at the only home she had ever known before allowing Brook to lead her to the waiting carriage. He helped her in and sat down next to her. He was silent as they rode through the village. She held her breath as they crossed the border of the village. None of the patrols took any notice of them and she finally breathed again. As they arrived at the top of the hill, she gasped as she saw the city spread out below them. In the very center was a very large building surrounded by a wide green field and a wall. It had to be the palace. She glanced at Brook and saw the look on his face as he returned her gaze.

"What's the matter?" she asked as the carriage began descending to the bottom of the hill.

He sighed before saying, "Today you will learn who your father really was and why he was sent to Weston until he died. You will also learn who I really am. I can only pray that you can forgive both of us."

"What can be so terrible that I could not forgive you?" she asked, confused by his concern.

"I have been commanded to not tell you certain things," he said. "I only ask that you remember that no matter what you learn today, two things remain true. The first is that I love you with all of my heart. I would give up everything to be your husband. The second is that my name is Brook."

"But, that is the name I gave you because you wouldn't tell me your real name," she replied, not understanding why he should say such a thing. "I gave you the name because you were found near where the brook flows into the river."

"Yes, you are the one who gave it to me, but I choose to keep it," he replied. "I will stay with you as long as I am allowed. I must obey King Langward's will."

They rode in silence along the city streets. They paused at the palace gate. A soldier rode up to the carriage and saluted. It was a colonel that had visited Brook several times before he woke up.

"Welcome home," the colonel said.

"For some reason, Weston feels more like home to me," Brook replied as he saluted. "It will seem very strange for a while."

This exchange puzzled her. Had Brook grown up in the palace? They passed through the gate and over a bridge before entering the palace courtyard. King Langward and Queen Retanta were waiting for them. There was a pile of square stones sitting next to a gate. Brook helped her from the carriage.

"I have been both looking forward to this day and dreading it for many years now," King Langward said. "I can only pray that you can forgive me for what I have withheld from you for all of these years."

He nodded to a man who opened the gate. He led them into a small courtyard with a door into the palace and another gate.

"This will explain a few things," King Langward said as he stepped to one side, revealing two graves.

"In memory of the man who was King Burkhart before becoming a loving father. He died an honorable man who paid his debt to Brinley. May he rest in peace with the wife he loved with all of his heart," she read in a whisper. "In memory of Queen Aurita."

She felt Brook's arm around her as she began to cry.

"The man known as King Burkhart was a tyrant of a ruler. Although his reign was only five years, he made laws that caused much suffering among the people of Brinley," she heard King Langward say. "I captured the palace the day you were born. When I found him, Burkhart was holding the lifeless body of his wife in his arms. She died giving birth to you and in that moment, King Burkhart ceased to exist. No words were said as he knelt at my feet and offered the armbands to me."

She was led through the door into a large room. The room was dusty and the bed unmade. There were large brown stains on the bedding.

"It was in this very room that you were born and your mother died," King Langward said. "I had the room and the courtyard sealed after you and your father left the palace for Weston. What is done with it now is completely up to you, but you need not decide today."

She nodded, not trusting her voice. If her father had been king then she would have been a princess. Certain things he had said over the years began to make sense. The attitude of the villagers began to make sense as well. She had heard them talk about how evil the former king had been. She saw the blood stains on the floor near the door where her father must have knelt at King Langward's feet.

"Before you learn about your future, perhaps it would be best if you had a chance to think about what you have just learned," King Langward said. "Lunch is waiting for us in the dining hall."

Brook kept his arm around her as they were led to the dining hall. She sat quietly between Brook and Queen Retanta. She was feeling a little numb as she watched food being placed before her. She began to eat, but did not taste the food at all.

"Are you alright?" Queen Retanta asked in a concerned tone.

She shook her head and Queen Retanta put her arm around her shoulders.

"I don't know what will happen to me now," she said. "I understand now why Father was so hated and why the villagers hated me too. How could anyone ever like me, let alone love me?"

"Everything will turn out alright," Queen Retanta said. "I know it will."

"The reason I forbid anyone to tell you who your father had been was I knew he needed you to love him," King Langward said gently. "I also knew that you would need someone to love. I hope you will be able to forgive me by the end of today."

She just nodded her head. She looked at Brook, who had been silent. He was not eating, but just staring at his plate. He was acting very strangely. She looked back at King Langward and saw the concerned look on his face.

"I can see that neither of you are very hungry," he said. "I suppose we should just get you ready now."

This confused her. Queen Retanta took her hand and stood up. She did not argue as she was led to a large room with a tub of water in the middle of it. Several servants stood waiting.

"Do not be afraid," Queen Retanta said gently. "No one here will hurt you. We are just going to get you bathed and into a new dress."

She nodded and a servant began to undress her. She was too numb to care. She stepped into the water and found it to be warm. They bathed her and washed her hair. After she was dried, they dressed her in a white dress. The fabric was softer and smoother than any she had ever felt before. They sat her down and began brushing and tugging gently at her hair. They put a very beautiful necklace on her and the earrings Brook had given her. When they left, Queen Retanta led her over to a polished shield. What she saw startled her. Staring back at her was a beautiful woman she did not recognize.

"That's not. . ," she said, then stopped.

"Yes, that's really you," Queen Retanta said.

"I can't accept this dress," Aurita said. "It's far too fancy for me."

"It's just perfect," Queen Retanta said. "There's someone I want you to meet."

She was led into an outer room where a man and a woman were waiting. They both knelt.

"Rise," Queen Retanta said. "Princess Aurita, this is your father's cousin Stasha and her husband Garman. This is Princess Aurita."

"I have waited so long to meet you," Stasha said. "I will enjoy serving you."

"Serving me?" Aurita asked, confused by being called princess and the idea of having a servant.

"You'll soon understand," Queen Retanta said. "I must leave now to prepare, but Garman and Stasha will bring you to the throne room shortly."

She nodded and Queen Retanta left.

"You look so much like your mother," Stasha said and Garman nodded. "But so much healthier."

"You knew my mother?" Aurita asked. "Father never spoke of her. He would only speak of how he missed her."

"She was a very kind and noble woman," Garman said. "But she was sick a lot."

"Your father loved her very much," Stasha said. "And she loved him."

"She did not have much to say about ruling Brinley," Garman said. "That she left to your father."

"Queen Retanta is a very kind and noble woman too, but she is very involved in ruling Brinley," Stasha said. "We should be on our way now. I'm certain everyone must be waiting for us."

"Everyone?" she asked. "What is going on?"

"King Langward has personally overseen every detail," Garman said. "We are sworn to not tell you, but I know you should be happy when you find out what is happening."

She sighed and followed them to a pair of doors guarded by two guards who knelt. She glanced at Garman who nodded.

"Rise," she said.

They got to their feet and opened the doors wide for her. The room was large and full of people. There were stairs at the other end of the room. At the top of the stairs, King Langward and Queen Retanta sat on thrones. There was a man in white standing facing them. Everyone knelt as she passed. Garman and Stasha led her to stand beside the man at the top of the stairs. She gasped with surprise as he turned to look at her.

"Brook?" she asked in a whisper.

"Aurita?" he replied in a surprised tone before glancing at King Langward who smiled and nodded.

"I assume you two want this," King Langward said quietly and Brook nodded. "Aurita, this man whom you have named Brook is my son, Prince Brook."

Blood of Ancient Kings

King Langward and Queen Retanta stood. King Langward took Aurita's left hand and placed it in Brook's right hand. Queen Retanta smiled as she bound their hands together with an ornate strip of cloth that had a large blue stone on each end. She began to tremble as she realized that this was a wedding, her wedding, and Brook would be her husband.

"I, King Langward of Brinley give this woman, Princess Aurita of Brinley to this man, my son, Prince Brook of Brinley, that they might be husband and wife," King Langward said loudly. "As they kiss, let it be known to all that they are married. May their happiness increase daily and joy be with them always."

She looked up at Brook and he was smiling. He softly stroked her cheek before he kissed her. She felt almost dizzy as he broke off the kiss. She felt the cloth being removed from their hands as the people's cheers began to die down.

"Today, it is time for Queen Retanta and I to pass the throne to Prince Brook that he becomes King Brook," King Langward said with a smile as he slid off his armband and placed it on Brook's arm. "And to Princess Aurita that she become Queen Aurita."

The metal felt warm as Queen Retanta slid it into place on Aurita's arm. She did not know what to do or say, so she just began to cry. Queen Retanta hugged her tight.

"I have long waited to bring you home and call you my daughter," Queen Retanta whispered.

King Langward hugged her and whispered, "I hope you can forgive me. As soon as everyone is gone, I will explain everything."

Brook smiled as he took her hand and led her to the thrones. She was glad to sit since her head had begun to spin. People began to come to the foot of the steps and kneel to them before leaving. At last the only people left besides King Langward's family were Barna, Kon, Noka, Kennar, Carria and Monau. They all knelt at the foot of the stairs.

"We've known since the day after you were pulled from the river," Kon said after they had stood up. "It was very hard not to tell you."

"We're so happy for both of you," Noka said.

"Why don't we all go have something to eat?" King Langward said. "These two hardly touched their lunch."

Soon they were in the dining hall sitting at the head of the table. Aurita was still somewhat in shock as the food was being brought to the

269

table. She could not quite believe this was all for real. Brook took her hand in his and kissed it.

"Are you alright?" he asked her quietly.

"I just don't dare believe that you are my husband," she said. "Especially since you are King Langward's son."

"I know what you mean," he replied. "It was so difficult to not tell you who I was. I had been worried about how you would feel about me when you found out that what I would inherit by birth was rightfully yours by blood. For years I had been able to put it out of my mind, but for the last week it was the only thing I could think about, but I suppose that doesn't really matter now that we're married."

"All that matters to me is that you are my husband," she replied with a smile.

The food was strange, but tasted good to her. They talked while they ate. It was good to be surrounded by friends and her new family. When everyone said goodbye and left, King Langward and Queen Retanta led them upstairs to a large beautiful room with chairs and tables.

"Sit down and I'll explain the rest to you," King Langward said as he sat down on a seat large enough for several people.

Brook led her to another seat facing King Langward and they sat down.

As King Langward told her about the fortune teller's message Aurita felt a shock run through her.

"I knew then that if what she said was true, that you two would someday be married," King Langward said

"Why didn't you tell us sooner?" Brook asked.

"Remember what I had said about people whose parents chose their spouses?" King Langward asked and Brook nodded. "I knew that if I had told you that it was you I had chosen to marry Aurita, you might not fall in love with her. I also realized that Aurita might be afraid to fall in love with someone she knew to be my son."

"So that's why he would never give me a name or talk about his family," Aurita said in surprise.

"Actually the fortune teller said that only by true love could my son be named," King Langward said with a grin.

"That's what I couldn't remember," Brook said.

"So you really didn't have a name?" Aurita asked as she looked at Brook.

"Only a title or a rank," he said. "But I have loved you so much that I would answer to any name you gave me. I also now understand why Father said it was me who needed to comfort you when you were attacked and why I was allowed to hold you in my arms and kiss you."

"When I first saw you holding her in your arms, I knew that it was only a matter of time before you two were in love," King Langward said. "And when you kissed her in front of me, it was hard to not show the joy it gave me to see how much you loved each other."

"Things are starting to make sense now," Aurita said. "Things that had bothered me for a long time, but Father would never explain to me."

"I know that life has been hard for you, Aurita," King Langward said. "I can only hope that you can find it in your heart to forgive me and your father."

"I know that you have always done what you thought was best for me," she replied, surprised that it seemed to matter so much to him. "I forgive you and Father. I'm grateful to finally know the past and understand why he was so sad all of the time."

King Langward said, "We can talk about this another time. You two need some time alone."

They all stood up. Queen Retanta hugged her tightly.

"Good night, My Daughter," Queen Retanta said and kissed her forehead. "And My Son."

She hugged Brook tightly before they began to leave. Brook seemed a bit confused.

"But. . ," he said.

"You are king and queen now," King Langward said. "These are the Royal Quarters. Your mother and I have chosen other quarters. It's all yours now, along with all the responsibilities that go with it. You both have been well prepared for your future as rulers of Brinley."

They shut the door behind them. She turned to Brook who shrugged his shoulders. He led her into a bedroom so large that it was twice the size of the shop. On a table at the foot of the bed was her doll leaning up against Father's box. Next to it was the basket she had woven and Brook's empty scabbard.

"You kept the basket?" she asked. "And it was really you who sent the doll to me?"

"Yes," Brook replied with a smile as he picked up the key laying on top of the box. "Shall we see what is inside?"

She just nodded. She was a little nervous about what could be inside. He turned the key and opened the box. Inside were a book, pen, ink and two letters. When Brook lifted up the letters, there was something flat in the bottom tied with a ribbon. She took it and untied the ribbon. A lock of hair tied with a ribbon fell out as she opened it up. Inside was a painted image of a beautiful woman who looked very much like her.

"It has to be your mother," Brook said.

"Father said the box contained the only things he felt were important enough to take with him," she said in a whisper.

Brook opened the letter that simply said 'Prince' on the outside.

"My Prince," Brook began to read. "Again I swear my loyalty and allegiance to you both in life and in death. I know you love Aurita with all of your heart and in your arms she will be happy. The day she was born, I learned that the only truly important thing in this world is who you love. I have left my journal for the two of you to read when Aurita is ready. It has been an honor and privilege to know you. Your Servant, Burkhart."

She picked up the other letter with a trembling hand and opened it.

"My Dearest Daughter Aurita," she read as her voice cracked with emotion. "Now that you know the truth about what an evil ruler I had been, I hope that you can find it in your heart to forgive and love me. I know that King Langward's son will love and care for you as I have your mother, for as long as he lives. You taught me that there are more important things in this life than power and money. Love and family are the most important things in this world. Always remember that. I know that you will be a good queen, wife and mother. I love you with all of my heart and will watch over you always. Your Father, Burkhart."

She began to cry as she set the letter on the table. She felt Brook's arms around her pulling her to him.

"He is right. All of it," Brook said softly. "I will miss him."

She looked up and he kissed her tenderly. She realized that although she would miss her father, everything was as it should be. She was now the wife of the only man she could ever see herself loving as her husband. The thoughts and feelings she had been denying since the day General Kannon first brought him to Weston began to surface as she looked into his eyes. As she unfastened his tunic, she felt his hands at work on the buttons down the back of her dress.

"Oh, how I have longed to feel your hands on my skin like when you bathed me," Brook whispered in her ear.

"And yours on mine," she replied. "I give to you what is mine alone to give even though in my heart it has always belonged to you, My Husband."

He kissed her passionately as his tunic fell to the floor.

Chapter 23 – The Future and the Past

Aurita woke slowly. She felt arms around her and someone's body pressing closely to her back. She began to remember yesterday's events and realized that she was in bed with Brook who was now her husband. She opened her eyes slowly. There was a movement across the room that drew her attention. For an instant she thought she saw her father with his arm around her mother. They both smiled before they vanished.

"You jumped," she heard Brook's sleepy voice say. "Is anything wrong?"

"No," she replied. "Everything is right. I thought I saw Father and Mother standing near the wall. They looked happy."

"I'm certain that your father is very happy now," Brook replied as he drew her even tighter against his chest. "I know I am."

"I am too," she said with a smile. "Many of the unanswered questions I had have been answered. I know my father's past and what made him so sad. I know now my future is as your wife."

"From the day I first met you, I had worried about if you would be married to a man who wouldn't love you," he said. "It really didn't matter to me who I married, only that you would be loved and cared for. Many of my questions have been answered too. Now I am married to the most beautiful woman I know. I think I have always loved you and you are now both my wife and Queen of all of Brinley."

"I was told that when I got married, King Langward would give me a job in the palace," she said. "I sometimes dreamed that I would marry the prince and become queen, but I never believed it could ever really happen."

*****

When they finally left the bedroom, they found Garman and Stasha waiting for them. They soon were bathed and dressed. Aurita looked very beautiful and regal in the purple dress she was wearing. Brook was so very happy she was his wife.

"Shall we go have some breakfast my beautiful queen?" he asked her after kissing her.

"Actually, My King, it is lunch time," Garman said. "But the kitchen could prepare some breakfast if that is what you prefer."

"Lunch will be fine," he replied with a laugh.

As they were walking down the hall they heard two men talking around the corner.

"I heard rumor that Little Prince No-Name finally came back," one said as they stopped to listen.

"I thought he was gone for good," the other said. "No one has seen him in years."

"Yeah," the first man said. "I remember he had quite a punch."

"You had a black eye for a month once," the second said and began to laugh.

Aurita was obviously angry over what they had said. He shook his head and led her around the corner.

"My name is Brook," he said and they suddenly turned to face him. "But to you it is now King Brook."

"K. . . King Brook?" one of the men said.

"And this is my wife, Queen Aurita," Brook said as he struggled not to laugh at the looks on their faces.

They looked at each other before getting to their knees.

"Rise," he said after smiling to Aurita. "I stood guard in the throne room once a week for several years, and after being in the military, I've got a lot more than a good punch."

The two men's faces went pale as he lead Aurita past them toward the dining hall. Once they had turned the next corner, he began to laugh. That had felt even better than when he had given Nokar the black eye when he was a young boy.

"I remember you saying that you didn't get along with the others your age," she said. "You seemed to enjoy that."

"Those two used to tease me a lot about not having a name," he said. "I used to fight with them all of the time. It felt good to have them kneeling at my feet without even laying a hand on them."

They arrived at the dining hall to find Mother and Father talking to some men. He recognized them as the ministers and district governors. They one by one knelt and introduced themselves to him and Aurita. By her expression as the first one knelt, he knew that it would take some time for both of them to become accustomed to people kneeling to them. While they ate, the men asked questions about what changes he wanted to make to the meeting schedule and such.

"I don't see any point in changing anything right now," he said. "It will take time for us to get used to being king and queen. I had always known that someday I would be king, but I certainly wasn't expecting it so soon."

"I wasn't expecting to become queen," Aurita admitted. "I'm not even certain what is expected of me."

"We'll be around to help you for a while," Mother said. "I understand how you must feel."

"When you're ready, we'll move out," Father said.

"You're leaving the palace?" Mikan asked in surprise.

"I had never planned to stay in the palace after Brook took my place as king," Father replied. "I have accomplished what I set out to do and now it is Brook's turn to lead Brinley."

Brook was just as shocked as the others appeared to be. He had been preparing to be Brinley's king all of his life, but now the reality of it was finally apparent.

"What about your safety?" someone asked.

"Where will you live?" another asked.

"We had planned on returning to Weston," Mother said.

"The house that Aurita grew up in has always belonged to us," Father said to Brook's surprise. "We don't need anything more than that, although I think I'll probably put in a wood floor. I will miss the warm baths during the cold season though."

Everyone laughed at that. After lunch they went to the council chamber and met. Brook had never attended any of the council meetings and didn't know quite what to expect. He soon discovered that most issues were minor and easily cleared up. There were a couple issues that were hotly debated amongst the members of the counsel before being put to a vote. He was surprised that they seemed to respect his and Aurita's opinions in each matter even if they didn't agree with them. By the time the last of the issues were resolved, it was mid-afternoon. One of the things that was decided was that tomorrow morning Brook and Aurita would tour the city to allow the people to meet their new king and queen. The council had wanted them to do it today, but Aurita said she wanted to do it tomorrow. They remained in the council chamber until the last member left. Mother and Father hugged them before leaving as well.

They stood in silence for a while before Aurita said, "I would like to visit my parents' room and look around a bit."

"Alright," Brook replied.

*****

She wasn't certain why, but she just wanted to see if she could learn more about her parents. She was very curious about her mother since all she knew was that Father had loved her more than anything else in Brinley. There was a guard at the door who knelt before opening the door for them. There was a night stand with an open drawer next to one side of the bed. She thought perhaps this might be her father's. The night stand on the other side of the bed must be her mother's. She opened the top drawer with a trembling hand. Inside there was a journal and a few other things.

"We can read it when you're ready," Brook said as she picked it up and held it to her chest.

She nodded before handing it to him. There was a tall narrow chest of drawers next to a table that sat in front of a polished shield on the wall. She opened up the first drawer in the chest to find rows of rings. Each ring had at least one precious stone. The next drawer held earrings. She looked at Brook. Obviously her mother had a lot of jewelry to wear.

"It's entirely up to you," Brook said.

She went to the large cupboard and found it to be full of beautiful dresses that must have belonged to her mother and fine outfits that must have been Father's. In the corner was a table with a bowl and a pitcher on it. Next to the bowl was a ring. It looked as though her mother had been washing her hands before getting interrupted. She picked up the ring. It was very small with a very large blue stone on it. She tried it on several fingers before she found it fit on the smallest finger of her left hand.

"I heard you mother was not very healthy," Brook said. "She must have been much thinner than you are."

She nodded. They looked at some of the other things in the room before she was ready to leave. Some of her questions about her father's past had been explained, but she had so many more. It had been a long day and she was beginning to feel tired. As they left the room, they found Garman waiting for them in the hall.

"Your supper is ready when you are," he said after he knelt. "Where did you find your mother's ring?"

"It was on the table with the bowl and pitcher on it," she replied.

"When she was being prepared for burial, we could not find it," Garman said as he walked down the hall with them. "I had always worried that it had been stolen. Your father gave her that ring two months before his father died. Your grandfather wanted him to marry another woman, but when he died your father became king and then married your mother."

"He never spoke of his family," she said quietly. "Nor of my mother except how much he missed her. Did his father die suddenly?"

"King Hessgar was found dead one evening. It appeared he had fallen and hit his head against the wall," Garman said. "He had been drinking that day."

She glanced at Brook, who had a strange expression on his face. "What?" she asked.

Brook told her exactly how King Hessgar had died.

"When did he tell you this?" Aurita asked in surprise.

"The morning after he had gotten drunk," Brook replied as they stopped in front of the dining room doors. "He said he couldn't understand how his father could stand to drink so much, so I asked him what his father was like. That is when he told me. Apparently it was a painful memory for him. I think I am the only person that he ever told."

*****

Aurita had been very quiet during supper. Brook was worried about her. He knew that it would take time for her to accept her new life. When the servants had left, he drew her into his arms and held her.

"Are you alright?" he asked as he felt her trembling.

"I need to sit down," she said.

He led her to the settee and sat down next to her. She looked at him for a long time before speaking.

"What else did Father tell you?" she finally asked. "What do you know that I do not?"

"When Father spoke of Burkhart it was with kindness and respect, never anger or hatred," Brook said after explaining some of what he knew had been hidden from her. "You look tired. We should go to bed."

Aurita just nodded. He gently took her hand and led her to the bed. He held her closely in his arms until they both fell asleep.

Chapter 24 – Visitors and Confessions

Aurita woke up feeling disoriented. She had dreamed of her mother and father. Brook was still sleeping. She watched him as he smiled in his sleep. He was so very handsome, but more than that, he was kind to her. She knew he loved her as no one else could. She looked at the ring on her hand. It was a beautiful ring, but somehow she didn't think she should wear it. It was as though it held great sadness.

"What is it?" Brook asked her quietly.

"This ring," she replied. "I don't think I should wear it. I think I will keep it with her picture."

"I could get you one similar to it," Brook replied. "I have heard that sometimes a ring that a person wears all the time takes on part of that person. When someone else wears the ring, they begin to act like the owner of the ring."

"Thank you for understanding," she said as she sat up and took off the ring.

*****

She took the ring and placed it in the box with her mother's picture. Brook watched her from the bed. It was still hard for him to believe that the one woman he would have given up his claim to the throne for was now his wife and queen. He remembered some of the things that Father had said to him over the years and realized that if he had been paying attention, Father had been telling him that he was the one chosen as Aurita's husband. He got out of bed and took her into his arms before kissing her tenderly.

They found Garman and Stasha waiting for them out in the sitting room. He waited with Garman while Aurita was bathed. Soon he was the one in the warm water being bathed.

"Your bruises are looking better this morning, My King," Garman commented as he washed Brook. "I had heard that you took quite a beating in the river, but how did you get the bruises around your neck?"

"Prince Onan thought I was going to kill his father, so he tried to choke me," Brook replied. "When I woke up I was able to tell him that I had never intended to kill his father and understood his reaction."

"You and your father are very alike," Garman commented. "Most men would not forgive another for trying to kill them. I have noticed that your opinions are very similar to your father's as well. Brinley is fortunate to have such a king."

"What I worry about right now is how the people will take having Burkhart's daughter as their queen," Brook replied as they dried him off. "I know that the people of Weston should accept it without too much argument, but what about the rest?"

"Actually your father has been working on that ever since you entered the military," Garman said. "He knew that it would take time to change people's view about Burkhart. He made it a point to frequently remind the people how much Burkhart had changed. When Burkhart died, he had an announcement read around Brinley. I remember it explained that Burkhart had repaid his debt to Brinley and felt true sorrow for his past. It also told of how he lost his life protecting King Langward and King Anar. The other thing that it announced was that Burkhart's daughter would soon be your wife and their queen."

Brook was silent as they dressed him. He was very surprised. It seemed that Father had kept a lot secret from him. They went down to the dining hall to find Mother and Father already there. It seemed very strange to be sitting in his father's place at the head of the table with Aurita at his side.

"You're quiet this morning, Son," Father said when they had almost finished eating.

"It will take time to get used to sitting in your place," he replied and Father laughed. "Garman told me about the announcements that you had made and the one you made when Burkhart died."

"I have always known that the people would need time to prepare for your rule," Father replied. "There still may be a few who don't understand why Burkhart's daughter is now Queen of Brinley, but I know that you will be able to overcome that. I have kept very close track of you and I have been very pleased with the way you handle people. You are able to get them to obey you without making them feel forced."

"I realized that there must be almost as much that you have kept from me as what you kept from Aurita," he said.

"Yes," Father replied. "While you were still quite young, I realized that there were things that it would be best for you to learn on your own. I knew that although it was my duty to protect you and teach you what you needed to know to be king, it was important that you learned to make your own decisions. Part of why I kept certain things secret from you was that I did not want you to feel forced into anything. I also wanted you to learn to rely upon yourself and not me. I am very proud of you. You have become everything I could have hoped. You are your own man and not someone I control."

Brook glanced at Aurita and she smiled.

"I have kept a careful record of everything you need to know," Father said. "It is in the study waiting for you."

"Thank you," he said. "I will look at them later. We first need to present ourselves to the people of Brinley."

Once they had finished eating, he took Aurita out to the courtyard where the carriage was waiting for them. He was still a bit apprehensive as they passed through the gate and into the city. He was unprepared for the cheers that greeted them. He heard Aurita breathe a sigh of relief. As they returned to the courtyard, they were greeted by Garman.

"A message came from the western patrols," Garman said as he held out a piece of paper.

'Group from Okiah in route to palace,' the message said.

"Thanks," he said as they entered the palace.

He wondered who was coming and why. They went to the throne room where there were people assembled waiting for them to grant audiences. It was all fairly trivial and most came to bring them gifts. It was lunchtime by the time the people from Okiah arrived. Brook was glad to see Prince Onan had come.

"Welcome to Brinley," he said as Prince Onan and his group bowed.

"It is good to see you again," Prince Onan replied with a smile as Brook and Aurita stood. "We came to congratulate you on your wedding and coronation. We brought some gifts."

Prince Onan turned to one of the other men as he and Aurita joined them. When he turned around he held a sword across his upturned hands.

"I believe this belongs to you," Prince Onan said with a smile. "It was found sticking out of the cliff we went over. I felt it a bit plain to be the sword of a king."

Brook picked up the sword. Precious gems had been added to the hilt and the blade had been etched with a beautiful design.

"Thank you," he replied. "I hadn't even thought about what had happened to this."

"Our armorer asked me to find out who made it," Prince Onan said. "He was quite impressed with the workmanship."

"I forged it myself while at the military training camp," he replied in surprise. "It has always served me well."

Prince Onan laughed and said, "I am not surprised. I had heard King Langward was an artist as well as a good leader. It is only fitting that his son would be similarly talented."

Brook was surprised by that comment.

"I also bring some of our finest fabrics as a gift for you, Queen Aurita," Prince Onan said. "Both of you saved my life. For that I am forever grateful."

Aurita smiled as she ran her hand over one of the piles of cloth held by one of Prince Onan's men.

"It is very beautiful," Aurita said.

"Yet, I see that it is plain in comparison to your beauty," Prince Onan commented and Aurita blushed slightly. "Lastly I bring a gift of memorial. In my kingdom it is a practice to keep portraits of the prior kings and queens. One of the royal painters had seen your parents and painted this."

Prince Onan drew off a cloth covering a large portrait that two men had been carrying. Brook heard Aurita gasp as it was revealed. It was of a much younger, happier Burkhart and his wife.

"I know that you will always love your father," Prince Onan said. "Although the people of Brinley hated the man that was King Burkhart, I know that the man you knew as your father was a changed man."

"Thank you," Aurita whispered as she reached out and gently stroked the face of her father on the portrait. "I shall treasure this always."

"Would you care to join us for lunch?" Brook asked as several servants took the gifts.

"We would be honored to do so," Prince Onan replied with a smile.

Soon they were seated in the dining room along with the ministers and district governors. The conversation was light and cheerful. Brook was glad to see that Aurita was enjoying herself. Prince Onan and his men left directly after lunch. He and Aurita went to the study.

"I used to spend a lot of time here," he commented as he sat down behind the desk. "None of the children of the palace staff dared come in here."

"It's sad to think that you didn't have any friends until you were in the military," Aurita said as she looked around the room. "I remember you telling me you didn't get along with the children your age at home."

"My grandmother was my only friend. I was very happy to learn that Noka and Carria became your friends," he replied. "I had been very worried about you not having any friends. I knew how lonely that can be."

He picked up the stack of papers on the desk and began reading them. They were copies of the announcements Father had made over the years. Aurita read them after he had. After several he noticed that she had a tear rolling down her cheek.

"What's the matter?" he asked with concern.

"Your father actually had this announced to the entire kingdom?" she asked.

"Yes," he replied.

"I know how the villagers felt about Father," she said. "Yet your father was unafraid to admit that he was satisfied that Father was a changed man and his friend. Why didn't he release Father then?"

"He once said that he had thought about releasing Burkhart but knew that it would not make Burkhart any happier," he replied as he set down the papers. "He said that he knew the only release Burkhart wanted was through death. Perhaps we should begin reading your father's journal. We could read each of these announcements when we reach the date in his journal."

"That would probably make more sense," she said.

He stood and went over to kneel before her. He took her hands in his and kissed both of them. She smiled at him as they both stood up. They went to the royal quarters and got out the journal. The journal started the day after Burkhart became king.

'At last I am free of him,' the journal began. 'I can now do anything I please and no one can tell me I am worthless. I can marry Aurita and not a woman chosen by my father. Never again shall I be in fear or pain. Never again must I obey anyone else's wishes for I am King of Brinley.'

*****

As the journal continued, Aurita learned much about her father. She began to understand why the people of Brinley had hated her father when he was king. Brook held her in his arms as she cried. She had not wanted to believe what Father had said about being an evil man, but now she could see it was true. When they reached the first entry after the day of her birth, it was hard to believe that it was written by the same man.

'In this last week my life has completely changed. My eyes have been opened and I see the truth about myself for the first time. I now sit in a house smaller than my bathing chamber in the palace, yet I am grateful for the protection it affords me and my daughter. I am learning to care for myself and for her. It is hard work to live outside the palace. I never knew life could be so hard. For the first time in my life, I feel the desire to obey and please someone, King Langward. I have no doubt that he is worthy of the title of king. I also know that I was never worthy of that title. He has seen into my very soul and knows me better than I know myself. Although it is the blood of our ancient kings that flows in my veins, it is worth less than the dust that mars his boots.'

Aurita felt the tears coming again as she set down the journal. Brook drew her into his arms and held her tightly.

"I know this is hard for you," he said softly. "I also know that in the end your father was a changed man who died an honorable death."

"You knew who he had been the first time you came with General Kannon, yet you seemed very comfortable speaking to him," she said. "You always treated him with dignity and kindness."

"I also knew who he had become," he replied. "Father made certain that I understood how he had changed. Since Father saw fit to treat him with kindness, I felt I should do the same. After I got to know him better, I knew for myself that your father had become a good man who had seen the error of his past and changed."

The next morning as they were finishing breakfast, Brook said, "I think today we should go to the military training camp. It is time they learned my true identity."

"They don't know?" Aurita asked in surprise.

"Like your father, I was not allowed to reveal my identity while living outside the palace," he said as he shook his head. "A few figured out who I was, but the rest were satisfied when I told them that my father bet me I couldn't make patrolman without telling anyone my name. If they pressed me further, I told them that he had been a patrolman and wanted me to get through training on my own abilities, not his reputation."

"I remember Kon mentioning that the first time he came to Weston," she said. "It must have been hard for you."

"I entered the military a year younger than everyone else," he said as they went to the courtyard. "I had to work hard to prove I belonged there."

They put on hooded capes as they waited for the carriage. A carriage was brought and soon they were headed to the gate in the palace wall.

"I was very surprised to find out you were King Langward's son," she said. "You never acted like I thought a prince would act."

"I needed to hide my identity for my own safety," he said. "Besides, I enjoyed being treated like everyone else. It made me feel good to know that I had earned my rank like everyone else. I was tired of being around people that assumed that I thought I was better than them."

"Did Kon, Monau and Kennar know who you were?" she asked as they rode through the city streets.

"Not until the day before their wedding," he replied with a laugh. "I'm glad that Father was the one to tell them. I doubt they would have believed it if he hadn't been there to show them that we both have the same birthmark."

"The heart shaped one on your right shoulder?" she asked.

"Yes," he said as they approached the camp. "Someday that same birthmark will need to be found."

"Why?" she asked.

"There will come a day that you will need to search for that birthmark," he said as they stopped in front of a building. "I'll tell you more later."

She was puzzled but followed him into the building. He did not lower the hood on his cape, so she left hers up as well. She followed him up some stairs and to a door. He tapped twice on the door.

"Come in," General Kannon said as he opened the door. "I got your message."

"I thought I should introduce myself as king in person," Brook said after the door was shut behind them.

"It's probably best that way," General Kannon said with a laugh. "I've had an assembly called. The men should be ready soon. I already miss having you as an assistant. My new one can read and write, but is not nearly as efficient as you."

"Give him time," Brook said as the door opened.

"The men are assembled, Sir," a Private said as he saluted.

"My new assistant," General Kannon said. "Private Makki, this is your predecessor, Colonel Brook."

"K...King Brook?" the Private stuttered.

"Yes," Brook said. "Your job will require you to work twice as hard as everyone else, but I promise it will be worth the effort."

"Shall we go?" General Kannon asked as he walked past the stunned private.

"Yes," Brook said.

Aurita walked with them to a platform in front of many men assembled in neat rows. She felt a little uncomfortable, but she wasn't certain if it was the height of the platform or the number of men assembled. The men saluted, and then Brook and General Kannon returned the salute.

"Our new king has come to honor us with his presence," General Kannon said, speaking loudly. "We welcome his return to the place he has called home for the last several years."

She heard gasps as Brook removed his hood and took off his cape.

"Many of you asked for my name and now you understand why I did not give it," Brook said. "I know that some of you were puzzled by some of the things I said or did. I hope that they make more sense now. I will always count those who serve in the military among my brothers and friends."

There was silence as he paused and held out his hand to her. She understood his gesture and pulled the hood from her head before placing her hand in his.

"Some of you have already met Our Queen from your patrol duties around Weston," Brook said with a smile as a murmuring was heard. "I am proud to introduce my wife, Queen Aurita."

"All Hail, King Brook and Queen Aurita!" the men replied in unison as they knelt.

Aurita was shocked by their response. He kissed her hand before speaking again.

"You are dismissed."

There was much noise as the men began to disperse. Brook led her by the hand down the steps of the platform. Some men had begun to gather near the bottom of the stairs. They all saluted Brook before turning to kneel before her with swords resting across their palms. She glanced at Brook, who smiled and nodded to her.

"Rise," she said and they stood up, sheathing their swords.

"You are right," one of the older of the men said. "Your words and actions make a lot more sense now."

"You also understand that other than refusing to reveal my identity, I was always careful to be completely truthful in everything else," Brook said and the men nodded.

"No wonder you were acting so strangely at Lady Kara's funeral," one of the younger ones said. "She was your grandmother."

"Yes, Sergeant Caddaric," Brook said. "I know I didn't act like it at the time, but I was grateful for your presence. I know that if I hadn't had to take care of you and Corporal Adamok, I might not have taken proper care of myself."

"It also explains why you didn't want anyone to see your birthmark," a corporal said. "I had heard about King Langward's heart shaped birthmark."

"Major Fyodor, I thought you might like to know that Aurita is the woman I mentioned to you the night before we captured King Anar's camp," Brook said and the older man smiled.

"I thought as much," the man responded. "Your love for her is obvious. It is a bit of a shock to learn that we were chosen to serve directly under Brinley's Prince."

"I knew it would be," Brook said with a laugh. "That's why I decided I should tell you myself. I enjoyed the time I spent in the military, for it gave me a freedom that I never had growing up in the palace, but I know I am doing what I need to be doing now."

"You seem much happier now," the corporal who had spoken earlier said.

"I want to speak to you in private for a moment, Corporal Adamok," Brook said and the man looked surprised. "The rest of you had best get back to your assignments."

The men saluted before leaving. The corporal looked nervous.

"I know that you have stayed in the military because you are friends with Caddaric," Brook said and the man nodded. "I have noticed that there is something else that you are far better suited for. Can you read and write?"

"No, My King," the man answered in a surprised tone.

"I know that eventually the ministers chosen by my father will need to be replaced as they are all getting on in years," Brook said. "I would like to offer you the chance to learn what they do. You could start out as an assistant to Mikan, but you would need to learn to read and write."

"Mikan, the prime minister?" the corporal asked.

"Yes," Brook replied. "I have noticed that he has a hard time getting around even with his cane. I'm certain he would welcome an assistant who could bring things to him and it would give you a chance to learn. I have noticed your interest in politics. I will speak to him about it tomorrow. Think about it for a couple of days, and then send your response with General Kannon. You are dismissed."

The man saluted and hurried off. Aurita was a bit surprised by Brook's offer.

"I thought you said you didn't see the need to make any changes," she said as they returned to the carriage.

"That is true," he replied as he helped her into the carriage. "But when I saw Corporal Adamok, I remembered how much he seemed to know about politics. I noticed that although Mikan is very happy being Prime Minister, his health is not good. I think that in time, Adamok could become a very good prime minister. I do not want Mikan to think that we have already replaced him, because we have not."

*****

The next day at the council meeting, Brook waited for the right opportunity to introduce the idea of bringing in an assistant for Mikan. Once they had settled the current matters, they began talking about Brinley's future.

"There have been a lot of changes to Brinley during my lifetime," Mikan said.

"You've been around for quite a while, My Friend," General Kannon said with a laugh.

"I have noticed getting around has been getting harder for you, Mikan," Brook said. "Would it help if you had someone young who could assist you?"

"That would help me a lot," Mikan said. "I've tried putting everything I would need on my desk, but that leaves me no room to work. Inevitably there is something I have forgotten forcing me to get up to get it. And carrying things is getting harder as well."

"I know of a young man who has quite an interest in politics," Brook said. "He doesn't read or write, but I think he would learn quickly and be an able assistant for you."

"I would appreciate that," Mikan said. "I know that I am not long for this world. Perhaps in time he could take my place. How soon could he start?"

"Actually I saw him yesterday," Brook said. "I mentioned to him that you might want an assistant."

"That wouldn't happen to be Corporal Adamok, would it?" General Kannon asked.

"Yes," Brook replied.

"This morning I found him waiting for me at my office door," General Kannon said. "He wanted me to tell you he said yes."

"Tell him he can start immediately," Mikan said with a smile.

"I must warn you that he is very opinionated about politics and not afraid to differ with someone in that regard," Brook said.

"That sounds a lot like you, Mikan," General Kannon said and began to laugh.

"That it does," Mikan said as he began to laugh.

"Perhaps I could use an assistant as well," Nokar said. "I know that eventually you will want to appoint your own ministers."

"I will find an assistant for you, but I have no intention of replacing any of you anytime soon," Brook said. "I want the transition in leadership to go smoothly. I feel that to appoint all new ministers at this time would be a big mistake. I feel that in time Adamok might be ready to take Mikan's place, but he is still very young and there is much for him to learn. Whomever I find to assist you may or may not be suited to take your place when you are ready to retire, but we'll deal with that when the time comes."

Nokar smiled and looked a bit relieved. They had lunch before granting audiences. Things were fairly trivial until an angry looking man entered the throne room. He knelt only briefly and got up without waiting to be told to.

"What is your matter?" Brook asked.

"Why is Burkhart's daughter at your side as queen?" the man asked in an angry tone. "You must have married her just to make your claim to the throne legitimate. Will she cause the same suffering her father caused?"

"I married Aurita because I love her with all of my heart," Brook said. "I would have given up my claim to the throne to marry her."

The man looked genuinely surprised.

"I know that all of Brinley hated King Burkhart," Brook continued. "I also know that King Burkhart died with his beloved wife. The man who survived was a sad and broken man with no desire to live beyond serving King Langward and raising his daughter."

Out of the crowd, Barna's father appeared and stepped forward.

"Guard, come here," Brook said and one of the guards stepped forward and knelt. "On my night stand is a letter, bring it here."

"At once, My King," the guard replied and left.

Brook nodded to Barna's father.

"I too hate King Burkhart," Barna's father began as he turned to face the man. "Burkhart was sent to my village to live and raise his daughter. When he first arrived, many of the men in the village would beat him. I am ashamed to admit that I was one of those men. He did not fight back, nor even cover his face. I actually saw him smile as we beat him."

The man looked shocked.

"He never reported the beatings to King Langward," Barna's father continued. "When my leg was crushed, I was brought to Queen Aurita. She was able to save my life by cutting off my damaged leg. I stayed in her shop for a week while I was healing. When my wife could not stay the night with me, Burkhart did. At first I was afraid that he would want to hurt me, but he did everything I needed without complaint, most times without me even asking. His hands were gentle and his words

290

encouraging and kind. He prepared my food right there in the shop so I could see that he was not poisoning me. The last night I was there, I asked him why he was so kind to me when I had been so cruel to him. He replied that he knew it was his fault that people hated him and he deserved to be beaten. He said that he knew he could never hope to repay his debt to Brinley's people in whole, but caring for me while I was injured was a small payment of his debt. He carved this leg for me and refused to take any payment for it. He worked very hard for two days to make certain that it was a perfect fit and comfortable for me to use."

Just then the guard entered with the letter. He handed it to Brook.

"Garman," Brook said and the man came to stand at his side. "Have you seen this before?"

"No, My King," Garman replied.

"Do you recognize the hand that wrote it?"

"It is Burkhart's hand," Garman said in a surprised tone.

"Read it out loud," Brook said. "Although it was written for me, I feel that it will answer this man's concerns."

As Garman read the letter there were many stunned looks among the people in the throne room. Even some of the guards looked shocked.

"In his journal Burkhart relates that he had feared King Langward because he had heard rumor that Langward was cowardly and heartless, but he had learned that he was the one that fit that description. Burkhart finally saw the truth about himself and what he had done," Brook said. "The Burkhart I knew was a truly repentant man. I was witness to his death. He was killed by the branch that he saved King Langward and King Anar from. As he lay dying he asked King Langward for release from this world. It was by King Langward's command that he lived and that he died. He died as a king should, an honorable man in service to his kingdom."

"I came to the palace with King Langward's brother, Langford, to care for Burkhart's body. The two of us and King Langward himself washed the body and prepared it for burial. We also dug the grave and buried him ourselves," Barna's father said, "I stand here today and pledge my loyalty and allegiance to King Brook and Queen Aurita knowing beyond doubt that the throne is rightfully theirs regardless of blood line or birthright."

He then knelt before them at the bottom of the stairs. The other man soon joined him on his knees as did the others in the room. Brook glanced at Aurita and found her smiling, but saw the tear forming in the corner of her eye.

"Rise," she said. "Before I arrived at the palace after Father's death, I knew nothing of his past. I am still learning what an evil man he was before my birth. It was something he was forbidden to tell me himself. I know he felt truly ashamed for what he had done while he was king. I do not expect the people of Brinley to ever forgive him, but I want them to know that I will take care to not repeat his evil. The council set up by King Langward will remain in place which will prevent that possibility. The man I knew as my father always taught me that I should be in service to the people of Brinley and do everything I could to make their lives better."

"I am sorry that I misjudged you," the man said. "I pledge my loyalty and allegiance to you, King Brook and Queen Aurita. I will return home to relate what was said here to the people of my village so that they might learn the truth."

He knelt again before leaving. The rest of the matters were mostly simple and easily cleared up.

As they sat down for supper Aurita said, "I think we should visit the outlying villages. We could grant audiences to the people of the village, but our main purpose would be to let the people get to know us."

"I like that idea," Brook said. "I know it was hard for you today, but I'm glad that man came. What he says to his village will win their loyalty to us far better than any official announcement."

Chapter 25 – Return to Nordam

It took Brook and Aurita two months to prepare for the trip. There were many matters that needed to be settled before they could leave. Aurita was feeling anxious over how each village would react, but excited to see places she had never been before. The morning they left she was feeling nauseated before she ate breakfast. The first village they visited turned out to be the one that the man had been from. They were greeted warmly and were presented with gifts. The next morning she was nauseated again in spite of feeling a lot calmer.

"Are you alright?" Brook asked her in a worried tone as she sipped at some tea before breakfast. "You look pale."

"I've been very nauseated the last couple of mornings," she said.

"You were up a lot last night," he said.

"Is your nausea just in the morning, My Queen?" Garman asked as he and Stasha brought their breakfasts to them.

"Yes," she replied and Garman began to laugh.

"Stasha was the same way for a while before we discovered she was with child," Garman said. "It sounds like Brinley's throne will have an heir before the year is done."

Aurita looked at Brook to find him smiling. He took her hand and kissed it.

"For many years I had thought about being married and bearing children," she said softly. "I dreaded my wedding day because it was your children I wanted to bear, yet I never dared hope to be your wife."

"I didn't care who I married as long as you were happy," Brook replied. "Now both our wishes have come true."

He kissed her tenderly on the lips before they ate breakfast. They were back on the road soon after breakfast. Aurita found that she liked sleeping in a tent with Brook. At the next village it took a while before the people accepted that her father had repented of his past and that she was their queen. She was glad when the audiences were over, but she was surprised by how many people came up to her afterwards to personally introduce themselves. They stayed the night before resuming their trip. The next two villages were about the same as the second village had been.

It had been a week since they left the palace when they arrived in a village Brook called Nordam. It was set in a tiny valley halfway up the mountain. The air was cool and Aurita was glad for the warmth of her cape. Two men looked up from a field. One was older than the other. The younger one looked almost familiar to Aurita. Brook stopped at the edge of the field and dismounted. He helped her from her horse as the men approached.

"You were at my grandmother's burial," the young man said. "Uncle Langward asked you to help carry the coffin. You left before I had a chance to ask your name."

"I couldn't have given you one at that time, Rodan," Brook replied causing the men to look surprised.

He flipped his cape over his right shoulder exposing his armband. The two men gasped.

"My name is Brook," he said with a smile. "And this is my wife, Aurita. Aurita, this is my Uncle Dornor and cousin Rodan."

The men began to kneel.

"You are family," she said. "You need not kneel."

The two looked up at Brook who nodded.

"Katia and Talia will want to see you," Dornor said. "We're sorry we couldn't make it to your wedding, but Katia was very ill. Then just yesterday Talia burned her arm with some scalding water."

"We will be arranging for a village assembly later today, but we have some time now," Brook said with a smile.

They followed the two to a small house near the field. There was a woman sitting in front of it spinning yarn. She looked up before setting down her work.

"Aunt Katia, it's good to see you again," Brook said. "I'm sorry to hear you were ill."

"I'm much better now," she said as she hugged him.

"This is Brook's wife, Aurita," Dornor said and suddenly Aurita found herself hugged as well.

"So you now have a name," Katia said. "You look very happy now."

"I am," Brook replied as he put his arm around Aurita's waist.

"Dornor said your daughter burned her arm," Aurita said. "How is it doing?"

"She is in a lot of pain," Katia replied. "The healer seemed very worried, but didn't say much. She won't talk much and won't get out of bed."

"May I take a look at it?" Aurita asked. "I may be able to help. The blacksmith in Weston burned himself several times."

"Aurita is a very skilled healer," Brook said as Katia glanced at him.

Katia opened the door and led them inside. She led them through a doorway into a tiny room. The two men stayed outside with the guards and servants. The young woman lying on the bed looked pale.

"Talia," Katia said softly as she put her hand on her shoulder. "Your cousin, Brook, is here.

Talia opened her eyes and looked at them.

"His wife, Aurita, wants to look at your arm." Katia said. "He says she is a healer."

Talia nodded and Aurita handed her cape to Brook. She sat down on the edge of the bed and gently unwrapped Talia's arm. She could see that the burn was a bad one. It was blistered and swollen.

"I know it hurts," she said. "But I need to see if the heat is gone out of it. I will be very gentle."

Talia nodded and she carefully touched the arm. The heat was gone but the skin was stretched tightly over the blisters.

"The heat is gone," she said. "I know how to make an ointment that will speed the healing and relieve some of the pain. I will need to borrow some things from the healer to make it and I will need some plants gathered. I saw some of the most important ones just outside the village."

*****

Aunt Katia glanced at him and Brook nodded.

"I'm expecting the healer to be here any time now," Aunt Katia said.

"I'll sit with Talia while you get what you need," Brook said as he handed Aunt Katia their capes. "Tell the guards what plants you need and they can help gather them."

Aurita nodded before she stood up. She kissed his cheek and smiled before leaving the room. Aunt Katia followed her out.

"I didn't recognize you at Grandmother's burial," Talia said as he sat down on the edge of the bed. "Fordan said you helped dig the grave. He was surprised when Uncle Langward asked you to help carry the casket."

"Actually the minister noticed I looked a lot like Grandmother," Brook said with a laugh. "I told him who I was, but hoped that no one else would notice. I knew that for my own safety I needed to appear to be just a soldier in Brinley's military. It was very difficult for me to stand to the side and not say anything to any of you."

"You look a lot happier than you did then," Talia said.

"I am happier than I had ever hoped for," Brook said. "I had always known that I would become king, but didn't know who would be my queen. I have loved Aurita since I first met her, but never dared hope she would be my wife."

"I know what you mean," she said. "I love Fordan, but I doubt Father would let me marry him after yesterday."

"Why is that?"

"I was moving the pot of water when he asked me what man he had seen me talking to and what we were talking about," Talia said. "I was so nervous that I spilled the water on my arm."

"Things have a way of working out for the best," Brook said as Aurita entered with a man carrying a bowl. "I'll be outside with Rodan and Uncle Dornor."

He patted Talia on the shoulder before leaving. He took his cape off a hook near the door and put it on before going outside. He found the guards peeling leaves off plants and putting them in bowls. Garman, Stasha and their daughter, Ayla, were helping. Uncle Dornor and Rodan were talking to Aunt Katia.

"It was Fordan she was with, Father," Rodan was saying as Brook joined them. "I've seen them talking several times before. I saw him kiss her hand last week."

"She's been very quiet," Aunt Katia said. "I heard her crying last night. I asked her if it was the pain from the burn, but she said it was something she didn't want to talk about."

"She's in love with Fordan," Brook said. "But she's worried that you won't let her marry him after yesterday."

"I just want her happy and well taken care of," Uncle Dornor said. "I don't know anything about this Fordan."

296

"He moved here recently," Rodan said. "He makes and sells jewelry. He has been coming to Nordam at least once a month for several years. He moved here to be closer to the mines. He's paying some men to build his house and shop."

"It sounds like he has enough money to take care of a wife," Aunt Katia said.

"I want to meet him," Uncle Dornor said. "I need to find out if he loves Talia and will treat her right. I don't like him sneaking around behind my back."

"I doubt he is doing it intentionally," Brook said. "If he is new to the village, he may not know who you are."

"That's him," Rodan said pointing to a man Brook recognized.

"Let me talk to him first. He was one of the men who helped me dig Grandmother's grave," Brook said. "In my experience, it is best to be very open about such things. Perhaps I can make him understand that he needs to introduce himself to you immediately if he has any hope of asking you for her hand in marriage."

"Thanks," Uncle Dornor said. "I would appreciate that."

Brook whistled and his horse trotted over to him. He mounted and followed Fordan. He soon caught up to him.

"You look familiar," Fordan said.

"You helped me dig Lady Kara's grave," Brook said. "I hear you've moved to Nordam."

"It's closer to the mines," Fordan said, nodding. "And to Lady Kara's granddaughter, Talia."

"Her father was asking who you were when she spilled boiling water on her arm last night," Brook said as he watched for a reaction.

Fordan pulled his horse to a stop and asked in a panicked voice, "Is she alright?"

"My wife is making some special ointment to treat the burn," he replied, careful not to smile. "But Talia is very worried right now."

"I'm going to go check on her myself," Fordan said as he turned his horse.

"You will have to talk to her father first," Brook said as he turned his horse. "I suggest that you had best tell him everything. He thinks you have been sneaking around behind his back."

"Actually I have been very busy," Fordan said. "But, also I have been afraid to talk to him. I want her for my wife, but I've never met her family."

"He's a good man who just wants to make certain you will care for her and treat her right," Brook said. "Have you ever kissed her lips?"

"I haven't dared," Fordan said as he began to blush slightly. "I've been afraid he would catch me kissing her and forbid me to see her again."

"I'll give you a piece of advice I was given in a similar situation," Brook said. "You would probably get into more trouble for not kissing her and making her unhappy than you would for kissing her and making her happy."

"What did you do?"

"I kissed her right in front of her father," Brook said with a laugh. "Later that same day my father ordered me to do the same in front of him."

"Ordered?"

"I'm sorry, I haven't properly introduced myself," he said then flipped his cape over his right shoulder. "My name is Brook."

"King Brook?" Fordan asked and he nodded. "That's why you helped dig Lady Kara's grave. You are her grandson and Talia is your cousin. I was beginning to wonder how you knew so much about her and her family."

"I think Talia will heal faster knowing that you and Uncle Dornor have settled your differences," Brook said. "Aunt Katia caught her crying about you last night."

They urged their horses to a trot and were soon back to where Uncle Dornor was standing. Fordan dismounted and glanced at Brook. He nodded and smiled.

"Sir, my name is Fordan," he began. "I met your daughter, Talia not long after Lady Kara's funeral. I love her and wish her for my wife. I beg your forgiveness for not introducing myself sooner and ask that you grant me permission to marry her."

"How do I know I can trust you to take care of her properly?" Uncle Dornor said. "I heard you have kissed her hand and who knows what else."

"I would never do anything to dishonor her or you," Fordan said quickly. "I have not even held her in my arms although I have longed to do so. I have taken her every suggestion in the design of my home that is being built. I am not extremely wealthy, but I am not poor either. I am willing to make certain that she never wants for anything."

"Will you treat her right?"

"I promise she will be happy," Fordan replied. "I could never intentionally do anything to hurt her. I was very alarmed when King Brook told me she had been burned and that it was over me. I will care for her while she heals."

"A husband's duty is to care for his wife and family whether well or ill," Uncle Dornor said. "You have my permission to marry her. You had best go see her."

Brook began to laugh as Fordan ran to the house. Rodan was laughing as well, but he could see the tears in Aunt Katia's eyes as they followed him. When they entered the house they found Fordan kneeling at Aurita's feet.

"Rise," she said.

"My Queen, I did not know you were a healer," Fordan said as he stood up. "I want to thank you for helping Talia."

She looked at Brook with a puzzled expression.

"This is Fordan," he said. "He was very alarmed to hear Talia had been burned when Uncle Dornor asked her about him. I believe he has something to ask Talia."

Aurita nodded and said, "That would explain why she was so quiet. Perhaps now she will eat something. She needs to drink a lot of water and broth to help her heal."

"I will make certain she does," Fordan said.

"Fordan?"

They turned to find Talia standing in the doorway. Fordan knelt at her feet.

"Will you marry me, Talia?" Fordan said as he looked up at her.

She glanced at her father, who nodded.

"Yes," she said.

Fordan quickly stood up and took her gently into his arms.

"I'm so sorry you got hurt because of me," he said.

"It was my own fault," she began.

"Shhh," he said before kissing her lips.

There was a knock at the door and they turned to find the minister and his wife standing there. They quickly knelt when they recognized him.

"Rise," he said and they stood up. "This is my wife Aurita."

"It is good to see you smile, My King," the minister said.

"Brook said that he stayed in your barn when he came to arrange for his grandmother's burial," Aurita said.

"It was quite a shock to find out that we had royalty sleeping in our barn," the minister's wife said. "I would have given him our bed if I had known before everyone was settled for the night."

"At that time, I couldn't have done that without revealing who I was," Brook said. "And that would have been too dangerous. I needed to remain just a soldier, a uniform without a name or face."

"We came to invite you to lunch," she replied with a smile. "When we heard you were coming we arranged a lunch for the entire village."

"Perfect," Brook said with a smile. "We can hold the audiences directly afterward."

They all followed the minister and his wife over to the churchyard. They introduced themselves before the food was served. Brook noticed many surprised expressions among the people. Many people came by to introduce themselves. Some of them had recognized him from the burial. He was glad to see that none of them seemed concerned that Aurita was Burkhart's daughter. The audiences went smoothly since most of the matters were very minor. Afterwards Uncle Dornor said Aunt Katia had a large supper prepared for them.

They talked while they ate. Brook noticed that Fordan was feeding Talia since it was her right arm that she had burned and Uncle Dornor seemed to find it funny. He learned a lot about them that he had not known. Both Uncle Dornor and Rodan worked in the mines several days a week, then spent the rest of the week tending to the farm. Uncle Dornor showed them a large blue stone that he had found just yesterday.

"That is about the size of the one in Mother's ring," Aurita said.

"Fordan, could you make Aurita a ring and set this stone in it?" Uncle Dornor asked to Brook's surprise. "It will be our wedding gift to them."

"I'd be happy to," Fordan said with a smile.

*****

They spent the night in Nordam and decided to stay for one more day since there was a village festival that day. Ayla was doing Aurita's hair when Rodan came into the main room of the house.

"I'm sorry," he said quickly. "I didn't realize anyone besides Mother was in here."

"It's alright, Rodan," Aurita said. "Ayla is almost done with my hair. She has been very curious about what it is like to live outside the palace. I told her she could take the day off today."

"I could show you around, Ayla," Rodan said. "That is if you want me to."

"I would like that," the girl replied as she put the last clip in place.

"First let's have breakfast," Katia said. "Fordan asked if we would like to see his house. It is almost finished."

Soon they were gathered around a couple of tables set up outside. Aurita noticed that Rodan and Ayla kept glancing at each other.

"She was asking me about him last night before she went to sleep," Stasha said quietly. "I didn't know what to tell her."

"I only know that he is Brook's cousin," Aurita replied. "I gave her the day off after she had been asking what it was like to live in a village. He offered to show her around."

"We've worried about finding her a husband," Stasha admitted. "Garman is related to most of the palace staff."

Aurita heard Brook chuckle quietly to himself. Directly after breakfast they all went to Fordan's house. There were men working on the roof hammering shingles into place. Aurita was surprised to see how large it was. The house had a large main room for cooking and eating with space around the fireplace for chairs. There were three bedrooms and the shop was attached to the house.

"You did add the third bedroom," Talia said.

"Because it is what you wanted," Fordan said and kissed her hand.

After leaving Fordan's house, they went to the graveyard. Brook knelt for a moment at the foot of the graves of his grandparents. She was glad that he had been able to participate in his grandmother's burial. She knew he would have taken her death even harder if he hadn't been able to.

Aurita noticed that Brook seemed happy and relaxed as they spent the day at the festival. She saw Rodan and Ayla several times. Once they were even holding hands. The festival ended with a dance in the center of the village. She enjoyed dancing with Brook as the moon rose over the village. She noticed Rodan dancing with Ayla while her parents watched with pleased expressions on their faces.

*****

Brook woke before Aurita did. He thought about what lay ahead. They would visit the last village, Weston. He wondered how Aurita would feel about returning to Weston as Queen Aurita of Brinley.

Shortly after breakfast they said their goodbyes and left Nordam. Brook noticed that Ayla seemed reluctant to leave. Rodan kissed her hand and helped her mount her horse. They traveled along the road stopping briefly for lunch. At nightfall they were not far from Weston. As they set up camp, he noticed Ayla sitting on a rock by herself on the edge of the clearing. As a noise drew her attention, she turned and he saw something glittering on her cheek. Why would she be crying? He went over to where she was sitting and placed his hand on her shoulder.

"What is the matter?" he asked her.

"Nothing, My King," she replied with a tremor in her voice.

"You are crying," he said as he sat on a nearby rock. "That seems to indicate that there is something troubling you."

"It's nothing you should be bothered with," she said as she wiped away the tear on her cheek.

"You seemed to be having a good time yesterday with Rodan," Brook said watching her for a reaction.

She looked down at the ground.

"What did you talk about?" he asked.

"About what it was like to live in a village instead of the palace," she said without looking up. "And about you."

"Certainly there are much more interesting things to talk about than me," he said and she looked up in surprise.

"He said he didn't know you very well and thought that I must know you better since we both grew up in the palace," she said. "I told him that I really didn't know you either. He mentioned that you had once said you didn't have any friends."

Brook was a little surprised.

"My grandmother and your father were basically my only friends while I was growing up," he said, nodding.

"Since you became king you have never said a single word about the past," she said. "You have been very nice to me in spite of how mean I was to you. I never even thanked you when you stood up for me when Nokar was teasing me by taking my doll."

"You were nicer to me than most of the children," Brook said. "I remember the other girls would make faces at me and then laugh. I remember that you never did that. Is that why you've been so quiet and almost avoiding being near me this whole trip?"

Ayla nodded.

"I was afraid you would be angry with me," she said. "Mother and Father were asking me how I liked Rodan and Nordam. I know they want me to marry outside the palace, but only you can approve that."

"There really isn't a law saying the king must approve any marriage of palace staff, but I am aware that seems to be expected," Brook said. "If you and Rodan want to get married, I will approve of it."

"You wouldn't mind that I would become your cousin?" Ayla asked.

"No more than I mind Burkhart being my wife's father," Brook said.

"I had wondered about how you felt about that until I have listened to the audiences," she said. "I could tell that you respected the man Burkhart had become."

"I miss Burkhart," Brook said. "I know what evil he did while he was king, but I knew the man he had become. He was a good friend who cared for me in times when I needed someone I trusted to take care of me. Although he would not admit it until he was dying, he knew all along who I was."

"I have thought a lot about what a difficult time you had as a child," Ayla said as she seemed to be relaxing a bit. "I don't remember ever seeing you with any toys. I do remember seeing you out in the garden with your grandmother."

"I really didn't have many toys," he admitted. "I never took them out of my room because I knew the larger boys would take them from me. I spent a lot of time studying to become king."

"It seems you really didn't have a childhood at all," she commented. "That's sad."

"I know that the past cannot be changed," he replied. "I have no regrets. I see no reason to let my past control my actions, although I did enjoy telling Nokar and Larkin that I had been in the military and now had more than a good punch."

Ayla began to giggle and said, "That explains why they have stayed in the kitchens since you became king. It's the one place you never go."

Brook began to laugh and said, "Perhaps it is time I let them know that the past is forgotten. They are probably afraid that I want to punish them for the way they treated me."

Chapter 26 – Loyalties and Reminders

They had a quick breakfast the next morning before continuing their journey. They reached Weston before mid morning. They were greeted with cheers as they made their way to the church. By the time they reached the church, everyone in the village was there. Aurita was a bit surprised. She had been a bit anxious about how the people of Weston would feel about her becoming queen. Brook's grandmother and grandfather both hugged her. Noka, Carria and Barna all hugged her as well. They granted audiences before lunch, but most people wanted to congratulate them on their marriage. There were a few very minor issues that were easily cleared up.

They had lunch with Brook's grandparents. It seemed a bit strange at first considering the last time they had eaten lunch with them she had not known they were his grandparents.

"You're quiet, Aurita," his grandmother said as they were finishing their meal.

"It's just so strange to think that you are Brook's grandparents and knew all along that I would become Brook's wife," she replied.

"It was sometimes hard to not call you Granddaughter," the Minister said with a laugh. "We have always thought of you as our granddaughter."

"Then it would be alright for me to call you Grandfather and Grandmother?" she asked.

"Of course," he replied.

She glanced at Brook and found he was smiling.

"I think I have considered you part of my family even though I did not know I would marry you," Brook said.

"I have often wondered what it would be like to have more than just a father," Aurita said. "I had always hoped that my husband's family would love me."

"We always have," Brook's grandmother said.

"How long are you staying?" Brook's grandfather asked

Brook looked at her and said, "It's entirely up to you."

"We could stay another day. I would like to spend some time with my friends. I have enjoyed traveling, but I think I am ready to return home to the palace," she replied. "That is where I belong now."

"I'm so glad to hear you say that," Brook said before kissing her hand. "Besides, I found out that Larkin and Nokar have been hiding in the kitchens ever since I told them I had more than a good punch now."

"The ones who were calling you Little Prince No-Name?"

"Yes. I think I'll have them brought here," Brook said with a grin. "I spoke to Ayla last night about growing up in the palace. Many of the children I grew up being teased by are now palace staff. I want them to understand that I will not hold that past against them, but I want to have a bit of fun teasing Larkin and Nokar first."

After lunch Brook and Aurita went for a walk down by the river. It was a little strange to have the guards following them, but they stayed back and allowed them some privacy.

"So much has changed since the last time we stood here," Aurita said as they watched the brook flow into the river. "I still miss Father, but I wouldn't trade my life now for the way things were before."

"I'm happy to hear you say that," Brook said. "I will miss your father too, but I am happier now than I thought was possible. I know that ruling a kingdom can be hard work, but it is what we both were trained to do."

"I want to see the house and shop," she said.

*****

When they reached the house, she paused at the door. He knew this would be a bit difficult for her. When she finally opened the door, they found everything exactly as they had left it. She walked over to the bed and picked up one of the tunics.

As she held it up to her cheek, she whispered, "I can't believe he's really gone."

He took her into his arms and gently stroked her hair. They stood in silence for a while before she finally moved. He released her and she laid the tunic back on the bed. He followed her outside, closing the door behind him. She opened the shop door and stopped before entering. He stepped behind her and looked over her shoulder. The shop had been returned to the way it was before the war. All of the extra beds were gone and in their place were piles of things.

"Wedding gifts from the whole village," a voice said behind them.

They turned to find Carria's father standing behind them. He quickly knelt then rose to his feet.

306

"During the war, we all got to know you and Burkhart better than we had allowed ourselves to the whole time you lived in the village," he said. "We came to realize that Burkhart had become a good man who worked hard for what he had. We learned that he was a good father who taught you the value of service to others. We know that we can never take back the things we did or said, but we wanted you to know that we are sorry."

"We have been reading Father's journal," Aurita said. "I now fully understand why everyone hated Father so much. I understand why the villagers treated us the way they did. I see no reason to fault people for their past behavior in that respect and forgive them. I also learned that everything King Langward said about him being a changed man is true. We have been visiting all of the villages in hope that the people of Brinley will accept me as their queen even though the man I knew as my father was once an evil, selfish tyrant of a king."

"We were all very surprised to discover that you were King Langward's son," Rocar said. "We had all come to feel you were a part of this village and would someday make it your home. We didn't care that you would never give anyone your name."

"To me it had become home more than the palace ever was," Brook said. "Because I had no name, the children I grew up with in the palace teased me and would not play with me. I too have decided it is time to forgive the past. The two who were the worst still work in the palace. I found out that they have been hiding in the kitchens after they found out I had been in the military. I gave one of them a black eye once. I'm going to have them brought here. I thought I would tease them a bit before letting them know that I've forgiven them."

Rocar began to laugh and said, "Let me know if I can do anything to help. I wanted to thank you for what you did to change my opinion of Monau. He and I have become close friends. I went alone to visit my father-in-law. We have settled our differences at last. I learned that he had lost a young son before my wife was born that she did not even know of. Although he had never allowed anyone to mention his son, he was still mourning his death. He admitted that he was afraid to have another son for fear of losing him."

"In the end he must have realized that by driving you away, he lost his daughter as well," Brook said. "I'm glad I was able to help."

"I have seen that you are wise beyond your years," Rocar said. "Brinley will prosper under your rule."

*****

Brook sent a message to the palace to have Larkin and Nokar bring a wagon to Weston, then they spent the rest of the afternoon going through the wedding gifts. It was just before supper time when a guard informed them that the wagon was arriving. As he stepped outside, he was not surprised to see Kon, Monau and Kennar escorting the wagon. Larkin and Nokar suddenly looked nervous.

"It's about time you showed up," he said in a serious tone.

"We've been out on patrol and saw the message you sent," Kon said as the three dismounted. "We thought you would have signaled us when you arrived."

"I've been taking care of some business," he said as he saw Grandfather cross the bridge with Rocar.

"Supper will be ready to eat in an hour," Grandfather said.

"Leave the wagon here," Brook said with a nod.

"Which one of these two did you give a black eye to, My King?" Rocar asked.

'Play along,' he signaled before saying, "Nokar."

As he pointed to him, Nokar fell to his knees followed closely by Larkin.

"The other is Larkin, I assume," Kon said.

"Yes," he replied. "To your feet."

The two men looked a little pale as they slowly got to their feet.

"We could take care of them for you," Monau said.

"Perhaps we should take a walk down by the river," Brook said.

"You go have your fun," Aurita said. "I'm going to go visit with my friends."

"I'll see you in about an hour," he replied before he kissed her tenderly.

He could see a smile starting as she turned to leave. He signaled for the guards to follow Aurita and Grandfather.

Nokar and Larkin found themselves being escorted by Kon, Monau and Kenner. Brook was having a hard time not laughing. He could tell that Rocar was having the same problem. They soon arrived at where the brook met the river.

"You know many have lost their lives in this section of the river, My King," Rocar commented.

Brook saw Larkin and Nokar begin to tremble as he said, "It nearly cost me my life."

He frowned as he turned to face Larkin and Nokar. He could see they were beginning to sweat.

"I doubt you have heard how the war with Okiah ended," he said and the two shook their heads.

He began to walk back away from the noise of the river and the rest followed. When they reached the shop and tiny house, he stopped.

Brook told them how he had captured Okiah's king only to wind up fighting for his life in the river. He also told them about making friends with Prince Onan. After assuring them he wasn't still mad at them he realized it was time for supper.

They walked in silence toward the churchyard. When they arrived, almost everyone was there. Larkin and Nokar looked surprised as everyone except Aurita knelt.

"Rise, My Friends," he said. "I thank you for your gifts."

Soon they were seated at a table with Aurita and her friends.

"Uncle Langford confirmed what Garman suspected," she said before they began to eat.

Brook smiled as his friends looked confused.

"We are going to be parents," he said. "Aurita is with child."

"That makes all of us then," Kennar said with a laugh.

Larkin and Nokar glanced at each other. Brook watched them as they ate. He could see that they were quite surprised about how much respect people had for him and how well liked he was. They seemed even more surprised as he and Aurita helped the villagers clean up after the meal.

"You are king," Larkin said. "Why did you help clean up?"

"While living outside the palace I learned a lot of things about how the people of Brinley live," he replied. "I learned what it is like to be a part of a community and what I needed to do to be a servant to the people of Brinley. What you and Nokar never figured out is that I never felt that I was better than anyone else."

He took Larkin and Nokar back to Burkhart's shop to get the gifts. They loaded the wagon in silence. Several guards joined them and it was soon loaded. They reached the palace just before supper. It felt good to be home again.

"You've been quiet," Aurita said as they sat down to eat. "Is something wrong?"

"No," he replied and kissed her hand. "I'll explain when we get back to our quarters."

Once they had finished eating, he led her back to their quarters. He sat down on a settee and she sat next to him. He could see the worry in her eyes.

"I'm glad that I have made peace with Larkin and Nokar," he said. "But they reminded me of something."

"What is it?"

"After my grandmother was buried, I was sent to Weston," he said and she nodded. "On the way there, we met a fortune teller."

"I remember you mentioning that. What did she say?"

"I cannot tell you all of it," he said with a sigh. "What she did say let me know that regardless of how long I live, what I do as King of Brinley is very important and will eventually bring peace and prosperity to many."

"How long you live?" Aurita asked. "You're not dying, are you?"

"No," he said as he thought about what to tell her. "Not just yet. But I want you to remember what I am about to tell you."

She nodded.

"I was told that we would have two sons," he began and she looked surprised. "I was also told that I would see them grow up. She said that I would not live to see my true heir, but you would."

"I don't want to live without you," she said and a tear rolled down her cheek.

"I know," he replied as he wiped away the tear. "There is more and it is very important for you to remember this. My true heir will be unparalleled with the sword. My true heir will bring peace and prosperity to many nations without drawing blood. There will come a time when all seems lost, but you must not give up hope. You must find my birthmark to reveal my true heir. It will be hidden and the search will be difficult, but you must not give up."

"Your true heir would not be one of our children?" she asked.

"A grandchild," he said.

"I still do not understand," she said. "It worries and frightens me."

"It will be many years before I die," he said. "I do not mean to worry or frighten you, but it is important that you know about this. I do not want to die and leave you alone. I love you with all of my heart and could never intentionally do anything to hurt you."

Chapter 27 – Sons and Brothers

The months passed quickly as Brook and Aurita waited for their son to be born. His parents moved to Weston shortly after Rodan married Ayla. General Kannon began bringing his grandson, Caddaric, to the council meetings and an assistant was found for Nokar.

It was a stormy winter night when their first son was born. They named him Burkhart after Aurita's father. Brook was secretly relieved when Aurita was able to eat in the dining hall the day after she delivered considering her mother had died in childbirth. He was surprised to notice that although Burkhart had a small birthmark on his right shoulder, it was not heart shaped.

Two years later Aurita gave birth to their second son, who was named Langward after Brook's father. Langward had Brook's heart shaped birthmark on his right shoulder. As their sons grew, Brook noticed that Burkhart was very outgoing and Langward was a bit more reserved. They both learned to read and write quickly, but Langward learned the language of the Northern kingdoms more readily than Burkhart. Whenever there was mischief going on in the palace, it was usually Burkhart that instigated it even though sometimes Langward said it was him. Langward liked to spend time alone drawing. Brook and Aurita loved both their sons, but spent a lot of time training Burkhart to be king.

One evening Brook was standing on the balcony looking out over the royal garden when he noticed some boys running through the garden. Suddenly the boy right behind the leader caught the leader and threw him to the ground. The boy struggled to regain his feet, but the other boy was larger and soon had him pinned. Brook saw the larger boy hit the smaller one several times while the other boys watched and laughed. He didn't like what he saw and was about to shout out when the larger boy let the smaller one up. Brook drew in a quick breath as he saw the glint of the sun off the armbands of both boys.

When his sons returned to the royal quarters, Burkhart sat down and began telling them about what he had learned that day at the training camp. Langward went directly to his room. Brook realized that this is what the fortune teller had told him about. Although it pained him to know that Burkhart was beating up Langward, he knew he must not intervene.

As time went by, Brook noticed that Langward more frequently took the blame for any trouble that Brook was certain that Burkhart was responsible for. Langward took any punishment without a word in his defense. This troubled Brook, especially when one of the servants reported that Langward frequently had bruises that he explained as clumsiness on his part. Soon after that, Langward began to refuse any help from servants when he bathed or dressed.

One evening Brook went to his study to find Langward sitting in the window alcove, quietly drawing. He had come to study the reports that General Kannon had sent on Mannton. He was concerned that they might try another attack on Brinley. Langward wiped at his face after quickly shutting his drawing book. Suddenly, the reports didn't seem so important.

As Langward headed toward the door, Brook said, "I want to talk to you, Son."

Langward looked nervous as Brook locked the door. Although he was nearly as tall as Brook, he was still slender. When others were around, Langward appeared happy, but Brook sensed sadness behind the smile. His eyes betrayed the emotions he was trying to hide.

Brook sat down in a chair at the table and Langward sat down to face him. He wondered how much he should tell Langward and how to begin.

"Long before you were born a fortune teller told me about my future and that of my children," Brook said and noticed interest in Langward's eyes. "I wish I could tell you what she told me, but I don't think I should."

Langward was silent and looked a little disappointed.

"I do want you to know that your mother and I love you very much," Brook said. "I also need you to know and believe that even though you will never become king of Brinley, you are just as important as Burkhart."

"How could that be, Father?" Langward asked with a tremor in his voice.

"I cannot explain it to you," Brook said with a sigh. "I know that regardless of what you want everyone to think, you are not very happy."

Langward looked surprised.

"I know more about what goes on than I will admit," Brook said. "When I was growing up I did not have any friends until I entered the

313

military. There were things that I hid from my parents, just as you hide things from us. I do understand what you are going through. I wish that I could change things, but you need to make your own way in this world. I will not be here forever to shield you from pain and sorrow. It doesn't matter who you are related to or where you were born. What will matter in the end is what you have done with your life. I know that someday you will meet the woman who will become your wife and mother to your child."

"I doubt any woman could love me," Langward said softly.

"I promise you that you will have a wife," Brook said. "I promise you that you are much more important to Brinley and to this world than you could ever imagine. Even if one day you leave the palace and even leave Brinley, you will still be of vital importance to the future of Brinley and this world."

Langward was silent. Brook let him think about it for a while.

"Burkhart says that he is so much more important than I could ever be," Langward said quietly. "He says that my drawings are ugly and worthless."

"I know that your brother doesn't respect you," Brook said as he saw the tear glittering in the corner of Langward's eye. "Unfortunately I cannot order him to respect you. I can tell you that he is wrong. I have seen your drawings. You have your grandfather's talent. I had always wished I could draw. Sometimes a picture can say a lot more than words ever could."

Brook could tell that Langward still didn't quite believe him.

"I know that you feel out of place and lonely," Brook said. "I know that nothing I say can change that. Just remember that you are important to me. I know how hard it is to believe in the words of a fortune teller. I know that there are people who want others to believe that they can see the future even though they cannot."

"How do you know that the fortune teller was really able to see the future?" Langward asked.

"She knew exactly who I was even though I had never seen her before. Some of what she said has already happened. Because of what she told me, I know some things for certain. Because of your birthmark, I know that although Burkhart will sit on Brinley's throne, your life is just as important to the future of Brinley for it will be your child who will rule Brinley."

"How?" Langward asked.

"I dare not tell you," Brook said. "Just remember that it is more important to be in service of others than to rule over others. I have complete faith in what she told me coming true. I also have complete faith that you will become the kind of man that others will respect and admire. I know that what I have told you has confused you, but know that your life is worth living. You must know sorrow that you might know joy and pain that you might know pleasure. There is a price that must be paid for everything. Sometimes war is the price that must be paid for peace. I have reports to go over tonight. Mannton is again preparing to attack Brinley."

Brook stood up and so did Langward.

"Remember, Langward," Brook said as he placed his hand on Langward's shoulder. "I may not say or do anything to intervene, but I am aware of what is going on. When my mother could not admit that I was her son, she would smile and nod to me. It was her way of telling me that she loved me. Know that when I nod to you, I am telling you that I love you."

"I'll remember, Father," Langward replied before he left.

Brook sighed and shook his head as the door closed behind Langward. It pained him to see his son suffering. He was afraid that someday Langward might die at the hands of another. He sat down and began reading the reports. From them he knew that another battle would be inevitable.

The next morning, Aurita asked him what was wrong. He knew he must take care to not reveal everything to her.

"There's trouble in the south again," he said.

Later that day Garman reported that someone had tied all the laundry in knots while the servants were eating lunch. Brook knew it had to be Burkhart and his friends again. He called his sons and the other boys into the throne room.

"Does anyone here know how all the laundry got tied in knots?" he asked.

There were several snickers as Burkhart said, "I thought I saw Langward near the laundry."

"It was me, Father," Langward said and there was more snickering.

"I really don't know what I am going to do with you," Brook said as he nodded. "I think that you need to spend some time outside the palace.

Perhaps you don't appreciate what you have here. Pack your things and I will take you to Weston. You can stay with your grandparents for two weeks. Perhaps you will learn what one must do to live outside the palace."

"Yes, Father," Langward said and nodded as the other boys snickered.

"Burkhart," Brook said.

"Yes, Father?" Burkhart replied.

"Why don't you and the rest of these boys go down to the laundry and help the servants untie the laundry?" he said and the snickering stopped. "You should be aware of what the palace servants do."

"Yes, Father," Burkhart said, although he did not look so smug anymore.

Shortly after the boys left, he went to the royal quarters. Aurita looked worried.

"Why is Langward packing?" she asked. "Are you really sending him out of the palace?"

"Yes," he replied and kissed her forehead. "I think he needs to spend some time learning to live outside the palace."

"I worry about him," she said quietly. "He is in trouble all of the time. He spends a lot of time locked in his room by himself."

"I know," he replied. "I worry about him too. I'll go talk to him."

He found Langward finishing his packing.

"I thought you could use a break," he said quietly. "I thought you might enjoy some time away from the palace. I know that you take the blame for Burkhart."

Langward looked surprised.

"There will come times in your life when you are faced with difficult decisions," Brook said. "Everything has a price and you must be prepared to pay that price. I know that it seems that your mother and I spend all of our time training Burkhart to be king, but you too are learning what you need to know. That is why I am sending you to Weston. Your mother doesn't know, nor will I tell her."

"Thank you, Father," Langward said. "I know she worries about me."

"Come on," he said. "I'll take you out to Weston."

Aurita hugged Langward and kissed his cheek before letting him go. Although Langward looked like he was being punished while they were inside the palace wall, he relaxed and began to smile once they left the palace.

"Sometimes I wish I could leave the palace forever," Langward admitted in the language of the Northern kingdoms as they left the city. "I wish I could go where Burkhart could not find me."

"I know," Brook said. "That day might actually come. If it does, I want you to be prepared. You might consider going east."

"I heard some of the guards talking about seeing a large winged beast flying the night sky to the east."

"I've heard the same things, but if everyone fears the east they will be less likely to follow you. I remember stories about your grandfather spending time in the east before becoming king. He may be able to tell you more about the region."

When they reached Weston, Brook's father was outside chopping some wood.

"I didn't expect to see you today, Son," he said as he wiped his brow.

"I brought Langward to stay for a couple of weeks," Brook said as they dismounted. "Go let your grandmother know you are here, Langward. I need to speak to your grandfather for a while."

Langward went into the house while Brook and his father walked toward the river.

"What's going on?" Father asked. "Where's Burkhart?"

"Remember I told you about the fortune teller speaking to me after Grandmother's death?"

"Yes."

"It has a lot to do with that," he replied. "Because of what she said, I know for certain that someday Langward will leave the palace and never return."

Father looked surprised.

"She said that just as I hid things from you, my sons would hide things from me. Today, Garman reported that all of the laundry had been tied in knots while the servants were eating lunch," Brook said. "Although Langward immediately said he had done it, I am certain that Burkhart and his friends did it."

"Why don't you punish Burkhart?" Father asked.

317

"I know that I must not interfere," Brook said with a sigh. "I acted angry with Langward and told him that he should stay for two weeks in Weston learning how to live outside the palace. Then I told Burkhart that he and his friends should help the servants untie the laundry so he can learn what the servants do to run the palace."

Father began to laugh.

"Langward knows that I know more than I am willing to admit," Brook said. "He also knows that he is being prepared for his future, not being punished. He is not happy in the palace and I know someday fate will lead him to leave the palace. It is in part what the fortune teller told me. He needs to know how to live outside the palace and how to survive off the land. I know these are things he can learn from you and Uncle Langford."

"I'm glad that you are such a wise parent," Father said as they headed back toward the house. "I'll keep him busy learning."

"Give him time to draw," Brook said. "He needs to know that he is a talented artist. Burkhart told him his drawings were ugly and worthless."

"I'll make certain he knows the truth," Father said as Mother and Langward came out of the house.

Mother hugged Brook and smiled.

"Thank you for letting him stay for a while," Mother said.

"The men are starting to build another house tomorrow," Father said. "We can always use another pair of hands."

"Now, Langward," Brook said. "You will obey your grandparents while you are here."

"I won't cause any trouble, Father," Langward said in a serious tone and nodded.

"Good," he replied as he nodded. "I'll see you in two weeks."

When Brook returned to the palace, Burkhart was locked in his room. Aurita looked worried.

"What is going on?" she asked. "Burkhart said you were punishing him."

He led her out to the balcony before answering.

"I am just trying to teach him some of what he needs to know," Brook said with a sigh as he shut the door behind him. "Just as I am trying to teach Langward what he needs to know."

Aurita looked confused.

"I know that Burkhart needs to understand the lives of the palace servants just as he needs to know the needs of the people of Brinley," Brook said. "He may not understand why I had him and his friends untie the knots in the laundry, but I felt it was important for him to do it. I think that Burkhart needs to read your father's journal."

"What are you not telling me?" she asked.

"It has a lot to do with what the fortune teller told me," he replied. "I promise that in time you will understand. I also promise that Burkhart will not be punished for something he did not do."

"All right," she said at last. "I think you need to go talk to him."

He kissed her on her forehead before going to Burkhart's door. He knocked and waited. Just when he thought he would have to get the key, Burkhart opened the door.

"I need to talk to you, Son," Brook said.

Burkhart backed away from the door before sitting down on the edge of his bed.

"Why did you make us untie the laundry, Father?" Burkhart asked. "Langward admitted to doing it."

"I know you don't understand," Brook said as he sat down on the bed next to Burkhart. "As king, you will be responsible for everyone in Brinley. Not only does that mean ruling over them, but sometimes it can mean that you have to deal with the consequences of their actions. Don't think that Langward is getting any less. He will spend the next two weeks helping build a house and helping your grandparents. He will be awakened at or before dawn every morning and not go to bed until the sun goes down. He will work until he is sore and tired, only to have to bathe in the cold river. He will learn to hunt for food and prepare that food so it can be eaten. He will spend most of his time dirty and tired."

Burkhart began to laugh a little.

"Don't think it is funny," Brook said and Burkhart fell silent. "Many people work very hard for barely enough food to keep them alive and clothes to wear. They spend all of their time dirty and tired with little hope of anything better. I want you to read your mother's father's journal. It contains some very important lessons that you need to learn. I have noticed that you and Langward don't always get along very well. He is your brother and he always will be. There may come a day that he is gone and you regret that you were not better friends. You and Langward are two very different people. It is important for you to remember that even though he is different, he is still important."

"He will never be king, Father," Burkhart said. "Isn't being king more important than anything else?"

"No," Brook replied. "Just because your brother will never be king, doesn't make him any less important. He can still do great and important things in his life. He can do things that will make people remember him long after he is dead."

Burkhart looked surprised.

"Go to sleep," Brook said as he stood up.

"Is everything alright?" Aurita asked as he entered the bedroom.

"Burkhart has much to learn," he replied.

"I've seen that expression on Father's face," Aurita said. "There's more that you're not telling me."

*****

Brook looked very tired and very worried.

"Remember when you had to cut off Barna's father's leg?" Brook asked her and she nodded. "Cutting off someone's leg was probably not something you wanted to do, but it had to be done. You knew that you were the only one who could do it but in order to save his life, you had to put him through too much pain for a man to endure while conscious."

"Yes," she replied wondering what that had to do with Burkhart.

"That was the price that had to be paid to preserve his life," Brook said.

"Yes," she acknowledged.

"I know that through our lineage, peace and prosperity will be brought to Brinley and many other kingdoms, but there is a high price to be paid," Brook said. "I do not know the whole of it, but I know the sacrifices made by us and our sons will be worth it. As king and queen of Brinley, our lives are pledged in service to the people of Brinley, no matter what the cost."

"You are frightening me," Aurita said. "You are talking as though you know exactly what will happen, but you don't want me to know. You told me that you will die before I do. Is that what this is all about?"

"I do not know everything that will happen," Brook said with a sigh. "I do know more than I wish I knew. I do know that I cannot share that information in whole with anyone alive. I know that I must allow things to happen, even though I know the full consequence of the events. The eventual outcome is far too important."

Aurita knew he would not tell her any more. She could see the pain he felt in his heart and the conflict in his mind. She had seen it far too many times in her father to not recognize it in her husband. She stroked his face softly.

"Why don't you go down and talk to Father about it?" she said quietly. "Let him take some of the burden from your heart."

Brook nodded and kissed her forehead before silently leaving. She followed him out to the sitting room and watched him leave. She collapsed to the floor as she felt the tears begin to run down her face.

"Mother? What's wrong?"

She looked up to see Burkhart kneeling before her with a worried look on his face.

"Where is Father going?"

She slowly stood and led him out to the balcony. In the gathering dusk, she could see Brook as he knelt at Father's grave side. She pointed and Burkhart looked before looking back at her.

"What's wrong?" Burkhart again asked. "Is this about Langward?"

She went into the sitting room and sat down. He sat down next to her.

"Only your father knows what this is all about," she said with a tremor in her voice. "He won't even tell me. He said that there are things happening that must happen no matter what the cost and that the eventual outcome was far too important to try to stop these things."

"When he came and talked to me he said some things that were very strange," Burkhart said quietly. "Things I don't quite understand."

"He said that right now you are learning what you need to know and Langward is learning what he needs to know," Aurita said. "I know he is worried about both of you. I suppose we will eventually understand all of this. You had best go to bed."

Aurita went to bed and was asleep before Brook returned. When she woke the next morning, he was already awake. He kissed her and held her tightly in his arms.

"Are you going to be alright?" she asked quietly.

"Yes," he said. "I know what must be done and I am ready to do it when the time comes. There will be a letter and a scroll in the desk in the study that are sealed with the ring your father gave me. They are to be opened only by my true heir."

*****

Directly after breakfast he went to the study and wrote a letter to his true heir. He sealed it not with his signet ring, but with the wooden ring.

During the next two years, Brook watched his sons closely. Langward still took the blame for most of the trouble that Burkhart caused, but there were fewer instances. He occasionally observed a look on Langward's face that he knew all too well. He knew that Burkhart was still beating Langward. It broke his heart to know he should not stop it. He frequently sat at Aurita's father's grave to unburden his heart. He knew his time was swiftly coming to an end.

*****

It was before dawn one morning when he was awakened to news of Mannton preparing to attack again. He knew in his heart that he would not return home from this war even as he got dressed. He stroked the jeweled hilt of his first sword before buckling on his new sword.

"What is it, Brook?" Aurita asked after he kissed her goodbye.

"When all seems hopeless, search out my birthmark," Brook said. "Do not forget that Brinley's future depends upon it. It will be many years that you must remember this. You must not say anything to Burkhart. When you find my birthmark, you will find my true heir. Give my true heir my first sword."

"You're not coming back," Aurita said softly.

"Remember that I love you with all that I am. Not even death can change that," Brook replied. "I will be watching over you."

He went into the sitting room to find Burkhart and Langward looking confused. Langward knelt at his feet and was soon joined by Burkhart.

"Rise, My Sons," he said. "Burkhart, we are going to war with Mannton. Go prepare yourself. Meet me in the courtyard."

He watched Burkhart as he went to his bedroom.

"Come with me, Langward," he said.

"What is wrong, Father?" Langward asked.

322

He led him out to the balcony and shut the door.

"There are things I know that I cannot change even though I desperately want to," Brook said. "Know that if I could I would take your place."

Langward looked frightened.

"You must be strong, My Dear Son," Brook said. "Soon there will be important decisions that you alone can make. I pray that you have the courage and strength to make these decisions. I know that in time you will be faced with the choice between your own life and that of your child. At that time you may not remember this day or my words, but I know you will make the correct decision. Events that begin today will in time lead to peace and prosperity for all of Brinley and many other kingdoms. There is a great price for that peace and prosperity. A price that must be paid in blood, both mine and yours. My time is at hand, but yours is not. I know that you will have a wife and a child. I know that you will have peace and happiness that you have never known before that price is paid in full."

"I don't understand, Father," Langward said.

"Nor are you meant to right now," Brook said. "Know this, if you leave this palace and Brinley, leave it behind you and never look back. Your child will return someday to Brinley, but you will not. Take your armband with you for it will guide your child back here to the palace. In time it will be your bloodline that rules Brinley, not Burkhart's. It does not matter what title you hold, or who you are related to, you will be loved and remembered, that is what is important. Remember that your mother and I love you."

Brook hugged his son before leaving him on the balcony. He went down to the courtyard to find Burkhart waiting for him. Garman offered him a slice of bread and cheese, but he was not hungry. They mounted their horses and rode at a gallop to where General Kannon and Colonel Caddaric were waiting for them.

"A word with you, General," Brook said. "In private."

General Kannon nodded and turned his horse to follow Brook a short distance away.

"I know that look," General Kannon said in the language of the Northern kingdoms.

"Remember what I told you and Father in Weston after Grandmother died?" Brook asked.

"Yes," the general replied.

"I know that it is time," Brook said. "I will defend Brinley unto my death. I want you to do something for me."

"What do you need me to do?" General Kannon replied. "You need not die."

"You cannot say a word of what I am about to tell you to anyone, ever," Brook said and the general nodded. "Soon after my death, Prince Langward will leave. No one is to stop him or interfere."

"What do you mean?" General Kannon asked.

"It is the destiny fate has chosen for him," Brook said. "The price for peace and prosperity will be paid with my blood and his. Do not let him be forgotten. There will come a day when it will be time to find Prince Langward. Tell Caddaric that someday my true heir will be found and will need his guidance along with that of the other ministers."

"I don't understand," General Kannon replied. "I will obey without question because I trust you know what you are doing."

"Thank you, My Friend," Brook said. "One last thing, there is a letter and a scroll in the study desk drawer sealed with the imprint of my wooden ring. Burkhart is not to open them."

The battle started slowly, but soon both armies were fully involved in the battle. After several days, Brinley was finally beginning to drive Mannton's army back over the border. Brook was pleased. He was leading a final charge against Mannton's King's unit when he met their king face to face.

"It is time for you to go back where you belong," Brook told Mannton's King as they dueled.

"It is time you gave Brinley to me," was the king's reply.

"Never," Brook replied as he slashed the king's side deeply.

He saw General Kannon appear beside the king as he fell. With one last effort as he collapsed, the king drove his sword into Brook's chest. He felt the searing pain as he was lifted and carried away.

"Father!" Burkhart exclaimed as his face came into view.

"It is time for you to take the throne of Brinley, Burkhart," Brook said with difficulty.

With great pain he removed the armband and handed it to Burkhart.

"Never forget those who are gone, Son," Brook said. "The price for peace and prosperity is paid in their blood."

*****

Burkhart stood in shock holding the armband of the king. He could see the tears on General Kannon's face as Father's body was carried away. Colonel Caddaric entered the tent.

"Mannton's army is retreating," Colonel Caddaric said. "What's wrong?"

"King Brook is dead," General Kannon said quietly.

Colonel Caddaric fell to his knees with tears streaming down his face.

"We must go tell Queen Aurita," General Kannon said. "Caddaric, make certain the men know all Mannton's wounded and dead can be taken by Mannton's troops as they retreat. Remain here until I return."

"Yes, Sir," Colonel Caddaric replied as he got to his feet and wiped his face.

By the time they reached the palace, Burkhart was realizing that he was king of Brinley. Mother was on the balcony.

"Father died in battle, Mother," Burkhart said. "Mannton is in retreat."

"He knew when he left that he was not returning," Mother said quietly. "You are now king."

Several servants came and took Burkhart to the bathing chamber while General Kannon stayed with Mother. Soon he was bathed and dressed. The armband of the king was placed on his arm. He went down to the throne room and sat down on Father's throne. Langward entered and crossed to the stairs without looking up.

"Father is dead and I am now your king," Burkhart said.

Langward looked up at him, but said nothing.

"Shouldn't you kneel before your king?" Burkhart said. "I can make you, you know."

"Do what you must, I will obey the law, but I will not obey you," Langward said in an angry tone. "All my life, you have imposed your will upon me, but no longer. I will not take the blame for you anymore. I will not take your beatings either."

"Father was right, you don't appreciate what you have here," Burkhart said angrily. "Leave the palace before I have you thrown in the dungeon!"

"I will leave," Langward said. "Of my own free will, I will leave and never return."

He turned and left. Burkhart went into the study. He wondered why Langward was so stubborn. It angered him to think his own brother would refuse to kneel before him. After a while, there was a knock on the door.

"Come," he said as he opened the center desk drawer.

As General Kannon entered Burkhart noticed a letter and a scroll both sealed with what looked like Father's wooden ring. He placed them on the desk.

"Your father said that those are not to be opened by you," General Kannon said.

"Then who?" Burkhart asked.

"I do not know," General Kannon replied. "I suppose your mother must know. You had best go speak with her. Something Langward did upset her."

Burkhart put the letter and scroll back into the drawer before returning to the royal quarters. Mother was on the settee, crying.

"What's the matter, Mother?" Burkhart asked as he sat next to her. "What has Langward done?"

"He went into his room and I heard slamming," Mother said. "I went to see what he was doing. I have never seen him so angry before. I asked him what was wrong. He said that he was leaving and never returning. He said that he loved me, but could no longer live in the palace. Then he took his armband off and put it in a bag that looked like it had books in it. He took a cape from the closet and left."

"I'll send some guards to look for him," Burkhart said. "It must have to do with Father's death."

Chapter 28 – Finding Freedom

Langward felt a great relief as he left the palace wall. He tried to hunch over and blend with the crowd as he made his way east. As he left the city, night was falling. He found some edible plants and an outcropping of rock to hide in for night. He thought about Father's words to him as he ate the bitter plants. His heart ached as he realized that he would never see his mother again. The rising sun woke him the next morning. He followed the rocks up the mountain toward the border and a mountain pass. He heard the patrol before he saw it. He was able to hide in some low trees that grew against the rocks. They eventually moved on and he continued his journey. As the sun began to set on the third day, he reached the pass. He took one last look back at Brinley before leaving it behind.

By noon the next day he reached the other side of the pass and looked out over the thick forest. He noticed several columns of smoke in a group to the north. Perhaps it was a settlement. All he knew for certain was that it was not Brinley. It was the next morning before he reached the outskirts of the village. By that time, he was thirsty and hungry. He saw a woman drawing water from a well. As he approached the well, she turned around. He was stunned by the beauty of the young woman.

"Are you thirsty?" she asked in the language of the northern kingdoms. "You look like you have traveled far."

"Yes," he replied as she handed him a scoop full of water. "Thank you."

"Carita," a man from a nearby house said and she turned towards him. "Lunch is ready."

"Yes, Father," the woman said as she picked up the bucket.

The man came to the well and looked him over.

"Where are you from?" the man asked.

"A very long way away," he replied. "I am looking for work and a place to stay."

"The last man I hired left after only a month," the man said.

"If I found work, I would stay," he replied. "I am looking for a new place to call home. Some place like this."

"Come join us for lunch," the man said. "What is your name?"

"Langward," he replied with a smile.

"That's a strange name," the man said. "No matter. What do you know about cattle?"

"A few things," he replied. "But I learn quickly."

"Ethan, who is this?" a woman said as she stood by the door of the house Carita had just entered.

"Marriah, this is Langward," the man said as they entered the house. "He's looking for work. I've invited him to eat lunch with us."

"Welcome, Langward," the man's wife said as Carita put another plate and cup on the table.

"Where do you come from?" Marriah asked. "I've never seen a shirt like that before."

"I come from a place south and west of here," Langward replied hoping they would be satisfied with his answer.

"Why did you leave?" Ethan asked. "You didn't commit any crimes, did you?"

Langward had a sinking feeling in his heart. He had hoped he wouldn't have to explain why he left Brinley behind.

"I have broken no laws, nor committed any crimes," he said. "The one person who knows exactly why I left would not dare explain it to the one person who knows I am never returning. I left of my own free will taking only what is rightfully mine."

"You seem sad about it," Carita said.

"What is past is past and therefore not important," Langward said. "It does not matter who you are related to or what title or position you hold. Everyone must make their own place in this world. It is time for me to make my own place."

After they sat in silence for a while, Marriah said, "I've got some cloth. I could make you a new shirt, one that won't attract so much attention."

"Thank you," Langward replied feeling relieved.

"There's some wood that needs to be chopped," Ethan said. "Most men don't wear shirts to chop wood this time of year anyway."

They got up from the table. Carita began to gather up the plates as Langward took off his tunic. She looked up as he handed the tunic to her mother. She paused for a moment, staring at him before she met his eyes and her face began to turn red. She quickly turned around and took the dishes over to the tub of water near the fireplace. He heard Ethan chuckle as he opened the door.

"My daughter apparently finds your appearance pleasing," Ethan said as he led Langward around behind the house.

He was glad the man's back was to him as he felt himself blush. He had found her looks pleasing as well. Soon he was chopping the large pile of wood behind the house. He felt relieved that they seemed to have accepted him for now. He saw Carita walk away farther into the village.

*****

"What do you think of Langward?" Ethan asked his wife as she began to stitch the shirt together. "Do you think he's telling the truth?"

"I think that he has many secrets," Marriah said. "Yet, I believe that he has not lied to us either."

"Can we trust him? What secret could be so terrible that he would not tell us?"

"I don't know," she replied. "I think that if there was a crime committed it was Langward that was the victim of it."

"Yes, I think you are right," Ethan said. "There's something about his eyes. I see sadness in them like I saw in Wyman's when his father died.

"Let's give him a chance," Marriah said.

*****

By the time Ethan returned, Langward had only chopped half of the wood, but he was glad to take time to rest for a moment. He gratefully drank the water Ethan brought.

"Why don't you stack this wood against the front of the barn and then you can have the rest of the day off," Ethan said.

"Thanks," Langward responded.

"Come in the house when you're done."

Langward was glad to get the last of the chopped wood stacked. He wiped his face with his handkerchief before going to the door of the house. He knocked twice and waited for an answer. Marriah opened the door. She looked surprised.

"Didn't Ethan tell you to just come in?" she asked.

"Yes, but I didn't feel right about just walking in," Langward replied.

"Come in and wash yourself before trying on the shirt," Marriah said.

She handed him a small cloth and pointed to the clean tub of water sitting next to the fireplace. He wet the cloth in the cold water and began to wash the sweat from his body. The cold water felt good, but he wished he could bathe instead of just washing with the small cloth. He had just put on the shirt when Carita entered with two other young women. They whispered something and she nodded.

"This looks like it fits well," Marriah said. "Supper will not be ready for a couple of hours yet. Take your things out to the barn. There is a bed in the loft and a small trunk."

"Thank you," Langward said and put his tunic in his bag.

He was glad to get out of the house. He had noticed how Carita and her two friends had been staring at him. He climbed the ladder and soon found the bed and trunk at the back of the barn. There was an empty mattress sack and a couple of old quilts lying on the bed. He opened the trunk and found it empty except for a piece of string. He took his cape and hung it on a hook next to the bed before taking the rest of his belongings out. He picked up the armband and looked at it for a while. In Brinley he had worn the armband to show that he was Prince Langward, son of King Brook. Here it had no meaning at all. He rolled his tunic around the armband and tied it with the string before putting them in the bottom of the trunk. Next he put in the empty drawing book and empty journal. On top of them he laid the hand sized rectangle of metal that he used as a mirror when he shaved and his small hunting knife. The last thing left was the small narrow box his grandfather had given him. It contained a small bottle of ink, a pen and several sticks of charcoal. He sighed as he placed the box in the trunk and closed the lid.

He took the empty bag and climbed down the ladder. He turned around and was surprised to see Carita and her two friends each carrying a bundle of grass.

"We gathered some grass for your mattress," Carita said.

"Thank you," Langward responded in surprise. "I didn't expect you to do that for me."

"There's more outside," one of the friends said.

He went out and picked up the two bundles sitting next to the barn door. When he returned he found the three women up in the loft stuffing the grass into the mattress.

"This will take a while," Carita said.

"You really don't have to do that for me."

"She wants to," one of the friends started to say before Carita kicked her foot.

"Alright," he said. "I'll just wander around the village for a bit and stay out of your way."

He shook his head as he left the barn. None of the girls at the palace had even spoken to him let alone look at him as Carita had. He did not quite know what to think of her. As he walked through the village, people went about their business without paying much attention to him. At the other end of the village he found the church. When he saw the cemetery his heart began to ache as he thought about his father. He found a bench under a tree and sat down. Father had gone into battle knowing that he would not return home alive. Langward knew what he had meant when he said that Langward too would pay for Brinley's future with his blood. He knew in his heart that he would die that his child might survive to return to rule Brinley.

*****

"He is very handsome," Erta said after Langward had left.

"I bet he looks even better without his shirt," Marta said.

"He does," Carita admitted as she felt herself blush.

Her friends laughed. They talked while they finished stuffing the mattress bag with the grass and sewing it shut. When they finished they made the bed. She picked up the bag that he had left and put it on the trunk. She walked with Marta to the church. As they approached it they saw the minister walking over to the bench under the tree.

"I wonder why Father is in the graveyard," Marta said.

As they walked further they could see someone on the bench. They turned and walked towards the bench.

"Can I help you with something?" the minister was asking.

"No," a familiar voice said. "I was just thinking about my father. He died a week ago."

"Grieving takes time," the minister said as Carita stopped.

Langward looked up suddenly. She could see the tears on his face.

"Why didn't you tell us?" Carita asked.

"I didn't want to trouble you with it," Langward said with a sigh. "I thought it would be easier than this. I wanted to start a new life and leave my old life behind. My father was told what my future holds for me, but would tell me very little."

"No one can tell what the future holds," the minister said.

"Apparently some can," Langward replied. "Father said that some of what the fortuneteller had told him had already come true. Things he had no control over yet he had never told anyone. He knew he would die, but said that the chain of events that would begin with his death were far too important to stop. I do know that he was right."

"Certainly that is not why you left your home," Carita said as she sat down next to him.

"In part it is," Langward said as he looked at the ground. "He once told me that I would leave home and never return, but that my child would someday return."

"You're married?" Carita asked.

"No," he replied. "I've never even had a girl interested in me, yet Father told me that I would have a wife and child."

She placed her hand on his back. He looked up at her suddenly.

"I don't know why a girl wouldn't be interested in you," Carita said as she reached up and wiped his tears from his face. "It's almost time for supper."

He took her hand in his and softly kissed it.

"Let's go home, Langward," she said and he smiled.

"You can come by to talk to me anytime you want," the minister said. "Nothing said here will be repeated. Right?"

"Yes, Father," Marta said.

"Yes," Carita agreed.

"Thank you," Langward said as he stood up.

He was silent as they walked home. She had seen the pain in his eyes. She stopped before they got to the door.

"I can see that the past is very painful for you," she said and he looked at her in surprise. "I will not ever repeat anything you tell me about it, not even to my parents."

"Thank you," Langward said. "That means a lot to me. I know it will take time for me to make a new life for myself. I only hope that someday my wife will love me as my mother loves my father."

*****

Langward was quiet during supper, but would answer when spoken to. He was relieved to get through the meal without any more questions about his past. It was not quite dark as he made his way to the barn and up the ladder. He lit the small lantern that was attached to the wall next to the bed. He sat down on the bed and took out his drawing book and a piece of charcoal. He drew his father's and mother's faces. He sat there for a while just looking at them before he heard someone climb the ladder. He closed the book as Ethan appeared.

"It looks like you are all settled in," Ethan said. "Marriah and I talked it over. We don't know what makes you feel you don't want to talk about your past, but we will respect your feelings in regards to that matter. We don't think you have lied to us. I just wanted to tell you that you are welcome to stay as long as you like. We can't pay you much, but we won't charge you for food or staying here."

"Thank you," Langward said. "I appreciate that. I'll be happy with whatever you feel you can pay me. Maybe I'll build my own home here someday."

"A man certainly can't have a family living in the loft of a barn," Ethan said and Langward felt himself blush. "I've noticed that my daughter seems interested in you."

Langward was surprised that Ethan would say such a thing.

"There aren't any other villages nearby and not many visitors," Ethan continued. "She doesn't seem to like any of the single men in the village. She's said they're loud and obnoxious. You seem a bit quieter. I noticed the book when I came up."

"Oh," Langward said. "It's for drawings."

"Can I see?" Ethan asked as he sat on the bed.

Langward opened the book, handed it to him and said, "My parents."

"I've never seen someone who could draw so well," Ethan said. "Yet, I've never seen someone chop wood as quickly as you can either."

"I was afraid I hadn't chopped enough,"

"I'd better let you get to sleep," Ethan said with a laugh. "The cows need to be milked first thing in the morning."

"Where are they?" Langward asked as Ethan stood up. "I haven't seen any around."

"Don't worry," Ethan said. "They're grazing in the forest, but they'll be waiting at the door in the morning."

Langward undressed, blew out the lantern and settled into the bed. It was almost as comfortable as his bed at home had been. It was certainly better than sleeping on the ground.

Chapter 29 – An Unexpected Visitor

When Ethan got out to the barn in the morning he found Langward busily milking a cow. There were several containers that already had the lids put on them.

"How many cows have you milked already?" Ethan asked as he got the other stool.

"Six," Langward said as he carefully poured the milk into a container.

Ethan was surprised. He led a cow in and tied it to be milked. The last man he had hired had to be woken up every morning. They were finished milking before breakfast was ready. After breakfast, he got the harness and began to harness the horse.

"I can do that for you," Langward said.

Ethan let Langward finish the harness and put on the bridle. He seemed to know what he was doing. Ethan checked the harness before backing the horse up to the small cart.

"When I first spoke to you I thought I would have to teach you a lot of things, but you seem to already know a lot," Ethan commented as Langward loaded the last container of milk. "You carry yourself differently than the men in this village. You walk with your head held high and your shoulders back. The only other men I've seen carry themselves that way are the lords of Dracona."

"Who are they?" Langward asked.

"The forest to the east of the village belongs to them. Cattle that wander into their forest vanish," Ethan said. "Some of the older people remember that once the people of this village lived in a town around the castle at Dracona, but something happened. Some of them had burn scars. None of them talked about it. We occasionally see them, the older Lord Dracona and the younger Lord Dracona."

"Do they come into the village?" Langward asked as they led the horse and cart out of the barn.

"No," Ethan replied. "They stay in the forest and we stay out. They might herd a cow deeper into the forest occasionally. It's best to just let them. They both carry swords and are large men like you. Any one wandering into the forest is driven back out. A couple of men decided to go to their castle. A couple of days later they were found."

"Found?"

"They didn't have a mark on them anywhere," Ethan said. "They were both carefully laid out near the edge of the forest. They were left there in the night. After that no one has gone into the forest of Dracona."

"How will I know if I see them?" Langward asked. "I don't want to mistake them for one of the villagers."

"You won't," Ethan said as they approached the first house. "They ride tall dark horses and dress mostly in black. When it is cold the younger one is wearing a large black cape with a very large brass dragon clasp. They are almost always together."

Langward was silent as they delivered the milk. He seemed nervous when they delivered to the houses nearest Dracona's forest. The minister invited him to church later and Langward smiled when he accepted the invitation. They were on their way back when they saw some boys wrestling. Langward seemed very anxious until the two combatants began laughing as they laid down to rest. Perhaps Marriah was right.

*****

When they reached home, Marriah and Carita were waiting for them. Langward took the horse and soon had it unharnessed and brushed. He was quiet as they walked to the church. He sat down next to Ethan and was surprised when Carita sat next to him instead of her mother. She was very beautiful and smiled when she looked at him. He listened to the sermon and hummed along with the hymns as he listened to the words. As everyone began to leave the church, the minister walked over to him.

"How are you doing today, Langward?" the minister asked.

"Better," he said as the last of the people left. "Ethan seems pleased with my work. He and his family have been most kind."

"Carita seems to like you," the minister said and he felt himself blush. "I've never seen her sit anywhere except between her parents."

That surprised him.

"Ethan told me that I was welcome to stay as long as I liked," Langward said as they began walking towards the door. "Apparently Carita thinks the young men of the village were loud and obnoxious but I seemed quieter."

The minister laughed as he opened the door. Langward saw three young men around Carita. She looked annoyed.

"You've got to marry someone, Carita," one of the men was saying as Langward approached.

"I've got a large house for a lot of children," another said.

"I've got a large farm," the third one said.

Langward approached the group and the men looked at him. He recognized the anger in their eyes. He bowed to Carita before holding out his hand. She smiled at him as she placed her hand in his. He softly kissed her hand before placing it on his arm. As he began to lead her towards her parents he felt a hand roughly grab his shoulder.

"Go to your parents, Carita," Langward said before turning around.

"Who are you?" one of the men asked.

"You have no right to interrupt us," another said.

"You are not her father," the third said in an angry tone.

"My name is Langward," he replied in a voice that was a lot calmer than he felt. "I work for Ethan."

He tensed up as one of them punched his stomach. Another tried to grab his upper arm. He tensed his arm and the man lost his grip.

"What have you got under that shirt?" the one asked as he shook his hand as though it hurt. "You must have a board hidden under that shirt."

"His arms are as thick as branches," the other said.

"I wish you would stop this foolishness," Langward said. "Fighting does not accomplish anything but injury, hatred and death."

They looked stunned.

"When Carita is ready, she will choose a man to be her husband," Langward continued. "She should not be forced to marry someone she does not love."

"Most marriages here are arranged," one said. "Ethan should have chosen her a husband already."

"I'll choose when I'm ready to," Ethan said as he joined them. "Come, Langward. It's time to be going."

Langward followed Ethan, grateful to get away from the men and the stares of the villagers.

"Did they hurt you?" Ethan asked. "You didn't seem to react when you got punched."

"I learned to tighten my stomach muscles," Langward said. "Bruised muscles are a lot better than a bruised stomach. I also learned the less reaction they get the sooner they will stop."

"I have been observing you today," Ethan said. "My wife thought that if there was a crime committed in your past you were the victim. I do believe she is right. From what you just said I gather that someone has beaten you more than once."

"Yes," Langward admitted with a sigh. "Part of why I left was I knew the only way I could have the respect of others was to leave and start a new life."

"I guarantee that no one here today would be foolish enough to try to beat you," Ethan said. "We all work too hard to have much energy to waste on fighting. It is a hard life here being so isolated. Other than the occasional peddler, we must grow or make what we need or go without. We are not subject to any king here, so we do not have to pay any taxes."

"I will never kneel before a king again," Langward said. "I think I will look for a good place to build a house."

"Let me show you someplace that might suit you," Ethan offered.

Langward followed him as he turned west and entered the edge of the forest. They soon came to a small level clearing. It was just large enough for a small house, a small shed and an outhouse. There were pink roses growing along the eastern edge of it.

"It's perfect," Langward said.

"I thought so, but you'll have to ask Carita first," Ethan said with a laugh.

"Why?" Langward asked.

"It's her favorite place," Ethan said. "Let's go home. Lunch should be ready soon."

*****

Langward wondered why Ethan had showed him the clearing. Why would he suggest Langward build a home there if it was Carita's favorite place? He followed Ethan to his home. As they reached it, Langward saw a man approach on a horse leading a pack horse. He recognized the tunic before the face.

"Stay here," Langward said to Ethan.

"Why?" Ethan asked as the man dismounted. "He's got a sword. Do you know him?"

338

"Yes," Langward said. "He was probably sent to find me, but I will not leave here of my own free will."

Ethan nodded and Langward approached the lone traveler. He could see him begin to bend his knees and reach for his sword.

"Don't," Langward said in Brinley's language. "Here I hold no title or position."

"But, you."

"That life is gone, General Kannon," Langward said. "No one here knows what title I held in that life and I don't want them finding out. This village is not ruled by any king. Since I will never again kneel before any king it is exactly where I want to spend the rest of my life. I will not return to Brinley with you."

"Nor do I expect you to," General Kannon replied. "It was by my order that you were allowed to leave Brinley without interference. The palace guard reported to me which direction you had gone, but your brother will never know. It was what I promised your father."

"Why have you come then?"

"Your grandfather was wounded in the battle with Mannton," General Kannon said. "He died the day after your father. Before he died he told me where to look for you and asked me to give you this."

General Kannon turned and untied a long narrow box from the pack saddle on the second horse. It was heavy as he handed it to Langward.

"It's your other grandfather's tools," General Kannon said. "He wanted you to have them."

"Lunch is ready, Langward," Marriah called to him. "Does he want to stay for lunch?"

"It's up to you," General Kannon said. "I will obey your command."

"I only ask that you do not speak of my title or where I am from," Langward said. "I do not want them to treat me differently than anyone else."

"I swear," General Kannon said as he led his horses to the house.

"Take his horses to the barn and feed them, Langward," Ethan said.

General Kannon hesitated for a moment as Langward held out his hand for the reins, but handed them to him with a nod. Langward took the horses to the barn.

"Come in," Ethan said. "What is your name?"

"Kannon," the man responded.

"You know Langward?" Marriah asked as she set another plate on the table.

"Since his birth and his father before him," Kannon answered.

"You are welcome in our home then," Ethan said.

He hoped he could speak to Kannon alone. He still had some questions about Langward. There was very little conversation during lunch. Kannon sat on one side of Langward and Carita on the other. After lunch Ethan, Langward and Kannon went outside while the women cleaned the dishes.

"Why don't you work on that wood, Langward?" Ethan said. "I'd like a word with your friend in private."

Langward looked at Kannon with a serious expression on his face and Kannon nodded in return. Langward left without saying a word.

"I know that Langward does not want to talk about his past," Ethan said. "I'm guessing that he has mentioned that to you."

"There are certain things that I am sworn to not reveal," Kannon replied as he nodded.

"The reason I wanted to talk to you is that I am thinking that Langward would be a suitable husband for my daughter," Ethan said. "There are questions I need answered before I can make my decision."

Kannon began to laugh and said, "I'll answer those that I can."

"You will tell me the truth?" Ethan asked.

"What I can not reveal, I will say so," Kannon said.

"Good," Ethan said as he led Kannon to a shady spot with a bench near the house. "What kind of man is Langward?"

"Langward is a good man," Kannon said as they watched Langward begin to chop wood. "I know of only once that he has raised his voice in anger. He is a very peaceful man."

"Why did he leave his home to come here?" Ethan asked.

"I do not know the exact reason, but I know he will never leave this village," Kannon replied.

"He arrived yesterday, but in the short time I have known him, I have observed certain things about him," Ethan said. "I noticed that he

340

does not like conflict and fighting. He said something that led me to believe he has been beaten by someone. He did admit to that much."

"I did not know that," Kannon said. "I think I know by whom. It does explain a lot, but I am sworn to secrecy in that respect. I cannot tell you nor anyone else living."

"You said you know his father," Ethan said.

"He was my assistant for a while," Kannon replied.

"Assistant?"

"I was a general and Minister of Defense," Kannon said. "I was there when Langward's father died. I would have given my life to save his. He knew he would not return from battle and he knew that Langward would leave, never to return."

"I have noticed that Langward carries himself differently than most men," Ethan said. "From what you have said and some things he has said, I am guessing that his father was a very important man and that Langward holds a title where you are from."

"I am not allowed to reveal what title he held," Kannon said. "I can tell you that his father and grandfather were both very good friends and extraordinary men. They were born to lead men and men were completely loyal to them. I'm afraid his brother does not get the same loyalty his father and grandfather did, nor has he earned it. Langward seems happier here than I have ever seen him."

"He said he wanted to start building his own home. I showed him a place just before you arrived," Ethan said. "Most marriages are arranged in this village. I watched Langward bow to Carita and kiss her hand today. I've noticed that she seems to like him. Has he had any interest in any other women?"

"Langward was always very quiet and seemed to prefer solitude. I don't think I've ever seen him talking to a girl before," Kannon replied. "I doubt he'll do anything more than kiss her hand unless he is given your permission."

Ethan considered that as he watched Carita bring some water out to Langward. He put down his axe and smiled as he took it from her. As she left, she was smiling. She glanced their direction and blushed when she saw them watching her. Kannon began to laugh.

"They remind me of his parents before they knew they were to marry each other," Kannon said. "It took his father four years to kiss his mother. Her father finally had to tell him that he would get into more trouble for making her unhappy than kissing her and making her happy."

"Why would her father tell him that?" Ethan asked with curiosity. "Wouldn't her father be the person who would get angry with him for kissing her?"

"I can't tell you all of it, but it was the king's idea that they get married to each other when they were old enough," Kannon said. "It was the king who told him her husband had already been chosen and he was to protect and watch over her, so he reported every contact with her to the king in detail."

"That must have been embarrassing for him," Ethan said as he began to laugh.

"It was," Kannon acknowledged. "The king wanted to make certain that they loved each other before they got married."

"Had he ever loved anyone else?" Ethan asked.

"Never," Kannon said. "I can tell you that both Langward's father and grandfather loved their wives and no other. I'm certain that if Langward loves your daughter, he will love only her and no other. Even living here he will treat his wife as a prince treats a princess, with kindness and respect. He will never raise his voice or hand in anger to her. He would give his life to protect hers. She will never doubt his love for her."

"You've answered my questions," Ethan said. "I have decided that Langward and Carita should be husband and wife. He is a very hard worker and I know he will provide for her."

"I'm certain his father would be pleased," Kannon responded.

"Would you like to stay the night?" Ethan said. "You've probably got a long journey to get back home."

"Yes, thank you," Kannon said as they both stood up.

"There's room in the loft in the barn," Ethan said. "Langward can help you get a cushion of grass."

"A smooth wooden floor would do," Kannon said. "I'm getting too old to sleep out on the rocky ground."

"Langward, after you stack that wood, help Kannon get a cushion of grass to sleep on. He's staying the night," Ethan said. "It's too late in the day to travel very far. You can have the rest of the day off."

*****

"Thank you," Langward said and began stacking the wood.

Ethan left. General Kannon began helping him stack the wood.

"What were you talking about?" Langward asked in Brinley's language as they finished.

"I did not reveal your title or birthplace," General Kannon replied. "As far as he knows, your father was my assistant, nothing more. I was careful to tell him the truth without revealing too much. I told him that you would not leave this village."

Langward was silent as they entered the barn and carried General Kannon's bedroll and saddlebags up the ladder.

"He told me some things about you I did not know," General Kannon said as he set down the saddlebags.

Langward was both curious and anxious.

"Burkhart beat you, didn't he?" General Kannon said.

Langward felt like he had been hit.

"I see that I am correct. Why didn't you tell anyone?"

"Father knew," Langward said quietly. "He told me that he wished he could take my place. He knew I took the blame and punishment for most of the things Burkhart did. He also told me that even though he knew, he could do nothing about it. He would not tell me why."

"I know that he loved you," General Kannon said. "I knew he was very worried about you. When I asked him about you he would say he couldn't talk about it, but I know it hurt him to know what Burkhart was doing to you."

"He began sending me to Weston to stay with my grandparents," Langward said. "He told Burkhart that I was being punished, but I knew he was not punishing me. He was preparing me for the day that I would leave Brinley behind. He once told me that it would be my child, not Burkhart's that would return to rule Brinley."

"How could he know that?" General Kannon asked.

"He said that his birthmark that I bear would be passed to my child," Langward said. "Burkhart has a birthmark, but it is not heart shaped."

"It looks like you won't be a single man much longer," General Kannon commented. "I can see that Carita likes you."

Langward felt himself blush.

"No woman has ever looked at me like she does," Langward said. "The minister commented that she always sits between her parents, yet today she sat beside me."

"I think Ethan likes you. He commented that you might make a good husband for his daughter," General Kannon said. "What do you think about Carita? Do you like her?"

"Yes," Langward admitted as he blushed again. "Her hands are so soft and she smiles when she sees me. She and her friends gathered the grass for my bed and then stuffed the mattress for me."

"If she brought her friends over to look at you, she definitely likes you," General Kannon said. "If you are to have a choice in the matter, I suggest you make up your mind quickly."

*****

"What did you find out?" Marriah asked Ethan as Carita left to find her friends.

"Kannon assured me that if Langward loves Carita, he will be faithful to her. He will treat her well and care for her," Ethan said. "I'm thinking that we've found Carita a husband."

"Good," Marriah said. "I like Langward. There's something about him that is very different from anyone else around here. I've never seen a man bow to a woman or kiss her hand. Carita seems to like him. I heard her say his name in her sleep last night."

"When should we tell them?" Ethan asked.

"Why not tonight after supper?" Marriah said.

"I've invited Kannon to stay for the night," Ethan said. "He is a friend of Langward's family. He seemed to approve of the match."

*****

"I saw Langward bow to you and kiss your hand," Marta said. "I've never seen any man do that before."

"Nether have I," Carita responded. "A man came looking for him today. I hope he doesn't leave."

"You like him," Marta said and laughed as Carita blushed.

"He is everything I've ever wanted for a husband," Carita said. "He is quiet and very gentle."

"And handsome," Marta said as she laughed again.

"Very," Carita admitted. "I dreamed about him kissing me last night."

Blood of Ancient Kings

"I think you're falling in love with him," Marta said. "You know your father would have to approve of him."

"I think Father likes him," Carita said. "He had six cows milked before Father got out to the barn this morning."

*****

Ethan looked up from the garden in surprise as a shadow crossed in front of him. He found Langward starting to pull up weeds.

"I thought I told you to take the rest of the day off," Ethan said.

"I wanted to talk to you," Langward replied. "I didn't want to talk to you while you worked."

"Come sit down," Ethan said wondering what it was he wanted to talk about.

Langward sat down on the ground facing Ethan. He seemed a bit nervous.

"I know I've only been here for two days," Langward said and paused. "I'm not certain about how this sort of thing works here, but I do know what is expected where I come from."

Ethan waited, curious as to what Langward was trying to say.

"I know that as Carita's father, you would be the one to approve of her husband to be," Langward continued.

Ethan was beginning to understand what he wanted.

"I would like to ask your permission to ask Carita to marry me," Langward said.

"Here most marriages are arranged. The parents work out the details before telling the children. It is rare for a man to ask a woman's father for her hand in marriage," Ethan said, careful to not laugh. "Marriah and I have already decided that you should be Carita's husband, but I think it would mean a lot to Carita if you asked her yourself."

"Thank you," Langward said, appearing very relieved. "I'll never give you any reason to regret your decision."

"I know," Ethan said with a smile as he stood up. "Kannon made that very clear to me. I think that Carita went to the minister's house to visit with Marta."

Ethan grinned as he watched Langward hurry towards the minister's house. Marriah came out to help in the garden. Kannon showed up and began helping as well.

"What's got you so happy?" Marriah asked after looking at him.

345

"Langward asked my permission to ask Carita to marry him," Ethan said. "He's on his way to ask her now."

"I'm glad to hear that," Kannon said.

Marriah began to laugh and Ethan joined in.

*****

"Look," Marta said as she looked behind Carita.

Carita turned to see Langward approaching. He had a very serious expression on his face.

"Carita," he said as he got to where they were sitting. "I was wondering if I could ask you something."

"What is it, Langward?" she asked.

"Not here," he said. "In private."

She glanced at Marta before taking the hand he offered her and standing up. She walked with him through the village and into the edge of the forest. She was very surprised when he stopped in a clearing that she frequently went to when she wanted to be alone. He turned to her and took both of her hands in his. She noticed that he was trembling.

"I've already asked your father's permission," Langward began. "He said that I should ask you myself."

"Ask me what, Langward?" Carita asked.

"Will you marry me?" Langward replied.

Carita was stunned.

"I know I can't promise you a castle or wealth," Langward said. "I can promise to build you a home and I will work very hard to care for you."

"Yes," Carita said as she felt the tears begin to run down her cheeks. "I will marry you."

She threw her arms around his neck and felt his arms draw her closer to him. She felt him kiss her hair and looked up to meet his gaze. He leaned down and kissed her lips softly. She laid her head on his shoulder and heard his heart beating rapidly.

"Your father suggested that this might be a good place for me to build a house," Langward said. "He said that it is your favorite place."

"It would be a perfect place to build our home," Carita agreed.

*****

Ethan and Marriah watched as Langward and Carita walked towards them. They were both smiling and looked very happy. Ethan knew that soon Langward would be his son.

"So, when should we have the wedding?" Marriah asked as the couple stopped in front of them.

"It will take some time to build the house," Langward said.

"I'll get some men to help," Ethan offered. "We can start it the day after tomorrow."

They talked about the wedding and the house over supper. Ethan noticed that Kannon seemed pleased. He was glad that Kannon had come. Even though there were things he might never know about Langward's past, he now knew that Langward would be a good husband for Carita. He smiled as Langward kissed Carita goodnight before he and Kannon went out to the barn.

*****

"Thank you for talking to Ethan, General Kannon," Langward said in Brinley's language as they entered the barn. "I was worried when I first saw you today. I came here to make a new life for myself and I didn't want my old life to follow me."

"And now I understand why," General Kannon said as they sat down on their beds. "I'm not certain why your father handled things they way he did. You are more like your father than Burkhart is."

"I am?" Langward asked in surprise.

"Your father didn't have any friends until he left the palace and entered the military," General Kannon replied. "Many of the boys would beat him up and none of the girls would talk to him. I know that he was very lonely as a child. The children in the palace didn't understand that he didn't think he was better than them just because he would become king someday."

"He never spoke of his childhood," Langward said.

"I know that he worked very hard to teach Burkhart to be king, but now I see that it was just as important to him that you learn what you would need to know," General Kannon said. "I always wondered why you spent so much time in Weston. He told everyone that you were being punished."

"He once told me that he was sending me to Weston to learn what I needed to know," Langward said. "He said he thought I needed some

347

time away from Burkhart. I think he realized that if Burkhart thought I was doing something I felt was a reward that he would have beaten me worse. I always tried to act like going to Weston was a punishment until we left the palace walls."

"I hope that someday Burkhart realizes that he should have spent time in the dungeon for how he treated you," General Kannon said.

"I don't think he would dare do anything to let Mother know that he had been beating me. Father did not want her to know. I wish I could tell her why I left. I know I probably hurt her by leaving, but I just couldn't stay. Father once told me that the day would come that I would leave the palace and Brinley forever. He told me he was trying to prepare me for that day."

"And I can see that he has," General Kannon said. "I will keep your secrets. When I return to Brinley, I will not tell anyone that I have seen you. I will never reveal that Burkhart beat you."

"Thank you," Langward replied gratefully. "Once you have left, I may never speak of Brinley or my past again. I have kept my tunic and armband. They will remain hidden until I die. At that time I hope that my child will understand my silence and forgive me."

"I hope so too," General Kannon said. "I have told Caddaric that someday your child would return to Brinley and would need his help and guidance. He knows that your child will be your father's true heir. I swore him to secrecy. He knows it is your father's will and will not disobey."

"Father once said that I was more important to Brinley's future than Burkhart was. It was then that he told me that it would be my child that would sit on Brinley's throne," Langward said. "I didn't know how it would be possible for me to have a wife and child considering no girl would even look at me. Not even the girls in Weston dared speak to me. It is so hard for me to believe that Carita will be my wife. I never thought it would be possible for any woman to love me."

"Here you can be the man your father knew you could be," General Kannon said with a smile. "I know that you will be happy at last."

Chapter 30 - A Kindness Rewarded

Langward had milked several cows before General Kannon woke up. Ethan came in about the same time and started milking. Soon they were sitting down for breakfast. He was kind of sorry to see General Kannon leave. He did feel better knowing that no one would be coming to try to take him back to Brinley.

He paid close attention to the route that Ethan took as they delivered the milk and collected payments from the villagers. He was surprised when Ethan gave him ten percent of the money he had collected. That night he opened the box that General Kannon had brought. He was surprised to find a paper on top of the tools along with a beaded pouch that he knew had belonged to his father. He opened the paper and began reading the letter.

'My Dear Langward,' it began. 'I wanted you to know that I have cherished the time I have spent with you over the years. You remind me of your father so much. I know that you will soon leave Brinley to begin your new life. Your father gave me his pouch to give to you. Langford has filled it with some things you might need if there is no healer where you have gone to. I know that your mother's father would want you to have his tools. Know that your grandmother and I love you and will miss you. Love, Grandfather.'

He felt the tears begin to run down his cheeks as he heard steps on the ladder. He looked up to see Ethan step up into the loft.

"Are you alright?" Ethan asked and pointed to the letter. "What's that?"

"A letter from my grandfather," Langward said quietly. "He must have written it before he went into battle. He died the day after my father did."

"I didn't know you could read," Ethan said.

"I know that other than the minister, probably no one else around here knows how to read or write," Langward said. "I probably shouldn't tell anyone I can."

"That's probably best," Ethan said as he nodded. "What's in the box?

"Tools," Langward replied as he drew back the cloth that covered them. "They belonged to my other grandfather who died before my parents were married. Grandfather also sent a pouch of things to use if a healer is needed."

"Are you a healer?" Ethan asked.

"My mother was a healer as is my grandfather's brother," Langward explained. "I know some of the basics, but I am not nearly skilled enough to call myself a healer."

"You didn't mention that your mother had died," Ethan said.

"No," Langward said. "She still lives. She has more important duties now."

"From what you and Kannon have said I know that your father and grandfather were both very important men and that you must hold a title where you came from," Ethan said. "I can see that you will miss your mother and father."

"Yes," Langward said. "But that was another life for me, a life that is forever gone. My life is here now, in this village as Carita's husband and your son."

"Tomorrow we will begin to build your house. Many have volunteered to help. They are very curious about you and quite surprised that I chose you as Carita's husband."

"I wasn't expecting any help building the house," Langward said in surprise. "I don't know anyone except you and the minister."

"It's time you became part of the village," Ethan said as he patted Langward's shoulder. "I'll see you in the morning.

*****

Langward awoke early and had most of the cows milked before Ethan entered the barn. He harnessed the horse as Ethan finished milking the last cow. They talked about the house as they delivered the milk. People were beginning to smile as they saw him and some even called him by name. It made him feel good to be accepted as a part of the village. He was surprised to find a dozen men waiting at Ethan's house when they returned from their deliveries. Langward got his father's pouch and an axe out of the box before leading the men to the clearing.

By evening they had cut about a quarter of the trees needed to build the house. Instead of cutting them into boards, the trunks were cut to length and notched on the ends so they would interconnect when stacked to form the walls. There would be a main room, a small bedroom and a sleeping loft for any children.

After supper, Langward decided to go for a walk around the village. As he approached the east side of the village, he thought he could see movement in the trees. When he was turning to return to Ethan's house, he heard crashing in the forest and a man cry out. He did not think as he ran towards the sound. He soon found a horse that struggled to its feet revealing a man sitting on the ground holding his arm. The horse's knees were scraped and its legs wet from the stream it had stumbled in. Langward could see the blood seeping from beneath the man's hand as he eyed Langward suspiciously. He could see a plant whose leaves had a numbing effect next to where the man sat on the ground.

"I can help you if you will allow me, Lord Dracona," Langward said.

"You know who I am, yet you are offering to help me?" Lord Dracona finally spoke.

"I have had some training in the healing art," Langward replied as he knelt next to him and plucked several leaves from the plant. "I have always been taught to be in service to others regardless of who they are."

"I know most of the villagers by sight, yet I have not seen you before," Lord Dracona said as he watched Langward select a round and a flat stone from the edge of the stream. "You carry yourself differently, prouder."

"I arrived a few days ago. My name is Langward," Langward said as he scrubbed the rocks together in the water to clean them. "I have been told of you and your son. I know that your past with the villagers is something that you probably would prefer to forget. I too have a past I wish I could forget."

Lord Dracona was silent as Langward ground the leaves and added some water to make a paste. He could see the long gash in the man's arm as he moved his hand so Langward could apply the paste. He washed his hands in the water before getting out a needle and some sinew to stitch the wound closed.

"This will hurt," Langward said.

"Do what you must," Lord Dracona replied. "It cannot match the pain in my heart."

"I too know what it is to have unseen pain," Langward commented as he began to stitch. "I left behind my mother knowing I

351

would never see her again. Although I know my leaving must hurt her deeply, I will not return because of how my brother treated me."

"I had a brother," Lord Dracona said. "He went insane and I had to take his life to spare others."

"My brother used to pin me to the ground and beat me in front of his friends," Langward said softly. "Before coming here, I had no friends and girls wouldn't even speak to me, but here I met a young woman who loves me. When I learned this village did not belong to any kingdom, I decided I would make it my home. I know that occasionally you and your son might take a cow belonging to the village. It is a small price to pay for that freedom. The man who soon will be my father-in-law told me about that. He also said that two of the villagers once entered the forest and were found a few days later carefully laid out next to the trees. I know you must have been the ones who returned them. Evil men would not do such a thing. I cannot hate you."

He looked up and found Lord Dracona looking at him. He tied the last knot before washing the blood and paste from the wound.

"I should go now," Langward said. "Try to not use that arm much until the wound seals. Have your son use a knife to remove the stitches on the outside. Have him cut one side and gently tug on it. If it does not pull out, just cut it off at the skin. The thread is sinew from a pig. Sometimes it will pull out, but it will not cause any problems if it does not."

"I know most of the villagers must hate us, but you have given me some hope. Perhaps someday my own son might find happiness as you have," Lord Dracona said. "Come to where this stream meets the forest the day after tomorrow at this same time. My son will bring you a gift."

"There is no need," Langward insisted.

"To show my gratitude and as a wedding gift," Lord Dracona said as he turned his horse and walked deeper into the forest.

Langward shook his head and left the forest. He said nothing about his encounter to anyone. He knew that no one would believe him if he had. By the time he was due to return to the stream as Lord Dracona had asked him to, the house was almost ready to put the roof on. He wondered what kind of gift Lord Dracona would send and how he would explain it. He hoped it was something small. When he arrived at the stream he saw a man in the edge of the forest. He looked somewhat like Lord Dracona, but much younger. He was about the same size and stature as Langward, but his hair was golden and his eyes were a piercing blue.

"You are Langward?" the young Lord Dracona asked.

Langward nodded and he gestured Langward forward. Langward followed him a short distance to where a horse and two cattle were tied.

"Thank you for helping my father," the young Lord Dracona said. "He has been so bitter towards the villagers. He did not expect anyone to help him when he was injured. He thought at first that you would kill him."

"I am a peaceful man," Langward said. "I have heard some about you and your father, but I know that what is seen and said is sometimes not the entire truth. Know that I am willing to be of assistance, you only need to ask."

"Always mark your cattle as these two have been marked," Lord Dracona said as he handed the lead ropes of the two cattle to him. "We will drive them out of the forest and not keep any."

"Thank you," Langward said as Lord Dracona mounted his horse. "I will not tell anyone of meeting you. They probably wouldn't believe me. I'll say that I found these two coming out of the forest."

Lord Dracona nodded and turned his horse deeper into the forest. Langward shook his head as he led the cattle back out of the forest. Ethan was coming out of the barn as he approached.

"Where did you get those two?" Ethan said as he led the cattle into the barn. "I recognize all the cattle in the village, but I don't recognize these two. They are a different color."

"I went for a walk and found them wandering out of the forest on the east side of the village," Langward said.

"Maybe they're Dracona's," Ethan said with a laugh. "I suppose this village is about due to get a couple of cattle in return for the ones they've taken over the years. They will give you a good start on your own herd. It looks like one is a bull and the other a cow. Both seem to be yearlings."

Langward just smiled as Carita and Marriah walked in.

"Where did you get these?" Marriah asked.

"Look at these strange markings burned into their shoulders," Carita said.

Langward examined the marking. It looked like two mountains with a vertical line between them.

"I found them wandering out of Dracona's forest," Langward said.

"Most cattle bear their owner's mark," Ethan said. "I don't recognize that one."

"Then I'll use it as my own mark," Langward said.

*****

Langward was surprised at how quickly the house got built. Many of the men were surprised by how quickly he could split wood into shingles. They all seemed to like him. Even the young men who had been bothering Carita now treated him as a friend. When they found out about his cattle, most thought it was funny that he might have gotten some of Dracona's cattle. The minister seemed worried though.

"What if the Lords of Dracona want the cattle back?" the minister asked Langward after church. "They tend to take what they want and they both carry swords."

"If I explained it to anyone, I doubt they would believe me," Langward said.

"I would," the minister said as he led Langward to a small room with a desk and a few chairs in it.

"I was walking near the forest several nights ago and heard a crashing and a man cry out," Langward said as the minister shut the door. "I went into the forest and found that the older Lord Dracona had been injured when his horse fell in the stream."

The minister looked surprised as he stopped halfway down to his chair.

"I have had some training as a healer, so I stitched shut the gash in his arm," Langward said. "He told me to meet his son two nights later where the stream meets the forest."

"You spoke to Lord Dracona?" the minister asked. "He didn't kill you?"

"In some respects we're not that different, he and I," Langward said. "He knows that most of the villagers hate him and his son. He said that my kindness gave him hope. He gave me the cattle as a gift of thanks and for a wedding gift as well. The young Lord Dracona told me to mark all my cattle with the same mark that was on those two and they will be driven out of the forest instead of being taken."

"You're right," the minister said. "That story is very hard to believe."

"That is why I'm just letting everyone think I found them wandering out of the forest," Langward said. "I don't like lying to anyone, but I don't see how anyone would believe the truth in this case. I know that most of the villagers hate and fear them, but I know that they are not evil men. I cannot hate them."

"You are a rare man, Langward," the minister said. "Most men are quick to judge and see the worst in others. Have you been a minister?"

"My great-grandfather was a minister," Langward said as he shook his head. "I have always been taught that I must be in service to others no matter what their position or social status."

"I can see how different you are from most men," the minister said. "Before I settled here, I did some traveling. You carry yourself as though you are of royal blood. You act that way too."

"I will tell you the whole truth of my past if you will swear to take that knowledge to your grave," Langward said, knowing he could not hide the truth from the minister.

"Part of being a minister is keeping the secrets of others to myself," the minister replied. "I swear I shall not tell anyone."

Langward began telling the minister about his past and why he had left Brinley to live in the village.

"I now understand the sadness I see in your eyes and the unseen burden you bear," the minister said quietly. "I also know within my heart that what you have just said is the truth. I will keep my silence in this matter. I shall pray for you."

"Thank you," Langward said. "I do not ask that others support me. I feel that if they knew my past they might think I expect that of them or that I was trying to create my own kingdom. I may never have much money or wealth, but I would much rather have the respect and friendship of others. I have chosen this life of my own free will. The man who served as my father's Minister of Defense came looking for me earlier this week. He is the only one from Brinley who knows where I am and that I still live. I know that he will take that information to his grave by my father's order. I will live and die in this village."

"I know you will be a good husband to Carita," the minister said as he stood and opened the door. "Marta told me that Carita said she loves you."

"She did not hesitate to accept my proposal of marriage," Langward said with a smile. "I am very happy to have found a wife who loves me and I love her."

"Where have you been?" Carita asked as they left the church. "I was worried about you."

"Just talking to the minister," he replied as she put her hand on his arm and leaned her head on his shoulder.

He felt happy and at peace as they walked home together. The house was almost finished and he had begun to build the furniture and doors. Soon they would be married and would move into the house. He worked while Carita watched. She smiled when he looked up at her. To him she was a princess regardless of her bloodline. By evening he had finished the two doors and the table. He had cut most of the pieces for the chairs and would start the bed once they were finished.

Chapter 31 – The Truth Revealed

Every afternoon he would work more on the furniture and preparing to make the house into a home. Carita helped sometimes, but spent a lot of time sewing a new dress to wear to get married in. He was surprised to discover that she was also making him a new pair of pants and a shirt. Once he had finished the chairs and bed, he began to build a cradle. He found some time to write in his journal and draw as well. He knew that the day would come that his child would need to learn the truth about the past. He wondered if he should tell Carita about his past, but decided there was time after the wedding for that.

The day of the wedding finally came. Langward was very nervous as he stood in the church waiting. Carita was so very beautiful in the white dress she was wearing. Her dark hair was crowned with a wreath of flowers. Ethan smiled at Langward as he placed Carita's hand in his. The ceremony was very different from Brinley's, but Langward didn't care. All he cared was that Carita was his wife.

He was very surprised by the gifts given to them by the villagers. There were a couple of quilts, some plates, cups and a cooking pot. They thanked the villagers before everyone sat down to a feast. Afterwards, Ethan and Marriah helped them load the milk cart with the gifts and walked them home.

"Don't worry about the milking tomorrow, Son," Ethan said. "I'll see you tomorrow afternoon."

"Thank you," he said. "For everything."

Carita took his hand and led him into the house. He thought he heard Ethan's laugh before he heard the milk cart creaking as they left. Carita turned to him and smiled. He took her into his arms and kissed her.

"I don't know where you came from, Langward," she said. "But I know that my prayers were answered when you walked into the village."

"I think it's time I told you more about my past," he said and led her to the table. "I only ask that you don't tell anyone because what is past is past and therefore no longer important."

"I promise," she said as she sat down with a worried expression on her face. "What could be that horrible?"

"I came from a kingdom named Brinley," he said as he opened the trunk and drew out his tunic.

He untied the string and unwrapped the armband.

"What is this?" Carita asked as she stroked the smooth metal.

"My father was King Brook of Brinley," Langward said and she looked up at him with surprise. "I wore this armband as Prince Langward of Brinley."

"Why would a prince want to leave his kingdom and become a poor villager?" Carita asked.

Langward explained how Burkhart treated him and why he left Brinley.

"Oh, Langward," Carita said as she softly wiped the tears that had begun to run down his face.

"I know that someday our child will return to Brinley to take the throne," Langward said. "Until that time, I will never mention Brinley or my past again."

"Wouldn't it be Burkhart's child that would rule after him?" Carita asked.

"A fortune teller once told Father that his true heir would be hidden, but would bear the same heart shaped birthmark that Father had on his right shoulder," Langward said as he removed his shirt.

He turned around so Carita could see the birthmark. He could feel her soft touch as she traced it with her fingers. He turned and found her standing. He stood and she placed her hands on his chest before sliding them up to his shoulders.

"So, My Dear Wife, you are now Princess Carita," Langward said before he leaned down to kiss her lips.

When he broke off the kiss, she led him into the bedroom saying, "Come, My Dear Husband. I will help you forget the past and put happiness in place of the sorrow that I see in your eyes."

*****

It had been almost a month since Langward left and he still could not be found. None of the guards had seen which way he went after they lost sight of him in the crowded streets. None of the border patrols had seen him leave Brinley and he was not to be found in any of the villages. General Kannon resigned and his grandson, General Caddaric took his place. General Kannon went to search out Langward, but when he returned he had no news of him. He died two days after returning. It had been far longer than Langward had ever been gone before.

Burkhart had been reading Grandfather Burkhart's journal and came to a passage that surprised him.

'In this last week my life has completely changed. My eyes have been opened and I see the truth about myself for the first time. I now sit in a house smaller than my bathing chamber in the palace, yet I am grateful for the protection it affords me and my daughter. I am learning to care for myself and for her. It is hard work to live outside the palace. I never knew life could be so hard. For the first time in my life, I feel the desire to obey and please someone, King Langward. I have no doubt that he is worthy of the title of king. I also know that I was never worthy of that title. He has seen into my very soul and knows me better than I know myself. Although it is the blood of our ancient kings that flows in my veins, it is worth less than the dust that mars his boots.'

'King Langward is the father I never had. The father I pray I can be to Aurita. I must now learn everything I can from King Langward. It must be his example that guides me as I raise Aurita to someday become queen of Brinley at King Langward's son's side. My own father hated me and called me worthless. He beat me and took from me everything I cared about. From him I learned to think only of myself. I now understand why the people of Brinley hate me.'

The next entry was two days later. The handwriting was not as clear and strong as the previous entry. It was as though Grandfather Burkhart's hand was shaking as he wrote it.

'Last night I dreamed about my mother and father. It was something I thought I had finally erased from my memory. I was still very young. Mother was putting me to bed and I noticed bruises on her neck. I touched them and she began to cry.

I remember she was trembling as she held me. Suddenly Father came into the bedroom and began to yell at her. He pushed me back into the bed as he grabbed her by the hair. When she protested he began to beat her. Her pleading and screaming still echo in my mind. I remember the blood as it splattered across my bed and body. When he finally left, she lay still and silent on the floor. I crept from the bed to comfort her, but found her face battered past recognition and no life left in her. I returned to my bed as I heard Father returning. I watched as he roughly wrapped her in a sheet and carried her out. I never found out where he buried her. I know the only reason he didn't kill me is he needed an heir. After my father died I never returned to visit his grave after he was buried. I pray that such violence and abuse stops with his death. To pass that down would be far worse evil than what I did while I was king.'

Burkhart closed the journal. He knew that he had done to Langward the very thing that Grandfather Burkhart had suffered as a child. He quietly took the most direct path out to the garden and the courtyard graveyard. He knelt at the graves as he felt the tears coming.

"I'm so sorry," Burkhart whispered. "If ever I see Langward again, I will tell him I understand and how much I regret it."

*****

The next morning Burkhart needed to look up a law before the council meeting. He took out the book of laws and was surprised to see a folded paper showing above the pages at the top of the book. He opened it to the paper. His name was written on it. He opened the paper and found it was a letter.

'Burkhart, I know that Father will die in battle and you will return as king of Brinley. I know it is now time for me to leave and find a place to call home. I've never told Mother what you did to me. She never saw my tunic that was torn and covered in blood, but it remains hidden. I pray that someday you will understand that one does not have to be a ruler over others to deserve the same respect and courtesy. I pray that you do not treat the people of Brinley as you have treated me. You should have been someone I could look up to and my protector, instead you abused me and humiliated me every chance you got. Still I can feel nothing but pain and sorrow when I think of you, never hatred. What is past is past and therefore no longer important. What is important is that Brinley is now in your hands. I pray that you make a better king than you did a brother. I pray that you will guide and protect Brinley as you should have me. The day will come for another to take the throne and I pray it will not be with a sword at your throat. You are forever rid of me. I will never return to the palace even though it pains me to know I will never see Mother again. It is the price I am willing to pay to at last be free of you. I know that someday I'll pay the same price Father did for Brinley. I pray that when that day comes I can face it as bravely as Father did.'

Although the letter was signed Prince Langward of Brinley everything except the name had been crossed out. Burkhart sat staring at the letter for a few moments. When he moved the letter to fold it, he found that it had been marking the page that contained the law defining the punishment of one found guilty of beating another. The punishment was two days in the dungeon for every bruise counted on the body of the victim. Burkhart felt the blood drain from his face as he realized the message Langward sent by leaving the letter to be found marking that particular page. Although it was the very law he was going to look up, it took on a meaning that left Burkhart with a knot in his stomach. He folded the letter and put it in the pouch that hung from his belt. He found his hands trembling as he closed the book and put it away.

Burkhart stood and went over to the window. Langward's words kept repeating in his mind. He had thought that Langward would return as usual, but he had not. Now he was gone just as Father and Grandfather were gone.

Burkhart sighed as he looked out over the garden to the courtyard where Father had been buried. Grandfather had died the day after Father. Mother had locked herself in her bedroom shortly after Grandfather had been buried and had not eaten anything but bread and water. She stayed locked in her room for an entire week. It was hard to look at the empty chair in the dining hall knowing it was his fault Langward was gone. He decided that the chair should remain empty to remind him of his failure.

Burkhart shook his head as he went to the chest holding the maps to look for the map he needed. As he unrolled the first bundle of paper he discovered that instead of maps the pages were drawings. The first one was of Mother and Father. Burkhart dropped the drawings on the table and sat down. His heart ached at the thought that he had been lying to his father all his life. He noticed the signature at the bottom of the page was Langward's. He moved aside the drawing of Mother and Father to find one of himself. The drawing was almost like looking in the mirror except the expression was happy and confident instead of the sorrow and doubt he now felt. He decided they should be hung and displayed.

He sighed as he stood and went back to look for the map. After finding several more drawings among the maps he found the map he needed. He turned to go to the council meeting knowing in his heart that Langward would never return. Brinley's future was now in his hands, but Burkhart was no longer certain he should be king. He was beginning to see in himself too many of the traits that had led to Grandfather Burkhart's downfall. As he paused at the door he hoped that wherever Langward was he would be happy.

There is a price to be paid for everything, each life affecting so many others. The price for some choices is paid in regret. The price for peace is paid in blood. No bloodline is exempt, not even the blood of ancient kings.

The Tales of Asculum and Map

A group of refugees stranded in the hostile snow covered north divide up hoping to find shelter on this world they call Asculum. All of the dragons and some of the people fly south in search of warmer climates while the rest of the people face a journey they are ill prepared for. They are lost and freezing as their leader urges them forward through the blizzard into the mountains for as a seer she knows that they will find temporary shelter there. They manage to stumble out of the snows into a paradise created by a ring of active volcanoes. Their magical talents become vital in building a city they name Glynis.

As they begin to settle into their new home their leader sends out small scouting parties to discover who inhabits this world. They find that while the people of Asculum look very much like them, they are a short lived primitive people. The people of Glynis learn what they can from these people without revealing that their past and magical abilities. They begin to make wagons and carriages for cargo and people. They even learn to make and use swords along with bows and arrows they've seen the people of Asculum using. As the people of Glynis search for a new home away from the volcanoes that could destroy their valley their past is forgotten.

It is in this environment that the Tales of Asculum are set. Each book is meant to be a standalone book involving a particular region of the planet and the characters that inhabit that region.

The last Lord of Dracona is a lonely man with a dark past who is thrust into unexpected responsibilities. He lives alone in an empty castle in the center of the deserted town of Dracona. He faces tasks that he has no hope of accomplishing on his own and no one to turn to for help. Lord Dracona's story includes a nation in search of the answer to an ancient riddle and another nation in the grip of a tyrant king. When he falls in love with a mysterious woman he goes from desperate for companionship and purpose to overwhelmed by new responsibilities as new citizens begin to arrive.

The new King of Burton is in search of a wife but is dissatisfied with the spoiled princesses sent by neighboring kingdoms to court him. At a dear friend's funeral he falls in love with a beautiful servant girl that had a life of slavery and abuse. Through their love and perseverance they are able to unite several kingdoms in peace.

In the dying kingdom of Mannton women are not treated as people. They work for scraps of food and sleep on woven mats that will become their burial wrappings. This all changes after Li is purchased by the king to provide him an heir. He soon finds that she is no ordinary woman.

For more information and social links see www.vjogardner.com

Asculum

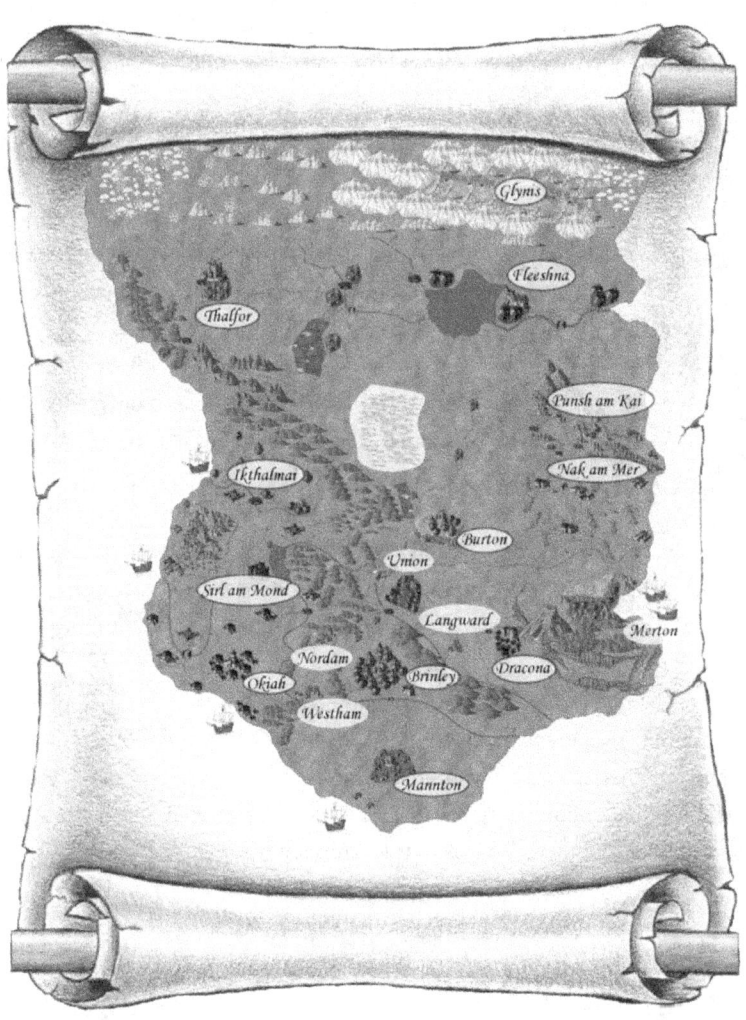

About The Author

Writing under the pen name V.J.O. Gardner, Valerie is an award wining author of full length fractured fairy tale fantasy novels. She has self published Blood of Ancient Kings which won an award in the very first contest she had ever entered. Her second book, Dracona's Rebirth, is published by Ink Smith Publishing.

Always fascinated by both medieval times and sci-fi she was an avid reader and enjoyed a wide variety of literature and authors. She began writing in in the late 1980's after graduating from Dixie State University in St. George, Utah, where she studied Fantasy Lit and Writing. Valerie is a member of the League of Utah Writers. Although she thought she was writing a short story when she began Dracona's Rebirth it blossomed into the full novel it is today.

The good values Valerie was brought up with she instilled both in her children and in her writing. One of her first professional reviews commented that the story reminded him of the Boy Scout Law. While Valerie has been both a Boy Scout leader and a Girl Scout leader the story was written before then. You can visit her at www.vjogardner.com.